Praise for The Lenticular

"Keith brings energy and invention to one of my favourite genres. Space Opera done right. Intelligent, thrilling with heart." **Trent Jamieson**, award-winning author of *The Stone Road*

"… wild and expansive, and just so utterly out there." *Aurealis Magazine*

"A potent SF depiction of humanity victimizing peaceful aliens." "The author's gift for xenofiction matches that of genre grandmasters like Hal Clement, Larry Niven, and C.J. Cherryh." *Kirkus Reviews*

"… if you're into epic space tales with a fresh spin, *Traitor's Run* should be your next binge. It's got drama, heart, and makes you think twice about where humans fit in the universe." **Dirk Strasser**, author of *Conquist*

"The novel's strengths lie with Stevenson's thoughtful and intelligent depictions of various aliens and their cultures, particularly the worldview, religion and social mores of the empathic Kresz." **Carol Ryles**, award-winning author of *The Eternal Machine* "a vast galactic canvas with a myriad of extremely well-drawn alien societies, interstellar travel, and plenty of political machinations." **Nathan Burrage**, author of *The Hidden Keystone*

"… space opera done as space opera should be done" **Richard Harland**, award-winning author of *Ferren and The Angel*

"… weaves a complex and enticing web of future humanity, alien races, and murky motives …" **Mitchell Hogan**, award-winning author of *A Crucible of Souls*

THE LENTICULAR

BOOK THREE

TRAITOR'S WAR

KEITH STEVENSON

First published in paperback in Australia in 2024

by coeur de lion publishing

www.coeurdelion.com.au

© Keith Stevenson 2024

www.keithstevenson.com

cover artwork and design by Jeff Brown Graphics

Print ISBN 978-0-6457466-2-4

Ebook ISBN 978-0-6457466-3-1

A catalogue record for this book is available from the National Library of Australia

Prologue

Troels Volmar's desk was filling up with reports from across the Hegemony and beyond, including the latest information on Fleet's advance into Hanloi space.

Close to home, events were running according to plan. His assassination of Representative Minch on Mars had weakened the Inclusionist political party and set the stage for their demise. His operative Denev Antwer was busy radicalising young Inclusionists to undertake a terror attack that would see the entire party outlawed.

But Volmar still had something to prove. He'd overstepped his authority in Cygnus Sector when he'd entered into a treaty with the Maagba – the same aliens who had destroyed the Brell colony system – to police that sector for the Hegemony. He'd been keen to show Permanent Head Breslaw that the Hegemony Diplomatic Corps could deal with military threats without any need for Fleet intervention, all on the pretext of freeing up Fleet resources to be used elsewhere. But Breslaw hadn't been fooled. He'd reminded Volmar that the latitude he allowed him to do whatever was needed only functioned as long as the results were invisible. A treaty with the Maagba was hardly that.

At Volmar's urging, Fleet Admiral Vargas had directed Admiral Gart Lowrans, his adjutant, to sign off on sacrificing the illegal Brell, Sissilak and Totek battleforce to the Maagba raiders as another means to gauge the Maagba's combat strength. But Vargas hadn't known about the treaty and had been less than impressed when he found out; and Undersecretary Laneaux, who commanded Sol

System Security, had called Volmar out on it at a special meeting of the executive. That had stung the most: that the permanent head had been forced to issue him with a rebuke.

Breslaw came to see him afterwards and his warning had been plain. Play nice with Fleet and show how the different arms of the Central Administration can work together successfully. Fleet strength bolstered by HDC intelligence.

Easy enough to say, but there was nothing more high stakes than the Hanloi campaign. The Hanloi currently controlled all of space around galactic centre. If the Hegemony couldn't dominate them, Earth's expansion would fail. Supposed allies would turn away and enemies would be emboldened. But information on the Hanloi was sparse, despite HDC's best efforts. As a result, tactical scenarios could only take them so far. In short, Volmar was worried though he would never admit it to anyone.

He crossed his office to the internal window and looked down through the galleried levels of the Datahive. The holopit image of the galactic arm shone bright, showing tac icons plotting Fleet's advance: one group on a direct approach to Hanloi space, while the other had taken a more circuitous route through the region the local aliens called the Lenticular.

Volmar sighed, fogging the glass. It wouldn't be long before all the pieces were in place. They *had* to succeed.

1

"Udun!"

I woke, disoriented at the sight of the dull blue shield metal on the ceiling above me. Then I remembered where I was and rolled off my mat to push aside the door hanging.

It was Rhees who had woken me and she stood beside Tzek, longtime advisor to Czerag, our house hierarch who had been killed when the Hegemony invaded.

Rhees and I had found Tzek and others from my house sheltering from the Hegemony invaders in this refuge below the deep desert – one of a network of hides that House Czerag kept as a place of last resort. It spoke to a lack of trust inherent in the hierarchs that, even after cycles of peace on Homeworld, places like this had still been stocked and maintained, their locations kept secret from rival houses. Now we were grateful for them.

"This is no time for sleep," Tzek told me. "You'll be leaving soon and I have to show you both something."

His staff thudded rhythmically on the stone floor as he led the way along the main corridor of the hide to a set of steps spiralling down to another level. Most of the lower corridor was filled with stacks of cargo podules, leaving just enough room for us to pass through.

"This is where most of the supplies are kept," Tzek said. "We have enough for our current complement to last three cycles. But I'd rather not be here long enough to use them all up. In any case, we keep him down here, well away from the others."

"Him?" I asked.

Tzek stopped in front of a heavy door clad in the shield metal that covered the hide's ceilings. He operated the lock and the door swung wide to reveal a small room with a weak globe set into the ceiling. Inside sat a Kresz, about the same colour and size as me, but he still had his hood. He wore a finely wrought green torque around his neck.

"This is our guest," Tzek said. "His name is Amaroc."

It was clear from the colour of Amaroc's torque that he was House Kergis and a senior house functionary.

Hierarch Kergis had betrayed us all when he sided with the Hegemony ships as they invaded Kresz space. Now he ruled Homeworld with the Hegemony's support. It was still a mystery how he'd managed to keep his plotting with the enemy a secret, given the empathic connection between all Kresz who retained their hoods.

Amaroc's attention focused immediately on Rhees. "A Human." His voice was hoarse but gained strength as he spoke. "Something tells me you're not here to liberate me, Human. You could have brought some food though. I'm starving in here."

"You have to prove you're worth the rations," Tzek said.

Amaroc raised his claws and glared at Tzek. Even without my mantle I could see he was consumed with hate. If he wasn't restrained he would have attacked us as soon as the door had opened.

"When Kergis comes, he'll roast you slowly in your shell, old one," he snarled. "And I'll be there to watch."

"We get nothing from him," Tzek said to me. "Even on an empathic level. He hates us as much as we hate him. That's all."

"What do you know about him?" I asked.

"He was with the Defenders on the frontal assault of the escarpment and clearly in charge of his contingent, maybe more. The authorities he carried said he was part of a unit called the 'stek-la'. It's not clear what that is but the permissions were signed by Kergis. I'd know his mark anywhere."

Which meant Amaroc was close to Kergis and could be a good source of information. "We'll take him with us when we go," I said.

"Oh, you'll take me, will you, cripple? How fortunate for me."

"Not really," I said. "I don't think you'll enjoy our cargo locker. It's smaller than this cell."

Amaroc screamed obscenities at us as Tzek pushed the heavy door shut.

"He's a charmer," Rhees said. "Is it worth the trouble to take him?"

"He's no use to us here," Tzek said. "He's told us nothing. And not for want of trying on our part. He's been on subsistence rations for a season now, but he's still sure of himself, and full of fight."

Tzek may have had no luck, but my sister, Isza, could be very persuasive. "He must know information that could help us," I said. "It's worth a try."

As Tzek led us back to the upper level I remembered how tense things had been between us in the escarpment when I returned from Telsan space. I'd seen a different side to him here. He'd protected the excisees and led the other House Czerag Kresz to safety.

"Come. We should eat."

I thought Tzek meant just the three of us would dine, but when we got to the commons the room was full, everyone already seated. Even Reka, Djidka and the rest of the excisees – those, like me, who'd had their empathic mantles severed by the Hegemony – were present. Though I noticed that no intact Kresz sat at their tables. Still, the difference between now and our first day in the hide was palpable. No strained silence, no stares. The conversation level barely dipped as we headed to the servery, picked up our platters and selected preserved fruit and dried fish.

It was only when we sat at our table and Tzek remained standing that the talk stilled.

"You're leaving soon, Udun, and everyone wanted to join together before that happens," Tzek said. "You may not fully realise it, but you've brought hope to us again. Hope that the fight's not over.

And you've completed a change that our enemies started. I thought I was too old for lessons. I thought the excised were to be pitied. Many here wanted to end their lives. But you've shown us that even with the communion shattered we are still strong. And those that have lost the most are strongest of all. That's a hard thing to come to terms with after so many years of no change.

"I wish you could feel what I feel in this room, Udun. Because you'd know that what you and the other excisees have been through was worth it. Kergis and the Hegemony tried to break us. You've shown that they failed."

The skin beneath my chitin tingled as I saw the looks on the faces of the other excisees. I couldn't sense anything of course, but this simple act of coming together – sitting among the intact and hearing Tzek's words – was enough.

Tzek said I'd caused this change. Some of that may have been true – I'd certainly been changed by what was done to me, by everything I'd seen – but one change was more than anything else. This feeling of belonging. Of being Kresz.

"I'm just doing what I can to fight our enemies," I muttered.

"That's fine, Udun. Eat. Let us all enjoy this evening together," Tzek said, and sat down.

Rhees was looking at me with her teeth bared, an expression I'd come to associate with humour. "My friend, the saviour of his people," she said.

It was ridiculous and I stuffed some preserved fish into my feeder mandibles to avoid having to say anything else. Thankfully Rhees and Tzek turned to their own meals.

As I ate I thought about what Rhees had said. Were we friends? Was friendship even possible between two beings whose species were at war? I didn't think it was. But we'd agreed to cooperate and further each other's interests. And given what we'd been through together so far, I trusted her.

We finished our meal in silence. As Rhees and I rose, the others all stood too. It was a sign of deep respect that I would never have thought possible.

No doubt Tzek had influenced this change in the assembled Kresz more than anything I'd done. I could imagine him moving between groups, seeking out those with even a tiny amount of sympathy for me and the other excisees, using his influence and clever words like blowing on a warm coal until the fire sprang to life and spread.

Yes, if there was a saviour here, as Rhees put it, it was Tzek, doing what he needed to give his people a fighting chance. But next time I returned home, I wouldn't feel like an outsider any more.

∞

When I arrived at our final session with the excisees the next day, I was struck with how different everything was from our first meeting. Then, the only thing the excisees had in common was the thing that shamed them in their own eyes and the eyes of the intact. They'd been thrust together by the others in the hide who wanted nothing to do with them. But after sharing their struggles and acknowledging the simple triumph of staying alive, they'd found something that bonded them more closely than before. There was healing here.

Now they had a chance to do something that would show the intact Kresz just how valued they should be. That would be a kind of healing too. Not just for the excised but for everyone.

Djidka and the Cultivator Galok sat with Rhees and most of the others, studying maps showing the locations of the other hides we'd been able to discover. Djidka looked up at me as I entered and her feeders spread wide. I spread my own feeders in return. It wasn't exactly the common sending – I knew I'd never feel that again – but this would do. We excised were learning how to be together with others again.

I saw Reka in the corner in deep conversation with a female excisee. Sazu was her name and I knew they would be travelling together. It was good to see Reka had a friend. He'd always been quiet and withdrawn when we were growing up together and I hadn't realised that he'd struggled with the empathic link just as much as I had. I'd grated against the feelings of others who viewed me as odd and that had made me stronger. But Reka had blamed himself and turned inward. It would have been unthinkable before, but it seemed that losing his mantle had freed him.

I joined Rhees at the table. Djidka and Galok moved to make space for me to view the charts.

"I spent a lot of time working those marshlands," Galok said, pointing a claw at the region beneath the southern shore of the Inland Sea. "Once we get there it's less than a day to the hills."

"Sounds good," Rhees said and bared her teeth at me. "Groups are set, routes are clear."

I looked around the table at the faces of the others. How many would survive the journey or the fight to come?

"Gather round!" It was Tzek.

He dropped a basket on the floor, filled with what I guessed must be newly made at'heka rods. They were about the length of a lower forearm, painted with lines of twisting colour for each house, and topped with long braids threaded with bleached and dyed ah'lok feathers.

"One each," Tzek called as the excisees jostled to get close to the rods.

"It's like kindergarten," Rhees said, but the voder didn't provide a translation.

"At the first sign you've entered house lands," Tzek explained, "take the rod from your pack and hold it above your head like this." He lifted a wooden rod as high as he could despite his thickened shell. "And shake it continually so the feathers dance. Try it."

The excited talk among the group rose in volume as they all held up their at'heka rods and shook them vigorously.

"That's right," Tzek said. "As long as the feathers dance you will be given fair hearing by those who guard the house."

The plan was for the excisees to carry our communications equipment to the other hides we'd identified so we could make contact with the remaining free Kresz on Homeworld and – hopefully – coordinate a counterattack against the invaders. The fact the excisees had no hoods meant any intact Kresz they met wouldn't be able to sense their emotions or tell that they were keeping the real reason for their journey secret. But excisees were often euthanised on sight and it would be a dangerous trek across the desert and into other house lands, even with the at'heka rods.

The excisees had gained so much in the past few days and still they were willing to risk all of that for all of us. For all of Homeworld. I knew there were many more like them out there. Victims of Kergis and the Hegemony. Broken and lonely, just like these excised had been when we arrived. If I survived, I would do everything I could to make sure those others found the same friendship and love I saw here.

"All right, all right," Tzek said loudly and the group quietened. "Stow your rods in your packs and get ready. It's time."

I crossed to Reka, who was refastening the straps of his pack. He glanced at me then focused on his task again.

"You're happier now, brother," I said.

He paused, considering my words. "I am. And sometimes it puzzles me. That the worst things can happen, but time passes and one day there is something to be grateful for. That's how I feel now."

I placed my claws on his shoulder plate. "That's how I feel too."

I thought about asking him not to go with the others. To stay here and be safe. His life had already been enough of a struggle. But when he rejoined Sazu and the rest of the excisees and I saw how they were together … He wasn't a scared child any more. He wanted this, and who was I to deny him.

When everyone was ready, we walked together to the hide entrance. Two Defenders lifted the glassy plug above our heads, pushing it through the ceiling and sliding it aside. All the moisture in the room was instantly sucked through that hole and my desert eyelid slid into place to cut the sudden glare.

Rhees accompanied us onto the surface. No part of her skin

was uncovered. She'd wrapped a thick cloth around her head and borrowed a pair of dark-lensed goggles from the workshop. She'd also tied thick slabs of leather to her boots to keep the soles from melting.

A baking wind pushed at us, shifting direction. All three suns were up and the sky was perfectly cloudless, glowing like an arch of molten metal.

"It's like standing in a furnace," Rhees said. "I don't know how they're going to make it anywhere in this."

The excisees wore their packs strapped across their shoulder plates. Each carried one of our communications devices along with the at'heka rod and a pathetically small stock of supplies. It was true that a Human couldn't survive crossing this desert. But what the excisees had was enough.

Tzek's voice rose above the wind. "If Czerag were here, I know he would be proud. You have proved your strength, and that strength will sust–"

He stopped at a loud cracking noise.

I turned back to the entrance to see more Kresz emerging. They walked forward to gather around the smaller group of excisees. No one spoke, but soon it felt like the entire hide had joined us. None of the intact Kresz knew what the excisees were doing, but it was clear they were going on some kind of mission. And they'd come to bear witness to their departure.

I felt suddenly proud. Here was a group of intact Kresz paying silent respect to a group of excisees who normally wouldn't be spoken to or acknowledged, and more than likely dispatched without a second thought by any intact with a blade. I caught Reka's eye and it seemed to me he stood a little taller.

Tzek spoke again to the small group now in the middle of a larger one. "The house needs you. Do well."

And that was it. The travellers, as Tzek called them, turned and walked into the blistering heat, already splitting up onto their separate headings. We all stayed to watch until their images broke apart into abstract pieces of movement in the rippling heat and were gone.

They would cross out of Czerag lands in three days or maybe a little longer, their paths diverging south and east. Then the going – while physically easier – would get more dangerous: skirting settlements, avoiding Kergis or Hegemony patrols, staying alive. Not all of them would make it. I hoped Reka wasn't among those who fell.

∞

Rhees hurried back underground as soon as the excisees had gone. I found her hunkered against the rough wall, unwrapping the bindings from her head and pulling the thick leather from her boots, as the rest of the Kresz streamed past us into the tunnels.

I passed her a waterskin and she took a swig, tipping her head back and making a strange bubbling noise before swallowing.

"Are you all right?" I asked.

She took another drink. "I am now. How can anything live out there?"

Tzek appeared, leaning heavily on his staff. "It finds a way." He reached his claws down and helped her up. "You'll be leaving now?"

"We'll wait until nightfall," Rhees said. "I'm not setting foot out there again in daylight if I can possibly avoid it. But yes. It'll be easier to monitor the travellers once we get back to the Jantri station."

"And we still need to organise our forces off Homeworld," I added.

"They need more than organising," Rhees said. "Me, a small group of Kresz refugees and an advanced species that prefers to stay in the shadows isn't going to be enough."

She was right, of course. Nok of Jantri'va had brought us together, offered his station as a base of operations and fabricated the communications devices that would avoid Hegemony detection. The instrumentality he commanded was far beyond any technology the rest of the Lenticular possessed, but he guarded his privacy.

Partly to avoid undue attention, but partly – I thought – because he was so different from every other species in the Lenticular that his motivations couldn't be understood within a normal frame of reference. That made him difficult to trust. Still, he was the only ally we had so far.

2

Rhees and Udun emerged onto the glassy desert in full darkness. The ground was still hot, and a dry wind blew in from the north. The cooling glass pinged and tinkled around them. The other Kresz from the hide stood together, a deeper mass of black in the total darkness forming a path to the invisible ship. The whole scene felt surreal to Rhees.

Individuals spoke softly as she and Udun passed between the group of Kresz: "Sakat guide you." "Go safe to your destination."

Rhees recalled her conversation with Nok before they met up with the Kresz refugees. Nok had described Udun as someone who was changing the course of history for his people. She had to admit he'd been right.

Tzek, holding a glowing lantern, waited for them at the end of the line, just in front of where the ship sat, still invisible.

"We'll be in touch by comms," Udun said to him. "And we'll meet again."

"Count on it," Tzek said and clasped Udun's lower forearm.

Tzek did the same to Rhees. His armoured claws felt smooth and strong against the fabric of her onepiece. "Be safe, Reeks."

Rhees looked into his dark eyes and felt a mix of emotions. Gratitude that he'd accepted her so easily, concern for his safety and that of the others hiding out here, and shame for how the Hegemony had destroyed the lives of these people.

When she'd first encountered Kresz in real life, they'd been so alien to her. Taller than any human, covered in thick shell-like articulated armour, arms and legs that bent strangely with twice as many elbows and knees, and their faces … The eyes were human enough but their mouths were a mass of articulated claws like something out of a nightmare. And yet living among them she'd learned they were just like her or anyone. They all had dreams, things they regretted. They were people, no matter what they looked like, and they deserved to be respected.

Tzek turned and raised his voice. "Bring the prisoner. He'll present no trouble," he added to Rhees and Udun. "He was easily captured and didn't put up much of a fight."

Two of the largest Kresz Rhees had seen cut through the group, each holding Amaroc tightly by an arm.

His mouth parts rippled as he spoke. "You are all going to die."

"I'll show you where to stow him," Rhees said to the guards.

Guided by her disc, she walked up the invisible entry steps. The large Kresz hesitated for a moment then followed her with Amaroc. Inside the ship, Rhees palmed open a locker just past the internal airlock and the Kresz guards pushed Amaroc roughly inside.

She followed them out again. Udun and Tzek were grasping forearms one last time.

"Thank you, Tzek," Udun said. "For now and for all those cycles you were around when I was growing up. You've given me a great deal."

The old Kresz blinked. "I have a feeling you'll return whatever I gave you many times over."

Udun had told Rhees about how much of an outsider he'd felt growing up on Homeworld. It seemed he'd found his way back into his family. She was glad for him. But she couldn't see a similar path for herself. Her father, who'd been distant all the time she was growing up, had all but given up on her when she crashed out of Fleet in disgrace. Her time working in the Hegemony Diplomatic Corps had ended disastrously when Volmar tried to kill her, and she had no doubt that if she turned up anywhere in human space she'd be shot on sight.

She re-entered the ship and sat in front of the displays, prepping for flight. Udun sat in the crash-chair beside her.

"You're a hit," she said.

"Hit what?" he asked.

"I mean you're popular with your Kresz friends there. Hell, they were even nice to me because I was with you."

Udun ignored the remark. "Now all we have to do is get back to the Jantri station."

"And hope our couriers do their job," Rhees added.

"They'll do it. Nothing but death will stop them."

"The Hegemony's going to regret picking a fight with you and Tzek."

What about her? It was all too likely she'd die alone, perhaps right here on Homeworld. At best she'd be forgotten by everyone who knew her. At worst she'd be reviled by humanity as a species traitor.

Fuck, she was getting maudlin. And anyway, Denev would care. He'd helped her when they were investigating the raider attacks in Cygnus Sector. And when he'd found out she was still alive after Volmar tried to kill her, he'd kept helping her. Despite the fact she'd killed Petar – his brother and her boyfriend – in a training accident. Another messy set of emotions she'd rather not look at.

She activated the drive and the ship lifted silently into the dark.

Safely out of atmosphere, Rhees negotiated their way past the shell of satellites and ferry craft in near-orbit. Far off to port they could see the beanstalk elevator decelerating in readiness for docking with the Kresz station – the Hub, Udun called it. A pretty standard spoke-wheel configuration of cargo bays studded around a central disc. The beanstalk cable passed straight through the centre of the station and kept on going until it met the counterweight asteroid a few more thousands of clicks above. A Hegemony Hurricane Class corvette was docked at the Hub and a flight of singleships flew past it as she watched, heading for the planet. Their own ship had gone completely undetected and landed in plain sight in the middle of an arid wasteland. Volmar would freak if he knew.

She checked her setting and accelerated, leaving Udun's world behind. "I think we'll take the conventional route back," she said.

"You mean the Point? Is that wise?"

Rhees shrugged, but wasn't sure if he understood her gestures. "It'll be crowded, but they can't see us. And we'll get an idea of Hegemony deployment around the Point and on the immediate Voss Space side."

"The Point it is then."

With the Hub and everything else safely behind them she punched for maximum acceleration. She was almost used to the lack of any sensation of speed now. But if whatever generated the inertialess field failed, they'd be a colourful paste of human and Kresz insides smeared across the back of the cockpit.

She became aware of a steady thumping from the rear of the ship. Amaroc. They flew on for several minutes and the sound didn't let up.

"Is he going to keep doing that all the way back?" she said.

"House Kergis is known for its stubbornness," Udun said, unlocking his harness.

She laid a hand on the smooth chitin of his middle forearm. "No, I'll go."

She walked aft to the storage locker, opened the door and dodged as Amaroc's foot lashed out at her. She stamped on it, bringing her full weight to bear. The Kresz's other leg and arms were still bound.

"Are you going to be quiet?" she said.

He glared at her.

She used her arms to brace against the walls, lifted her other leg and kicked him hard across the feeder mandibles. His head rocked back, and she kicked it again on the rebound.

"Your face is going to wear out before my boot does."

She stomped on his lower knee joint and kicked his free leg

back into the locker.

"You're going to die," he said.

"Shut up or I'll break both your legs. We don't need you to walk where we're headed." She slammed the door, cutting off his response.

Back in the cockpit, she said, "Message from Amaroc: we're going to die."

"At least he's consistent."

"We could space him. He didn't tell Tzek anything. Maybe he's not worth the trouble."

"I've been thinking about that," Udun said. "It's hard to believe they got nothing out of him."

"He's tough."

"You don't understand," he said. "Empathic interrogation is about more than what you say or don't say. You have to be in complete control of your emotions. Even reactions to words spoken by the interrogator can give away vital clues."

She hadn't thought about that. "Is there any way to block being read like that?"

"Strong emotions, like hatred directed at the interrogator, can blanket the rest. But it's not something you can keep up day in, day out. Eventually something will slip past your guard."

"Maybe he's just a foot soldier and doesn't know anything."

"No. Tzek said he was part of the stek-la."

"But he didn't know what that meant," Rhees said.

"No, he said it wasn't clear what it was. But you see what 'stek-la' means?"

"I'm not getting a translation."

"Ah." Udun paused. "It's from a pre-Emergence dialect. It means a person or group that is special because it is close to the middle. Trusted by the leader so able to access more secrets."

"Not a foot soldier then. So how do we get him to talk?"

"Isza will think of something."

Rhees had to agree. Udun's sister wasn't the type of person to give up easily.

They were approaching the loose globe of satellites that balanced gravity for transit and she dropped speed.

"This is where Kergis betrayed us," Udun said. "The Hegemony came through the Point and our Defender ships were containing them. Then the Kergis ships broke ranks and started firing on our own ships." He looked at Rhees. "We still don't know how they did that without any warning."

"Sensors read increased radiation," Rhees said, "but nothing else. Fleet would have cleared the debris. Hazard to naviga–"

The ship shuddered.

"What was that?" Udun asked.

"We just launched something. Or the ship did." Rhees looked at the boards, trying to make sense of the readouts. "Nothing on the screens. Wait … I'm getting a signal. Fuck." The ship had launched something all right. Autonomously. "It's a probe. Cloaked, luckily. It just attached itself to one of the Point satellites. I'm getting data packets. But no alerts on any of the Hegemony channels. That I know of anyway."

"A surveillance device?"

"I guess it makes sense, but ships don't generally act autonomously. Is Nok operating this thing remotely?"

"That or …" Udun paused again. It was clear he knew something she didn't.

"You're scaring me now. Or what?"

He seemed to be considering what he should tell her. She bit down on sudden anger. The trust they'd spoken about was still problematic in practice.

"I don't think it's something to worry about," he said finally. "Nok can split his consciousness. He's not just in the armoured suit you see."

"He could be with us – in the ship?" Rhees looked around the cockpit, expecting some ghostly form to appear. *Come out, come out, wherever you are.* She almost laughed.

"Nok?" she said. But if Nok was there he wasn't answering.

"Or it could just be a protocol," Udun said. "To release surveillance drones at useful targets when it's safe."

"I'd class this as a useful target," she said, still spooked but relaxing a little. "Good thinking, ship. Or disembodied alien spirit." She keyed the transit drive. "Let's get out of here."

The satellites failed to register them as they slipped between them and gently into Voss Space.

The chamber on the other side displayed all the mind-bending architecture of a non-three-dimensional space where energy and matter swapped places in a chaotic dance. But still there were safe channels and it was here that two System Class Hegemony battlecruisers, three Planet Class destroyer escorts and a standard complement of singleships waited. There could have been more in the darkness.

The ship vibrated again.

"Son of a —" Rhees said. "Another cloaked probe. Fuck, it's attached to the cruiser. Nok, if you can hear me, it's *our* lives you're risking."

Of course if he could hear her he'd know they didn't trust him. And that they'd contacted Denev on the outward leg. The second didn't really matter, and the first … Well, it was pretty obvious given all of their backgrounds. Maybe it was easier to be upfront. At least about some things.

She moved the ship invisibly past the Hegemony vessels and into the network, making best speed for the Jantri station. They passed more sentry ships on the way out, but she was confident of their own ship's abilities now. Nothing could see them if they didn't want to be seen.

Once they were clear, Udun spelled her on the controls and she slept.

It was a dream she hadn't had in a long time. The training mission over Neptune. Fleet singleships flying in precision formation – Petar to her right, Jute to her left – wingtip to wingtip as they weaved a path through a sky too full of icy rock. Bogies on tac, centre screen and closing.

No. She knew what was coming.

Cannons cycling up. The sudden rattle of pellets on her hull as the bogies fired. Wingtips touched, the barest kiss of contact. And through the canopy Petar's face. Focused concentration turning to surprise, the first inkling that everything was going to shit.

She couldn't look. She pulled on the controls, her dolphincraft executing an inertialess turn that would have pulped a singleship pilot. But three of the bogies were in pursuit, following her out of Neptune's rings. Except she wasn't there. It was Voss Space. A spitting chamber of violent energies, like being caught in an electric storm dialled up to a thousand. The Fleet ships were still on her tail, somehow keeping up with her physics-defying moves.

A comms window opened on her forward screen. The face of her father, pale and drawn, clearly pulling heavy gees in one of the singleships behind her.

"Rhees." It was hard for him to talk, the word drawn out in a groan. "What are you doing?"

"You don't understand," she said. But his eyes said he did. She was betraying everything he stood for. Everything she'd believed in.

The transmission cut.

More dolphincraft appeared, flying out of the Jantri station dead ahead, angled towards the singleships.

Rhees brought her own ship to a complete stop, flipping over and back towards the Fleet ships. Towards her father.

She tried comms. "Nok. No! Call your ships off."

Nothing.

The singleships bunched closer, taking an attack formation. On the tac, the dolphincraft vectored down from both flanks.

Rhees dived directly at the singleships, but they didn't veer off. So she slewed her ship around, leading them now and placing herself directly in the path of the oncoming Jantri ships.

"Nok!"

The dolphincraft fired and the singleships erupted in flames as her own cockpit disintegrated.

∞

She woke with a start and looked quickly over at Udun, who was steering them down a Voss Space corridor. That had been a bad one. And it didn't take a psychoanalyst to work out where it had come from. She could keep telling herself she was doing the right thing, but sooner or later innocent people were going to die because of her.

But what was the alternative? She hadn't been able to think of one. Not since Volmar had left her to die on the Maagba cruiser.

"We're here," Udun said, and she realised they were negotiating the final twisting channels that led to the chamber holding the Jantri station.

It came into view like some storm-blasted lighthouse. Plasma raged around it, strikes concentrated on the two furthest points of the structure, like anodes in some long ago experiment. It was hard to understand how the station withstood such violent energies. Hegemony Voss bridges took advantage of the relative peace of stable transit nodes. Even the sentry installations in the channels approaching Earth had taken years of exotic engineering, incrementally dampening the local fields and slowly building a beachhead that could be extended. The Jantri station stood dead centre of untamed Armageddon. Not only surviving, but sucking hungrily at the energy expended. The Jantri hadn't tamed Voss Space, they'd harnessed it. It was a huge tactical advantage in a place that still claimed hundreds of Hegemony ships every year.

They docked in the same bay they'd left and Udun cut the controls. Rhees felt exhaustion close in. They still had such a long way to go.

3

Denev dropped by his dorm only long enough to change into his uniform, then he was on the slidewalk to Vigilance Plaza and the HDC Datahive.

All he'd wanted to do was warn off Preem and the other young Inclusionists so they didn't throw their lives away on a terrorist attack that was really an HDC trap. But he'd been grabbed and knocked out. And when he came round he'd met Rapskel.

Think of us as the real Inclusionists, Rapskel had said. Did that mean they followed the Inclusionist manifesto without Central Administration's interference? Or did he just mean they were the real opposition and their aims were something different? The topic hadn't been open for discussion.

There was a point when Denev had considered Rapskel and his people might be part of some twisted plan by Volmar to test his loyalty. He could have lied to them, protested his loyalty to HDC, but his gut told him that would just get him shot. So he'd gone with the truth: that ever since Rhees – though he didn't name her – had shown him just how fucked the whole system was, he no longer worked for HDC or the Hegemony. He was working for himself.

Rapskel hadn't been entirely convinced. He'd injected a monitor and bomb into Denev and right now the device was in his neck or his bloodstream or maybe even nestled in his brain. The deal was simple: Denev could prove he wasn't loyal to the Hegemony by assassinating Cerise Laneaux, the head of SolSec, and the bomb would come out. If he did anything else the results would be messy.

If Rapskel's group could evade SolSec and HDC surveillance, why hadn't they moved against the CA before now, Denev wondered. There was only one tactical reason that made sense. They weren't as powerful as they made out. They could hide, but they couldn't strike back. Which meant they could be bargained with, especially if Denev had something they could use.

He took the sideband down towards the plaza. All this would be academic if the Datahive security systems detected or triggered the device. It would either go off or Rapskel's people would detonate it remotely. But there was a third option. If the Datahive scanners were able to neutralise it as soon as it was detected – which wasn't outside the bounds of possibility – he could claim he'd been captured, implanted and released to target the Datahive as an unwilling suicide bomber.

There'd be questions, of course. Why hadn't he just sacrificed himself instead of bringing a lethal device to HDC headquarters? There were a number of arguments he could use – the strongest and perhaps most believable, but ultimately damaging to his career, would be that he panicked.

But all that was in a tentative-looking short-term future. He had to get through the Datahive doors alive first.

His mouth was dry. That would help with the panic alibi. He clamped down on a manic laugh and, without slowing his pace, walked through the glass doors as they parted and into the cool foyer.

His head was still firmly on his neck. No klaxons. No rushing guards with rifles levelled at him. The operative behind the long black reception desk looked up from his screen, eyebrows raised.

Denev took a deep breath, nodded to the operative, headed for the farthest elevator, which travelled only to Volmar's office, and pushed the contact.

The car halted on its way to the topmost level of the Datahive. Somewhere above, Volmar was being notified of the elevator request and who the occupant was. Denev would be scanned again.

Again, his head remained intact. The car continued its ascent.

Volmar was seated at his desk and concentrating on screens when the doors opened.

"In-person reports aren't necessary," he said, then looked up when Denev didn't reply immediately. "What's happened?"

"A slight hiccup," Denev said, moving to the centre of the room. To his left, the angled window looked down on the steeply raked tiers of the Datahive. "Preem and my other co-conspirators have gone a little cold on the plan."

"Scared?"

Denev shook his head. "More like other things to do. Not as committed to the cause as we'd hoped."

Volmar put down the stylus he was holding and pushed his chair back from the desk, watching Denev all the while. Calculating.

"Can their resolve be hardened?"

"I'm not sure it's worth the effort. But I have thought of something that might be more … sensational than a group of boys blowing up a power relay. An assassination."

Volmar picked up his stylus again and tapped the end against his bottom lip.

Denev knew he mustn't overplay his hand. If he appeared too keen, Volmar's antennae would twitch. And the comptroller had very good instincts.

"You have my attention, Antwer."

"We have enough surveillance and DNA data on the boys. They were very vocal at the rally and the records of their interactions can be moderated to suit our needs."

"You're not telling me anything I don't already know."

Here it was then. Volmar was still focused on him, giving nothing away.

"SolSec were responsible for Alderman Minch's safety on Mars. Ultimately the responsibility for his death rests with Cerise Laneaux."

The silence stretched. Volmar replaced the stylus on his desk and laced his fingers together. A crease appeared at one side of his thin lips.

"It would certainly be … provocative. Why Laneaux?"

"She's visible, so relatively easy to get to – and culpable in the eyes of the Inclusionists. And she deserves it for challenging you."

The crease by Volmar's mouth deepened. "Two birds with one stone."

The desk chirped and Volmar waved a hand over it. "What is it?"

"You asked to be informed when the Fleet was ready to transit, sir."

"Indeed. Sit down, Antwer." Volmar indicated a chair. "You picked the right time to visit. You can view the fruits of your labours."

As soon as Denev sat, the desk linked with his band and opened a neural pathway, just like a datanook. He was blind for an instant and gripped the seat arms to reassure himself the reality of Volmar's office persisted. Then he had a ship's-eye view of a Voss Space chamber strobing with violet bands of energy. An armada of ships floated around him. Massive Omega Class heavy carriers, still dwarfed by the crackling columns of plasma spanning the dark void, were flanked by destroyer escorts, while Sector Class battleships – which were little more than giant self-propelled guns – flew in clouds of darting singleships. He quickly saw from the composition of the Fleet that this was the main force that had taken the more direct route to the Hanloi border.

Ships began winking out, transiting to space. In seconds the chamber was empty.

Denev's view jumped – flashes of distended energy twisting and spinning, then gone. Blackness. Stars crowded far too close together – and in front of him the Fleet, forming up and under full thrust.

"No sensor contact."

That was Lamark's voice. He was the embedded HDC liaison. His ship – a Hurricane Class corvette, which was furnishing the images – was hanging back from the main force, monitoring.

The attack force spread in a broad line of engagement, singleships swarming around to cover every possible attack vector.

Denev dipped into the various sensor feeds available, some stretching across the full electromagnetic spectrum, others probing the subatomic structure of space, and yet others focused on the tightly wrapped dimensions below and above the visible three-dimensions. But still, there was no warning.

One moment the space ahead of Fleet was empty. The next, a vast structure blinked into existence. A Hanloi ship. Too big to comprehend and moving ridiculously fast, its leading edge leaped at the Hegemony force's flank. Ships bloomed into silent firebursts as the structure sliced through them, sweeping everything in its path and blotting out the rest of space.

The feed died.

"Get it back. Switch view!" Volmar shouted.

"The relays are down, Comptroller." The voice of the comms operator.

"Then reconnect them." Volmar's voice was quiet again after his outburst, and all the more dangerous for it.

Denev blinked, back in Volmar's office. The comptroller was staring at the surface of his desk.

"In light of events, it's important we get our domestic house in order," he said, and looked directly at Denev. "Your new mission is approved."

Denev stood. "At once, Comptroller."

He took the elevator down to reception again and rode another to one of the topmost galleries of the Datahive. The air was cool there and dim light picked out the curves of the datanooks that extended side by side around the inner wall of the walkway. The soft murmur of data interpolation was like waves lapping on a beach. Denev knew HDC would be throwing all its resources into analysing how the Hegemony had just been so easily beaten.

He sat at the nearest vacant nook, felt the seat unfolding around him and pulling him into the wall as the synapse shunts engaged. Laneaux was his primary objective and he opened a search to collate background details and her schedule for the next few weeks, before dipping deeper into the telemetry on the latest encounter with the Hanloi.

The relays were still dark and what ship feeds he could directly access told him no more than he already knew. The pincer movement had failed and Fleet had been caught flat-footed. Thousands were already dead, maybe tens of thousands, and no way to tell what was coming next.

He backtracked on the relay network to see how far the effect extended. It wasn't his job any more, but he'd run tactical analyses for Volmar and that gave him reason enough to be looking, particularly now. If there were lessons to be learned, he was best placed to learn them.

The relays were out for a hundred light years in all directions. The escape route through the Lenticular was still green. He studied a sub-file on force deployment there. Again, he had a good reason. If there were survivors from the Hanloi attack, it was vital the route was as secure as possible now. He committed the details to memory. He'd promised Rhees he'd get that intel for her and he couldn't risk making a copy.

Laneaux's dossier was ready. He moved it to his band and disengaged.

∞

It took less than half an hour to get back to his room in the dorms, where he ditched his uniform and changed into civilian clothes. A short walk from there to the hypertube station, where he caught a public car heading for the conurb, ready to drop back into his life as a renegade. What had Rapskel's people told Preem when they'd grabbed him and Denev at the rendezvous? Hopefully they had Preem and his two friends somewhere safe and out of the way. Particularly as their DNA would soon be all over Laneaux's murder site.

The car halted at a dimly lit urban station whose curved walls glistened with an abstract mosaic that shifted like an ocean current.

A hiss and the doors sealed and they were picking up speed again. It was then Denev heard the voice, like a whisper in his ear. "You did well."

He turned but no one was nearby. Just a kid at the end of the car with the blank-eyed stare of a shunt, and an older woman looking out the window at the tunnel flashing by. She may be shunted too, it was hard to tell.

"Don't freak," the voice said. It was Rapskel. "I told you we'd be watching and listening to everything you do. You can talk back. Just sub-vocalise. I know you HDC types are good at all that covert shit."

"What do you want?"

"Want? We own you. We want everything. What were you doing in the datanook?"

"Getting the Laneaux intel."

"The other stuff. You weren't reviewing those files for my benefit."

Rapskel wasn't getting out of his head anytime soon. Which meant he'd find out about Rhees as soon as she contacted him again.

"I told you, I'm not working for HDC any more. I have a friend. She needs intel on Fleet and troop dispositions."

"Oh no, you work exclusively for us now," Rapskel said. "I told you: we own you."

"So go ahead and blow my head off. See how that helps you." Denev waited. His head remained intact. "No? Maybe you're not as powerful as you'd like me to imagine. You can hide from the Hegemony but you can't act against them, or you'd have done so already. You're not a resistance, you're a parasite. You've found an ecological niche where you can survive, but that's all."

"And how are you any better?"

"Maybe I'm not. But just maybe, I'm an opportunity. I'm not going to expose you, so why don't you let me do what I need to do and we'll see what happens?"

"Because if you do something stupid, they'll find our device and it won't take long to figure out we exist."

"Or you could blow my head off before then. But the results would be the same, wouldn't they? It seems we *both* have something to lose if this goes wrong."

Rapskel's voice rose angrily. "Which is why you should do what we tell you."

"Not going to happen." The car slowed again and Denev stood. "This is my stop. Can you at least keep quiet for a while? I have an assassination to plan."

4

The main bulkhead doors opened on my breach sister, Isza. I unstrapped, and Rhees followed me through the lock and onto the deck.

Isza pulled me close as soon as I was clear of the ship. "You made it," she said, holding me at arm's length and looking me up and down as if inspecting me for damage. Then she turned to Rhees. "You kept him safe. Thank you."

"I had something to do with keeping myself safe, you know," I told her.

"I doubt that," Isza said.

"Don't argue with your sister," Rhees said, then turned to indicate a familiar banging from the ship locker. "We brought you a present."

I went back up the steps with Rhees in case she needed help. She opened the door gingerly, as if expecting Amaroc to lash out, but he was slumped against the internal bulkhead.

"Come on," she said, tugging on his manacles, and he pulled himself up and followed her docilely enough.

As soon as Isza saw Amaroc and the House Kergis torque he wore, she grabbed him by his chest plate and threw him skidding across the deck. A Defender appeared in the bay doorway and picked him up.

"Welcome to the free Kresz," Isza said and indicated for the Defender to march Amaroc into the corridor.

"Tzek couldn't get him to talk, but I hope you'll be able to," I said.

"You saw Tzek?"

"Yes. He's well. They're hiding out in the deep desert." I paused. "Czerag is dead."

"I'm sorry," Isza said. "I know how much he meant to you."

She was right. Our hierarch had trusted me when others wouldn't. But I knew how Isza felt about what Czerag had done when he set us against Kergis and the Merchants Lodge. I wondered if Kergis would have betrayed us to the Hegemony if he hadn't felt threatened by Czerag's plans to break the trade monopoly. I pushed that thought away. Might-have-beens wouldn't help us now.

"Come on. We have food," Isza said as she led us through the inner bay door. "You have to tell me how the mission went."

"We didn't go anywhere near Aktiuk," I said. "But from what Tzek told us, life is bad there and worse on the rest of Homeworld. Kergis has complete control and they've taken all the children for 're-education'. In a single generation, House Kergis will be all that exists."

"He has a nasty surprise coming," Isza said. "Nok's been a little more forthcoming. The Jantri are fabricating hand weapons for a ground assault."

"Ground attack's fine," Rhees said as we entered a lift and ascended to the Kresz habitat level. "But we'll need air support. We saw some of the ships the Hegemony have round Homeworld. The Jantri are going to have to supply pilots."

"We'll see," I said. I didn't think Nok would do that. But we did need ships and people to fly them.

As the lift door opened, I heard yelling coming from the converted cargo hold. Amaroc was surrounded by other Kresz who were shouting and pushing at him. He didn't look as belligerent as he'd been on Homeworld.

"This could get violent," I said. "We need him alive."

Isza was about to intervene when the door opened again and three suited instances of Nok entered.

The closest Jantri shouted, "Get away from him!"

The Kresz pushing at Amaroc fell silent and backed away. Amaroc froze at the sight of the Jantri bearing down on him. There was nowhere to run.

Two of the Jantri forced him to lie on the floor, their suit servos whining as he struggled against their grip. The lead Jantri, who I decided was Nok, kneeled next to Amaroc's prone body and ran a gauntleted hand over him.

"What is it?" Rhees asked.

"Unknown tech," Nok said. "Sensors picked it up in the lift. He has something … Ah."

"He's carrying a bug?" Rhees said.

An image hovered above Amaroc's abdominal plates and I could see something artificial inside him. A four-pointed star.

"Let's hope it's not a tracker," Nok said.

"Let me go!" Amaroc screamed.

One of the Jantri suits clamped a metal hand down on Amaroc's mouth, instantly silencing him.

"That's more like it," Rhees said.

"Is this Kresz tech?" Nok asked me.

I stared at the image but I'd seen nothing like it before. "Not that I know of."

"It has to come out," Nok said.

Amaroc strained harder to escape. It was clear he didn't want anyone to know what was inside him.

Nok held up his other hand and a crimson laser beam, barely three centimetres long, shot from his middle finger. "Be still," he told Amaroc. "Or I might cut something you'll need later."

The image of Amaroc's insides still hung in the air between us. Nok pulled aside an abdominal plate with his other hand to reveal as much flesh as possible.

Isza hunkered beside me, looking at the image. "This is strange."

"I know," I said.

"No, you don't. He's screaming and struggling – waves of fear should be flying off him. I should be feeling that, but all I feel is hate and a certain amount of fascination. Exactly what they're feeling," she added, indicating the other Kresz in the hold who had gathered around Amaroc's body.

Nok brought the laser beam down to part the flesh beneath Amaroc's plate. Even though he was gagged, we could hear his muffled scream of agony. I smelled searing flesh and tried not to think about it.

"We should be feeling that pain too," Isza said.

"You're not feeling anything of what he's experiencing?" Rhees asked.

"Nothing."

Something was interfering with the empathic link.

The beam cut deeper. Yellow rusz spurted from the wound, but not much. It seemed the beam cauterised whatever it cut.

"Nearly there," Nok said.

Another cut and then he thrust his gauntlet into the wound. On the image, we could see his hand, intensely bright. Finger shapes probed inside Amaroc then closed around the tech, pulling it free.

Isza gasped, falling back as Nok pulled the device from Amaroc's body.

I helped her kneel again. "Are you all right?" I asked.

"It's him," she rasped. "I can feel him now. When Nok removed that thing from his body."

Rhees took the small object from Nok and wiped it clean on her suit leg. She held the star up and we could see it was made of a dull alloy. The Hegemony's double circle was etched along one of the points.

"It's Hegemony tech all right," she said. "Some kind of empathy shield?"

Isza blinked. "Not a shield. I thought I could feel him before. But when Nok came in, Amaroc's reactions didn't match what I was feeling from him."

We stood and moved away from Amaroc.

"A more subtle effect then," I said. "What *did* you feel?"

"Hatred," Isza said. "Understandable. It's what everyone in the room was projecting."

"*He hates us as much as we hate him.* That's what Tzek said," Rhees reminded me.

Isza looked down at Amaroc. Nok was applying some sealant to the wound. "He knows exactly what this is," she said. "I can feel it."

Nok stood while his two other suits continued to hold Amaroc. He took the device from Rhees. "We'll analyse this. But if it's as Isza says …"

"It's standard Hegemony tactics," Rhees said. "Find a disaffected group within the target society and give them an edge." She pointed at the device. "However this works, it allowed secrets to be kept in what was an open society."

"It doesn't create an absence like a shielded room," Isza said. "That would be picked up easily. It's more like a synthesis of the prevailing mood. It picks up whatever is there and reflects it back."

"The stek-la," I said. "The inner circle. A group that could be briefed by Kergis and then move around freely without giving away a hint of the plan. This is a piece of the puzzle."

Isza grabbed Amaroc by his chest plate, hauling him to his hoofs. "You have some explaining to do." She pulled him along and signalled to two of the Defenders. "You come with me."

∞

Rhees watched as Isza pushed Amaroc ahead of her towards the far end of the hold. When he resisted, one of the other Kresz grabbed him violently, half-dragging him along behind. It looked like he was in for a long night.

Rhees had to get some rest. "Is there a cabin I can use?" she asked Nok. "Or I'll sleep in our ship."

The cabin Nok directed her to wasn't much different from her room on the other Jantri ship. She wondered how many other cabins like this one were on the station, and why Nok hadn't allocated some to the Kresz. Was the communal camp another experiment to encourage the survivors of the different houses to bond?

She was too tired to care. She lay on the chaise and it reconfigured, seeming to know how best to make her as comfortable as possible. She fell asleep almost immediately.

Waking was an indeterminate line. Her dreams had been full of jumbled images: Voss Space, Erdjis's head parting from his neck beneath the rapid fire of her flechete pistol, the intense bright of the deep desert, the ship firing a surveillance device in the Point. Something she'd said in the hide beneath the deep desert came to her — *an advanced species that prefers to stay in the shadows isn't going to be enough.*

Slowly her thoughts became more directed. The Lenticular was home to a lot of different aliens, and the Hegemony's action here was secondary to the Hanloi offensive. Unlike a full-scale occupation, penetration of systems in the Lenticular would be prioritised and targeted based on available resources and risk profiles. Some systems would escape interference completely. How could she separate the two? Now she had the campaign comms protocols from Denev, it should be easier to work that out. But it might not tell the whole story. Some HDC operatives went dark during missions — no comms at all, but plenty of latitude to do whatever was expedient.

She needed eyes across the Lenticular and the processing grunt to analyse the raw data they captured to reveal anything that might point to outside interference. Just like Emba had done when he'd found those unusual trades in the Telsus and Aphsan systems. But that kind of network wasn't easy to conjure out of thin air. Nok could do it, but it would take time. It would be so much easier if the network had been in place and monitoring before the Hegemony moved in. Not just to provide a baseline, but to catch the deep infiltrations that were already in place. If they stood up a listening station now, they'd completely miss those operatives.

Her eyes snapped open and she was completely awake.

"Nok, can you hear me?"

She wasn't as disconcerted as she should have been when the Jantri answered almost immediately. "Yes."

"Where are you?"

"I'm in station control. I can be with you in a few minutes."

"Never mind." She spoke quickly, outlining what she needed and the problems she'd identified.

"We already have a network like that," Nok said. "Stealth-equipped surveillance satellites have been in place around every planet and colony of the Lenticular for a very long time."

Rhees understood what she was hearing but she was struggling with the why. "So you saw the Hegemony coming?"

There was only a moment's hesitation. "As soon as they made their move, we saw it. But we had no hint of their preparations beforehand. That alone made them worthy of further study."

"Udun said he first met you when he travelled to the Lenticular Council to ask for help. If you knew what was happening then, you could have added your voice to his."

"And a hastily mobilised Lenticular force would have blundered into Voss Space. The Hegemony had just invaded Homeworld. A counterattack was a planned contingency for them. It would have failed."

"That's not why you kept quiet."

There was no reply this time.

"The ship you gave us launched probes into the Point and one of the ships on the Voss Space side," she said.

"The availability of data is its own justification for collecting it."

Rhees sighed. "I'm trying to understand why you're doing this."

Nok's next words exactly mirrored her thoughts. "Because you worry we're just like the Hegemony."

"Did you monitor my conversations with Udun on the stealth ship?"

"No. I could review the ship's log now, but I choose not to."

She was beginning to regret this whole fucking deal with the

Jantri. She felt less and less like she understood what she'd gotten into. "I feel like a lab rat in an experiment."

"There's nothing I can say that will convince you you're not being manipulated. Is suspicion a default for Humans?"

"Not without cause," she snapped back.

"Real or imagined?"

"You really are fucking annoying to talk to."

"If it's any help at all, everything is as I told you when we first met. Events turn around certain individuals. It is our design to supply those individuals with the resources they need and see what happens."

"There must be key individuals supporting the Hegemony's invasion. Volmar for one."

"There are always sides. But out of luck, circumstance or whatever motivation you choose to ascribe to us, we are on yours."

"Or you're lying to me and supporting both sides for your fucked-up amusement." She could go around in circles like this with Nok forever. "Look, I need my comms gear, access to your spy network, and logs of all the traffic monitored since before the invasion."

"It will be assembled and waiting for you in the cargo bay when you are ready."

Through a sliding door in her cabin there was a head and what she'd come to call a "light shower" during her time on the other Jantri ship. It was bright, definitely not wet, but it cleaned off the sweat and grit of Homeworld. When she tied her hair back and re-entered her cabin, a clean onepiece was waiting for her on the bed, courtesy of her creepy ally.

If Nok betrayed Udun and his people …

Fuck, there was nothing she could do if he did. They'd all be screwed.

5

Amaroc screamed again and fell to the deck. The other Kresz surrounded him, their hoods fully erect. Though I couldn't feel it myself, I could imagine what he was experiencing. I'd suffered an empathic interrogation when Kergis's people took me and it had almost driven me mad. The same thing had broken Reka.

The corridor door opened and Rhees hurried in. She came to a halt as a keening wail rose from the knot of Kresz around Amaroc. I raised a claw to her.

The screaming stopped abruptly, replaced by low, guttural sobbing.

"Is that Amaroc crying?" Rhees asked.

"Imagine if you fell among your victims and were forced to relive all the death and violence they'd witnessed," I said. "All the pain and suffering as if you were experiencing it yourself for the first time. Everyone here has seen horrors too terrible to imagine. They've felt their loved ones die beside them. You Humans can only imagine the suffering of others. We share it. That's what Amaroc is feeling – the consequences of what he and Kergis have wrought."

"And I thought the Hegemony's torture techniques were harsh," Rhees said.

I gestured at the puckered scar across my shoulders. "No. They're still worse."

She paused for a moment. "I'm sorry. You're right."

Isza joined us. She looked exhausted. The interrogation had been going all night. The stek-la relied on more than Hegemony tech to keep their secrets safe.

"Are you all right?" I asked her.

"It's as hard on everyone. We're living through what happened again. But it's working. The empathy devices were supplied by the Hegemony. At first only Kergis's most trusted, his stek-la, were fitted with them. But then the Kergis Kresz in the Defence Force got them. They couldn't have turned on us otherwise. And now all Kergis Kresz have them."

"So they can't feel each other?" I said. "They've chosen to become like Humans."

"No offence taken," Rhees said.

"The devices can be switched off," Isza said. "And they are when Kergis Kresz are together in a shielded location. Kergis wouldn't want to give up the control he can exert as hierarch through the communion."

"It gives Kergis an unbeatable advantage, I can see that," I said. "But it's a dangerous thing to do to our people. It's returning them to a pre-Emergence state even if it's temporary."

"And it can be switched on if they want to avoid some particular empathic event," Isza added. "Some feeling they don't want to acknowledge."

"It weakens what we are," I said. "It makes the communion optional for intact Kresz."

I understood the irony of my words. My younger self would have welcomed a device that could hide my feelings from others.

"It's what the Hegemony does," Rhees said. "They find the weak links in a society and weaken them more. By the time you realise what you've lost, it's too late."

"You think the Jantri can replicate this tech for us?" Isza asked.

She meant for us to use the empathy reflectors. I could understand why – right now we were at a huge tactical disadvantage – but it felt wrong. It would be a betrayal of everything Kresz had become since the Emergence. And an insult to those the Hegemony had excised.

"No," I said. "We're not using this, even if we can."

"How can we hope to win if we don't?" Isza said.

"Even if we defeated Kergis's forces, using this tech wouldn't be winning."

"I agree," Rhees said. "You don't want to use Hegemony tech. But maybe Nok could help jam the effect, render the devices inert."

"You trust him now?" Isza asked.

Rhees made the human sound for laughter. "No, I do not. He told me he knew about the Hegemony invasion before you went to the Lenticular Council, Udun. He could have helped. He chose not to because …" She sighed. "I have no idea why."

"You see?" Isza said. She'd already made it clear to me how little she trusted the Jantri.

"I trust him only so long as our interests are aligned," I said.

"And you are the same as Nok," Isza said, rounding on Rhees. "If we stood in the way of achieving your ultimate goal, I'm sure you wouldn't hesitate to sacrifice us."

"I'd like to think I'd at least hesitate," Rhees said. "We owe each other that much after what we've been through."

"We'll see," Isza said. "Amaroc is subdued for the moment. I'm going to get some rest."

She left to join the others who were bedding down on sleep mats in the shelter of the podule wall.

"You agree with her?" Rhees asked.

I didn't. Rhees and I had spoken before about using others and being used in return. Ultimately it led to betrayal because there was no trust. So we'd agreed to cooperate beyond the satisfaction of our own needs and desires. We'd promised to make each other's goals our own.

"I keep my word," I said, then nodded towards the open podules that contained a comms array. Three of Nok's suited incarnations had delivered it during the long night. "This comms array – can it sync with the slaved comms unit we left with Tzek? I'd like to check in."

"It should."

Rhees sat before the array and activated it. A holographic representation of the Lenticular phased into the space between us. She reached into the holo display of planets and grabbed Homeworld, drawing it close and turning it to reveal the deep desert.

There was a bright point where Tzek's hide lay, and two-one other points – the excisees' units – lit up too. We couldn't tell if the excisees carrying them still lived. All but one, on the extreme edge of the Inland Sea below Aktiuk, had travelled far. Two were still in Czerag lands, one near the polar tundra and one far west of Tzek. Of the others, two were just south of the Inland Sea, three were spread in a line across Haketiug lands, with another two below the marshlands of Ukat, and three in the mountains of Dageru.

"Looks good," Rhees said.

"Let's raise Tzek."

She prodded the bright point in the deep desert and a section of the array lit up.

"Tzek," I said. "Can you hear us?"

There was the sound of air running through a tunnel, or some exotic radiation that sounded just like that. Then Tzek's voice came through loud and strong.

"Udun. I'm glad to hear you made it back safely. How is the traitor Amaroc?"

"Much more cooperative. We found a device in his body. An empathic shield that's undetectable to other Kresz. It's how House Kergis kept their secrets from us."

"Ahh." There was a scraping noise and a pause as Tzek considered the implications. "Kergis has gone further to destroy what we had than I'd ever imagined."

"We can see the locations of the excised," I said. "Do you have any word from them?"

"Yes. It's better than we'd hoped. We've made contact with House Ukat, Dageru and Akczek, and re-established contact with some of our own hides we'd thought uninhabited. One of the units isn't responding. I'm assuming the worst. I'm in communication now with hides that can pass messages along to other house members if we need. Though we haven't done so yet. I wanted to limit the chance of news spreading to unwelcome ears."

"And Reka?" I asked, afraid of the answer.

"He's well. He and Sazu are making friends with House Ukat."

My feeder claws stretched wide.

"I do have more news," Tzek said. The sound of airflow increased and I wondered if we'd lost the contact but then he spoke again. "One of our travellers was killed. Her communication device is in the possession of others."

"Does Kergis have it?" Rhees asked.

We both knew that if Kergis or the Hegemony had our device, our whole infiltration was for nothing.

"Wait," Tzek said, "I'm setting up a direct link now. Gatiku, can you hear me?"

I looked at Rhees. Gatiku was the renegade Defender who'd split from the Defenders Lodge after their dean, Resgtu, sided with Kergis and the Hegemony.

"I am here. Speak." The voice was deep and powerful, and filled with suspicion.

Rhees manipulated her array and pointed to the device marker on the holo near the edge of the Inland Sea. This was where Gatiku was broadcasting from. What had happened to the excisee?

"I'm joined by Udun, the Kresz I told you of, and his ally Reeks," Tzek said.

"Fuck," Rhees whispered beside me. "I hope that name's not going to stick."

"The alien Hegemony," Gatiku said.

"I'm an alien," Rhees said, "but I hate the Hegemony and everything they've done to your people."

"The Hegemony lie as easily as air passes through spiracles," Gatiku said.

"He's not wrong," Rhees whispered. "I guess I'll shut up."

"Gatiku," I said, "I'm Udun. I was excised by the Hegemony and I have fought them ever since on Homeworld and in space. We've heard what you've done since the traitors Kergis and Resgtu brought the Hegemony to our world. We should be allies."

"And exchange one group of alien masters for another? This device your dead scout carried. It's Jantri."

Again I wondered how the excisee who carried the communicator had died. Did Gatiku believe all excisees should be euthanised? No, he wouldn't be talking to me if he did.

"I understand your caution," I said. "We can't trust aliens to save us. But you can see what Kergis is doing to our world. The houses and lodges, everything we know, will not survive unless we stop him."

There was silence on the channel and then a low rumble. "Kergis must die."

"We have more chance of achieving that together," I said.

"I have a counter-proposal then. Leave your alien helpers. Let Kresz fight Kresz. We need no outsiders."

Spoken like a true Kresz, I thought. But it was impossible. We needed the Jantri and anyone else we could ally with to have any chance against the Hegemony and Kergis. But we had to keep contact with Gatiku.

"You've given us a lot to think about," I said. "Tzek will keep in touch and we'll talk again."

"He's gone," Tzek said.

"Tzek, we can't do this without the Jan—"

"I know," he said. "Leave Gatiku to me. I'll try to bring him round. I have to go now."

"Take care," I said, and Rhees broke the contact.

She stretched back in her chair and showed her bony teeth. "That Gatiku is a tough nut. But at least my excisees made it. Not bad."

"It's about time we had some luck," I said. "But now we have contact with forces on the ground we have to work out how to mobilise them without alerting Kergis. Once they leave their hides in any sort of numbers they'll be picked up by the worldmind."

"I see what you mean." Rhees waved her hand through the holo and it disappeared. "I need to contact Denev again."

I looked at the ceiling. Here on the Jantri station, nothing could escape Nok's notice.

"I'm pretty sure Nok already knows about Denev," Rhees said. "Or could know if he wanted to."

"I hope your friend is safe," I said, and left her to tell Isza the good news about Reka.

6

The sun was coming up on Conurb Town XT67#. Deep in this cosy suburbia controlled and regulated by the Central Administration, Denev sat in a safe house in a surveillance dead zone and plotted the murder of Undersecretary Cerise Laneaux, Head of SolSec. He brought up another data overlay, matching with times and local topographicals, and stopped. This was hopeful. The engagement was two weeks away but it was the first open-air event Laneaux was confirmed for. And he had his choice of sightlines. The fact it was a SolSec graduation ceremony sharpened the political angle.

"You still there?" he said aloud.

There was a pause and for a moment Denev considered he might be alone inside his own head. But then Rapskel spoke, sounding like he was standing just over his left shoulder.

"Still here. Plan coming together?"

Denev focused on the overlay again. "Maybe." He flipped the relief map out of the screen to hover at eye level so he was looking across the plane near the top of a south-facing rise. Three hundred metres from the podium.

An icon blinked on the screen. Not HDC but carrying an encrypt key.

He let his breath out slowly. He'd been waiting for this call and couldn't ignore it even with Rapskel piggybacking in his skull.

He accepted the encrypt key and a window opened. Rhees looked out at him. Her blonde hair was sleep-rumpled but she still looked good.

"Hey," she said and grinned. "You're still alive."

He smiled too. "You look happy about that. But before we go any further, we're not alone."

"Careful," Rapskel said.

"Or what?" Denev replied.

"There's a point where blowing your head off will be worth the risk."

"Who's with you?" Rhees said.

"I made contact with the Inclusionists. Or the opposition at least. They haven't really told me much. They're in my head. Along with a small bomb."

Rhees sat back, looking lost for words.

"Rhees Lowrans, former Fleet pilot, now … Shit, what are you?" Denev said. "Earth freedom fighter? Meet Rapskel. Is that a first or last name?"

"Last," Rapskel said. "Eon Rapskel."

"Eon Rapskel," Denev echoed. "He's with a rebel cell. They grabbed me and forced me to work against the Hegemony." He smiled again. "Except you'd already convinced me to do that."

"What do they want you to do?"

"Prove my loyalty by killing the head of SolSec. After that, who knows? I'm hoping they'll disable the bomb at least. And maybe get out of my head."

"What the fuck is going on?" Rapskel said.

"Rapskel wants to know what's going on. You want to tell him?" Denev asked Rhees.

"Do you think I should?"

Allies were thin on the ground, and they needed all the help they could get. "Yes. I really do."

Rhees didn't hesitate and Denev was grateful. It showed how far they'd come since Herakli.

"The Hegemony invaded a planetary system in a part of space called the Lenticular. I'm working with the aliens here to kick them out again. After that I hope the aliens will help me bring down the

Central Administration."

Denev waited for Rapskel to respond.

After a few seconds, Rhees asked, "What did he say?"

"I think you surprised him."

"You could say that," Rapskel said. "We need to think about this."

"So maybe he can deactivate that bomb and we can work together," Rhees said. "We're all on the same side."

"Not so fast," Rapskel said. "This could all be bullshit. And either way, killing Laneaux is the right move. It puts you in tight with Volmar. That makes him vulnerable. And it's never not a good idea to kill a CA official."

"Yeah, he's not going to do that," Denev told Rhees. "Besides Volmar's expecting me to kill Laneaux too. It's all very complicated but I'll be fine. What about you?"

"We need allies out here," Rhees said. "I have to find out which worlds HDC have compromised."

Denev thought about where that information would be kept. Way above his clearance. "That's not something I –"

"It's okay. We have that part figured."

"I do have the Fleet and HDC ship deployment for the Lenticular for you," he said. "Unless you have that part figured too."

She smiled. "That would be a help."

He pushed the file from his board into the transmission feed. "I didn't have the chance to tell you last time we talked." He hesitated. "I met your father. He was with Ten Vargas. I thought you were dead then. Offered him my sympathies."

Rhees's lips pressed into a thin line. "It's better if he thinks I'm dead. I've disappointed him enough. And he … He's as much a part of the Hegemony machine as Volmar."

It was the first time Denev had seen her looking lost since Herakli and he wished he could offer some comfort. It wasn't a feeling he'd anticipated. He'd hated her when they'd first met. He'd hated himself too.

"There's something else," he said. "The action against the Hanloi went badly. I'm not sure how badly yet. They're still piecing things together, and now I'm on the Laneaux mission I'm in deep cover. I can't go back in to find out."

"But?" Rhees said.

"Unless our forces were completely annihilated, expect some Fleet ships making use of the escape route through the Lenticular."

"That could complicate things." She paused, no doubt aware Rapskel was listening. "Are you going to be all right? I can come if you need –"

"Save your aliens," he said. "When the fight brings you this way, I'll be waiting."

She nodded and raised her hand, breaking the connection.

"She's the daughter of Admiral Gart Lowrans?" Rapskel said.

"Yes, you know him?"

"Know of him. I want you to tell me everything about you and her."

"I bet you do," Denev said.

∞

Rhees stared at the comms board. She didn't like feeling helpless. But there was nothing she could do from here to help Denev. He could take care of himself. He had to.

As for her father … That was just too complicated to even think about. Their relationship had been fucked up even before she was reportedly killed in action.

She looked at the files Denev had sent her and fed them into the data array. Nok's spy satellite network showed a reasonable deployment, but she could see now there were other Fleet ships running silent deeper in the Voss Space network that could give any attackers a nasty surprise. The campaign comms protocols meant she could tag and decrypt most of the Hegemony comms Nok's network had picked up.

She ran her analysis back two Earth months before the

Hegemony invasion of the Kresz Homeworld, building up a timelapse map of Hegemony incursions and growing networks across the Lenticular. Not all systems and planets had been compromised, and some looked to be under surveillance only rather than full infiltration. But Fleet and HDC had penetrated further than she'd expected – like an infestation of rats or a disease.

She took a break when it was done. The Kresz were sleeping, so she went back to her cabin, slept for a couple of hours and took another shower. Then she called Nok and Udun to meet.

7

I was eating breakfast when two Jantri entered the cargo hold pushing a long table. The other Kresz were used to the Jantri coming and going by now, but I watched the way the suited figures cooperated to place the table beside Rhees's comms array and arrange chairs around it. I knew both suits were extensions of Nok's consciousness – something like the Kresz worldmind but much more sophisticated – but they acted like autonomous beings. It was a charade Nok had kept up across the Lenticular worlds for how long I didn't know. He'd revealed his true nature to me in order to gain my trust, or so he said. But why choose to hide it at all? Was it because he didn't want to scare the other Lenticular species? Did he think they might attack him out of fear or misunderstanding? Or did it indicate motivations that were so unconnected to beings with physical bodies that we couldn't possibly understand?

One of the suits left and the other sat and raised a gauntleted hand to me. Clearly this was the suit designated as Nok for any other Kresz who may be watching.

I put the remains of my meal aside and sat opposite him as Isza and Agik joined us.

Agik had saved Isza during the Hegemony invasion and they'd escaped Homeworld with a small group, hiding out on an asteroid until the Jantri found them. I was grateful to him and I knew he had feelings for Isza, but things had been strained between them since before I'd gone on my mission with Rhees. Agik was opposed to any sort of action that would result in more Kresz lives being lost.

But he and Isza had been talking quietly together all morning and when he sat with her it felt like a good concession.

Rhees entered, pulled the chair from her comms array and sat opposite Isza and me. "All right," she said, "now that we have complete data on Hegemony ship deployment, access to their comms and campaign protocols *and* all the records from Nok's Lenticular-wide spy network, it's clear the whole Telsan system is compromised."

"Which means the Aphsans too – they're close trade partners," Nok said.

"That matches my analysis," Rhees said. "I'd also count out the Dray, P-vvarni, Oclath, Gen'sh and Mentari. And the Fvel. I can't be certain about them."

"Which leaves …" Isza said.

"The Jantri and the Svestans. And the Ophids."

"The Ophids are barely able to get off-planet so not much use as an ally," Nok said.

Despite what Gatiku had said, we needed allies and the Hegemony had neutralised all of them except for Svesta. The last time I'd seen Tol Imnan was when I'd warned the Lenticular Council about the Hegemony invasion. He'd been completely uninterested in helping.

"Tol Imnan was right," I said. "The Hegemony isn't interested in their methane worlds."

"The Hegemony doesn't care what gas a planet's covered in," Rhees said. "But from what you told me, the Svestans are almost as insular as the Kresz. That would limit exposure opportunities, especially if the Hegemony didn't have a Kergis equivalent on Svesta to play with."

"Or a particular need," I said. "The Svestan worlds are furthest from the main tenspace channels. Let's not forget why the Hegemony are really here. A combination of difficulty to reach and low strategic advantage might have saved the Svestans for now. And if they don't feel threatened, why should they join us?" I turned to

Nok. "Have the Jantri received overtures from the Hegemony, no matter how heavily veiled?"

"The Telsans have become interested of late in pushing for a joint project in some of the asteroid fields between Telsan and Jantri space," Nok said. "We're making noises that the idea has potential, but negotiations on the details of such an undertaking have a habit of becoming … protracted."

"Are these Svestans handy in a fight?" Rhees asked.

"I'm sure they could be," Nok said. "But they'll take some convincing."

We didn't have much of a choice. "Nok and I can go there to talk to them," I said. Though I had no idea what I could say to make them join us. "What about Homeworld? Can we get an overlay of the equatorial region around the Inland Sea?"

Rhees leaned over to her array and tapped the interface. A holo appeared and she dragged it over to the tabletop. "Thanks to the Jantri satellite network, comms chatter from Kergis buildings was the most helpful, correlated with hi-res scans of the planet surface. Each of the hierarch strongholds have Kergis garrisons, with larger contingents at the spaceport and the skystalk. Kergis has Defenders stationed at his 're-education centre' on the site of the Academy, and another group on the northwest outskirts where they've set up a prison for political dissidents – basically those who refuse to pledge loyalty to Kergis as Rector."

Isza spoke up. "From what Amaroc's said so far, the dissident group are mainly Adepts and other specialists. Kergis hasn't excised them yet because they have useful skills. They're regularly tortured and kept on low rations. He's trying to break them."

"Garrisons, brainwashing facilities and concentration camps," Rhees said. "Kergis is a fast adopter of Hegemony tools."

"I know from personal experience that he worked some of this out before the Hegemony got involved," I said. "He kidnapped and broke Reka, my brother, and tried to do the same to me."

"Amaroc says the Hegemony troops are low in number," Isza

said. "Some are dispersed among the Kergis-loyal Defenders, a few in each cadre. Most are concentrated at the escarpment."

"They're pretty well dug in there," Rhees said. "Ground troops are concentrated on Aktiuk and immediate surrounds. I've been reviewing transport movements. There's a hell of a lot less troops on the planet now. Most have been withdrawn to the ships in Homeworld orbit, ready for fast-deployment to other Lenticular worlds I'd say. If the need arises. From the Hegemony perspective, if Kergis loses control they can withdraw the remaining troops quickly and raze the planet from orbit if they want to. But why bother? The main aim is to protect the tenspace corridor and they have that covered."

"It's why they haven't poured resources into finding the hides either," I said. "They're not strategically important to them."

Isza blinked. "And Kergis hasn't pressed them to help with that because – like any Kresz – he doesn't feel the need for assistance from outsiders. From what Amaroc told us, his optimal path is to ease the Humans out rather than rely on them. Not only because the alternative means Humans becoming more entrenched on Homeworld, but politically he needs to be seen as strong enough to rule without outside intervention."

"Because of the troop drawdown, the Hegemony is relying on air superiority to maintain control," Rhees said.

"Then these need to be taken out early." I pointed to the escarpment on the map, then the spaceport, and finally the Kergis and Haketiug strongholds. "We destroy the Hegemony airfields and Kergis's command centres. Once the strongholds are gone, whoever holds Aktiuk holds the planet."

"There are significant Hegemony forces in low orbit round the Hub," Rhees said.

"And the Hub is directly above Aktiuk," Isza said.

"And more Hegemony ships in tenspace near the Point," Rhees added.

"We need to neutralise the Hegemony in the air too and stop

anything coming in from orbit," I said. "If we achieve that, the ground battle will be for Kresz only. No outside help, even from Rhees."

"Udun, are you sure?" Isza asked, and I saw that Agik had gripped her lower arm, clearly upset at the way the discussion was heading.

But on this point I was convinced Gatiku was right. "Kergis took Homeworld deceitfully and with help from outsiders. He knows how that looks to other Kresz. If we're to win convincingly, we have to do it as Kresz."

"You don't know what size force Kergis can field on the ground," Rhees said. "You need the air superiority we can give you."

"You can stop the Hegemony interfering," I said. "But that's all you can do."

"You realise how many Kresz will die because of this?" Agik said, looking at me as if I was a monster. "What gives you the right?"

"They do, Agik," Isza said, indicating the other Kresz in the hold. "You can feel it if you try. They were scared for their lives, traumatised. But now they know what Kergis has done to our home, they want to stop what's happening there."

"I want to go home as much as anyone," Agik said. "But are we prepared for what it will cost?"

It was a fair question. So many Kresz had died in the first wave of the Hegemony invasion. And then the excisions had started and those Kresz unable to live with what had been done to them had suicided. There were still safe havens on Homeworld – Tzek and the others were in the deep desert, and other house hides persisted – but they couldn't last forever. Meanwhile those Kresz under Kergis's rule had two choices: submit to his will or be killed or excised. Our people would not survive unless we fought to free them.

"We have to be," I said.

"So we have a war on three fronts," Nok said. "The surface of Homeworld, low orbit and tenspace. All the more reason to get the Svestans on side."

"The question is: how do we get the free Kresz in the hides to Aktiuk without alerting Kergis and every other Kresz on the planet?" I said.

"If we could mass produce those Hegemony empathy reflectors –" Rhees began.

"No." I moved my head from side to side, a Human gesture I'd seen Rhees use many times. "I've already said we won't use them."

"What if we sedated the Kresz and moved them that way?" Rhees asked.

"Sedation wouldn't help," Isza said. "Even asleep, that many Kresz coming out from behind the hide shields would resonate in the worldmind."

"So they don't come out from behind the shields," I said. "We have shielded carriers take them to a staging area near Aktiuk."

"How will they –" Isza began.

"I think Udun means invisible ships," Nok said.

"Can it be done?" I asked.

"I'm sending the specifications to our shipyards," Nok said. "We have something that can adapt to our needs."

"We're talking about a lot of ships here," Isza said.

"You'll have a lot," Nok said.

"So we have a ground war, and we need ships to engage in low orbit," I said. "What about tenspace?"

"Rhees and I will handle the Hegemony in tenspace," Nok said.

"We will?" Rhees asked.

But the Jantri said no more.

The meeting broke up and Rhees returned to her comms array.

"When do you want to leave for Svesta?" Nok asked me.

"Now," I said, standing.

"I'll meet you in the bay when you're ready," Nok said.

Isza stood close beside me and curled her claws around mine. "You're leaving me again. This is becoming a habit."

I held her claws against my chest plate. "I'll be safe. Svesta is free from Hegemony spies and I'll have Nok with me."

"That's not what I meant. Things are happening fast now."

"And they're going to happen faster. We're committed. All or nothing."

She paused and I could tell she wanted to say something more.

"What is it?" I asked.

"Just now, in the meeting – I've never heard you speak like that before. You sounded like a hierarch preparing for battle. I wish I could still feel you. I worry what's going on inside you. I wish I could help."

I knew I'd changed since that first trip to Telsan space I'd taken for Czerag. I'd learned so much about trust and friendship, and the price the universe extracted for trying to change the way things were. Emba and Atalna had died to protect what was good and right. Rhees, Tzek and Isza would do everything they could to fight for the same cause. I could do no less.

"You do help," I said and the air passed through my spiracles in a low hiss. "This is what I need to be to free Homeworld."

"You're not going to throw your life away in this battle, are you?"

I'd thought about dying before. But that had changed too.

"No. I'd have let Tzulak kill me on the Jantri ship if that's how I felt. I want to fight and live."

"Then we'll fight side by side this time."

"That's how it's always been." She'd watched over me when we were growing up, and taken my side when the other younglings ridiculed me because I wanted to travel beyond the horizon of our planet.

"Has Amaroc told us all he knows?" I said, changing the subject.

"I think so."

"And how does he feel about what he's done?"

"He obeyed his hierarch and acted in the best interests of his house," Isza said.

"Those two things aren't always the same."

"You and I know that, but a lot of Kresz grind their thoughts along well-worn paths. That's the problem with traditionalism."

"*The different, the injured and the deformed weaken us and must be destroyed,*" I said. "Sakat's golden rule."

"Bad as this war has been, the viciousness and death we've witnessed has at least shown the stupidity of aiming for a single mode of perfection," Isza said. "It's stupid for an individual. It's even stupider for a whole species. There's strength in difference. In the unexpected."

"If we win, Homeworld will be a very different place," I said. "It's already changed but that change was uncontrolled. The mould has been broken. People will be ready for a new way."

"Listen to us," Isza said. "Changing the world."

"I think our world was ready to change, but it didn't know how. I wouldn't wish the Hegemony invasion on us again, but you and I were already a product of that desire for change. One can't exist without the other."

"The times make the person?" she said.

"Something like that."

"I'm just glad we're together to see this."

She touched my arm. I almost didn't mind the fact I couldn't feel her through the contact.

"Stay safe," she said.

8

In the holo display Admiral Gart Lowrans saw a shower of sparks erupt from a ceiling panel behind Frey's shoulder. Someone shouted, "Lock that short down!" and a uniform ran to obey.

Commander Frey of the System Class Battlecruiser *Hyperion* grimaced. "Whatever the Hanloi hit us with cut through our shields like they weren't there. I've got wounded from most of my escort backed into the corridors, the environment systems are strained beyond capacity, and the drive's running at forty per cent at best."

"Hang in there, Tom," Gart said. "If anyone can bring those people home safe and sound, it's you. I'll check in again soon."

"Appreciate it. Frey out."

The holo display closed and Gart clenched his fists in helpless anger. *Hyperion* was only one of dozens of ships limping back from galactic centre. The remnants of Frey's group were retracing their steps through the direct route between there and Hegemony space. What relief ships Gart could spare were already heading out to meet them. But with ship drives compromised, days became weeks of trip time. Tom Frey and his crew were staring at a long slow death if their already stretched luck didn't hold.

Gart's name had been on the orders that sent all those men and women out there. Not that he'd had any choice in that. Vargas had relayed the wishes of the Central Administration and Gart had turned them into deployment commands.

He crossed to the picture window and looked down at

the checkerboard of parade grounds spreading out from the administration hub. Twenty squads were working through close-formation drills in the sunshine. More fodder for the Hegemony war machine.

Vargas said the Central Administration had voted unanimously for the Hanloi campaign. But Gart had sensed Volmar's fingers all over the decision. The HDC comptroller had supreme self-confidence and fuck anyone else's opinion. He wouldn't be satisfied until the whole galaxy was under Hegemony rule and if that meant tens of thousands of Fleet personnel died, it was just the cost of doing business. And to top it all, Gart had put Rhees under Volmar's control and in harm's way. It was another mistake in a long line of mistakes he'd made with his daughter, right back to how he'd behaved when Rhees was a little girl.

When Catriona – Gart's wife and Rhees's mother – had been killed during the Battle for Earth, Rhees had been left alone just like him. All she needed was someone to love her and take care of her, but he couldn't do it. He was too wrapped up in his own grief and anger. So he'd pushed her away, telling himself it was for her own good. When she contacted him some years later, he didn't know what he could possibly have in common with a teenage girl he'd barely spoken to for years. What could they offer each other, except a reminder of past pain? And by then he'd already become a traitor to the Hegemony in his mind.

Then he'd seen Rhees among the cadet intake on the *Nimitz*. Saw how she'd grown into a strong, capable woman like her mother. Someone who had friends who would look after her. He was proud, but he'd pushed her away again because … Well, it was safer for her if the two of them weren't seen to be close. Not after what he'd been doing for the past few years.

The last time they spoke was after Petar Antwer had died and she'd been court-martialled. He had to intercede then. It was dangerous, but she was looking at years in prison. Which was why he'd arranged for her to work for HDC. Bury her inside that vast surveillance machine – just another cog as far away from Gart Lowrans and anything he might do or say as humanly possible. Safe under Volmar. And then she'd died on Volmar's watch.

"Fuck," he said, the word sounding powerless in his empty office.

His desk chimed and he crossed back to it, sitting slowly as he saw the codestring on the holo display. He initiated full encryption. The comm was sound only.

"Rapskel. Can't say I was expecting to hear from you."

"Likewise, Admiral."

Gart winced. "Gart, please. Or Lowrans will do."

"Sure. I came across some news I think might interest you. That is, if you're happy to trade some intel."

"Same deal as before," Gart said. "You tell me what you have and I'll do my best to get you what you want."

"Fair enough." Rapskel paused. "It's about your daughter, Rhees Lowrans."

"Yes?" Gart felt the familiar tightening across his chest.

"She's alive."

Two words he never thought he'd hear. "You're sure?"

"Positive."

"How?"

"Through a recent contact. He still needs to prove himself before I can fully trust him. But when I know more, you'll know more. Now here's what *we* need."

A window opened and an encrypted list appeared, decoding as it scrolled. A series of security protocols and patrol routes for supply bases spread across several southern hemisphere conurbs.

"An update on these would be useful," Rapskel said.

Gart scanned the list. It was doable. "It'll take a little time."

"Then we'll talk again in a few days."

The comm ended.

Gart sat back in his chair. Just maybe he'd been given a second chance.

9

The open lock to the cloaked ship stood like a door into another dimension. Nok was waiting inside, seated in the pilot's chair. I strapped in quickly and the ship lifted, manoeuvring across the deck towards the opening hull.

"How long till we get to Svesta?" I asked.

"Not long. Rhees is an able pilot, but the biological form has its limitations."

The ship shot through the force wall and into a storm of light. I'd flown through this space three times now and even though I couldn't feel the acceleration I knew we'd never travelled this fast. Great arcs of plasma speared out at us but before they hit, the ship was always somewhere else. Then the wall was rushing towards us and we angled at the last moment, slipping into the narrow channel and then into the broader tenspace corridor. At least here it was a little calmer.

"I think I prefer a human pilot," I said. Nok's gauntlets were holding the controls but I realised they hadn't moved during our flight from the station. "You're not steering with your hands, are you?" But of course he had no hands. There wasn't even a "he".

"I'm interfaced directly with the vessel. As I said –"

"The biological form has its limitations," I echoed.

Nok had revealed his true self to me: pure thought and pure energy. But not just of an individual. The memories, thoughts and brain power of an entire species. He – or they – didn't need armoured suits. They didn't need to concern themselves with corporeal beings at all.

"You could go anywhere in the universe, or other dimensions even. Why choose to stay here and concern yourself with the Lenticular?" I asked.

"I told you before there would be secrets between us. There are some things beings like yourself couldn't possibly understand."

"But you could stop all this if you wanted to, couldn't you?"

The glowing visor turned to me as if in question.

"You could stop the Hegemony," I clarified. "Make them go away. Put everything back the way it was, or arrange things in any way you wish."

"Perhaps we could. But would you thank us for it?"

"You'd stop a lot of suffering."

"Now, yes. But after. If the Lenticular saw us for what we really are, wouldn't they come to resent us, or rely on us, or both? We'd be gods, but not gods of their choosing nor in their own image. Tell me, do you think the Kresz need more gods?"

I thought of Sakat. The wars, cleansings and sacrifices that had been carried out in his name.

"Imaginary gods are bad enough," Nok continued. "No. If we've learned anything in our long evolution, it's that each species must learn to stand on its own. To find and finally be its true self. We can help. But we don't want to be worshipped for it."

I'd judged Nok as I'd judge any Kresz or Telsan. But he didn't need a hidden agenda, and maybe he didn't have one. He didn't think like individual limited beings. It was still possible he could betray us without seeing it as betrayal simply because he was so very different.

"And if you had unlimited power?" Nok asked.

"If it didn't change who I was, I'd destroy the Hegemony in an instant. And Kergis and all the other Kresz who imposed their will on others. Who robbed them of their freedom, or their lives."

"And would you know when to stop?"

It seemed a simple question. But the evidence that it was not was all around me. Kergis had pursued power at all costs and he'd made an alliance with the Hegemony that gave him control of

Homeworld. But the Hegemony weren't interested in him or his dreams. They'd sweep him aside when he was no longer useful. Had he realised that yet?

And the Hegemony itself. From what Rhees said, it had been born out of a simple desire for self-protection and grown into something that subjugated and fed on its own people.

Those with power always cautioned those without about its dangers. But the Jantri'va had avoided the obvious pitfalls. Which meant it was at least possible.

We sped down the tunnel, brightly glowing plasma ghosts keeping pace with us, spinning around each other and beneath the ship like a shoal of luk'ah following a fishing vessel on the Inland Sea. We entered a chamber webbed with sparkling energy channels and barely slowed before plunging into the next tunnel and going even faster judging by how the walls glowed as they flashed by.

I looked at Nok's gauntlets again, still immobile. A tiny irregular patch of plating on the back of his left glove slowly detached and floated away, letting a strong light shine from within. It was joined by another and another. Flecks of metal breaking off. Pinpricks of radiance beneath, pushing them out. What was happening?

"Nok?" I said.

"Don't be alarmed. You'll be safe."

I pulled my harness tighter. That's when I saw the same thing was happening to me. Flakes of chitin detaching. My torso plates turning into a lattice. My arms and legs the same. I was glowing too. A light from within. I felt panic. My body was slowly flying apart but there was no pain. Was I hallucinating?

"Nok?" I said again.

"Watch," he said.

What was left of his gauntlet swept across the controls, which started to disintegrate. The ship pulled apart. The tenspace corridor was visible through the fragments that swirled and coalesced into a stream of light. I looked down again. My body was gone.

This will be faster.

The voice was Nok's. But he had nothing to speak with and I had nothing to hear with. It was his thoughts I heard.

The fish-like streaks of plasma spun around me then shot off ahead and we were flying with them, streaking faster and faster. Tunnel walls and chambers blurring past.

We're the same medium as tenspace, Nok thought. *Part of the plasma flow.*

You could have told me first.

Difficult to explain. Easier just to experience.

Particles flew by, flowing out of an invisible point ahead. The only constant was the creatures – I thought of them as creatures – that accompanied us.

Nok answered even as the question formed in my mind.

Natives of this energy level. I don't know much more than that. They can't or won't communicate. The universe is alive, Udun. At every level. Beneath the quantum and above the macro. Understanding that is what truly absorbs me. The trials of the species in the Lenticular … His thought trailed off as he considered how to explain. *There's a vestige of me that remembers how it was to be corporeal.*

He was silent then, but I thought I understood. It was why he helped us in his way.

Suddenly the creatures peeled away from us. The corridor walls glowed brighter and then we were flying across infinite black studded with stars, streaking towards a dark red eye that swelled rapidly to reveal planets and moons. One moon in particular, rushing for us, the surface suddenly visible in all its dead, rock-strewn detail as we plunged into it, like diving into a mist and just as insubstantial. We emerged into space again as the ship coalesced around us and an instant later I was looking at my claw held up before my eyes. I was whole again.

"We're here," Nok said.

A torus-shaped space station hung in front of us. The moon we'd flown through lay directly behind, and the station floated above a cloud-wrapped planet. Bands of vapour in brown, orange and dirty yellow swirled across its face, twisting, shredding and reforming as I watched.

"This is the Svestans' most secret installation," Nok said. "Cloaked from observation by the disturbance the moon behind us causes in the planet's magnetosphere. It's an effective barrier against approaching ships too. Unless that ship is composed of pure energy. But for our purposes now, I've neutralised our ship's invisibility."

On the surface of the torus, weapons bays opened and three ships emerged, spreading out in an attack formation.

"We have their attention," Nok said, keying open a comms channel. "This is Nok of Jantri'va. We're unarmed and here to see Tol Imnan."

The ships were still closing on us. Sharp-nosed lozenges.

"You think that will stop them?" I said.

"They can't harm us."

A screen opened up in front of us: a schematic of the station with one of the hold locks ringed in red.

"Proceed to this location," a voice said. "Offer no resistance."

The approaching ships sheared off, circling to provide an escort.

The plating on the station shone with a dull lustre, refracting different colours across its surface like a smoky jewel. The hold lock was more conventional: open and leading into a large hangar filled with a pale pink smoke. Svestans were methane-breathers.

I looked at Nok. I didn't suppose he needed to breathe, but his armour suggested to others he carried his own atmosphere with him.

"Do you have a spare suit?" I asked.

"Nothing so mundane. We want to impress our hosts with the technology we have. The method of our arrival already has them guessing, so we'll press our advantage. A self-replenishing force bubble will suffice. You'll be quite safe and able to breathe."

I had no doubt Nok could do what he said and I followed him out to the small ship lock. I felt nothing unusual, but as the internal atmosphere vented and I looked down at my body there was a shimmer of colour across my shell. I could still breathe even though we stood in near vacuum. Then the Svestan atmosphere seeped in, pink tendrils curling around my legs and rising in coils, but never quite touching me. The air tasted strange in my spiracles but that was probably my imagination. If there had been any leakage, I'd be dead.

The outer hatch opened. A group of Svestans – their heads free of the bubble helmets they wore off-world – stood in a half-circle, their spines rattling as they levelled long-snouted weapons at us. I felt exposed and wished I had Nok's armour.

"This way," one of them said, walking backwards. As we followed, the other Svestans formed a circle that moved with us through the fog. The escort was an obvious show of force. I imagined the nature of our arrival had frightened the Svestans, though they'd never admit it.

Indistinct shapes passed us in the gloom. I wondered what it was like to live on a world where you could never see the horizon. To always feel enclosed. Leaving their planet for the first time and encountering limitless space must have been challenging.

The group rearranged formation as we passed through a door and were led into a bare room. The circle of weapon muzzles reformed around us. No one spoke and time stretched. Nok seemed content to wait.

The door opened again. I'd only seen Tol Imnan once, in the broadcast space of the Telsus IV spire, and that was just a projection. He was more physically imposing here. A head taller than Nok, and broader than Isza. His spines rattled as he pushed through the ring of guards and walked straight up to Nok.

"You knew the location of this facility and you knew I was on it. How?"

There was a soft hum as Nok's helmet tilted back to regard Tol Imnan. "There are a great many things I know. The alloy of this station is being developed as an alternative to tekla. You're testing it in the energetic zone between the moon and the planet below. The alloy shows promise, but ultimately the atomic structure will break down when subjected to true tenspace conditions."

"I could have you executed for coming here," Tol Imnan said.

"You can try," Nok said. "But this facility, the moon above and the world below would be reduced to dust shortly after."

Tol Imnan grunted. It may have been a laugh. "So why are you here?" He looked at me then. "And why have you brought your little Kresz runaway?"

"Udun warned the Council the Lenticular was under secret attack," Nok said. "What he said was true. The Kresz Homeworld has been occupied by alien invaders. Their ships control Kresz space and tenspace around it. Other systems have been infiltrated: Telsus, Dray-helm and the P-vvarni worlds. We have proof that even Oclathi space on your border is under covert Hegemony control. For the moment your own system is clear. That's why we're talking."

"They leave us alone because they fear us," Tol Imnan said. "Why should we care about the other worlds?"

"They leave you alone because you don't have anything they want yet," Nok said. "But that can change. And Svesta isn't as independent of the wider Lenticular as you claim. You still need tekla and you have none of your own. You still need the Jantri to service the power stations we set up on Atva and Atva Minor. There are vital components in those plants that need regular replacement. It's a simple truth: you need us more than we need you."

"We can do without your power stations, Jantri."

"Yes, and run your own at a quarter of the efficiency and ten times the cost."

This wasn't going well. It struck me that Tol Imnan was a contrarian. He'd turn aside any appeals to mutual interest.

"We didn't come here to threaten Svesta," I said.

"It doesn't sound that way, little Kresz. Are you going to plead for your Homeworld now?"

"No. I already know you don't care about us. But Svestans claim to be great warriors."

"That's no claim. We are."

"But where's the record that bears that out? When the Lenticular was in its infancy there were plenty of wars and border skirmishes. Minor systems changed hands regularly. Some more than once in a single cycle. The P-vvarni and Telsans fought hard over mining rights to systems along their borders, with great loss of life on both sides, but they kept fighting. Where was Svesta when all this was going on? When species were flexing muscles and grabbing planets on a daily basis? You were sitting on the same small collection of methane worlds."

"You know nothing about us."

"Because there's nothing to know. You're a footnote in the history of the Lenticular. You have no influence beyond your borders because you've done nothing beyond them."

"I don't have to listen to this."

"No. You don't. But we're about to wage a war that will decide the future of the Lenticular for cycles to come. You're lucky enough to have a choice. You can cower on your ball of dirty gas or you can join us. Show your warrior prowess and share in the glory."

"Or the defeat," Tol Imnan said.

"Staying out of this war means you're already defeated."

Tol Imnan stood to his full height, spines vibrating. Finally he said, "And what is it you need from us?"

"Ships and pilots," Nok said. "To fight alongside our forces and destroy every enemy vessel we find."

"And the spoils?"

"They will be beyond your imagining. The Jantri'va pledge it."

Tol Imnan waved a spine-encrusted arm and the guards around us lowered their weapons.

He pointed a finger at Nok's visor. "We want you to make our alloy work."

"It's possible," Nok said.

"And we want the means to manufacture it ourselves. We will not be reliant on the Jantri or anyone else."

"Agreed."

Tol Imnan raised his hand and his guards levelled their blasters at us again. "You'll have your answer soon. You can go." And he was gone too.

We walked back out into the misty corridor with our Svestan escort leading us.

"I think we'll have a deal," Nok said.

"You can do what he asked?"

"Oh, yes. Quite easily. But we wouldn't have gotten this far if you hadn't provoked him."

I blinked. "It was the right thing to do. You knew that."

"Yes, but the point is you did too. I told you before, you're one of those individuals around which the events of the universe turn."

"If you keep testing me, at some point I'll fail."

"Some things can't fail. It's not in their nature."

We were at the ship now, the lock door opening for us. The task ahead was overwhelming. The solution, according to Nok, was "be yourself". But it couldn't be that simple.

I'd been broken, lost and somehow I'd survived. But I could lose everything again. Lose more. I didn't mean my life – there were worse things than dying. But if I failed again, it might break me forever.

10

Rhees sat at her comms board but didn't see the data flowing past her eyes. She was thinking about the battle to come. It had a definite shape now and she would play a major part: pushing the Hegemony out of Homeworld airspace and near-orbit. And doing whatever Nok had planned for the forces in Voss Space. There was no turning back. She'd known that for a long time. The Central Administration was ultimately responsible for what happened next. But how many humans would die because of her involvement? The question had already invaded her dreams. She had no idea how she'd cope with the reality.

She pushed back from her console. She needed to stretch her legs. A flight outside was out of the question, so she did the next best thing – walking through the corridors until she came to the ship bay. The stealth ship still hadn't returned.

Isza sat on the deck just inside the doorway, leaning against the bulkhead wall.

"Waiting for Udun?" Rhees said.

"I am."

"Are you worried?"

"I've been worried for him all my life. It's my job."

Rhees laughed softly.

"What?" Isza said, looking at her.

"Nothing. I'll wait and worry with you." She slid down the bulkhead to sit beside Isza.

The Kresz dwarfed her, even reclining against the wall. Isza's chitinous plates slid over one another as she shifted, unfolding her double-kneed legs and stretching. The skin beneath her plates was dotted with pinprick openings that hissed gently with respiration. She was so alien, and yet she sat there worrying about her brother and waiting for him to return. It was such a familiar scenario. The Kresz had an emotional framework that was understandable in human terms. It made what the Hegemony had done to them all the more horrible – or it seemed to. Perhaps that fact pointed to humanity's inherent weakness, Rhees thought. We ascribe more value to things we can understand on our own terms. But killing and subjugating a species that is truly alien – that, unlike the Kresz, has a set of responses humans can't relate to – is surely just as bad. It's just harder to care about.

The CA understood that. The xenophobic hysteria that gripped humanity after the K-Chaan war had given them their cue. An empire was strongest when it had something to oppose, to push against. Keeping aliens off Earth made it easier for the CA to objectify them as something "other". And humanity – traumatised and, at heart, emotionally stunted when it came to the truly alien – fell in line. Really we're the worst possible species to be in charge of a galactic empire, Rhees thought.

"They're back," Isza said.

The bay door opened and the force shield that held in the atmosphere glittered. Outside, rings of energy were twisting against an angry, roiling wall of cloud. Rhees couldn't see any sign of a ship, then remembered it was cloaked. Perhaps there was a shimmer at the shield wall – only perceptible because she was looking for it. Or imagining it.

And then there was no doubt. A rectangle opened in an empty part of the bay and Udun stepped onto the deck followed by Nok.

Isza stood to greet them and Rhees followed her, watching as the much bigger Kresz pulled her brother into a quick embrace. Their shells clacked together.

"Another successful mission?" Isza asked.

"We'll see," Udun said, glancing at Nok beside him. "We gave the Svestans a few things to think about."

"They didn't need to think too hard," Nok said. "I've just received their answer."

"And?" Rhees said.

"They'll join us."

That's it, Rhees thought. The last piece had fallen into place.

Nok turned to her. "It's time to show you your command post. You need to familiarise yourself with the control interface."

Rhees felt a weight pull at her chest. Each step in the process took her closer to the point where she'd fight her own people.

∞

Nok led her to a simple room that held something like an eviscerated dolphinship crossed with a datanook. A couch lay inside the device surrounded by panels that looked slightly melted. She took Nok's offered gauntlet and stepped inside.

As she reclined on the couch it flowed around her. A hum intensified and interfaces powered up, filling the enclosed capsule with a dome of holo displays.

"This may be disorienting," Nok said.

She was expecting a 360-degree view to emerge as it had when she'd flown the dolphinship. But then – there was no other way to describe it – the dome of holos exploded into her head. Her eyes stopped working, her perspective was all wrong. She gagged. Tasted vomit. Swallowed. Images of space strobed past her, revolving faster and faster.

"Wait," Nok said.

The spinning was making her nauseous again. Then it stopped. Blackness. And then … she could "see" multiple points of view – different images of space from different locations. If she thought about it too hard she was sure her brain would burst. But somehow she knew each point of view was her own and – somehow – she could make sense of them all, separate but existing alongside all the others.

"What you're seeing," Nok said, "is the view from seventy-three Jantri flyers nearby in normal space. A simple feed only, but it can be enhanced with tactical and haptic overlays. That comes next."

"How are you doing this?" Rhees asked, flipping between conscious views.

"Study of human physiology and brain structure. Yours. You'll need this to control the ships."

"Control? You mean command the Jantri pilots?"

"There are no pilots. These ships are slaved to your will. You've already seen they have a level of autonomy."

She remembered the dolphinship saving her from Emba's crumbling residence.

"But," Nok continued, "you will *be* the attack force."

Which meant the battle would be much more personal. "I don't want to kill Hegemony pilots," she blurted.

Nok was silent for a moment. "That may be difficult."

"I know but …"

How could she explain? Fleet command and HDC were culpable. The pilots were only following orders. But it was a hollow excuse. If any of those pilots cared to find out, they'd see how the Hegemony was brutalising the Kresz and how they'd done the same to countless species. They had choices: ignore it, or accept and be complicit; or do what she'd done. Though she couldn't recommend the specifics of how she'd defected from the Hegemony war machine. Still, killing them felt wrong.

"If I can disable their ships – take them out of the fight – the effect will be the same," she said.

"The Svestan ships fighting alongside you will not be so merciful."

"Do we even need their help now if I can control so many dolphinships?"

"There's a limit to how far your consciousness can be segmented," Nok said. "We'll still need their help if we're to be sure of winning against the ships the Hegemony has in Homeworld orbit."

Which sounded reasonable. Although Nok could deploy more Jantri ships to help her without involving the Svestans if he wanted to. Unless he had some other reason to get them involved. The multiple points of view suddenly felt like they were pressing in on her.

"How do I …"

"Just think 'disengage'," Nok said.

Her vision cleared. It was just her and Nok in an unremarkable room again. The engineering behind such a direct brain interface was at least equal to the Hegemony-built empathy reflectors. Perhaps more advanced, as she had no idea how the Kresz empathic sense functioned.

"Have you been able to crack the empathy reflectors?" she asked.

Nok's suit folded to sitting position and his faceplate reflected the same golden glow as usual – beyond inscrutable.

"It's not possible to block the effect remotely. The devices are linked by some highly exotic means involving higher-dimensional channels and the signal has random phase shifting."

"That sounds overly engineered for what it does. It's almost like Hegemony Voss Space comms tech – too much for devices confined to a single planet. But …" A number of worrying thoughts blossomed in her mind. "HDC *could* use the devices to eavesdrop on conversations by every Kresz fitted with a reflector. Or broadcast a kill switch if they wanted to deactivate the units. Hell, if the units contained explosives, they could even …"

It was too horrible to think about, but easily something Volmar could do. An assassination wave spreading across the planet, killing all the Kresz who had accepted the HDC implant.

"They don't contain explosives," Nok said.

That was something at least.

"But analysis indicates they're slaved to a central unit, which we suspect is held by Kergis."

"That makes sense," Rhees said. "The devices facilitate betrayal in an empathic society. Kergis would want to make sure he could turn them off if he suspected his own people were plotting against him."

"I've discussed this with Udun," Nok said. "When they're on the ground, he will need to find the central unit and neutralise it if they're to have any hope of winning."

"If Kergis has it, they'll need to get very close. It'll be difficult."

Rhees regarded the unchanging glow of Nok's faceplate again. Was remote deactivation of the reflectors *really* beyond Jantri tech or was this another of Nok's "manifest destiny" moments? Udun was all for a Kresz-only hand-to-hand battle. Having an alien switch off the reflectors remotely at a crucial moment would rob him of that. Was *that* what Nok and Udun had discussed?

Ultimately it wasn't her concern. And she had her own problems to worry about. Where was her father in all this, she wondered. Would he be directing the forces she came up against?

11

Denev was woken by an insistent bird call. Two plaintive peeps repeated over and over. Then another bird started up: a single tone like a breathy flute but modulating up at the end. A koel he was pretty sure, though his bushcraft was based on three trips only: two to the Tasmanian Reserve and one to the Galapagos Islands while he was still at school.

He opened the tent flap and pushed through the anti-static shield that had repelled most of last night's downpour and kept him warm inside while he slept. It was still dark and the air was chill, smelling of damp growing things. He switched on the solar stove and set a pot of water on it to boil.

He'd been out here for four days now, following the hiking trail. Setting up camp, striking it the next day and walking to the next site. He'd met a few other walkers on the way but had discouraged more than simple hellos. He was inside the SolSec surveillance perimeter that had been put in place for the week running up to Laneaux's appearance. The Academy was twenty kilometres away, but the park that bordered its grounds was a popular bushwalk site. There was no need to close it down as long as the walkers were tagged and accounted for. None of his camping equipment threw up a red flag. It was all perfectly innocuous. The cache of mission gear had been buried by HDC three days before the perimeter was raised.

The water was boiling now and he tipped a caf concentrate into his mug and topped it off, swirling the mixture a few times before standing and walking to the edge of his camp. The calls of the birds that had woken him were joined by others and early dawn light was turning the clouds pink. He took a sip of coffee and waited as a band of weak sunlight illuminated the hills in the distance – tree-covered for the most part, but a few bare outcrops of rock glowed rose-coloured. Wisps of morning mist clung to the treetops.

A kookaburra call echoed from below, quickly answered by others. Denev was standing on the edge of a cliff looking over at an escarpment on the other side of a deep, wide gorge filled with gum trees, palms and tall ferns. Sunlight was streaming in now through the gorge's narrow neck. A flock of lorikeets suddenly took flight, pushing through the canopy to congregate in the air above and sweep across the treetops in a slow climb.

"Thinking of jumping?"

Rapskel was in his head again.

"It's an option," Denev said and took another sip of coffee. "Laneaux's assassination will be pinned squarely on the Inclusionists. I still don't understand how that's going to help your cause."

"Understanding is not required. Only obedience."

"I *could* jump," Denev said. "I mean, you're going to blow my head off once Laneaux's dead."

"The Inclusionists are a creation of the CA. We could never engage with them let alone use them. It would compromise our security. Some of us suspect the only reason the CA created them was to draw out dissidents to 'join the cause'."

"Like a Judas goat."

"Just like."

It was more than possible Rapskel was right. HDC taught it was a poor tool that didn't have at least two uses. The Inclusionists offered citizens the comfortable fantasy of living in a democracy with a viable opposition party to keep the government honest. And any true believers the group attracted were tagged and surveilled to make sure they didn't do any real harm. Or got used in turn themselves, like Preem and his friends.

"So what *do* you believe in?" Denev asked.

"Freedom. The rule of law balanced equitably against the rights of the individual."

"And what about aliens?"

"What about them? Why should their rights be any different to the rights we aspire to for ourselves? The lessons of history are plain. No good ever comes from vilifying a group or creating second-class citizens."

"And if they attack?"

"We have the right to defend ourselves against aggressors. But if they come in peace, why not welcome them?"

"It's that simple?"

"It really is."

"I think you and Rhees would get along," Denev said.

It was true. She shared the same clear moral vision he'd lost somewhere along the way. He still doubted he'd get out of this alive. But perhaps there was hope for humanity.

"So what *is* the end game?" he said.

"The goal is clear. The means …" Rapskel sighed. "That's the trick, isn't it?"

"Yes. It is."

A warm breeze picked up from the valley floor, rushing at Denev where he stood on the rock edge. He ate a soya bar and had another cup of coffee, enjoying the stillness and the sunlight filtering through the branches. Then he struck camp, folding everything into a hip bag, and struck off along the trail.

The route was flat for most of the morning, skirting the edge of the gorge. But after a brief stop for lunch he started climbing and the trail became narrower, with bushes and ferns closing in around until finally he pushed through the tree cover onto a ridge.

A drone paced him for half an hour as he followed the trail along the ridge, climbing slowly towards the peak that dominated the surrounding countryside, then it peeled off as he followed the path curving back into the trees along the side of the mountain.

He wasn't worried about the surveillance. And if they were worried about him, they'd have done something about it.

In the late afternoon, he made camp in a small clearing that was relatively flat. A stream chattered along the edge of the site. He couldn't remember water ever tasting so good. After quenching his thirst, he set his tent, climbed in and fell asleep.

His band woke him in darkness. The readout showed two minutes after midnight. Six hours till dawn. He tapped his band and it glowed, providing a dim illumination. Making sure the fastening into the tent was secure, he activated a stud in the lining. Any drone passing overhead and employing infrared or more exotic wavelengths would now see a man sleeping peacefully inside.

He ran a finger along the central seam of the tent's groundsheet. It parted and he pulled it back to show the undisturbed turf underneath. Except it *had* been disturbed just ten days before. He took a small folding spade from his pack and began to dig.

The tip of his spade hit something hard half a metre below the turf. He scraped dirt back from the surface and undogged the latches on the lid, lifting it off the case beneath. On top lay a onepiece shimmer suit. The camo-cloth activated as he pulled it on, pressed the seals and drew the hood to fit snugly over his head. He fitted HUD lenses before pressing the rest of the hood flap over his face.

There were four other items set into the thick foam interior of the case. He took out the launcher: a standard rifle stock, but studded with controls and attached to a short, thick barrel around twenty centimetres long and pierced in a regular pattern from the business end to halfway down the dull metal. The second item was a black pipe as long as his forearm that clipped onto the side of the launcher muzzle. The other two items were black spheres, no wider than a fingernail. Last time he'd used these, he'd been infiltrating the alien rebel base with Rhees. That had felt dangerous then, but now it seemed like a memory from simpler times.

He tapped both spheres and they rose to hover a metre above the case. The HUD sprang to life. He tapped his band to kill the illumination, now painfully bright, lengthened the launcher's strap as he shouldered the weapon, and pushed through the tent flap to the outside. The spheres followed him, hovering at head height for a moment. Then one moved off into the trees to scout the path ahead. He watched its progress in the HUD's window. The other sphere took up a position behind him, waiting for him to move off in pursuit of its sibling while it followed at a discreet distance.

He crossed the stream and turned uphill. The HUD showed his bearing, elevation and distance to the outward post. The forest around him was silent but he could see glowing IR ghosts of birds, possums in the branches, smaller mammals in the undergrowth, frozen in place, sensing his passing if not actually seeing him.

The way got steeper and he fell into a steady gait, pushing upward, stopping frequently to hunker down against a tree trunk, drink and catch his breath.

He followed an animal trail angling up for about half an hour that ended in a sheer outcrop of rock ten metres high that looked unscalable. He waited as the spheres scouted left and right until they found a way that was manageable.

After four hours of climbing he reached the edge of the tree cover. The peak was another twenty metres up but he stayed at this level and skirted the treeline to the other side of the mountain and started down.

He came across a fallen ghost gum. A big one, maybe eighty years old. The trunk leaned at an angle against other sturdier gums. Laying the launcher on the ground, he shinned up the trunk until he was level with the treetops and could see down to the valley below. Forest gave way to a neat undulating lawn running up to a series of low glass buildings in front of which a white canopy curved over a broad stage. A single podium stood dead centre.

He made his way back down, cutting away branches that might snag him while maintaining what cover the remaining foliage afforded. Back on ground level, he opened a line of pockets around the waistband of the shimmer suit and pulled out carefully sealed forensic evidence that would implicate Preem, Torp and Medge, the three young men with Inclusionist leanings that HDC had chosen to frame for the assassination. He scattered ration wrappers bearing the boys' smudged fingerprints among the leaf litter, along with a nut kernel coated in Preem's saliva, unchewable and spat out; poured three containers of urine against a nearby tree; and placed hair and skin scrapings from Preem along the tree trunk to indicate he'd pushed through the branches to sit and wait to kill Laneaux for the Inclusionists. In the trial to come, the prosecutor would show Torp and Medge had gone back up the hill before dawn to wait with the escape craft.

Denev had no idea where the boys were. Rapskel's people had Preem, or maybe he was already dead. The other two were probably at home wondering where Preem was. They might have alibis for what was about to happen, but records could be easily changed – and eyewitness accounts too if HDC needed them to.

He recovered the launcher and walked on until he was fifty metres below the summit. One of the spheres rose above him to watch the canopy below. He lay down in the soft leaf litter and waited.

∞

This side of the mountain was still in shadow even as the sky burned bright blue. Denev checked his band: 9:45 a.m. Time.

The ghost gum's trunk was solid beneath him as he settled at canopy level and looked down to the lawn below. Neat rows of white chairs had been set up facing the stage. A crowd was milling around, some civilians, but mainly graduates in sky-blue SolSec uniforms. He could see a few techs on the stage and behind it, making final preparations for the ceremony.

"We expect a clean kill," Rapskel said in his head.

"Even with state-of-the-art gear, it's not going to be easy."

"That's your problem. You need to prove your loyalty. If Laneaux survives, you will have failed to do that."

Her life for mine, Denev thought. A devil's bargain, but still his choice. It could end here. Should it? But he was fooling himself. Something had shifted inside him. Petar's death had woken him from the life he'd been sleeping through and set him on the path to this place and this moment. He wanted to live. He wanted to find out what had happened to his parents. And Laneaux wasn't worth dying for.

There was a flurry of activity below: the crowd untangling itself into ordered lines, filing between the rows of chairs. In a few seconds everyone was seated. Then quickly stood to attention as Laneaux strode onstage and took her place at the podium. She looked out at the assembly, then spoke – the amplified sound not quite loud enough to be more than the suggestion of words to Denev. The SolSec grads and their families sat and Laneaux began her address.

Denev lifted the launcher, sighted along the barrel at the podium. The targeting system linked with his HUD and the scene below jumped into sharp focus like the immersion of a datanook.

"Here's one for all the lookers," he whispered.

He sloped the barrel skyward and pressed the trigger contact. The stock kicked against his shoulder as the rocket fired, gases side-venting through the pierced barrel. His perception shifted to a payload-eye view, arcing into the blue sky then turning towards the scene below, everything happening at an accelerated pace.

The counterattack systems at the Academy were committed. Already missiles were launching from the roofs of the low buildings, vectoring up on intercept.

Denev's fingers played along the studded controls set into the launcher barrel and the rocket swerved in its course, erratic but still hurtling towards Laneaux. She was still on the podium, startled in a half-crouch and looking up intently, watching the race between weapon and counter-weapon. An aide was running towards her across the stage.

The rocket swerved again, released a bloom of mini-warheads

and the nearest counter-missiles exploded. Denev's view shuddered, cleared. Laneaux was turning. The aide had reached her, was pulling at her arm. Another wave of counter-missiles was zeroing in on Denev's rocket. There was no way through.

The immersion cut out as Denev's rocket exploded midair in a gout of smoke and flame, still two hundred metres from the target. The EMP it delivered was small but close enough now. His HUD showed the defence grid offline.

Laneaux stopped near the back of the stage, looked up towards Denev's position. He sighted along the thin barrel attached to the launcher. A jet of gas hissed past his ear and a sharp crack sounded behind him, launching the hypersonic needle. At the same time Laneaux jerked her arm up and looked at the back of her hand. She dropped to the stage.

Denev turned quickly and ran down the trunk, dropping the last few metres to the forest floor.

"A distraction," Rapskel said. "Nicely done."

Denev had no breath to answer. He ran uphill as fast as he was able. He could hear the drones' tortured engines as they raced up from the SolSec buildings below. Even the shimmer suit couldn't shield him when they knew for certain there was someone up here.

He saw blue among the treetops ahead. The summit of the mountain. He crossed the tree line into bright sunlight. Didn't dare look back. The sound from the drones stepped up a notch. His lungs were burning.

Then he was at the top and skidding down the other side, running full tilt. The slope levelled out ahead, ran flat for a few metres, then terminated at a rocky outcrop. A tree fifty metres to his left exploded in a gout of flame.

He hit the flat, not slowing down, then jumped, flying out over the edge of rock. Freefall.

He hit solid deck, knocking the wind out of him. He twisted onto his back, saw a flash of sky, then the roof closed over and turbines roared, pushing him down as the vehicle thrust into the sky. He closed his eyes, pulling in huge gasps of air like a salmon thrown up on a riverbank.

Slowly his heartbeat quieted and the acceleration eased, the auto-pilot levelling the flight out. He was still travelling at multi-sonic speed but the smooth course suggested he wasn't being actively pursued.

There was a chime and a viewscreen lit up on the wall beside his head. Denev twisted to look as the image cleared and the face of Admiral Gart Lowrans appeared. He didn't have time to wonder how the admiral had accessed this channel before the older man spoke.

"We need to talk. I hear my daughter's alive."

12

Isza had piloted us undetected and unmolested past the Hub and the Hegemony ships that guarded near-space, and brought our transport to rest on the northern edge of the plain. The forest was a blue smudge on the horizon and the slender needle of the skystalk rippled in the heat-haze. The wall of the transport appeared transparent, as if we were standing on the lip of a cargo deck with the doors open on the world. But the wind that picked up dust and whirled it into eddies that spun across the plain didn't touch us. And the heat of sura, djel and ataz high in the clear sky went unfelt.

Every Kresz from the Jantri station stood ready behind me, armed with weapons the Jantri had supplied. Somewhere in the clear air above, a small group of Jantri fighters waited, slaved to Rhees's console on Nok's station. But it was down to the Kresz on the ground to fight for Homeworld.

"The other transports are coming in now," Isza said.

Out on the plain, only the dust stirred. Nok had been true to his word, dispatching stealth transports to the hides we'd identified and contacted through our emissaries, loading all those able to fight and bringing them here.

I reached into my travel pouch, claws closing around the studded elongated disc Nok had given me before we left. If he was right, this would block the empathic reflector field that Kergis relied on so much. But I had to get close enough to trigger it.

"Incoming signal," Isza said.

"*Udun?*" It was Tzek.

"We're here," I said. "Where are you?"

"*The machine that flew us here informs me we are right beside you, though it doesn't seem possible.*"

I looked at Isza. "Let's meet outside. It's time we made our presence known."

Isza touched her controls and the wall of the transport moved back with a hiss then cantilevered up. The heat rolled across us, the air suddenly dry in my spiracles.

The Plain of Ak'ra occupied a liminal territory that was bordered by Czerag lands to the north and west and nudged against the forest that edged the Inland Sea around Aktiuk. Like Treaty Mount it was claimed by no house, and the two sites were inextricably linked. It was here that the last great House War was fought with such violence some believed only one house would have survived its conclusion. But amid the heat of battle and carnage a miracle happened. The Emergence. As Kresz battled Kresz their empathic sense blossomed – the first connections that would eventually build the worldmind. The battle ground to a halt as the weight of suffering across the plain bludgeoned the consciousness of everyone left alive. Later the hierarchs met at Treaty Mount and pledged an end to war on Homeworld.

Now it was time to wage war again.

Isza came to stand beside me and took my claws in hers. A silver comms bar sprouted from her ear gap.

"The worldmind," she said. "It feels so dark. Alien ..."

We stepped out onto the dusty ground, followed by the others.

"How long before we're discovered?" I asked.

Isza looked over at a doorway hovering above the ground that was disgorging Tzek and his group. "Not long."

Behind us, our transport was lifting off, though it barely made a sound.

Tzek came forward and gripped my forearm, then Isza's. "Thank you," he said. "Today we take back what's ours."

"And cast out the Hegemony," I said. We had to. "Any word

from Gatiku?" It would be good to have his renegade Defenders on our side.

"None," Tzek said.

We walked further out onto the plain, Agik beside Isza, and the others from the Jantri station following us, talking in low murmurs.

Isza glanced behind her. "They're excited to be home."

Tzulak, who had challenged me when I first arrived at the Jantri station, broke from the group and approached us.

"If you'll allow it," he said to me, "I'll stay by your side and protect you and the others."

We'd all come such a long way, I thought. But the longest journey was leaving our prejudices and preconceptions behind.

"Thank you, Tzulak," I said, laying my claws on his shoulder plate.

We turned together to watch the disembarkation. The unremarkable plain was broken by a series of large rectangles floating in the air and disgorging Kresz of all castes. They were equipped with blasters and heavy assault rifles supplied by the Jantri, but they also carried more traditional weapons. Ha'ga: long clubs with heavy weights at the end, used for smashing through shell; and czid-ga: spears with a hooked end and a sharp outer edge to slash between armour plates.

"I think we've reached critical mass," Isza said. "The worldmind knows we're here."

There was a sharp crack and three contrails appeared in the sky in the north-east – coming from the direction of the escarpment. With my secondary eyelid I could see they were Hegemony singleships.

Isza touched the silver bar at her ear gap. "Rhees is moving to intercept."

Despite this, the air above us appeared deceptively empty.

The Hegemony ships lost altitude, pulled together and banked towards us. Then all three exploded. Debris rained down on the plain ahead of us but three small shapes remained in the sky: hard to see but floating beneath billowing cloth canopies and powered somehow, turning and flying into the distance. It was Rhees's first engagement and the enemy pilots would live, which I knew was what she hoped for. But all of us would witness deaths we'd rather not see today.

The ground shook and a rolling sound like a thunderstorm hit us. A plume of smoke grew over the horizon. Then two more further south.

"The airfield at the escarpment's gone," Isza said. "And Rhees is attacking the Kergis and Haketiug strongholds. Oh, and she says, 'you're welcome'. She'll be moving on to neutralise the spaceport and the base of the skystalk now. After that, we're on our own."

Everyone on the plain was silent, staring at the columns of smoke. Then voices were raised: Defender Kresz taking command. The others moved quickly, forming up into cadres.

"All of the hides have been training hard," Tzek said. "The old ways – battle tactics, weapons." There was pride in his voice but also regret. "I'd thought the days of Kresz killing Kresz were behind us."

I saw Reka with Sazu and Djidka – two of the other excisees from Tzek's deep desert hide – marching past in a nearby group. I was glad to see they'd survived.

I raised my arm to them and they broke away and came to join us. Isza hugged each in turn, and I grasped Reka and pulled him into an embrace.

"Stay with us, brother," I said. I didn't want to lose him again.

"I will," he said, then reached out and took Sazu's claws in his. "And Sazu too."

It was clear they'd become close and I was happy for them. They deserved it.

Together with Tzulak, Isza, Agik and Tzek, we walked further out onto the plain. When we looked back, our force was ready, standing in massed ranks. Different houses, different castes, excised, intact – they were together in this single cause and I could not have been more proud.

The ground shook and the air rang with deep explosions. Rhees doing her work around Aktiuk.

"I think the Hegemony have discovered they have a fight now," I said. I raised my voice and shouted, "We march on Aktiuk."

The answering cry from the assembled Kresz rivalled the thunder of the explosions.

∞

Rhees set the stealth fighters to autonomous patrol and shifted her attention away. She'd destroyed most of the Hegemony flyers while they were still on the ground – the beauty of being invisible on all wavelengths. The three fighters headed for Udun's forces had been trickier but she'd watched each of the pilots ejecting. From now on it was going to get harder to save lives.

Back in Voss Space, in the Jantri station, her body was hooked into the consciousness expander – or splitter – but it was hard to remember she had a physical form. She was seventy-three dolphinships on approach to Homeworld orbital space and mixed in with fifty Svestan fighters – long, thin-bodied craft with a rear section bristling with spear-like weapons surfaces, just like the aliens that flew them.

While the stealth fighters had been useful in atmosphere, practical invisibility in space would make coordinating with the Svestans too difficult. Besides she wanted to drive off the Hegemony with superior flying rather than target them like sitting ducks with invisible fire. If Fleet couldn't see what they were fighting, they wouldn't run. They couldn't. They'd dig in and that would mean suicide.

A tactical window opened, showing ground troop transports being launched from the Hegemony's System Class battlecruiser hanging close to the Kresz skystalk – the Hub. She counted three transports, no doubt returning troops to bolster their garrison. They'd be easy targets if the Svestans got to them first.

Her ships accelerated, outstripping the Svestans and breaking into three groups with three targets: the transports heading to atmosphere, the battlecruiser and – past them and strung around the planet's curve – the rest of the near-orbit Hegemony force of three gunships and a Planet Class destroyer already showing signs they'd detected the incoming attackers.

As her groups diverged she tried to ignore the weirdness of encompassing different perspectives. It was simpler when the ships were in one group. Even so, she could still make sense of it.

Her ships heading for the transports pulled together approaching maximum speed then split apart, firing particle beams across the transports' path and forcing them to turn away from the planet.

The battlecruiser loosed a swarm of Typhoon ramcraft, which quickly split, one flight headed to support the transports and the other making best speed towards Rhees's second group, which was vectoring on the battlecruiser.

She kept firing at the transports, herding them towards the Hub, but their pilots were determined to break through and it was hard to keep them together.

Her third group spread out on approach to the gunships and destroyer, flew in among them and forced them to change vectors and react defensively.

"A little help anytime you can, Nok," she said.

The ramcraft engaged her second group and she threw her dolphinships around, dodging and firing lasers, feeling the ships respond to or even anticipate her will. Or maybe it was because the interface had zero latency. Whatever, she was evading cannon strafes, swapping vectors as the Hegemony singleships overshot and were too slow to react as she fired with pinpoint accuracy, targeting drives with pinhead missiles. Her attackers tumbled away into darkness.

Her transport group split again, three still harrying the transports while the others met the incoming ramcraft head-on.

A sudden flare from the planet distracted her for a millisecond – a web of coruscating energy leaped across the face of the globe. Nok had been augmenting his stealth satellite network for the past few days and now Homeworld was encircled by a defensive shield of lasers, effectively closing it to space traffic. She hoped whatever Udun was doing down there was enough.

The transports, seeing they had no other option, turned for the Hub. The elevator cars down to Aktiuk were docked against the bottom of the station. One of Rhees's ships targeted the cars, slicing through walls and cable motors, and she threw the rest of her ships against the ramcraft.

More were streaming from the battlecruiser, but two dolphincraft from her second group managed to find a gap, spearing through to kamikaze into the drive section of the massive ship. The engines erupted in a silent bloom of fire and she piloted more ships through in the confusion to work their way up the remaining hull, lasers and missiles tracking and trashing weapons batteries and sensors.

The Svestan craft rushed in to join the battle and the Hegemony destroyer and gunships were also closing.

A line of fire from the destroyer's massive railgun cut a swathe through the centre of the battle, indiscriminately shredding whatever craft were in the way. The gunships leaped forward, still taking hits from Rhees's dolphincraft but ignoring them, and any sense of tactics dissolved as the battle became a contest of brute strength, speed and manoeuvrability.

Rhees gave herself over to it and her sense of sequential time broke down. A single ramcraft looping towards her. Dodge in close. Close enough to see the pilot through the canopy. Then flip, flying below the craft, belly to belly. Brake. Fire. Drive section disintegrated. Gel capsule ejected, spinning into black.

Triple view. Strafing down the destroyer's length. Particle beams slagging the railgun housing. One dolphinship exploded. One spun on its long axis, firing backwards at the incoming ramcraft. Forward guns targeting its nose, taking out guidance control. Ramcraft veering off. Dolphinship flipping back, following the first to smash into the railgun's business end.

Three Svestan fighters peeled off from the main group and headed for a bunch of crash capsules. Five dolphincraft in pursuit. One accelerated ahead, braked on a one-eighty and flew towards the lead Svestan, forcing it to break off. Two dolphinships on each of the other Svestans, coming in close and pushing at the weapons surfaces, sending them spinning out of control.

An angry shout over the comms from Tol Imnan. Rhees ignored it.

Two ramcraft paced a dolphincraft, cannon firing. Shots went wild as the pilots tried to follow her inertialess flight.

Gunship hull burst open and she flew through the expanding fireball, counting escape pods and vectoring more dolphincraft in to help.

Turn. Fire. Accelerate. Vector shift. Brake. Fire. Fire. Fire.

So many views and then just one. The remaining dolphincraft strung together in a defensive line. Behind them, a clutter of gel capsules and other escape pods being shepherded together by her massed ships in an almost unconscious ballet. In front, a tumbling debris field of drive sections, hull fragments and more than a few bodies, dominated by the cracked hull of the battlecruiser. Interspersed with Svestan fighters bristling with weapons and all oriented towards her ships.

"It's over," Rhees said.

"You!" Tol Imnan's voice. She couldn't determine which ship he was in, but she *could* tell he was furious. "You fought against us. Protected the humans."

"I didn't harm any of your ships," she said. "The battle's won. Those that survived are prisoners of war. They will not be harmed."

"You don't have the right —"

"Take your victory, Tol Imnan." Nok's voice broke in over the comms. "Our agreement still holds. You have your glory. And soon you'll have your alloy."

Seconds stretched and Rhees waited for the Svestan ships to attack. But the moment passed and the Svestans turned tail, accelerating away from near-orbit, leaving the humans alive in the capsules and pods to be gathered up by her ships.

She doubted those inside would thank her for saving their lives.

13

Rhees saw the last of the Hegemony ships' capsules and escape pods into the open bays of the Hub. The skystalk was cut off from the ground and the remaining Hegemony troops would be trapped there until she could figure out what to do with them.

She pulled her consciousness back, disengaging as Nok had taught her. She was in the room again, surrounded by standard feeds from her remaining ships. But the main feed was what commanded her attention. The station had been moving through Voss Space and, judging from the tac view, it was closing on its destination. Rhees was under no illusions. In Voss Space it would be near impossible to prevent casualties.

Progress to the Kresz Sector had been slow. The station was so big only a junction chamber could hold it comfortably, but somehow the Jantri were able to coax the narrower channels to extrude and stretch around the station as it moved through them. Rhees wouldn't have thought it possible if she hadn't seen it herself. But the station was coming to a stop now.

"Phase three," Nok said. "This will be rather more delicate, given where we are."

They were close to the end of the tunnel where it opened into the transit chamber held steady by the Point satellites. Rhees had been through here twice before. After Nok had picked her up in her Maagba ship and brought her to the Lenticular for the first time; and later with Udun, after their mission on Homeworld. Both times she'd been undetected, moving invisibly between the Hegemony ships.

The chamber was dim but brightened by intermittent plasma flashes. Rhees could make out the two System Class battlecruisers – ugly, blocky expressions of brute force – and the three sleeker Planet Class destroyer escorts she'd seen before. The ships were surrounded by smaller ramcraft, too many to count. They were powered down to avoid a field discharge.

"They must have heard what's happening in orbit around the Kresz Homeworld," she said. "But they're staying put."

"Remember, Homeworld is a secondary objective for them," Nok said. "Holding the Voss Space corridor is their main objective."

The fight around Homeworld would have been much harder if they *had* transited, she thought. "Something isn't right."

"That may be," Nok said. "But we have no other options. I'll try to keep damage to a minimum but we must drive them out of here. Once they break and run, it will be easier to keep them moving."

It'll be like herding cats, Rhees thought, but the tactics were sound. If they could flush them out of the stable chamber into the tunnels, the Hegemony ships would have no easy transit options back to space.

The Jantri station released a cluster of dark, spiked objects which drifted into the junction, moving slowly towards the Hegemony ships. They covered half the distance to their target before some sharp-eyed gunner saw them. Particle-beam fire lanced out from the two closest cruisers. Short, controlled bursts. If you had to fire energy weapons in Voss Space, this was the way to do it.

But the spiked objects dodged the incoming blasts, expanding as they moved to fill the space between the Jantri station and the ships. Ramcraft darted towards them, firing in a circumspect way, but those spikes they did hit moved on unfazed.

The ships started to retreat, but there wasn't much manoeuvring room and one Storm Class gunboat got too close and a spike attached to its hull. The other ships moved away quickly – just as a searingly bright Voss Space discharge hit the attached spike, destroying the gunboat.

A ramcraft was next. A spike latched onto it, and Voss Space energy lashed out and vapourised it. Rhees realised the spikes concentrated the field potential on anything they touched until the ship reached threshold and Voss Space did what it did to any unwanted trespassers.

The remaining ships were still retreating behind the line of spikes. The tunnel back towards Earth was behind them, but instead of turning tail and running, the other ships started firing indiscriminately at the spikes.

More plasma flares leaped out from the junction walls. Another Hegemony ship was gone. And another. The smaller ships darted around looking for a target.

"Why are they staying put?" Rhees shouted.

"Maybe they need more persuasion," Nok said.

The station moved out into the chamber, which was crackling with Voss Space energy now, the walls beginning to distend.

A comms screen opened up in front of Rhees. Multiple Hegemony broadcasts – from within Voss Space.

"Oh, fuck," she said. "That fleet the Hegemony sent to Hanloi space. I think it's coming back."

She stared as the junction filled with ships. The Hegemony must have been just as startled to see their local tenspace garrison engaged in battle. From the feed, Rhees could see a lot of the fleet was badly damaged. Hulls scored from heavy fire, and nacelles buckled or simply missing. But it was still a formidable force.

It only took a second for the fleet to see what was going on and start shooting. The whole chamber was a mass of discharge sites.

"You have to leave," Nok said. "Now."

Rhees hadn't expected that. "What? What are you going to do?"

"Even here, the Hegemony ships will prevail. They have the numbers and if they transit to Kresz space, Udun and the others will die. This station is fully charged with Voss Space energy. I'm going to release it."

It took a second for Rhees to understand what Nok was saying.

"That's crazy. You'll die."

"No. You'd die. That's why you have to get out."

"But –"

"Now!" Nok said. "I'm starting the energy cascade."

"No!" Rhees shouted, but the feeds shut down around her and the eviscerated dolphincraft suddenly shifted, reconstituting itself and sealing her inside.

A screen opened up. She was outside the station, ejected somehow and drifting in the Voss Space junction. A plasma charge speared across the empty space and struck a Hegemony cruiser right above the primary missile battery, which exploded in a bright plume.

The dolphinship kept turning until Rhees was looking back the way she'd come. None of its controls were responding.

The Jantri station was the brightest thing in the chamber. Brighter than a sun.

Then darkness. Stars wheeled around. A scream of static. Space split apart. An otherworldly blast of light and energy shattering the firmament.

The dolphinship spun wildly until Rhees thought it would fly apart. She held on, screaming at the top of her lungs, but couldn't hear a thing above the roar of the universe.

The shaking stopped. The ship stilled its spin. The silence was almost as deafening as what had gone before.

The stars were back, but among them was a rip in space. A bright rupture bleeding energy. A white hole.

Rhees keyed the comms. "Nok. Nok, can you hear me?"

She kept trying. But there was no answer. The radiation from the rupture was off the scale. Nothing could have survived.

She felt her link with the rest of her dolphincraft around Homeworld orbit re-establish itself. Her own dolphinship responded to her now and she set course for them, accelerating rapidly.

Nok had pushed back the Hegemony, but Rhees was under no illusion the war was over. Thousands of humans had just died in that blast and she'd been a part of it.

14

We didn't see any Hegemony ships after the first attack. Rhees and the Jantri had established air superiority. There was only the ground war left.

Our forces marched in a series of units that were split – predictably – along house lines. The dust raised with our passing meant I couldn't see where the ranks finished. But I could hear the ancient karak – war drums from before the Emergence that some had brought – rapping out an insistent rhythm.

"There's no fear here," Isza said as we walked. "All I feel is total commitment. They've been in the hides for so long. They want justice."

"Whatever the cost," Agik said beside her.

I saw Isza stiffen, biting down on whatever rebuke was in her head.

Tzek had said the hides had trained hard and that showed not only in the orderliness of their formations but – as forward scouts signalled movement at the distant edge of the forest – in the way several Adepts moved quickly to both flanks with hoods raised. Within seconds I felt the distant vibration in my chitin as their mantles laid down an interference pattern: an old defence to neutralise mass blasts of mantle energy from an opposing force.

My desert eyelid flicked over and I could see a darker line at the base of the forest. A Kresz war party marching out to meet us.

"I don't see any Hegemony troops," Tzek said.

"It's hard to see how many there are," Isza said. "Or what else might be hiding in the tree line. Should I ask Rhees –"

"No," I said. "This part is not for outsiders."

I called out to Reka and he trotted over with Sazu and Djidka. "Stay close. Protect Tzek," I told them.

"Yes, brother," Reka said.

As we drew closer I could see more of the enemy Kresz. Their shells glistened in the suns, polished to a rich lustre. Kergis banners flapped in the wind above them, and their gaszti blades were unsheathed, clacking noisily against their chest plates.

I was no battle commander, even though it was Rhees and I who had started the events that had brought us all to this plain. That role fell to Tzek. He spoke into his comms bar and the ranks began to split up, reforming behind us.

Hulking Defenders moved to the front, their outsized claws raised before them and locking together to form a solid wall. They hefted long-shafted ha'ga in their lesser claws, ready to swing forward and smash at the opposition.

Behind them, two rows of Cultivator caste formed up, their longer arms and legs giving them superior reach to thrust over the defensive line with hooked, sharp-bladed czid-ga. They were backed up by an assortment of other castes with Jantri blasters, gaszti blades, simple clubs and anything else that could be used to stab and smash.

Agik said something I couldn't hear.

"*This* is worth dying for," Isza responded angrily.

By unconscious agreement, both sides stopped and faced each other across the plain. The drums stilled. Gaszti blades were sheathed for the moment.

"Do you feel anything from them?" I asked Isza.

"Only what I've been feeling all morning. They're a perfect mirror."

"They're fully protected by the Hegemony device," I said. "They think they can attack us with impunity."

There was movement in their ranks as four tall Defenders made their way to the front. They parted to reveal a Kresz standing stiffly between them, plates burnished a deep black. Kergis.

"He couldn't stay away," Tzek said. "He's like a pre-Emergence lord of war, leading his house into battle."

"With the Hegemony neutralised, it's his time to prove he still leads," I said. I opened my travel pouch again. The Jantri device nestled inside next to a gaszti blade.

Kergis's amplified voice echoed across the plain. "It seems you have found help from outsiders, Tzek."

Tzek used his comms bar to amplify his reply. "Weapon matches weapon, as the saying goes. It is only fair after your Hegemony friends killed so many of our fellow Kresz for you."

"There are no Hegemony here," Kergis said.

"No. They've deserted you."

"They are not necessary to defeat you."

"Yet you still carry the outsiders' weapons," Tzek said.

"As do you. But House Kergis holds close to tradition. I make you this offer. Drop your alien weapons and we will do the same. Let us battle in the ancient way."

"He thinks the empathy reflector gives his forces an edge," Isza said.

"It does," Agik said. "This is all madness."

I agreed. I took the comms bar from Tzek.

"Nothing will be gained by Kresz killing Kresz. Give up the traitor Kergis, and let us leave the plain together and rid the planet of the Hegemony invaders."

"Ah," Kergis said, "the excisee who murdered Erdjis. Why do you stand with him, Tzek?"

Tzek took the comms bar again. "Udun has done more for our people since the Hegemony took his mantle than you will ever do if you lived three-two lifetimes, traitor."

"He is outside," Kergis said. "He always was, even when he was intact. Submit to the will of Sakat. Or die in this place."

"I had to at least try," I said. "I'm sorry, Agik. Sometimes the only option is to fight."

The Cultivator stood silent. He was still angry and I saw disgust on Isza's face.

"We have to get close to Kergis," I told Tzek. "Blasters will make that harder."

"We refuse your offer to surrender, Kergis," Tzek said. "But we agree that outsider weapons have no place here."

"Then ask Sakat to prepare the way for you," Kergis said.

A gust of wind plucked at the Kergis banners and threw up grit to rattle against our carapaces. We saw the Kergis ranks drop their blasters and other charge weapons and the noise of gaszti blades against chitin started again. Kergis turned and was followed by his Defenders behind his lines.

Our own Defender line opened to let us through to the relative safety behind the front ranks. As we passed, Tzek placed his claws on the nearest Defender. "Hold fast," he said.

Tzek had been Czerag's advisor for more cycles than I'd been alive. He knew how to command and how to inspire loyalty. While the Kresz on board the Jantri ship and in the deep desert hide had accepted me as one of their own, I knew this army was here because of Tzek and the work he'd done to convince the other house hierachs and hide leaders to join us.

The wind dropped. Stillness. The high-pitched karak drums started again.

And then the armies were running towards each other, screaming, closing the distance swiftly. We followed behind, Tzek leaning heavily on his staff to keep up.

There was a deafening crunch as the front ranks clashed together, then our ranks fell back, reeling as the psychic shock of combat pain spread out. Reka and I and the other excisees were immune, but Isza screamed and Tzek almost fell to the ground. Agik turned and ran back the way we had come.

But our force was committed now and the front ranks moved forward again, pushing through the pain and fighting for all they were worth.

I crouched beside Isza. "What do you feel?"

"It's hard," she said. "But we can survive it. We must. At least the Hegemony device means we can attack the Kergis Kresz without empathic feedback. They're blank. It's the wounds and deaths of our own soldiers that hinder us."

Reka and Sazu had helped Tzek to stand and the old Kresz was shouting into his comms bar, directing the battle.

"Guta!" he shouted. "Watch the left flank – it needs support."

A small group of Defenders and Cultivators waiting behind our forces suddenly mobilised, heading towards part of the line that was under heavy assault and being forced back. Some of the Cultivators jumped on the backs of the Defenders, leaning over the heads of their comrades and thrusting hard with czid-ga at the Kergis fighters in danger of pushing through. The breach halted, then pushed back. There was a shout from our Defenders at the front who pushed back harder and gained ground, grinding the bodies of fallen Kresz – Kergis-aligned and our own troops – into the ground as they advanced.

The roving group commanded by Guta pulled back, looking for another potential breach they could reinforce.

I helped Isza get to her hoofs. She patted my brow ridge then pushed me away. "I'll be fine." Her feeder claws spread wide, but I could see the pain on her face as she lived the woundings and deaths in front of us.

"We need to end this," I said.

There was a shout and a breach opened in our lines directly ahead. Kergis Defenders concentrated their attack and pushed through, hacking and slashing at anyone standing in their way.

Isza screamed and ran straight for the melee, her gaszti blade held above her head. Djidka was right behind her.

I lost sight of them and took a step forward, but Tzulak pulled me back. "No, Udun. You must be safe."

I tried to pull away, but Tzek grabbed my other arm even as he doubled over and fell to the ground again, eyes screwed shut against collective pain.

"Madness," he said. "We'll all be mad soon. Or dead."

Reka and Sazu kneeled beside him and helped him to stand again. And still the fighting continued. I couldn't comprehend it: the will to keep going when every moment was filled with agony. Kresz pushed against Kresz, bodies transformed into meat to be bludgeoned, hacked and sliced. Weapons rose and fell and the air was thick with the smell of death.

Isza was beside me again. I saw rusz on her shell but it wasn't her own. "Djidka is dead," she said.

One more death amongst this madness seemed infinitesimal, but I felt it all the same. Even excised and shunned, Djidka had fought for her world. She'd given everything she could.

"The breach is closed," Tzek said. "We're holding."

"We need to do more than hold," I said.

Beyond our lines and behind an impenetrable wall of Defenders I could see Kergis's banners. The hierarch was there, but he may as well be standing on the Hub. There was no way we could get to him.

A high scream, hoarse and dying, and the line pushed forward then pitched back like an angry wave.

Isza doubled over and I held her. She screamed in pain. "Sakat, Udun. We have to stop it!"

I could see our forces were being beaten back. The Kergis Kresz were hacking and slashing. Our side was severely hampered, fighting the empathic assault as well as the physical.

A shout came from our left, behind our lines. I saw a group of czid-ga pointing skywards like a stand of thin endar saplings and moving towards us.

Isza stood and pulled me close, and Tzulak stood between us and the advancing lances with gaszti drawn.

The crowd parted and a group of Defenders stopped in front of us, breath whistling heavily through their spiracles. They wore no house colour.

"They're like the Kergis Kresz," Isza said. "Reflecting the emotions around them."

The lead Defender – as big as Gurud had been but with a darker shell – looked at Tzulak who was still holding his gaszti like a stick against a mountain.

"Brave but unnecessary," he said. "I am Gatiku."

"You came," Tzek said as Tzulak sheathed his weapon and stood aside.

"You use Hegemony empathy reflectors," Isza said.

Gatiku focused on her. "You know of them? We tore them from the bodies of dead Kergis Kresz. They help us hide and fight."

Despite what I'd said to Isza about using Hegemony tech, I wasn't about to challenge Gatiku on it. We were staring into the face of defeat.

"Will you fight with us?" I asked.

Gatiku looked at the line, which was being pushed relentlessly back towards us. "Can you stop this, and quickly?"

I pointed at the Kergis banners. "Get me to Kergis. I'll end it."

"Form up," Gatiku said. "Stay behind us. But stay close."

The Defenders moved to form a shape like the tip of their czid-ga. Isza, Reka, Sazu, Tzulak and I stood between them. I held Isza's claws tightly in mine, knowing these could be our last moments together.

"Ready," Gatiku said. Then, "Forward!"

They moved swiftly but together and we stayed with them, leaving Tzek to control our forces. The Defenders bellowed as they ran. Startled faces of Cultivators and Defenders turned to us and got quickly out of our way.

We smashed into the Kergis lines, barely slowing as our momentum and the sheer weight of Gatiku's group carried us through. They pushed forward with their czid-ga or slashed and stabbed at the enemy, and we stumbled after them over ground strewn with bodies and body parts and slick with gore.

I caught a glimpse of a Kergis banner and we surged forward, then crashed to a halt as Gatiku's group smashed into Kergis's personal guard. The noise was deafening. Kresz smashed and stabbed, swaying back and forth as they pushed and grabbed for leverage. Our small group kept low, crouching in the middle of death and suffering that had not been seen on Homeworld since the Emergence.

And then a gap opened in front of us and we saw Kergis. Isza leaped and crashed into him, dragging him to the ground. Reka, Sazu and Tzulak moved quickly to help, grabbing at Kergis's limbs to hold him down, while around us his Defenders frantically beat at Gatiku and his fighters, trying to push through to save their hierarch.

I fumbled in the pouch as Kergis bucked and struggled beneath me and pulled out Nok's device and the gaszti. An imager window opened up above Kergis's chest and I slashed quickly between his torso plates. Kergis stiffened as I reached into the rent in his flesh, my claws visible in the imager, closing around the Hegemony reflector control.

Something struck me from behind and I pitched forward, dropping the Jantri device. But I'd pulled the reflector control from Kergis's flesh. I scooped up the Jantri disc and held the two mechanisms together, pressing the contact.

There was no indication it had worked – until Isza screamed beside me and went limp. I dropped the mechanisms and reached for her, twisting to pull her against my chest.

As I turned I saw the Defenders around us falling to their knees. Beyond, the frenzy and noise of battle stilled. The only sounds were groans of pain from the wounded and dying.

Isza's eyes opened and stared up at me. "It's done," she gasped.

Gatiku lifted the still living Kergis like a toy, holding the hierarch above his head. "It's over," he bellowed.

Those of Kergis's guard that remained threw down their weapons.

We had succeeded.

Slowly I helped Isza to her feet and we looked over the devastation. Twisted and smashed bodies lay all around us. Isza clutched at her head and moaned like a wounded animal. I could only imagine the pain and suffering she was experiencing. What came next *had* to be worth all of this.

15

The escape craft levelled out. Denev, still short of breath, pulled himself off the deck and fell into the webbing strung against the bulkhead. The craft was moving slower now, the drones that had been chasing him after Laneaux's assassination left far behind. But Denev's mind was still spinning in high gear, considering the words Admiral Gart Lowrans had just spoken: *I hear my daughter's alive.*

The only way Lowrans could know that was if someone in the Hegemony had monitored Denev's communications with Rhees. Which meant Volmar knew Denev was a traitor, and may have known ever since he'd come back to Earth. So now he was going to die. Probably after being tortured to give up Rhees's whereabouts.

Lowrans's image still stared at him, waiting for a response.

"Relax," Rapskel said inside his skull. "Your cover's not blown. Gart Lowrans is what you might call a fellow traveller."

Admiral Gart Lowrans, adjutant to Ten Vargas, chief of the combined Hegemony forces, was a traitor?

"You told him," Denev said, forgetting to sub-vocalise, and Lowrans's expression became quizzical.

"We share information from time to time when it suits us," Rapskel said. "I needed some Fleet intel, I thought it was a suitable price. So did he."

"You traded my safety," Denev said.

"What's going on?" Lowrans asked.

"Mute," Denev ordered and the image was silenced.

"I did not trade your safety," Rapskel said. "The only reason you're alive now is because I allow it. That can change if you like. Telling Gart Lowrans about you is no more dangerous than the risks my people take every day. But if you want out, just say the word."

Denev knew what "out" meant. "Fine," he said angrily, "but I want you and that bomb you planted out of my head. I've proved my loyalty: Laneaux is dead. Now you meet your part of the bargain."

Rapskel was silent and Denev braced for a refusal. The rebel leader was going to string him along until he was no longer useful and then blow his head off.

But then Rapskel said, "Okay. The bomb's dissolving into your bloodstream and you'll piss it out soon enough. Our little head-share will go the same way as soon as we're finished with the admiral here."

Denev looked at the image. Lowrans was still waiting, but by the clench of his jaw he wasn't happy about it.

"Unmute," Denev said. "I'm sorry, Admiral —"

"Gart," Lowrans interrupted. "That title belongs to a hierarchy I don't support."

Denev stared at the man he'd met only once before, at the Security and Defence Group meeting with Vargas. A man like that didn't turn traitor on a whim. How long had he been part of this secret rebellion and why had he joined?

"I asked you about my daughter," he prompted.

There was no point denying it. Rapskel had already confirmed Rhees was alive.

"The last time I spoke to her she was working with some aliens," Denev said, "pushing back against the Hegemony in the Lenticular."

Lowrans's bushy red eyebrows climbed up his forehead. "The Lenticular! We just lost … Well, we don't know how many ships we lost, but we lost control of that entire area of space."

So she'd done it. Rhees and the Kresz and the other aliens — they'd all done it.

"What's she doing that far out?" Lowrans asked.

"It was the only safe place for her after Volmar tried to have her killed."

Lowrans's brow furrowed angrily. "Jesus. I thought the safest place for her after your brother died would be sifting data in the HDC. Cataloguing intel for a living isn't meant to be life-threatening."

"She has a talent for finding trouble," Denev said, thinking of their time together on Herakli. Lowrans grunted agreement. "But to be fair, Volmar took an instant dislike to her. I think he was intent on getting rid of her from the moment they met."

"That fucking snake," Lowrans said. "Look …" He paused, trying to find the right words. "I've not been a good father, and I can't excuse that even though I had reasons. But if she contacts you, tell her I'm sorry. Tell her to stay safe."

Denev could see the pain and worry etched on Lowrans's face. He barely remembered his own mother and father, but when he'd found out they were dead, it was like a stone dropping into his gut. He knew he'd lost something he hadn't even realised he'd had — a feeling of being loved. A feeling he could see all too plainly on the screen.

"I will," he said and broke the contact.

"Touching," Rapskel said.

Denev felt a hot surge of anger. "And now you're leaving my skull."

"As agreed. But since we won't have these cosy chats any more, we need to see each other the old-fashioned way. I'll send you details," Rapskel said.

Denev felt the craft losing altitude, heard the tone of the whisper-quiet engines dropping. He waited a full minute as the escape craft angled down more then levelled off, prepping for landing. "Rapskel?"

There was no reply, but he couldn't be sure the link was truly gone. Fuck, he couldn't be sure the bomb was gone either.

He cued up an exterior view as the thrusters kicked again and the craft tilted nose up slightly and descended. In the grey rainy light he recognised the hangars of the Bathurst Island launch facility he'd used with Volmar when the comptroller had travelled to Mars to kill Minch. He was only two thousand kilometres from Laneaux's cooling corpse. Most of the flight time had been simple evasion just in case.

A floodlight flared on the runway. Volmar became visible, flanked by two HDC security officers armed with blasters.

The craft touched down and the rear split open, forming a ramp. Denev exited and stood to attention in front of Volmar. Rain ran down the comptroller's cheeks and pasted what little hair he had left to his skull.

"Mission accomplished," Denev said, half-expecting Volmar to order him gunned down on the spot. After all, he'd killed Laneaux. Volmar could expose him as a traitor – particularly if he knew Denev had been helping Rhees, or about his meetings with Rapskel – and wipe his own hands clean of the whole affair.

The comptroller looked angry, but it was a tightly controlled anger. His lips parted and he paused for a moment before saying, "You did well, Antwer. SolSec don't know what hit them."

"Thank you, sir."

Volmar scowled. "But things have gone badly elsewhere. The occupation in the Lenticular has turned to shit." Denev had never heard the comptroller swear. "And from what I can gather, it's all because of that Kresz we met at Minch's … demise. Fleet have lost control and it doesn't reflect well on HDC."

Which meant it didn't reflect well on Volmar. It had been his call to let Udun go free on Mars. And Denev now knew Udun's and Rhees's plans to take back Homeworld had succeeded. He only hoped Rhees was still alive.

A ground car stopped beside them and Denev followed Volmar inside, leaving the guards behind.

"Their victory indicates the aliens had detailed intel on Fleet and HDC placements," Volmar said. "And now they've begun degrading our surveillance network across the Lenticular, which speaks to an even greater security leak. That information is known only to me, the HDC strategor team, you, Vargas and a handful of his top staff." Volmar looked directly at Denev. "I want you to find that leak. But the investigation must be above reproach. I'm bringing in two auditors. Everything will be crosschecked by each of you independently. I want triple redundancy on the outcome. I want to be sure."

"I understand, Comptroller."

Volmar had just named Denev as one of the potential leakers, which was why he'd decided to bring in the auditors. But Volmar suspected everyone else as well, including Vargas. Denev had used all his skill to encrypt and hide the signals he'd sent to Rhees, but nothing was ever completely hidden if you knew how to look for it. Would the auditors be smart enough to discover his treachery?

"As for Udun," Volmar said, breaking into Denev's thoughts, "he must die."

"Would you like me to prepare a strategy?" Denev asked.

"No." Volmar's eyes were cold blue and hooded, all trace of anger gone. He was in control again. "I still have an asset on the Kresz Homeworld. I'm going to handle this myself."

An asset, Denev thought. Who?

The car pulled up at the hypertube station and the door on Denev's side swept open.

"Oh," Volmar said casually, "SolSec want to interview you. Or rather they wanted to interview me but I said they'd have to make do with my aide."

Denev was already feeling off balance. Was Volmar throwing him to the SolSec wolves after all?

"I said you'd meet them at their headquarters at 2 p.m."

Three and a half hours from now.

"Did they give you a reason for the meeting?" Denev asked.

"It's connected with Laneaux. I imagine everything they do in the next forty-eight hours will be connected with Laneaux. Help them of course, but not too much." Volmar nodded at the open door. "This is where we part company."

"I'll see you at the Datahive, sir," Denev said, but Volmar was silent.

Denev crossed the rain-slick footpath to the shelter of the station canopy. The concourse and the platform beneath it were empty. A single hypertube car waited to take him back to the Datahive. He realised he was still wearing his shimmer suit and he stank of sweat. As he sank into the padded seat of the hypertube car, his thigh muscles ached from his frantic dash to the summit of the hill pursued by SolSec drones.

He might have been alone again inside his skull but his head felt heavy and too full of thoughts. If he closed his eyes, he could see Laneaux through the HUD, startled by the micro-missiles' explosions moments before the hypersonic needle killed her.

If the auditors found proof against Denev, Volmar would have him executed immediately. But maybe SolSec knew what Denev had done and would get to him first.

∞

Sadly, HDC Operative Rhees Lowrans was killed in the final action to neutralise the Cygnus Sector rebels. Her body was not recovered.

Gart closed the service file and let his gaze drift towards the sun-filled window of his office. *Body not recovered.* Volmar had tried to kill her. That little shit would get what was coming to him. But somehow Rhees had escaped.

Thousands dead in the Hanloi campaign and more in the Lenticular. And Rhees was out there fighting against Fleet. What must she be feeling?

He'd hoped to keep her out of this. But maybe she was more like him than he'd realised. In the years since the K-Chaan war, he'd built a shadow network in Fleet to work against the Hegemony, but they'd achieved nothing tangible. Breslaw and the others were still in charge and more powerful than ever. Real action meant people were going to get hurt and killed. Rhees was out there, taking real action. Living with the consequences.

He keyed his comms. "Sasha, come in here, please."

Seconds later, his aide stood in front of him at parade rest. Gart closed a contact on his desk. Their discussion couldn't be monitored.

"I need you to contact Colonel Anyo at the Jupiter listening station. But this is off the books, you understand."

"Yes, sir." Sasha's expression barely changed.

"I want everything they get from the Lenticular to come through my office *before* it's released to the rest of the Central Administration."

Sasha saluted, turned smartly on one heel and left.

With any luck Gart might see some sign that Rhees was still alive. But beyond that, the Lenticular had been able to push back the Hegemony occupying forces – something no other sector had ever been able to do. Whatever happened next out there could be very important. It was time they all got their hands dirty.

16

I'd only seen the inside of the Council chamber at the top of Treaty Mount on vuscreen before now. It seemed smaller in real life. And different. The benches for the hierarchs and deans had been pushed back to make room for Kergis's throne on the central dais.

Tzek followed my gaze. "That's one of the things we'll have to change."

"Back to deans and hierarchs?" I asked.

Isza said, "Maybe we can work out a new way together."

"It's time to rebuild," Tzek said as we climbed onto the dais. "There are spiritual as well as physical wounds to heal."

There was a crash from outside and then Kergis was brought in, held closely by two Defenders and led by Gatiku. Kergis's shell was scuffed and dirty, and stained with rusz from where I'd cut him to extract the Hegemony's empathy device, but the old hierarch still walked as if he owned the building.

"Sakat," Isza said quietly, "we might have defeated him but he still scares me. The sheer energy of his personality. It's like everything around him dims."

The Defenders halted Kergis in front of us.

"Is this some kind of joke?" he said. "Tzek, your puppet's served his purpose. There's no need to sully this chamber with his presence."

"I think you are under a grave misapprehension," Tzek said. "Your alien allies are defeated. Your house is rubble. Wake up to yourself."

"So what now? I'm to be excised like him?"

"Excision is not a punishment," Isza said. "It's a badge of honour worn by those who resisted your invaders."

I couldn't have loved my sister more in that instant.

"I've spoken to the remaining hierarchs and they've agreed," I told Kergis. "You're to be taken to a shielded room where you'll live out your days cut off from the worldmind. Your jailors will be excised Kresz, immune to your personality. You'll never know contact with the Kresz again."

Kergis's feeders splayed wide and he shrugged off the Defenders holding him. "Sakat damn you. Sakat damn all of you. He will sweep you all from Homeworld. His Way will see all the crippled Kresz destroyed."

"No," I said. "You will be the last of your line."

"You have no right –"

"Silence him," Tzek said and Gatiku grabbed Kergis's feeders. Kergis struggled, but it was useless against the big Defender.

"Udun has earned the right," Tzek said. "Take him away."

The Defenders led Kergis, unresisting now, from the room.

Isza, Tzek and I walked out of the chamber, across the reception hall and through the burnished bronze doors onto the summit of Treaty Mount. The roars from the crowd were suddenly deafening. The souk was filled with Kresz, and they spilled out onto the streets beyond, stood on rooftops and leaned from open windows.

We stood together, looking down at them all, and the cheering slowly abated.

"Every Kresz in Aktiuk is here," Isza said. "Are you ready to face them?"

I was glad Isza would be with me through this. And Tzek. I'd need their perspective. Nok had told me I was different, that events would turn around me. At the time I'd thought he was mad and I wouldn't live to see Homeworld retaken. Against all the odds, he'd been right. But nothing was finished.

"Brothers and sisters," I said, "Homeworld is ours again."

Roars greeted my words, the sound reverberating until it peaked and finally quietened.

"But our victory has come at a terrible price," I continued. "Many of our people lie dead on the plain, and countless others were mutilated or murdered during the Hegemony occupation. Those Kresz who fought alongside the invaders have betrayed all of us."

"Excise them!" came the shouts. "Cut them off from us!"

I raised a claw. "No. There will be no more excisions. Look around you. Too many of us have been excised through no fault of our own. Those Kresz traitors will have to live with their deeds and the judgement of us all. I can think of no better punishment."

I paused. We could survive the past, but how could we build our future? How could we heal what was broken? And then I knew.

"We have to realise that the communion no longer represents all that we are. The excisees must have a voice now. And so must the remains of House Kergis and House Haketiug and anyone else unhappy with the way things are. Our society is the sum of all its parts. It includes all of us, not just those Kresz who have a mantle or who think and act in a certain way.

"In the past it was the communion that brought us together, but it also made us complacent. We relied on the worldmind to tell us how others felt instead of taking the time to build true and lasting relationships. We've seen how fragile the bonds between us were, and how that laid us open to attack. House Kergis's betrayal shows us how little we've progressed since the days of house rivalry. If we are to survive now as one people it's up to those who rule to go beyond the communion and listen to the differing voices among us. And it is up to all of us to overcome our divisions and work together to strengthen the ties between us, to become a true community with a common understanding and purpose. Only then can we stand and face a foe with the knowledge we can never be divided again."

Isza placed her claws on my shoulder plate. "Oh, Udun," she said.

"I couldn't have said it better myself," Tzek added.

I looked down at the crowd, hanging on the words of an outcast and excisee. I could see other excised standing among the intact and hoped my words brought them the comfort they deserved.

"The war isn't over," I said. "The Hegemony still exists in the Lenticular. And beyond that their empire waits. They won't forget the wounds we've dealt them. Enjoy this brief respite, but know that we must rebuild. We must be ready to fight again. We must be ready to win."

∞

Tol Imnan and his Svestan ships were long gone, and Nok's satellite laser shield was gone too. Did that mean he was still alive, Rhees wondered. Or had it deactivated when the station exploded?

Her dolphincraft had started the clean-up, moving debris from the battle to a higher orbit where it wouldn't threaten Homeworld below. She needed to check in on the captured Hegemony pilots and the other troops now marooned on the Hub to make sure they were safe. But first she had to see what was happening at the escarpment.

She left the rest of her ships to continue clean-up and piloted her command craft down towards Homeworld. Plumes of smoke tens of kilometres long trailed into the upper atmosphere from the strike sites around the Inland Sea, in Aktiuk, and the airfield at the escarpment. She accelerated, flames licking at the dolphincraft's hull as she pushed the ship as fast as she dared go in atmosphere. Her view expanded, magnifying the land around the escarpment. There were bodies between the rows of damaged ships – ground crew, unable to get away before the blasts. Nok would have said it was unavoidable. But all of this was avoidable. She just didn't know how.

Then she was above the escarpment and descending to the desert close to the main entrance. There'd been fierce fighting here. She could see that from the scoring on the bare rock walls and the blast craters in the sand around the cliff base. But it was quiet now. Hardly any movement. Just a couple of Defenders standing idly by a ground transport.

She landed and her ship opened around her. The heat struck her instantly, but nothing like what she'd felt out in the deep desert. The Defenders looked her way. One raised an outsized pincer to her then turned back to its comrade.

The air smelled like cooked meat. Rhees hadn't seen it among the smoke from the airfield, but there was a pile of burning bodies past the entrance to the house. She took a step closer. Then clamped a hand over her nose and mouth. Charred uniform, armour, flesh. A pale flash of bone among the flames. It was impossible to count how many dead there were.

She fell to her knees and vomited on the sand, then drew a shaky hand across her mouth, wiping spit away. She stood again. The Defenders watched her approaching.

"Where –" Her voice sounded raspy and she coughed and spat. Tried again. "Where are the prisoners?"

The closest Defender looked down at her. His eyes were a beautiful golden colour. He gestured over her head to the pile of smoking corpses. "That's what's left of the ones who surrendered."

Rhees felt disgust and a deepening pit of guilt opening up inside her. They'd surrendered then been butchered like animals?

"On whose orders?" The words were almost a snarl.

"Orders," the Defender said, then turned to his comrade. "We should go. Join the celebrations."

Rhees walked back across the sand to her dolphincraft. Could she blame the Kresz for taking revenge? This was no more barbaric than what the Hegemony had done many times over. But Udun had known she wanted to do everything possible to minimise loss of life. They'd promised to make each other's goals their own. This felt like a betrayal.

In her ship, she opened a comm to Udun but it was Tzek who answered. She could hear crowds roaring in the background.

"Udun is busy," he said. "You've done well. You should come and join us."

She felt a sudden surge of anger. "I'm at the escarpment. What

I've found here doesn't make me feel like celebrating."

"Ah," Tzek said. "Would you spare the lives of those who tried to destroy us?"

"The ones who *surrendered*," she said. "I'd spare those. And Udun —"

"Udun had nothing to do with this. I ordered all captured Hegemony executed. This is a war."

"Fuck." She cut the connection, her fingers curling into fists. But there was nothing she could do. Nothing she could have done differently. This was the result.

The dolphincraft closed around her. She had to get back to the Hub and make sure those pilots and troops were safe.

You got yourself into this mess, girl. She could hear her father clearly, his voice laden with disappointment but also resignation. *How're you going to fix it?*

Rhees had no idea.

17

The shower was hot and hard and Denev played the jets over tired muscles. After leaving the hypertube at Datahive station, he'd been directed to the decon level. His very top layer of skin had been snap-burned to powder and washed off in a chemical shower, which didn't deserve the name because the thick, sloughing goop sprayed onto him was anything but refreshing. Then came the mouthwash and some other chemical he had to swallow a litre of that would do things to his gut and intestines he'd rather not think about. After that, another chemical shower, pink and foaming and tepid, which he'd used to scrub under finger and toenails and rubbed the foam everywhere possible. The last stage was a light dusting of particles consistent with living in the city and working in the Datahive, and an inhaler of the same for his mouth, throat and lungs. It was like he'd never set foot outside of the conurb these past few days.

His band vibrated and he cut off the water reluctantly and dressed in a fresh onepiece. There was just time for a quick bite. He hadn't eaten since yesterday evening.

The Datahive canteen was below ground level but it was bright with natural light reflecting from white tiled walls beneath light wells in the ceiling. It was also well used because the food was prepared by human chefs. Denev took a bowl of stroganoff and a glass of sparkling water and sat at an empty table, savouring the meaty sharp taste after days of reconstituted camping rations.

He noticed two strikingly similar men at the servery looking his way. Both were tall, blondly Nordic and well-built, dressed in matching grey business suits. Each had a visitor's tag on his suit lapel. They picked up their trays and headed his way.

"Specialist Antwer," one said, before the other added, "Do you mind if we sit?" Their accents were identical too, placing them from somewhere in the North Atlantic Conurb.

Denev tried on a smile. "Not at all."

The visitor tags said they were from the Office of Security and Defence – Rejak's office. The auditors. So Volmar had brought in people from outside, but not too far outside. He and Rejak were allies. These were Rejak's men and could be trusted to do exactly what Volmar wanted. The question remained: were they good enough to catch Denev?

They sank into chairs opposite and each placed what looked like the same sandwich choice on the table.

"I'm Hel and this is Stin," the one on the left said.

Even close up, Denev couldn't tell them apart. "Are you twins?"

They graced him with dazzling identical smiles.

"Clones," Hel said. "But we're really quite different when you get to know us. I'm the talkative one and Stin's –"

"Not so much," Stin interrupted.

Denev wasn't sure if he was admonishing his partner or just finishing his sentence.

"Right," Hel concluded. "We're here to plug your leak." Again the bright smile.

Denev wouldn't have trusted these two an inch even if they didn't work for Rejak.

He returned the smile. "Glad to help." He tapped his band and shunted access logs to them, heard their bands vibrate in response. "These should get you started."

He picked up his spoon and scooped another mouthful of stroganoff, eating quickly.

Hel studied his band while Stin started on his sandwich.

"A start, yes," Hel agreed. "We need to map the entire communications structure. We have whatever clearance is necessary."

"That'll make things easier," Denev said, finishing up his bowl and taking a long gulp of water. "We can meet later. I have a meeting with SolSec now that I can't be late for."

Both men nodded amiably at him and he left. He should be worried, but he'd felt under suspicion for so long now – ever since Volmar freed him from the Maagba – it was like he'd reached some limit. This was his new normal.

That didn't mean he wasn't alert to the dangers. Stin and Hel may be gene-tweaked to be smarter than him but they didn't have his field experience. They were just another obstacle. So be it. He was an enemy of the Central Administration now. If he came out the other end of this alive, that would be a bonus.

He took the slideband out of Vigilance Plaza, skipping across the accel strips to the main band that carved its way between the elegantly twisted skyscrapers of the central district. The sky was dappled with cloud, shafting sunlight through the negative spaces of the city and gilding the building fronts so they looked hyper-real.

The strip was almost empty and Denev leaned on the rail to look back the way he'd come. No obvious tail but that didn't mean anything. If HDC or SolSec wanted to, each organisation could watch and record him while he ate, slept, went to the toilet. The problem for universal surveillance was – as always – bandwidth and resources. Those who "had to be watched" were watched 24/7. For everyone else, active surveillance only happened if they became even tangentially connected to someone on the watchlist. Passive surveillance took care of the rest. They were still watched but the brain behind the eyes was an AI. If you did nothing that raised a flag for the algorithm, your records would never be viewed by a human consciousness. Denev wondered if he was on the active or passive list; and if it was the latter, where on the scale the algorithm placed him right now.

SolSec HQ was a tall isosceles of a building that thrust above its neighbours in an unapologetic manner. The sunlight was swallowed whole by its matte black, windowless surface. Its only adornment was a stylised golden sun halfway up the edifice.

Denev was barely inside the foyer when someone called, "Specialist Antwer!"

The man walking to greet him was young, maybe early twenties, with close-cropped ginger hair and a pink freckled complexion above the sky-blue SolSec uniform. The tabs at his shoulder indicated he was a lieutenant investigator. Denev shook the outthrust hand. A firm grip.

"Comptroller Volmar said you'd agreed to help us. We really appreciate your time. I'm Investigator Tor Elvann, but please call me Tor."

Just one big happy inter-agency collaboration, Denev thought as he fell in step with Elvann through a security wall and into an open office area.

"My condolences on the death of Undersecretary Laneaux," Denev said. "She'll be very hard to replace."

Elvann nodded. "Yes, yes, of course." He sounded distracted.

He ushered Denev into a small, windowless interview room that was sparsely furnished with a table and three chairs. Denev sat. As Elvann closed the door, Denev's band buzzed once. He looked and saw it had been deactivated.

"We're not really here to talk about Laneaux," Elvann said.

"Oh?" Denev had a feeling the door behind him would be locked, and if he did get through it there'd be guards waiting outside.

Elvann reached into his pocket and pulled out a holo disc, placed it on the table. "We wanted to ask you about this."

He activated the disc and an image filled the space between them. Denev recognised the location. It was an external view of one of the countless monitoring hubs – a cube structure that controlled distributed services across the conurb. The view was from above, maybe an aerial drone. A man appeared round the corner, staying close to the wall. The view zoomed in. Denev knew that face. It was Beloc, the HDC operative who'd followed him from the Datahive to his dormitory shortly after he'd returned to Earth.

"This next bit is very interesting," Elvann said.

Denev knew exactly what came next.

Beloc turned and looked back around the corner. A door opened in the cube wall behind him and Denev emerged and attacked, punching Beloc in the kidney and kicking at the back of his knee. Beloc pulled a blaster as he fell, the gun arcing round. Denev caught his wrist, twisting and flipping Beloc onto his back, and wrenched the gun from his grasp.

"Nice move," Elvann said with a smirk.

"What do you –" Denev began, but Elvann interrupted.

"Watch."

Holo-Denev ripped the band from Beloc's wrist, then hesitated. He couldn't shoot because even if he'd evaded surveillance up to now, that would definitely trigger the algorithm. Beloc kicked him in the chest, then he was up and running round the corner, heading for the strips. The drone view pulled back and followed Denev as he ran after Beloc, skipping up the accel strips and gaining on his quarry. Other riders got out of their way, startled. Then came the junction. Beloc fell and Denev halted at the barrier. The drone's-eye view zoomed in on him as he broke the strap on Beloc's band and threw it down to join its owner.

Clearly SolSec had brought Denev here to blackmail him. But it was a gamble on their part. Denev could simply stonewall and say what they'd witnessed was part of a sanctioned HDC operation. Beloc had gotten in the way and been killed for it. But that wouldn't tell Denev what SolSec were up to. So he'd show them what they wanted to believe. He was sure his vitals were being monitored so he shortened and quickened his breath to raise his pulse and blood pressure. He thought about being pursued up the hillside after killing Laneaux. About crash-landing on an unknown planet with Rhees after the Maagba had destroyed the rebel fleet. About the barfight in Herakli where he'd nearly lost his life. His growing agitation should convince them they had him.

"What do you want?" he said.

"Beloc was our man," a new voice said.

Startled, Denev spun in his chair to see who had entered the room.

A small, slim man in a conservative business suit, brown hair combed forward over his forehead. He had small eyes and a pointed nose over a protruding top lip. The effect was rodent-like. He looked vaguely familiar.

Denev considered what the man had just said. He'd thought Volmar had set Beloc to watch him. If Beloc was SolSec, it explained why Volmar hadn't so much as mentioned his disappearance. Why had SolSec been surveilling Denev?

"I don't understand," he said, still playing agitated.

"Your boss," Rat Man said. "He's a piece of work." He rounded the table and Elvann stood to attention. "You can go, Elvann."

Elvann actually clicked his heels. "Yes, Undersecretary," he said and left.

So whoever this was had taken over from Laneaux. Denev dredged up a name to match the face. Ceed Felman. He'd been director of ops. Looked like he'd got a promotion.

Felman sat in Elvann's vacant chair, glanced at Denev, then looked at the frozen holo-Denev and the dead Beloc. "Looks like you've been a naughty boy."

"Wait," Denev said and held a hand towards Felman, letting it tremble slightly. "You've got it wrong."

Felman sniffed and leaned back in his chair. "Nah, it's written all over you. Now, I don't really care what you get up to in your spare time. But your boss definitely would. I imagine your life wouldn't be worth living."

He was right there. But clearly Felman had no intention of telling Volmar as long as he felt Denev could be of use. Time to show him his instincts were right.

Denev let out a long sigh. "All right. What do you want?"

Felman smiled, showing small rodent teeth. "That's more like it. But it's not what, it's who. Laneaux was a good boss, but she was too subtle. She tried to outmanoeuvre Volmar, but he's a sneaky fuck. He had her killed, I know he did." His voice had grown angry, and he sat forward and shook his head. "Subtle's not my way. You'll learn that about me. I'm gonna kill that fuck. And you're going to help me."

18

It had been one-four days since we'd taken back Homeworld, but each of those days had been so filled with meetings and arguments it seemed as if seasons had passed in an eyeblink. So much time and so many words, with so little progress to show. Perhaps I'd been hopelessly naive.

When I'd watched public sessions of the Kresz Council on the vuscreen as a youngling, it had seemed to me that the pronouncements made by the house hierarchs and lodge deans sitting together in the grand and ancient chamber envisioned a better future for all Kresz. A future that would come to pass because of the intelligent consideration and rational debate exhibited by the Council members on the chamber floor. It was only when I grew a little older – and more so when Czerag brought me into his scheme to sell tekla direct to the Telsans – that I'd realised the sessions I'd witnessed were carefully managed public events, not the reality of the Council. The real business was conducted by hierarchs and deans from their shielded rooms, and they'd send carefully instructed delegates – with no real knowledge of their leaders' true plans to prevent any empathic spying – to argue on their behalf. Altruism and belief in a shared destiny had little to do with what went on in the Council chambers. Beneath the surface, the houses and lodges fought each other for advantage, making and breaking alliances and deals whenever it was convenient.

That was why I'd insisted the house and lodge leaders attend this reconvened Council in person. There could be no secrets between us, and surely – after all we'd experienced – we could work together for the common good.

Kergis had been replaced, of course. And even though the new House Kergis hierarch sat on the benches, the voting rights of that house had been suspended. They were on probation.

House Czerag's bench stood empty. I was house leader until a replacement could be agreed, but I was also "prime hierarch", a new role voted by the Council. It wasn't one I particularly liked with its echoes of the position Kergis had given himself when he seized control. But it gave me some authority and I needed that.

Hierarch Akczek had died in the Hegemony's first bombardment of Aktiuk and had been replaced by his successor, while House Haketiug had been absorbed by House Kergis during the invasion when their hierarch had been killed at the Point. I'd chosen Tzulak – who had tried to kill me on the Jantri station before becoming one of my most loyal supporters – as the new leader of House Haketiug.

Hierarchs Ukat and Dageru had survived the invasion, as had most of the lodge deans. The only changes there were Dean Ha'ik of the Adepts – his predecessor, Djelad, had been tortured and killed in one of Kergis's camps; and Gatiku, the Defender who'd been so pivotal in our final battle with Kergis, was now dean of the Defenders Lodge. Defender Dean Resgtu and his aides had suicided on the lodge spikes shortly after their defeat.

There was one other new addition to the Council chamber. Many of the hierarchs and deans refused to acknowledge her directly, though as a female with a Defender body plan, she was hard to miss. Rasa was hierarch for the House of the Excised. When the houses refused to re-admit excised Kresz, I'd been forced to create a separate house to represent them.

The Council was in session again and Hierarch Akczek was holding the floor. It was clear this new Akczek liked the sound of his own voice. He was young – so young his shell still held a tinge of orange – and excited perhaps by his new role.

"It is impossible to enumerate the debt this place and the Kresz people owe to Prime Hierarch Udun," he said, standing in the midst of the other hierarchs and their advisors.

But, I thought. There was always a but.

"But our people are traumatised by the recent unpleasantness, weary and sick in spirit. They need time to heal. They need certainty. They need things *not* to change."

Beside the young hierarch sat his advisor, old Czel, listening with eyes closed. I had no doubt Akczek's words – and most likely his sentiments – were straight from Czel. He was deeply traditional, and heavily invested in keeping a tight claw-hold on Akczek's mineral wealth.

Akczek was still speaking. He used a lot of words to say very little. "… any healing cannot truly begin until the threat of the Hegemony is gone forever. Prime Hierarch, every house and lodge here has pledged its unswerving support for the war that must come to our vanquished invaders. We will follow you into death if that is what Sakat wills."

The Council chamber echoed with shouts of agreement. I knew those at least were genuine. However much we'd suffered during the Hegemony invasion, we knew we couldn't rest until they were defeated forever.

"But these other things you want," Akczek finished. "They must wait."

More shouts of support, but to my ear gaps they felt weaker. Or perhaps that was wishful thinking. I couldn't sense the emotion in the room, which meant there was a whole silent level of debate that passed me by. I relied on Tzek to brief me later.

During the morning session Tzek and I had laid out the reform program that seemed so clear to me. First we had to ensure our security. Those Kresz who fought for Kergis had been rounded up and processed for trial. At the same time we had to root out and neutralise any remaining Hegemony forces across the Lenticular. That meant closer cooperation with other Lenticular worlds:

welcoming and establishing embassies in Aktiuk to work together and protect against further invasion; setting up an early warning network in tenspace against further incursion; and planning and mounting a coordinated counterstrike on the Hegemony. At the same time we had to open up membership to the lodges to all houses and body types in order to increase personal choice and freedom *and* ensure recognition of and equal treatment for excisees. These last two were the hardest to achieve, but after everything we'd suffered I couldn't fail.

If Akczek wanted me to call a vote on the reforms now, he was to be disappointed. But he seemed content to keep talking.

"The House of Akczek has a proud history of –"

"Is there a question in all this, Hierarch Akczek?" I interrupted.

Akczek faltered but recovered quickly. "The alien embassies you have invited to Aktiuk –"

I cut in again. "You mean our Lenticular allies?"

Akczek looked briefly at Czel. "It is not right that aliens should walk on Homeworld. Not after we have reclaimed our planet from other aliens."

I stood from my bench in the centre of the chamber and looked around at the assembly. "I'd hoped the recent war would have demonstrated to the young hierarch that there are good aliens and bad aliens. The embassies are necessary to ensure close coordination for the war against the Hegemony. We're mounting a multi-species fleet to travel to the far ends of the galaxy." I paused and looked again at Akczek. "That takes a bit of planning."

"So," Akczek said, unabashed, "when the war is won, these embassies will be invited to leave Homeworld?"

Tzek shifted on the bench beside me. I knew he wanted me to give a non-answer.

"No. If the Hegemony are defeated, we will still benefit from the closer ties these embassies provide with the Lenticular. We are stronger when we are together."

"And why do we keep Hegemony prisoners in camps?" Akczek

asked. "Why don't we just kill them?"

There were shouts of support from the Council. I knew Tzek agreed with the sentiment. We'd argued when Rhees told me what she'd witnessed at the escarpment, and I'd issued new orders and initiated the camps immediately after.

I was saved the necessity of answering as Gulatesi, High Priest of Sakat, stood and Akczek sat.

Tzek cleared his throat in warning. He sensed something. Were Gulatesi and Czel working together?

The high priest's shell was black but thin, almost translucent, revealing dark spotted hide beneath his plates. He leaned heavily on an obsidian staff.

"Sakat created Homeworld for the Kresz," Gulatesi said. His body may be weak but his voice was deep and strong and smooth. The main weapon of a practised orator. "And for the Kresz alone. That is why our fight against the Hegemony invaders was rewarded with victory. Sakat stood with us on the battlefield that day."

I hadn't seen Sakat among the heave of bodies but I kept that thought to myself.

"Sakat may have stood with us on the Plain of Ak'ra," I said, "but the Hegemony would have destroyed us from space if the Jantri and Svestans hadn't attacked their ships. Could they not be part of Sakat's plan too? And what about all the excisees who gave their lives so we could sit here once more in freedom? Weren't they instruments of Sakat?"

"Udun," Tzek said quietly beside me. But I was sick of this. We'd been going round in circles all morning.

"Aliens and excisees are not part of Sakat's plan," Gulatesi insisted.

On her bench, Rasa stared impassively at the high priest, her thoughts and feelings known only to herself.

"You say that, but the evidence is all around us," I said. "The excised cannot be ignored after what the Hegemony did. And not after what the excised did for all of you here today."

"It is impossible to ignore them when you create a House of Excised and bring their leader into this place," Gulatesi said.

Even without my mantle his anger was obvious. But I was angry too. "They won't be ignored any longer. Whether Sakat wills it or not."

"Udun," Tzek warned again.

I turned to him, but was distracted by a shout and a sudden crash.

At the entrance to the chamber, a Defender stumbled back, overbalancing. Another ran forward, pincer raised, and a Cultivator-caste Kresz leaped between them, long legs fully extended as he sailed over the deans' heads and landed awkwardly on the dais beside me. Tzek made to stand but I pushed him down and shifted to shield him.

The Cultivator swung a long, hooked czid-ga towards me, shouting, "Death to the excisee!"

I froze, waiting for the blade to slice into me. Then the Cultivator jerked sideways and at the same instant my hoofs left the ground as I was lifted bodily and pulled back, held in a strong grip.

Gatiku grasped the Cultivator in his dominant claw, but the Kresz kept shouting and raised the czid-ga to throw it. Gatiku's pincers closed with an audible snap. The czid-ga clattered to the ground and the Cultivator split in two, yellow rusz spraying between the body halves, then quickly stopping as the cut flesh sealed. His legs kicked uncontrollably, slid down the steps of the dais, then stilled. The rest of him was still alive, lying beside my bench.

Tzek shouted, "Clear the chamber and seal the doors!"

My hoofs found solid ground again, and I realised it was Rasa who had pulled me away. "Thank you," I said to her.

Gatiku kneeled beside the torso. He must be experiencing the pain of his own attack on the Cultivator. I kneeled beside him and placed a claw on his back. I couldn't feel anything, of course.

"Are you all right?" I asked.

Gatiku looked at me. "I felt nothing." He pulled at a travelling pouch the Cultivator wore over one shoulder. Inside was a Hegemony empathy reflector.

"Destroy it," I said.

Gatiku crushed it in his pincer, then groaned as he felt whatever the Cultivator was feeling.

"Are you in pain?" I asked the Cultivator.

His gaze locked on me and his feeder claws spread wide. "It is Sakat's divine will that you die. You are an abomination in his sight. You are outside, and the Way must be cleared –"

Gatiku clamped a claw over his mouth to silence him.

"He's filled with hatred," Tzek said beside me. "Almost insane with it."

By now the chamber had been emptied and the two guards the Cultivator had evaded arrived beside Gatiku. One of them lifted the Cultivator's torso, maintaining a grip on his feeder claws to silence him. Gatiku said nothing, but it was clear he was unimpressed with the door guards.

The one not holding the Cultivator stammered, "H-h-he surprised us, Dean. He was quicker and more agile."

"He was wearing an empathy reflector," Gatiku said. "You didn't think to search him?"

The guard looked at the floor. "He had not yet been searched."

Tzek stooped, picked up the czid-ga and passed it to Gatiku. "Or his weapon taken?" Gatiku said.

"He took that from the wall display in the antechamber," the Defender said, a note of pleading in his voice.

"Then dismantle the display," Gatiku said angrily. "And search all who would come here *before* they enter the building."

"Searching wouldn't find a reflector if it was implanted like the stek-la," Tzek said.

He was right. Who knew how many reflectors were out there?

"There is a possible solution," Gatiku said. "The Adepts have been studying the device the Jantri gave you, Prime Hierarch, that ended the fighting. Replicating the technology. We could use units to protect the chamber and other buildings. Reflectors would become non-functional."

"Do it," I said, then glanced at the now unconscious Cultivator. "But I need to know why he attacked."

He'd grabbed a nearby weapon, which indicated an opportunistic attack, but he'd also carried and used an empathy reflector. That told me he'd planned this. But had he planned it alone?

"I'll conduct the interrogation personally," Tzek said, and he and the guards left with their prisoner. Or the half that mattered.

"Judging by what he said, his insanity's tinged with a heavy dose of religion," I said.

"And a hatred of excisees," Rasa added. "The two thrive together, like divides before the split."

"Do you think the priesthood sent him to assassinate you?" Gatiku asked me.

I thought about it. An attack here in the Council chamber felt like a desperate move. Gulatesi was more subtle than that.

"Whether they did or not, their stance on excisees certainly contributed," I said. "Anyone with deeply held religious beliefs can't fail to hate excisees when the sermons they hear are filled with that hatred."

"I don't know how to change that," Rasa said.

"I don't either." I looked at Gatiku. "You were quiet during the debate."

"I'm a warrior first and a politician last," he said. "And many things in-between."

"When I first asked you to fight with us, you refused and made a counter-proposal," I reminded him.

Gatiku blinked slowly. "I asked you to walk away from your alien allies and fight as Kresz alone."

"So you oppose the alien embassies? You'd want them to leave after the war?"

"I do. But I would never vote for that."

"Why?" I asked.

He laid a heavy claw on my shoulder. "Because regardless of what I think, we have to change. And you have been sent to change us."

19

Ten days as the Kresz reckoned time and Rhees had been awake and in her dolphincraft for most of it. She had to be everywhere she could. It was her responsibility if more lives were lost.

She hadn't spoken to Tzek since that day at the escarpment. She understood why he'd done what he'd done, but it still horrified her. At least Udun kept to his promise when she talked to him about it later, though she knew opening up internment camps instead of just slaughtering captured Hegemony invaders would cost him politically.

Using the intel Denev had provided, she'd run sortie after sortie on those ship and base locations that had stayed out of the big fight. For the most part she'd been successful in neutralising Hegemony forces, sending those she captured back to Homeworld, where they would be treated far better than they had a right to be.

There was no way to know how many other Hegemony ships or operatives had gone deep cover and still lurked in the Lenticular spaceways. Rhees couldn't use Denev to help flush them out. Every time he sent information, he risked being discovered. So she'd split her dolphincraft force, spreading half of them out across the Lenticular to sniff out anything unusual and tug on her consciousness if they found something.

Isza had insisted on sending – and accompanying – a group of Luk'ah fighters with Rhees's smaller flight of dolphincraft. Rhees didn't need the extra protection, but Isza wouldn't take no for an answer. Besides, she insisted it was ideal training for her and her fellow Kresz pilots to shadow someone as experienced as Rhees. It was hard to argue against flattery, but Rhees wondered if Isza was keeping a close eye on her because she worried Rhees would revert to type and betray Udun. It was possible, although Rhees felt they'd moved past that.

Right now the combined dolphincraft and Luk'ah flight were on patrol near what had been the Point and talking tactics about the Lenticular coalition fleet's journey to Earth.

"All I'm saying is given the number of Hegemony monitoring satellites we've found spread across the Lenticular, you can expect a string of them all the way back through the Voss Space passages to Sol system," Rhees warned.

Isza was silent for a moment. "So we take another route."

"Difficult. When the fleet gets underway it'll need a network of passages big enough to navigate. It can't squeeze through side tunnels or waste time fumbling down uncharted networks."

"Okay, then we find the monitors and jam them or subvert them."

"Not an easy task. I don't –" Rhees paused as the dolphinship's sensors pushed against her awareness. A moment ago there'd been nothing. But this part of the Kresz outer system was weird. The fabric of spacetime had twisted and ripped when Nok detonated his station. The resulting white hole bleeding energy from higher-dimensional space made Rhees queasy just looking at it.

There it was again. Like a sensor ghost, but more. She willed the fractured data to make sense. Then she saw it.

"All ships, attack formation."

Even before her last word the dolphinships leaped forward, leaving the Luk'ah fighters behind, and Rhees's consciousness fully expanded into the other Jantri-made ships in her flight. She had full control now, integrating multiple points of view as her ships weaved past the interspatial tendrils of the shattered Point's edge and into the clear space beyond – right on top of a Hegemony Hurricane Class corvette, a Storm Class gunboat and a flight of twenty Typhoon ramcraft. Their sensors hadn't picked up her dolphinships, but once Isza and the other fighters cleared the spatial rip she'd lose any advantage.

She split her flight into three groups. The first – and largest – vectored down towards the corvette and opened fire with lasers and point missiles to target the ship's hangar nacelles and stop any more ramcraft launching. The second group zeroed in on the much more manoeuvrable gunboat, which looked like a heavily armoured swoop-winged bird of prey. She concentrated the dolphincrafts' powerful nose lasers on the aft main engines, shearing through exhaust fairings and slagging the main thrusters, then picked off point cannon emplacements. The gunboat was dead before it could fire a single shot. This dolphinship group rejoined the first to continue worrying at the corvette, destroying sensors and weapons.

The ramcraft were alert and already peeling off under full acceleration, rounding on Rhees's third group, and this was where she threw most of her attention. She could sympathise with the pilots. They were just getting into the fight and already their gunboat was dead and the corvette wasn't far behind. But then they were shooting at her.

Her own ship dodged and weaved, firing as she dived straight through the centre of the enemy flight, then executed a one-eighty that would have pancaked a ramcraft pilot even in the most advanced gel capsule. The rest of her group flanked the ramcraft at speed, firing with pinpoint accuracy at drives and weapons. Within seconds it was over, her dolphincraft moving in to nudge and shepherd the ramcrafts' now powerless hulls in a manoeuvre she'd perfected over too many missions since they'd beat the Hegemony over Homeworld.

Isza's voice came over the comms as her flight of fighters finally caught up. "You could have left us some for target practice."

But that was just it: Rhees couldn't. When she counted the returning Fleet ships caught in the Jantri station blast and the ships and grunts killed at the escarpment and elsewhere on Homeworld, thousands of humans had died in the fighting so far. She couldn't say exactly, but her mental tally put over sixty down to her directly and many more indirectly. It was war, certainly. But it wasn't *her* war. It was a means to an end. Stop Volmar, stop the Central Administration. Save lives. Not kill people.

She'd convinced herself she was doing the right thing. The ideals were sound. The arithmetic was harder.

∞

Rhees's pod of dolphinships nestled together in one of the Hub's main hangars. Through the force-shielded opening she could see the crippled Hurricane Class corvette floating nearby, tethered by multiple umbilicals. The crew had already been transferred off-ship. And the dead too. Six of them. Four had been burned alive in an engine-room fire when the main power bus blew. The other two were ramcraft pilots.

"You're not to blame," Isza told her.

"No one else fired on that corvette." Rhees sighed. "Let's go see the captain."

The corridor arced around the curve of the station and opened onto one of the concourse segments holding a rail of cargo cars ready for the skystalk. They passed through a pressure door into the administration section, where offices had been hastily converted into holding cells and interview rooms. Most of the captured Fleet personnel had passed through here on their way to the internment camps on the surface.

Two Defenders stood guard at one of the interview room doors. It felt like overkill to Rhees. What could a human prisoner possibly do against even one of these giants?

The guards stood aside and Rhees entered the room followed by Isza. She stopped dead when she saw who the corvette captain was.

Jute.

Rhees remembered Jute flying beside her, Petar on her other wing, as they weaved through the rings of Neptune, ramcraft swerving and diving like a ballet – until that one slip. Petar's ship spinning off. Crashing.

"What the fuck are *you* doing here?" Jute said. She was frozen, half-standing.

They were both stuck, Rhees thought, neither sure how to progress to the next moment – but she had to say something.

"You're a long way from home," she managed.

She sat, and Isza sat beside her. As Jute considered both of them, Rhees looked at her old flight partner. Jute had always been classically beautiful: flawless skin, full lips, large dark eyes that slightly bulged beneath thick tapered eyebrows. None of that had changed, but she wore captain's pips on her collar now. Clearly being caught up in the mess on Neptune hadn't harmed her career. But then Jute hadn't been to blame for killing Petar.

"You're not a prisoner," Jute said. "You're … working with them?"

"It's a little more complicated than that," Rhees said.

"What have you done with my crew?"

"They're safe planetside. They won't be harmed."

"Safe?" Jute said the word as if Rhees had spoken an alien language. "With them?" She cast a look at Isza, who shifted in her seat. "And where are my dead?"

The dead I killed, Rhees thought. Would Jute work out it had been Rhees leading the attack?

"They're nearby. You can see them soon."

Jute sank back into her chair, shock giving way to suspicion. "What do you want, Rhees?"

"I'm trying to stop the fighting. The battle's over. No one else has to die."

Jute's lips compressed in a thin line.

"If you can tell me the position of other Fleet ships in the Lenticular," Rhees went on, "we can bring them in safely."

"You mean capture them. Why would I help you?"

"You and your people would all be dead if it wasn't for her,"

Isza said.

Jute glared at Isza, then tapped her ear. "No trink. *No hablo* crab."

"Have you been planetside?" Rhees asked, suddenly angry. "Have you seen the aliens mutilated and killed by our troops? This world was never a threat to us. The Kresz didn't even know we existed before Fleet invaded and started killing."

Jute regarded her for a handful of seconds, then gave a short laugh. "Fuck you, Rhees. You always thought you knew better than anybody else. That's what got Petar killed, but it was just the start, wasn't it? Now look at you."

Rhees felt like she'd been slapped.

"You don't feel in any way responsible for what's happened here?" she asked.

"I do my job," Jute said. "I try to keep my people safe." She sat forward, her beautiful face twisted in hatred. "And *I'm* not a traitor."

Rhees had imagined a meeting like this in a hundred different ways with a hundred different faces confronting her, and it always came down to that word.

"You're wrong," she said. "What I am is someone who's trying to end this butchery. All of it – here and in the rest of the Hegemony. The sooner that happens, the sooner you and your crew can go home."

Jute took a deep breath and let it out slowly. "This war isn't going to end until you and every one of these fucking aliens is burned down and their planet is dust. If you can't see that you're fucking naive. Now I want to see my dead crew."

If Rhees hadn't washed out of Fleet, would she be thinking and saying the same things as the woman she'd called friend? She couldn't tell any more.

She stood. "Someone will take you to them shortly."

Isza followed Rhees back into the corridor. "I meant it," Isza said. "That Human's lucky you're with us."

But Rhees knew that a lot of people in the Hegemony thought like Jute. How many would agree with Rhees?

20

I need some time to think. That's what Denev had told Felman and they'd let him go.

Denev knew Felman was sure he could tug on Denev's leash whenever he wanted, but for now SolSec were playing nice. Or perhaps Felman just wanted Denev to stew on the situation to soften him up for their next conversation.

Killing Volmar was a bold move. But Denev was sure that if they succeeded, Felman would orchestrate events so Denev was blamed. And if Denev was killed as well, all the better. A dead traitor who'd killed his own boss was an open and shut case.

Still, Beloc had been SolSec and he'd infiltrated HDC under Laneaux's command. She'd wanted to discredit Volmar. Was Beloc's infiltration part of a bigger plan? Were there other SolSec operatives in the Datahive?

Volmar and the clones Hel and Stin were looking for a leak. Maybe the existence of a SolSec mole could point their suspicions away from Denev. That would be tricky to manage though. If they got a whiff of Beloc, they could also find out he and Denev had met and what had ultimately happened to him.

It was too much to think about now.

Denev took a decel strip that looped down to a quiet street – mostly houses, with a vendory on the corner of a cross-street and a comms booth beside it. Inside the booth, he set up his security and encryption protocols and keyed in the codestring for Elna Darrow, the HDC identity he'd given Rhees. It wasn't the smartest thing he'd ever done, but he had to know she was still alive.

The codestring played across the screen, the image flashing as handshakes and connections were made. And then Rhees was there, a tired smile on her face.

"Hey, we're both still alive," she said.

"We keep beating those odds," Denev said, returning the smile.

He knew he sounded flip, but that was mainly to cover the sudden unwinding of a tension he hadn't known he'd been holding until he saw Rhees alive and safe. She meant a lot more to him than he could easily admit. He was used to working in the field, living lies from waking to sleep. To have one person he could be completely honest with was an unaccustomed luxury.

"From what I hear, you and your aliens have been making a nuisance of yourselves," he said. "Volmar is mightily displeased."

"Is your friend Rapskel still listening in?"

Denev thought about it. If Rapskel were still there he would have found it impossible to stay quiet after Denev's little chat with Ceed Felman.

"No, he's gone. Laneaux is dead and things are just getting more complicated. How about you?"

Rhees frowned. "Complicated is the word." She slumped back in her chair and rubbed her face. "I don't know if I'm making things better or worse. When the Kresz took back their world they killed every human they could."

"You can't blame them for that. Not after what the Hegemony's done."

"I don't. A lot of those that died deserved it. But their deaths are on my hands too."

"They're not —"

"I helped!" Rhees snapped, and Denev could see the pain on her face, the second-guessing that led to sleepless nights. He knew that feeling.

"You helped stop a terrible wrong," he said.

"Yeah." Her eyes lost focus for a moment. "I ... ran into an ex-friend from Fleet. I hoped – maybe – she'd understand." She gave a bitter laugh.

"You remember what *I* was like when we first met," Denev said. "Most people are so wrapped up in their own lives they can't see how fucked up the Hegemony is."

"But I've made it worse. The Lenticular is sending ships to go to war with the Hegemony. And if they win, I'm not sure I can stop them from wiping out the whole of humanity."

"How long have you been awake?" Denev asked.

"What?" Her eyes were bloodshot and red-rimmed. "I don't know. Three days? It's hard to keep track when I'm off-planet."

"You sound defeated, but that's the exhaustion talking. The fact is, you've given the aliens a fighting chance. Which means they'll listen to you. And you're not alone. You've got me."

The tired smile returned.

"And if there *is* a death armada on its way from the Lenticular," he added, "maybe there's a way to tamper with whatever sensor intel we get from out your way. Remove any data on ship movements."

"Don't put your life in danger," Rhees said.

"No more so than usual. Besides, I'm not alone now. I've got Rapskel and his group of whatevers, and …" He paused. There was no easy way to bring this up. "I spoke to your father."

Rhees's brow furrowed and she leaned forward. "You what?"

"He contacted me right after I killed Laneaux."

"How? Why?"

"He was worried about you," Denev said and ploughed on before she asked the inevitable question. "Rapskel told him because … it seems Gart Lowrans is a traitor."

Rhees sat back again, considering. "He's the adjutant for Ten Vargas."

"Apparently you can be both. From what he told me, this has been going on for a long time. Maybe that's why he kept his distance from you."

"Convenient."

"Or he had some other reason. I don't know the man."

"Neither do I really," Rhees said.

"He … asked me to pass on a message, assuming you were still alive. He said he's sorry. And he wants you to stay safe."

Rhees barked a short laugh. "Staying safe is pretty much off the table." Then, "I don't know if you should trust him."

"I don't. But if he's a traitor, he's right in the middle of Fleet high command. The more allies we have, the more we can steer events. And maybe not destroy humanity and all get killed along the way."

Rhees let out a long sigh. "All right. You know what you're doing."

"And so do you. Look, we can't communicate like this for a while. Volmar's brought in a couple of auditors looking for a leak in the Datahive and I have to help them."

"And by help them, you mean –"

"Not get caught, yes."

"Will you be all right?"

"I think so, but there's a couple of things you need to know. I told you Volmar's angry."

She nodded.

"Well, he's mainly angry at your friend Udun. Volmar has an asset on Homeworld and whoever it is will be tasked with killing him. I can't get any more details. Volmar's handling this one personally."

"I'll warn the Kresz," Rhees said. "What else?"

"SolSec are sure Volmar had Laneaux killed and they're blackmailing me to help kill Volmar."

Rhees was silent and Denev could see she was working through the implications.

"Do they have proof you killed Laneaux?" she said.

"No. They have something else on me that could make things uncomfortable if they leak it, but they won't do that as long as I'm useful."

"Are you going to be useful?" she asked.

"That I don't know."

21

As prime hierarch, I'd been given a private room dug into the rock of Treaty Mount and accessed by stairs leading down from behind the central podium of the Council chamber. It had been a small meeting room used by the representatives of hierarchs and lodge factions between Council sessions, so it was well furnished with benches and a long table I usually worked at when I couldn't return to the escarpment. The room was shielded of course, though here alone I had no need of it. The Hegemony had locked my emotions inside me when they took my mantle.

I sat at the table reading through the sheaf of reports that had framed my days since the fighting ended. My mind was full of disruption. Not just because of the incident in the chamber, but the disruption that spread through all of Kresz society. The disruption much of the Council was doing its best to ignore.

Even before the Hegemony came, the house and guild system was doing everything it could to preserve its sovereignty and ignore the fact the population was growing far beyond the limits that system imposed. If a Kresz was born with a Cultivator body plan to House Ukat, she didn't necessarily want a life fishing the Inland Sea as part of the Cultivators Lodge, no matter how many of her ancestors had followed the same path. Even without the Hegemony invasion we'd been heading for a collision between house/lodge needs and individual wants on a massive scale.

But the Hegemony did come, and they gained Kergis as an ally because he was already fighting for the old ways against progressives like Czerag. When we'd defeated Kergis and the Hegemony on Homeworld, I'd hoped the houses and lodges would realise that disruption was good because it showed you what needed to change. If we didn't address the root causes – the expansion of personal freedom and now the large contingent of disenfranchised excisees – those disrupting forces would tear us apart. But the old ways and old prejudices ran deep.

The doorway rolled open and Tzek took the last two steps down from the chamber, then sat on the closest bench, breath wheezing through his spiracles.

"The Cultivator's dead," he said. "I stayed with him till the end."

I imagined what that would have been like for Tzek, feeling my attacker's realisation that death was coming. The fears and regrets, or anger perhaps, that realisation would bring, and then the loss of focus as the dying Cultivator's personality unwound, falling into final chaos before it slipped into silence.

"Are you all right?" I asked.

Tzek looked at me and it was clear he wasn't. "I had to be sure. His motivations for the attack were purely personal. Deep-held religious beliefs. Pride in his work. A feeling that his world was changing beyond his capacity to control it."

"Change brings fear," I said.

"It also brings rage," Tzek snapped, then looked at the stone floor. Was he re-experiencing what the Cultivator had shown him or was this something else?

"Hiding out in the deep desert, there were days I felt reclaiming Homeworld would be impossible," he went on. "We did it but ..."

"But?" I asked.

"Winning the peace is harder. It could destroy us all."

I moved from behind my table to sit on the closest bench to him. "You're not talking about defeating the Hegemony, are you?"

"That part is easy by comparison. We have the support of the Council, the Telsans and the Svestans. Not easy allies, but they'll rub along as long as they get to fight. It's everything else," he said, suddenly angry again. "It's your Human. She fills our prisons with Humans when she should be helping us to kill them."

"I made my decision about that," I said firmly. "Rhees is our ally."

"Can we trust her when the real fight comes if she can't bring herself to do what must be done?"

"This is difficult for her."

"Difficult?" Tzek stared at me. "At some point it will become impossible. And if we share our battle plans with her, she will betray us."

"No," I said, my own anger at the suggestion pushing past my concern for Tzek. "She would never do that. But this isn't just about Rhees, is it? Why are you so angry?"

Tzek raised his staff and struck the floor. "Because you're pushing things too hard and too fast." He looked away again, leaning forward to rest his lower elbows on his thigh plates. When he spoke again his voice was more tired than angry.

"The Cultivator. His name was Adek. He was just like anyone else. When the Hegemony came, he was caught up in the fighting at Treaty Mount. Put into a labour gang. Beaten and tortured until he escaped and hid out on the fringes of Aktiuk. Free in a way. Free to starve. Free to be killed if he was recaptured. He could have hidden out like that, staying in relative safety. But when he heard about the great gathering of Kresz liberators, he stole a ground car and joined us. He was there, fighting alongside us. Against Kergis and the Hegemony, do you see?"

I did. There were many like Adek. And many who had died in that fight.

"And now, this morning, he was filled with rage," I said. "Enough to want to kill me in the Council chamber."

"Rage. Fear. Both. Adek was no hierarch. Politics and power didn't motivate him. He suffered through the occupation. He fought for his world. He won against all indications to the contrary. But when the fighting stopped, the world he found himself in was not the world he fought for. It was filled with too much strangeness. And it was being led by someone intent on changing it even more. Adek was not the only Kresz who feels this way."

The Kresz were conservative in nature. That was a fundamental truth. But there were other truths that couldn't be ignored.

"We all have to live in the world as it is," I said. "And deal with the problems we inherit. Do you get a sense of how things are from the worldmind?"

The overlapping empathic fields from all the Kresz bled into our dreams – or it had when I still had my mantle – like a sort of collective unconscious. Though during the invasion, it had made it hard to think, filled as it was with violence, fear and hatred.

"It hasn't been the same since the Hegemony came," Tzek said. "It feels …" He paused, trying to put the abstract into words. "Confused. Uncertain and dark. I agree we have to deal with what's in front of us, but there are ways and ways. And for all I dislike Akczek, there is a kernel of truth in what he says. We must bring the people with us, not force change on them."

I couldn't believe what I was hearing. "You want me to stop the reforms?"

"Not stop. Slow them."

I stood, unable to sit still. "No."

"Udun –"

"No. The excisees are the ones who suffered the most during the occupation and they're still suffering. They look to us – to me – to help them. Every day we *don't* change, excisees are abused, attacked or die of neglect. Not just in Aktiuk, but all across Homeworld. It's still legal to euthanise them, and you ask me to slow down? No. I regret Adek's death, but what he did was wrong."

Tzek planted his staff between his hoofs and stood. "We won't help the excisees by failing. And if you don't temper your ambition, we will fail."

At least he still said "we". But he didn't understand. He couldn't. He'd helped keep Reka and the other excisees who strayed his way in the deep desert safe. But they weren't real people to him. They were cripples to be cared for. It was an improvement on most Kresz, whose instinct was to shun excisees or even to "clear the way"– the polite term for mercy killings. But the needs of the excisees still held a lesser place in Tzek's mental hierarchy. Somehow I was an exception. Or he didn't see me as an excisee. But I knew what I was. And I knew what I had to do.

The door rolled open, interrupting us, and Rhees and Isza entered. I saw Isza's greeting die on her feeders as she picked up on whatever Tzek was feeling. I wondered which of his emotions dominated. Anger or frustration at how foolish I was being? Or perhaps disappointment that I was failing whatever standard of statecraft he expected of me. The ability to set aside whatever beliefs one held for political expediency. If so, it was a standard I was happy not to live up to.

Rhees broke the awkward silence. "How's things?"

"They are as you might expect," Tzek said, which did nothing to lighten the mood.

"We've just returned from the Hub," Isza said, still unsure of what she'd walked into. "More interrogations."

"Some of the Hegemony ships are breaking cover," Rhees said. "We're not sure why."

I glanced at the sheaf of reports on my table. "You've been busy."

"Yes," Tzek said, "you fill our prisons with more and more Humans. A drain on our resources. Tell me, when we fight the Hegemony fleet again, do you plan to capture all of them?"

"I certainly don't believe in killing for killing's sake," Rhees said.

"Your fellow Humans do."

"Yes, and I know some Kresz do too, especially with non-Kresz. I experience enough bigotry from Kresz who don't know any better. I don't expect it from you."

"You don't know me," Tzek said. "And I don't know you. I don't trust you to do what has to –"

"That's enough," I said, angry with him again. "Leave us."

Tzek looked at me for a long moment, then swept out of the room, the door rolling shut behind him.

"What was that about?" Isza asked.

I didn't want to discuss Tzek's outburst in front of Rhees. Instead I said, "I wish Atalna were still here. He was a politician. I'm not."

"I think we can do without politicians for a while," Isza said.

I took my seat behind the table and gestured for Rhees and Isza to sit. Isza still looked concerned.

"I want you to know how grateful we are for the work you're doing," I told Rhees. "I understand how difficult it is for you."

Rhees bared her teeth in what I knew was a smile. "I've got to live with the decisions I made. There's no turning back now."

"Tzek had no right to say what he did," Isza said.

"He was angry with me," I said. "And you bore the brunt of it. We're all on edge, preparing for war."

"There's a chance the Hegemony will leave us alone," Isza said. "They were only here to keep the way clear to Hanloi space. Their campaign failed. There's no reason for them to come back."

"It's already decided," I said. "The Council agrees on that at least. The Telsans want revenge after they discovered the extent of Hegemony infiltration into their society. The same goes for the Aphsans, Gen'sh, Dray, P-vvarni … every Lenticular species the Hegemony has impacted in some way. The Svestans just want to fight. But even if none of that were true, war would still come. We defeated the Hegemony. They can't let the other alien species they control see they can be beaten. We have to be punished."

"We just spoke to a corvette captain who'd agree with you," Rhees said.

"I thought she was more than a little deranged," Isza said.

"No. There's a type in Fleet. Fiercely loyal to crew and the Hegemony and fuck everyone and everything else. I thought she was different, but …"

Rhees lapsed into silence and I looked at Isza, wondering what had happened.

"I spoke to Denev," Rhees continued. "Volmar wants you dead, Udun. Denev says he has an asset on Homeworld who'll assassinate you on his orders."

I thought about Adek. But from what Tzek had learned, it was unlikely he was an agent of the Hegemony. I didn't really want to mention the attack, but Isza was bound to find out.

"There was a … disturbance in the Council chamber today," I said. "Someone tried to attack me."

"Sakat," Isza said. "Are you all right?"

I raised a claw. "Still in one piece. It wasn't a Hegemony spy. Just a misguided victim of the occupation."

"Which means whoever Volmar has is still out there," Isza said.

"They'll have to get through Gatiku and the whole Defenders Lodge if they want to kill the prime hierarch," I pointed out.

"Which very nearly happened today," Isza said. "Gatiku has to do a lot better if he's to keep you safe."

"We could really use Nok's help," Rhees said. "Do you think he died when the station exploded?"

"I don't know." I remembered when Nok had revealed his true nature to me. A being of pure energy and thought. The synthesis of the entire Jantri species. "I prefer to think he's passed into a higher dimension. He told me once there were things in this universe beyond even his understanding. And he wanted to explore them."

"For someone who didn't like getting involved, he certainly got involved at the end," Rhees said. "Maybe he decided to pull back after that. I'd like to know for sure."

"What are you thinking?" I asked.

She slapped her hands on her legs and stood up. "A little bit of exploration. There's a whole Jantri world nobody visits. If Nok's still around, there's a good chance he's there. Do you feel like coming with me, Isza?"

Rhees and Isza had grown close during the clean-up missions. I could see Isza was tempted, but she was still worried about me.

"I need a break from flying around in space," she said.

Rhees nodded. "No problem. It'll give me some time to think. Oh –" She held up a finger. "If you're getting a battle fleet ready, you need to start scouring the tenspace corridors for Hegemony devices. The closer you can get to Hegemony space without detection, the better."

I wished Tzek were still here. If he had been, he'd see he had no reason to question Rhees's loyalty.

"We will," I said. "But you'll be back before the fight?"

"You can count on it."

Rhees left, and it was just me and Isza. I knew what she was going to say and I raised a claw to head her off. "Gatiku has already increased security."

"And he'll have to increase it more when we tell him about Volmar's threat. Could there be Humans still on Homeworld?"

"I suppose it's possible. But they couldn't move in the open without being instantly discovered."

"Maybe they wouldn't need to. The Hegemony could have left all kinds of remote devices, bombs and traps."

"Every house and public building has been scoured for Hegemony tech."

Isza started pacing along the length of the table. "That doesn't mean we found it all. Or that a hidden Human couldn't still kill you from a distance, or there's a stealth satellite we've missed with weapons capability –"

"Or Volmar's convinced Sakat to strike me down with divine fire," I interrupted. "The Priests would certainly believe that could happen. I can't hide away from the world, Isza."

She stopped pacing and faced me. "You have to be safe. You need trusted guards with you at all times, limit outside travel and meetings, regular security sweeps of your chambers and public rooms, maybe have your food screened for toxins."

"I can't run a government from inside a prison cell." It was already hard enough trying to get anything done, particularly with Tzek in his current mood. "And I can't stop now."

Isza placed her claws on the table top and leaned forward to look into my eyes. I wondered if she was trying to pick up some vestige of empathic contact again. But there was nothing and the breath hissed through her spiracles.

"It's the excisees, isn't it," she said.

"It's the Council. Or most of them. Generations of reviling excisees, and they can't see how different this situation is. They won't allow them to rejoin their houses, most lodges are closed to them, and they complain about the House of Excisees and Rasa's presence in the Council chamber."

"How is she doing?"

"She's very capable. You know she was chosen by a majority of the excisee group? It's a new way of doing things."

"And another reason the hierarchs feel threatened," Isza said, dampening the enthusiasm I always felt when I thought about how the excisees were organising themselves.

I could see what she meant, but what the excisees represented – to me at least – was hope from hopelessness. I'd seen how it was after the Hegemony took my mantle. Newly excised Kresz standing like statues, unsure of what to do or how to navigate a world that looked totally changed and felt like nothing. Many couldn't live with that new reality and had suicided on the spikes. Others fell victim to gangs of intact, as cruel as the Humans. But those who survived – like those Rhees and I met in the deep desert hide – had found a way through their grief. They'd found a family – one that transcended house or lodge or body plan. That was threatening to some. But it was also something that needed to be protected and nurtured.

If the houses continued to refuse entry to the excisees, that might be a good thing, I thought. As long as we had strong laws to protect individual excisees, and broad recognition for the House of Excisees as a legitimate part of society. But all of that felt very far away.

"I'm surrounded by hierarchs and deans and advisors telling me what the people want," I said. "Tzek tells me the worldmind is a dark place filled with confusion."

"It is," Isza said. "But sometimes when I sleep, I feel … It's like a collective in-breath. Waiting." Her eyes were focused on the infinite. "A potential something not formed or understood." Her feeders spread wide. "I don't know. Who can make sense of dreams?"

"Do you think I should slow my reforms, give everyone a chance to catch up?"

"Is that what Tzek advises?"

"Do you agree with him?"

She blinked. "No. The Hegemony wounded us. We have to heal, I agree. But we have to heal the whole body, not just a part of it. The excisees are part of us. You're one of them and you're also prime hierarch. But the other hierarchs and lodge leaders are just like anyone else – rational argument only gets you so far. You have to show them how the excisees can help them."

"To do what?"

"To get whatever it is they want."

"Maybe you should be my advisor instead of Tzek," I said. "If he still *is* my advisor."

"He was angry. I certainly felt that. But he was scared too. Give him some time. He'll do what's right. But in the meantime, talk to Gatiku about increasing security."

"I'll do what I can to stay safe," I told her. "Believe me."

"I know you will." Her feeders stretched wide. "Sometimes the saviour of our people has to be saved from himself."

22

It felt good to be out in space again and not on a search-and-engage mission. Just flying, her and her dolphinship. She'd left the rest of her ship pod back on the Kresz Hub. She wasn't looking for or expecting a fight, but if she found one, her little ship had more than enough firepower and speed to get her out of it.

The Voss Space run between Kresz space and Jantri'va was pretty quick once she'd reached a safe transit area at the Kresz end. The white hole where the Point had been was still unnavigable. As soon as she transited she punched for maximum speed. Not because she was on a deadline or anything, but because she could. The power of the ship around her was exhilarating, even without a sense of acceleration. She felt free.

But it was an illusion. When she'd agreed to work with Nok he'd told her that if they won back the Lenticular, she would have to convince the others not to destroy Earth. She still had no idea how to do that.

If she failed, then everything Jute thought and said about her would be right. She'd be a fool who thought she knew better than everybody else *and* a traitor to her species. There was no doubt the other Hegemony prisoners Rhees had rescued would feel the same way. But what about her father? Was he really a traitor? And if so, would he agree with Jute or would he understand what Rhees was trying to achieve?

Long-range scans nudged her consciousness, correlating data with charts of the region. The Jantri star was an old red giant, its face peppered with massive sunspots. The space around it was relatively sparse: a bright orange gas giant wearing a gaudy cross of double rings guarding the edge of the system, followed by a broad asteroid belt – far wider than Sol system's. The sheer volume of debris spoke of the violent collisions and disintegrations of three or four Earth-sized worlds. Closer in to the star – so close its mantle must be perpetually molten – was a smaller planet, maybe twice the size of Earth's moon, and remarkable for its fast orbit: not just set at forty-five degrees to the ecliptic but also orbiting against the direction of every other body in the system.

Nok's homeworld sat between the orbit of the hot, fast planet and the inner edge of the asteroid belt. Half again the size of Earth, it shone with its own light, a scintillating pattern of pinks, purples and silvers that sparkled and roiled across the atmosphere, like ripples on a pond suddenly shot through with forks of violet lightning. It was beautiful. But it hid any glimpse of what the surface might be like. Sensors could make out major landmasses and what looked to be large, interlinked cities, but any more detail was masked by the ionising radiation that kept visitors away.

Near-orbit of the world was strangely free of anything artificial. No satellites, stations or skystalks. In fact, as Rhees sped closer she realised there was nothing like that in the whole system. No automated miners or manufactories in the belt or drilling into the inner depths of the gas giant. No bubble habs on larger planetesimals, no ships. If she didn't know better, she'd take it as the mark of a pre-spaceflight civilisation, confined to the single inhabited planet in the system.

As she entered final orbital approach for Nok's world, there was a signal so quick she almost missed it – maybe from the planet, maybe from something in orbit she couldn't see – which her ship responded to automatically. She slowed her flight, but nothing obvious happened so she kept going.

The beautiful glowing atmosphere sped by beneath her and then she dropped further and it was all around her. When she thought about the experience later, it was a bit like swimming. You're under the water, looking up at the surface. The sea is choppy so the image is broken up, disjointed. Still, you feel you have a good idea of what you're looking at. And then you swim up and break through the surface of the water and what you see is nothing like you imagined.

That topography, the linked cities, had to be a projection – because directly beneath her was a blast crater. The ship calculated the radius at two hundred and fifty kilometres. The force at the epicentre must have been tremendous. The ground was scoured back to the bedrock, slagged and glassy and gouged in long channels where stone had run like liquid. All around the edge was the remains of a city. What must have been incredibly tall, delicate structures now broken, melted, crumbling with decay and leaning away from the blast or completely collapsed.

She was still travelling high and fast. The dead city spread out for another thousand kilometres around the crater. Her current course showed it running right up to the edge of an ancient mountain range that looked more like a jumble of oversized boulders. She'd climbed mountains in the Southern Patagonian Ice Field during an Academy exercise years ago. The mountains there were deadly-looking, like rows of pointed teeth raking the sky. These mountains had been worn smooth by aeons of rain and weather.

Once she passed over the range, the landscape looked more natural, descending through foothills to a shoreline. Except the ocean the coastal shelf skirted was gone. Nothing but a vast, uneven bowl ten kilometres deep and three thousand kilometres at its widest point. What had happened here? A war? A city obliterated by an explosion? A sea boiled dry?

She understood from Udun that the Jantri had evolved from beings of matter to pure mind and energy. And that Nok was an amalgam: all the living minds of Jantri'va fused into a single consciousness. That sort of phase change might happen slowly at first, until it reached a threshold where matter became energy. Then the shift would happen very quickly. Would it release enough energy to flatten cities and evaporate oceans?

Or perhaps this all happened afterwards. Without bodies the Jantri wouldn't need cities. Was Rhees witnessing the result of some experiment? Some transformation she couldn't fathom? She'd struggled with Nok's motivations when he was around, and was sure she couldn't even guess at the truth of what had really happened. But was he still here?

She gazed down at the dry, cracked ocean floor and shuddered. The place was dead – she felt that strongly. Dead and haunted; not by the ghosts of the Jantri'va but by the violent events that had torn the flesh from this world until there was nothing left but crumbling bone.

Still, she had to try.

The ship opened a broadcast channel for her.

"Nok. Nok, can you hear me?"

Nothing.

She thought about returning to space. Instead the ship increased speed and dropped altitude.

She pushed at the control surfaces but they didn't respond.

The dead seabed fell away behind her and the ship – very low now – shot across an undulating desert of crystalline sand. She tried to gain control again.

"Fuck!"

The broadcast channel was still open. "Nok, what are you doing? Give me back control!"

But maybe it wasn't Nok. Had some automatic defence system grabbed her ship?

She was just metres above the dunes now, the coarse sand flashing beneath her. The craft dipped to follow the contours of the land, and then it broke over a high ridge and slowed above a level plain of sand dominated by a stark white dome a hundred metres high.

The dolphincraft landed, and the cockpit roof peeled back. Rhees gasped. The atmosphere here was radioactive and deadly to organic life. Ship sensors had confirmed that on approach. But she could breathe.

She looked at her hand. Rubbed her fingers together. A shower of rainbow fractals strobed up her arm, across her chest and faded. Her fingers felt strange, a little soapy maybe. She was enveloped in a force field. One that held a breathable atmosphere.

She grasped the edge of the cockpit and swung her legs over the side, sinking into the crystalline sand up to her knees. Above her the roiling sky looked like a bruise and the bloated sun was an angry red. The visuals in the ship had been colour-compensated for detail. Out here it was perpetual dusk.

She took a few awkward steps towards the dome, pulling her legs high to step forward only to sink again. The "sand" was more like small pebbles. She scooped up a handful. It looked like diamonds but was light like pumice. Each rock was maybe five millimetres in diameter and irregular in shape, but – she looked closely – they were all identical.

"What the fuck?"

She kept walking towards the dome, the diamond aggregate scrunching beneath her feet, making it difficult going. The dome wall was smooth and featureless. There was no way she was going to walk round it looking for an opening. Her thighs were already aching with the effort to walk from the ship.

"Nok!" she shouted. "Nok, it's me!"

Still nothing.

She placed a flat palm on the dome. It was vibrating. And the skin of the dome round her fingers looked brighter. She thought she was imagining it at first. But the bright patch was spreading. She pulled her hand away. Where she'd made contact was different. Rough and blurred. And this effect was following the brightness as it spread across the curved wall. Was it opening?

She looked down as the bright patch reached the pebbles, which started to roughen and blur as well. And then the roughened dome surface and pebbles split apart. Particles drifting as if weightless, bumping into each other and spinning away.

She stepped back to keep out of the way. Whatever was happening was accelerating. The dome was disintegrating. The sand beneath it too.

She stepped back again, then turned and ran. But the ground sucked at her, making her feel like she was running underwater. A sudden violent wind pushed at her, knocking her to her knees. She struggled to her feet again and looked back.

The dome was gone, particles whirling around each other in a column that grew higher and higher into the dark sky.

Rhees scrambled over the ground on all fours now, keeping her centre of gravity low, scooping gravel through her fists and pushing with her feet. Dusk darkened to night and somewhere above thunder rumbled in a deep long roar.

A gust of wind almost lifted her into the sky and she crashed against the dolphinship. She reached up to grip the side and pulled herself into the cockpit. The skin sealed over her, cutting off the roar of the building hurricane.

This time the ship responded to her commands, lifting quickly. The dunes were breaking apart and floating into the air – until she was flying above a dusty sea or a thick fog lit by flashes of lightning. Wherever she saw a flash, things emerged from the fog, flowing and taking shape as they rose. Dolphinships. More and more of them. Birthing from whatever was happening down there.

The effect was growing. Ripples of light like multiple laser blasts coursed through the transforming matter. Ships sprang into existence, crowding the space beneath, until suddenly it was over. The fog was gone.

Beneath the dolphinships, the planet surface was a blank plain as far as Rhees could see. Not one grain of sand remained.

She pushed back in her seat as she felt her perception expanding – that seasick doubling and trebling of awareness when she linked fully with her dolphinship pod. But there were too many here. Her mind would burst.

The sensation stopped as quickly as it had begun. Equilibrium. She knew, without knowing how she knew, that she could directly control seventy-three ships. The same limit as when Nok had first taught her about the interface. But the rest … The figure sprang into her mind. There were twelve hundred dolphincraft below her.

Something else opened in her mind. A command tree of sorts, but limited. The ships beyond her immediate span of control were slaved to her. Not enough to be useful in battle, but they'd follow, or wait, or … She felt the option and probed it tentatively. She could destroy them all. Right now.

She almost felt Nok's presence with her in the dolphincraft. "You bastard," she whispered. This was another of his experiments. Like when he'd left her alone with the Kresz on his ship, or when he'd introduced them all to the other group of Kresz on the Jantri station. Like chemistry. Mix the agents together and see what happens. If they go boom, start again.

Nok had given her tremendous firepower, but her control of it – beyond her direct cohort of seventy-three ships – was limited. He'd also given her the choice to destroy it all. All options were on the table. What was she going to do?

Fuck. She wasn't going to destroy this tool. She needed it too much. Without Nok, it was by no means certain the Lenticular could win against the Hegemony. They needed an edge. This was it.

But she was also sure she couldn't just turn the ships over to the Lenticular alliance. Udun might agree that not all humans deserved to die, but there were plenty of other Kresz, Telsans and Svestans that believed they did. Shit, the Svestans didn't even see a choice. They were in it for the death and glory.

Tzek had said he didn't trust her. Was this the moment she betrayed them?

No. She wouldn't desert Udun after everything they'd been through together.

The newborn ships still waited below her. She gave the command to follow and piloted her dolphincraft up into the bruised sky. The storm had gone as quickly as it had arrived and apart from the mass of ships climbing with her there was nothing left to signify the transformation she'd witnessed.

She climbed higher until the atmosphere thinned and she was back in space, the twelve hundred craft accelerating with her away from the planet until she brought them all to a complete halt and looked back. The beautiful pink, purple, silver atmosphere rippled across the face of the planet again, with vague suggestions of cities and landmasses, and no sign of the altered landscapes she'd seen.

Where to now? If she could go anywhere, what ally would she choose?

One that wanted to fight, but who understood not all humans were monsters. That meant familiarity with the Hegemony.

The Lenticular had experienced humanity at its worst. The aliens here had been an annoyance at best, something to keep out of the way while Fleet maintained a strategic foothold to support the Hanloi campaign. That had been the single driver for everything that happened here. Other alien species had a different experience. Particularly those encountered in the natural expansion of the Hegemony. In those cases there was the carrot of trade or mutual alliance and protection, or both. And the stick was only used if necessary. Of course, once the aliens who were open to HDC's sweet talk got on the inside of the Hegemony, they realised they were second-class citizens at best. But for many, that didn't figure in their day-to-day lives. If they were productive and useful to the Hegemony and kept to their own kind, they could live happily enough under Hegemony rule. It was only if they pushed against the status quo that things got ugly.

They'd gotten pretty ugly for the Brell, the Sissilak and the Totek when Volmar fed their rebel fleet to the Maagba. But they may still be a possibility. The takeover of the Brell system had been fairly bloodless. When the Hegemony destroyed their spaceyards, the Brell Conglomerate capitulated immediately. It was the only option left to them. The Sissilak and Totek had fallen in line when they saw what happened to the Brell. Since then things had been peaceful in Cygnus Sector apart from the Maagba problem, which meant the Brell, Sissilak and Totek knew the Hegemony as more than stone-cold killers.

If she could contact them, offer them a bargain: their freedom for their help. Maybe they could be the allies she needed.

23

There was a sharp chill in the air this morning that Denev hadn't felt even when he was camping. Early morning workers stood in conversational clumps along the slidewalk and he caught snatches of their talk as he passed: the weather, the latest celeb-scandal, office gossip.

If war came and the Central Administration and the Hegemony toppled, would these people feel liberated, he wondered. After all, a lab-grown rat knew nothing of the possibilities that existed outside the walls of its cage.

Rapskel and his group would say yes. Even if only at a subconscious level, the lab rat knows it's trapped, and the walls it lives within limit its choices and – consequently – its thoughts. Remove the walls and something wonderful will happen.

Maybe. But whatever else it did, the Central Administration kept the lights on, the hospitals running and the food stores well-stocked. Those who couldn't find work got basic and lived well enough comparatively. If the revolution was to be a success, it had to offer something better than the status quo. Denev didn't know what that was. But maybe Rhees did.

He took the sidestrip down and was deposited at the entrance to the Datahive. Inside, the foyer was busy. HDC uniforms lined up for the elevators, which opened and disgorged more uniformed bodies. Shift change.

Denev navigated through the crowds to the single elevator that had no one waiting, because it only travelled to Volmar's office at the top of the Datahive. The elevator opened and he stepped inside, turning to face the foyer as the doors started to close.

"Hold!"

A large fist grabbed the edge of one of the doors and they parted before Denev could react. Gart Lowrans entered, and the elevator closed and started its ascent.

The admiral was a bear of a man, but Denev had seen him fearful and worried for his daughter. He had his weakness like everybody else.

"Good morning, Admiral."

Lowrans half-turned, looking at Denev as if he'd never seen him before. Which made sense. Every inch of the Datahive was under surveillance. And Denev and Lowrans had only met once. It was unlikely someone like Lowrans would remember him.

"I'm Denev Antwer, Comptroller Volmar's aide. We met at a Security Review Sub-Committee meeting."

Lowrans grunted a good morning and turned to face the doors again. But Denev was sure that if he could Lowrans would ask if he had any more news of Rhees. It must be eating at him, sharing a lift and not being able to say anything. And there were no words and no signal Denev could give that wouldn't be analysed to the nth degree and endanger them both.

The lift stopped but the doors remained closed. After a second, Lowrans stabbed a finger on the single contact, but nothing happened.

"Additional security scan," Denev said. "We'll be moving in –"

The car started again and three seconds later the doors opened. Volmar stood at the broad window that angled vertiginously down towards the lower levels of the Datahive. He clasped his hands behind his back, his thin lips compressing as he nodded at them.

"Lowrans. Antwer."

Denev could have explained he'd met Lowrans in the elevator. It was something he'd say in normal conversation, calling out a coincidence. But Volmar would have watched them in the car. Any additional information volunteered by Denev would be viewed as dissembling. The mark of a guilty conscience. Better to stay quiet.

Volmar crossed to stand behind his desk and indicated chairs for Denev and Lowrans. "Lowrans, I wanted to gauge Fleet readiness for a counterattack on the Lenticular. The longer we wait, the longer the aliens have to regroup."

Lowrans remained silent and looked meaningfully at Denev.

"You can talk freely in front of Antwer," Volmar said with a note of annoyance. "He's completely familiar with the whole operation."

Lowrans cleared his throat. "There'll be no counterattack."

Volmar's lips compressed even more, his cold blue eyes narrowing. "Not good enough. The Lenticular needs to be put down, if only to show our member species we still have the means to control them."

"The Hanloi just handed us our arses on a plate," Lowrans said. "The losses we sustained aren't something you bounce back from. It's going to take years to rebuild, and smashing a few uppity aliens in a system no one's heard of is not high on the agenda."

"What about reserves?"

Lowrans grunted a humourless laugh. "What reserves? We threw everything we had into the Hanloi campaign. Right now we're spread thin across the territory we already hold. We're having to pull resources out of settled systems – telling any aliens who ask that the ships are needed for wargaming exercises and they'll be back soon. But the truth is, we're vulnerable."

"So you've failed. Despite Vargas's assurances."

"And despite your supposedly thorough tactical analyses," Lowrans countered.

"A plan is only as good as its execution." A slow smile spread across Volmar's face but failed to reach his eyes. "I told your daughter when she was alive that her faith in Fleet was misguided."

Denev glanced at Lowrans and saw the man's ruddy complexion grow darker.

"It looks like it's down to HDC to find a solution to our current woes." Volmar stood. "I'm sure you have duties to attend to."

Lowrans stood too and, without a word or a backward glance, walked into the waiting elevator car. The doors closed behind him.

Volmar took his seat again, leaning back and steepling his fingers. He regarded Denev for a long moment. "So much for Fleet. What did SolSec want?"

They want to kill you and I'm considering helping them.

"They're scrambling in the dark after Laneaux's death," Denev said. "They want access to whatever surveillance data we might have."

"Of course. Give them whatever you think corroborates our preferred version of events. Speaking of which, two of our scapegoat assassins have been arrested but one seems to have dropped off the face of the planet: Preem Renalds. You don't know where he might be?"

"I don't," Denev said. "But he can't hide forever."

Or perhaps he could. Rapskel's people had grabbed Preem when they'd introduced themselves to Denev.

Volmar sniffed. "In any case, the Inclusionist connection is playing out well. Kant, the party secretary, has been detained for questioning. The show trials should begin soon. But I'm more concerned about the Fleet situation."

He raised a hand above his desk, palm upward, and a holo star map sprang up in the space between them. A representation of Sol and the other systems that formed the stable boundaries of the Hegemony.

With one finger, Volmar rotated the view. "It won't be long until these busy alien minds notice the ships that keep them safe and obedient are missing. The more rebellious among them may well see an opportunity to move against us. Like your Cygnus Sector friends. Perhaps the Maagba can be of assistance. At least in that part of space." Volmar paused, staring at the display.

Wheels within wheels, Denev thought. Leaving no plot unhatched.

Volmar focused on Denev again. "HDC hasn't exactly covered itself in glory of late."

It was clear from Volmar's exchange with Lowrans that the comptroller was doing his best to lay the blame for the Hanloi defeat squarely on Fleet. But as Lowrans had pointed out, HDC had played a major role in providing tactical analyses for the battle plan.

"We need to focus on what we do best. Identify treachery before it occurs and neutralise it," Volmar continued.

"Of course." And work as hard as we can to prove to Central Administration that the Hanloi mess was an isolated incident – at least on HDC's part, Denev thought.

"I want you to prepare an analysis. Check in with the sector heads and develop risk profiles for each system. We'll show them we don't need Fleet to keep the Hegemony safe."

"What about the Lenticular campaign leak?" Denev asked.

"You've briefed Rejak's men. They're capable enough."

"Yes, Comptroller." Denev stood to leave.

"Oh, and I need you in my office first thing the day after tomorrow. I have a special meeting of the executive to attend. You can present your risk profiles then."

More arse-covering, Denev thought. He'd intended to work closely with Hel and Stin and nudge them away from any "unhelpful" line of enquiry. That wouldn't be possible now.

∞

Back in his nook, Denev queried for Rejak's auditors and the datastream reorganised around him, bringing the three of them together. The data architecture could do this regardless of where Hel and Stin were – even on another planet – with no perceptible communication lag. But the two clones were both sequestered on other levels of the Datahive. They had no choice in order to have the access they required for the audit.

The clones stood in a blank room, looking the same as they'd done in the cafeteria. But while visually neutral, the environment was far more information rich than the real world. Denev could tell just by looking at them the exact clearance they'd been granted. It was the same as his, which gave him a degree of comfort he hadn't felt a moment ago.

"Slight change of plans," he told them.

Hel – at least he thought it was Hel – raised a perfectly groomed blond eyebrow. Stin's expression remained neutral.

"The comptroller's tasked me with other urgent duties, so you'll be working on your own. Is there anything more you need from me to get started?"

Hel shifted to a broad smile. "Not a problem at all, Specialist," he said and nodded at Stin. "We are very good at sniffing out rats."

There was something predatory about Hel that made Denev quickly revise down his comfort level.

"Okay," he said. "Contact me if you have any questions. Good hunting."

He brushed the contact away and began organising separate streams on sector threat reports. He had a lot of work to get through before Volmar's meeting with the executive.

24

Rasa and I sat in my room beneath the Council chamber watching the vuscreen. The latest contingent of the combined Lenticular battle fleet was leaving on the long journey to Hegemony space. The ship group was dominated by two flights of heavy cruisers. The first was Telsan-built: massive ships composed of tiered layers of hull stacked on central tapered spines and backed with circle drives. Not to be outdone, the Svestan flight had more ships, each one a statement of aggression constructed from building-sized and knife-pointed planes of hull metal that mirrored their crews' armoured bodies. There were Kresz deeprange ships in among them, smaller but heavily armed I knew, and a few P-vvarni, Aphsan and Gen'sh ships, plus the distinctive crescent hulls of scouts purchased from the Jantri long before the invasion.

"That's a lot of ships," Rasa said.

"We'll need a lot more than that," I replied. "As much as they're fighting for themselves, they're fighting for us. For what was done to the excisees. That's how it feels to me anyway."

"Me too," Rasa said. "And there's hope on Homeworld as well. I know things are difficult here now, but some intacts aren't so bad."

My feeders spread wide. I liked Rasa. She reminded me a lot of Isza, without the more interfering aspects. And she'd been chosen by the other excisees to lead them.

Rhees told me the Humans had a word for it – democracy. With no house willing to take back its excisees, someone had to be their voice. It couldn't be me. I had to lead the intact *and* the excised.

And somehow bring them to a common understanding.

"The problem is, the intacts that 'aren't so bad' still aren't willing to actively support us," I said. "You saw that yourself at the last Council session."

"Gulatesi's definitely on the 'bad' side."

That was true enough. "I think it would be very difficult for Sakat's high priest to overturn generations of religious doctrine."

"But it's doctrine he believes in," Rasa said. "He wouldn't overturn it even if he could."

Again she was right. And the Priests were so hardline, there wasn't an alternative voice to Gulatesi's worth nurturing.

"Tzagse and the Scholars Lodge are a little more split," I said. "Some seem happy enough teaching excised."

"Or they're more interested in the act of teaching than who their pupil happens to be," Rasa said. "It's the same with the Cultivators. A worker is a worker and people have to eat."

"But tolerance is still short of active support." I paused, thinking. "Isza said if we want the hierarchs and deans to fall in line, I need to show them how support for the excised can get them what they want."

"It makes sense," Rasa said. "I mean, Priests will never change, but the Merchants were quiet at the meeting. It's hard to know what they want. I could set up a private meeting and sound them out?"

"That's a good idea. They certainly don't want their trade with the Lenticiular disrupted. Guaranteeing that could be a good starting point."

"I can manage that," Rasa said.

Ordinarily I'd have asked Tzek to meet with the Merchants quietly. Having no empathic sense made these kinds of discussions hard for excisees. But I wasn't sure Tzek would want to help. And excisees couldn't rely on intacts forever. We'd eventually have to do things for ourselves. We may as well start now.

"What about the houses?" I asked.

"Kergis is on probation, but I wouldn't want their support

even if they offered it, or had any influence in Council. Akczek is definitely against us. What about your house?"

"It's difficult right now without a hierarch, but they'll fall into line. And Haketiug will support us, that's a definite."

"Which leaves Ukat and Dageru. Neither of them have been very vocal one way or the other."

The comms sounded: an incoming signal.

"Interesting," I said. "Hierarch Dageru is calling on an encrypted channel."

Rasa stood. "I'll leave."

"No." I raised a claw. "Sit over there out of view."

She hesitated a moment, then sat on the bench near the door. It wasn't exactly protocol. Encrypted communications were meant only for the recipient. But I trusted Rasa to be discreet, and without Tzek I could really use another perspective on whatever Dageru wanted to talk about.

Hierarch Dageru was older than me, his body plates a deep crimson just starting to marble to black, but there was nothing in his manner to show he was feeling his age. His shell was finely polished and his skull plate and the ridges around his cheeks were inlaid with golden wire, curled in intricate patterns and framing lively green eyes. He'd been House Dageru hierarch for as long as I'd been alive and he wore his authority comfortably.

"Udun," he said, dispensing with my title and – as a result – any formality though we'd barely spoken to each other since I'd taken power. "Are we alone?"

"Yes," I said.

It occurred to me this was a perfect opportunity to follow Isza's advice and find out what House Dageru wanted in exchange for helping excisees. I needed to be circumspect though. I didn't want him to realise too early that we were bargaining. But it seemed he was already ahead of me.

"I want to talk to you about your excisee problem."

"I think the excisees are a problem for all of us, not just me."

"Yes, but it's you that's made them that way." His feeder claws spread wide. "To be fair, I don't see what else you could have done. I'm not criticising, Udun. Far from it. I sympathise."

"I see," I said, not really seeing at all. Rasa looked just as puzzled.

"I want to help. I've played the game of statecraft long enough to know things are not always as they seem. Particularly when it comes to hierarchs. I don't want to say too much over this channel. I can't risk anyone in Council knowing we've spoken privately, and neither can you. But I'll send a message soon." He ended the call.

"What do you think?" Rasa asked, resuming her seat beside me.

"I don't know. Dageru – and Ukat for that matter – both survived the occupation. From what I've heard they didn't actively support Kergis, but they didn't do anything to stop him either."

"Lots of people dug in during the occupation. Kept themselves to themselves. Just like those who fled to the hides," Rasa said.

"So he 'played the game of statecraft' to keep himself safe," I said.

"And to keep his house safe. If a hierarch can't do that, they're not a very good hierarch."

I thought of Czerag risking everything to break the Merchants Lodge trade monopoly. Isza had hated him for putting us all in danger. Was I doing the same thing with the excisees by forcing the issue? Tzek certainly believed that.

Rasa looked at me with her dark eyes. "I've heard rumours among the excisees that Dageru took in some of us who found their way to the southern reaches during the occupation and gave them refuge."

"Interesting. But it would be good to have more than rumours."

If Dageru was sympathetic he could be an ally. Or at worst I could use it to force him to support us.

"I'll see what I can find out," Rasa said.

"That would be good. And there's something else I could use your help with."

"Anything."

"I'm setting up a meeting with Lintal, the Telsan ambassador. I'm worried we'll be forced to remove the alien embassies from Homeworld if we defeat the Hegemony and I don't want that to happen."

"Being optimistic *and* taking the long view," Rasa said, her feeders wide.

"If a prime hierarch can't do that, he's not much of a prime hierarch," I said, returning her smile. "Having the embassies here brings the Kresz closer to the other Lenticular species and that's a good thing in and of itself. But I think it also helps the excisees. We need to get used to difference. Whether it's an excisee or an alien, it's harder to ignore the 'other' if they live alongside us."

"And by comparison, having an excisee living next door *must* be better than having an alien as a neighbour," Rasa said.

"That too. Though I hope there'll come a time when what a person looks like makes no difference to how they're treated."

"That's pretty much how you've lived up to now, isn't it?"

I thought about it. "I suppose. Growing up I was too excited by the prospect of leaving Homeworld and seeing and meeting aliens to care much about what they might look like. In any case, perhaps Lintal will have some ideas about how his embassy can make itself more welcome here."

"I'd be happy to come along," Rasa said.

"Good." I paused. "We'll keep this between us for now. About Dageru *and* Lintal."

"Of course."

"And not a word to Tzek if you see him."

I felt the betrayal as soon as I spoke the words. But I knew what Tzek would say.

25

Denev brought his auto to a halt. In front of him, the cracked roadway gave way to the smooth concrete of a curved dam wall. To his left was a sheer drop to forest below, and to his right scraggly bush choked what was left of the riverbed. Archer River had been dammed to provide drinking water for the surrounding townships and then retrofitted for pumped hydro in the bad old days. But the rain patterns had shifted and its operational life was over almost before it began. Without water, the townships went the same way soon after.

It seemed Rapskel had a penchant for abandoned large-scale infrastructure. It certainly had advantages, Denev thought. Out in the middle of nowhere; minimal if any passive surveillance; and lots of underground space well hidden from orbital eyes. As long as you could get out here without tripping the interest of the algorithm – and there was definitely a trick to that not everyone could accomplish – it was a relatively safe space.

But as Denev made his way to the concrete entry at this end of the dam wall, he found that the location still held its challenges. The steel door opened easily enough, screeching on rusted hinges, but inside he was confronted with steep concrete steps running down into darkness. Some of the concrete was crumbling away. More than once he had to grab for the handrail as his feet slipped on disintegrating rubble. His thighs were aching by the time he made it to the turbine hall level.

At least here emergency lighting showed the path he should

take. He pushed open another steel door – these hinges had been recently oiled – and entered the amphitheatre-like hall. Rapskel stood in a pool of light beside the nearest turbine housing.

The door shut and Denev turned to see a guard wearing an augment helmet, a rifle slung on one shoulder.

"You're late," Rapskel said.

"Have you tried to hurry down those steps? I nearly broke my neck."

"Save us the trouble," Rapskel said. He pulled a couple of chairs from the shadow of the turbine, sat and nodded for Denev to take the other one. "The Laneaux thing has SolSec riled up. Those poor Inclusionist dupes are getting hit hard. My own people are dug in, keeping a lower profile than usual."

"What happened to Preem?"

"Still on ice. Jail with us is better than a death sentence from the CA."

No doubt Medge and Torp – Preem's sidekicks – were being interrogated. Would they be executed even though SolSec knew they weren't guilty?

"SolSec know Volmar's to blame for Laneaux," Denev said.

"Do they now."

A smile played on Rapskel's lips and Denev wondered if he'd tipped Felman off. That was a conversation for another day.

"In fact, I had a chat with their new boss, Ceed Felman," Denev continued. "He wants me to help them kill Volmar."

Rapskel's face fell and he looked genuinely worried. "Fuck. Really?"

"You don't approve?"

"Are you going to help them?"

"I don't know. He deserves it." Denev was puzzled by Rapskel's reticence. "You don't think I should?"

Rapskel leaned back in his chair. "Before I answer that, what have SolSec got on you that makes them think you'll help them?"

"I had a tail, shortly after coming back to Earth. I thought I'd shaken him but he caught me doing something that would have been … problematic if it got reported. I killed him."

"Uh-huh," Rapskel said, wanting more.

"I thought he was HDC and I'd be discovered anyway. Turns out he was SolSec and they covered up the murder –"

"So they could use it on you later," Rapskel finished.

"If the opportunity came up, yes."

"And it's opportunity time and you're thinking about helping them."

Denev was certainly thinking about it, but it had the potential to complicate an already complex situation.

"Volmar will be attending an executive meeting tomorrow," he said. "Private hypertube car there and back. Just me, him, minimal guards. SolSec could interrupt the trip without too much trouble and do whatever they want."

Rapskel sighed again. "Volmar deserves it, I get that. But he's also a known quantity. He dies like this, not only will the Central Administration be on high alert – and all our operations will be jeopardised – but it's unlikely whoever replaces him will choose you as their aide. We'll lose our man on the inside."

That might be about to happen anyway, Denev thought, if Hel and Stin did their job right.

"Even if Felman lets you live after he kills Volmar," Rapskel added, "you're going to be under heavy scrutiny."

"I could just disappear."

Rapskel nodded. "You could. If there's a hole deep enough on this planet, no doubt you can find it. It's your call. But it's high risk, low reward. All I'm saying is, Volmar is the devil we know. Whoever replaces him could be much worse."

Denev heard footsteps at the far end of the hall and stood quickly.

"Jumpy, eh?" Rapskel said, smiling up at him.

"You didn't say to expect company."

Gart Lowrans appeared in a pool of light cast by one of the

emergency overheads, walking towards them. Denev noticed his boots were parade clean, not a speck of dust or scuff mark on them.

"There's an easier way in?" he said.

"That info's for close friends only," Rapskel said.

"I killed for you. Doesn't that make us close friends?"

Rapskel stood too, raising a quizzical eyebrow at Denev. "Do you listen to the words that come out of your mouth?"

Lowrans reached them and held out his large hand to shake Rapskel's and Denev's. A quaintly old-fashioned gesture, Denev thought.

Lowrans looked at Denev intently, still grasping his hand. "Sorry, I have to ask. Have you heard anything more from Rhees?"

"She's alive. I can't tell you more than that," Denev said, remembering Rhees's feeling that they shouldn't trust her father.

The look of relief on Lowrans's face was impossible to fake. Denev was sure this man would never do anything to endanger his daughter.

"Thank Christ," Lowrans said. "I felt like ripping Volmar's throat out when he brought her up yesterday."

"It was a low blow," Denev agreed as Lowrans finally let go of his hand.

"I thought I'd get us all together to talk about next steps," Rapskel said, inserting himself into the conversation.

Denev had the distinct feeling he wasn't too happy about the dynamic between himself and Lowrans. At least it confirmed Rapskel didn't have access to the inside of his head any more.

"The next step," Denev said, "is that you help me, as we agreed."

"We've got other priorities than cracking open a twenty-year-old file," Rapskel said.

"What file?" Lowrans asked.

Denev had only spoken to the admiral a handful of times but he was inclined to trust him, despite Rhees's misgivings. He was old-school military: honour wasn't just a word for him. And his presence here meant he was more loyal to an idea than a simple chain of command.

"Something happened on my father's last mission during the K-Chaan war," Denev said. "He and my mother were both killed. Volmar was there, but he lied to me and said he wasn't. And the information – whatever it is – is locked in the Datahive, encrypted to the personal brain scans of Volmar, Rejak, Vargas and Breslaw."

Lowrans whistled. "That's quite a secure file."

"Not you too," Rapskel said. "What Denev wants is impossible, even if it doesn't get us all killed."

"I was on the line twenty years ago when the shit hit the fan," Lowrans said, looking at Rapskel. "Suddenly the generals weren't giving the orders any more; it was Vargas and Breslaw in control. It turned the tide of the war, but … Vargas has never said anything to me directly, but a couple of times I got the feeling he'd been involved in something. Before he and Breslaw took over. Something very sensitive but off limits for discussion."

"So the file …" Denev said.

Lowrans nodded. "It's worth thinking about."

"With that kind of security? There's no way to open it," Rapskel said.

"Maybe not," Lowrans said. "But I'll think on it."

"There's something else you can do," Denev said, feeling grateful to Lowrans for backing him. "What you told Volmar yesterday about Fleet vulnerability."

"Yes."

"Rhees needs that intel. I don't know if you've figured it out yet, but she was instrumental in defeating the Hegemony in the Lenticular."

"I can still put two and two together," Lowrans said. "After you told me where she was, I reviewed all the logs from that battle. She's not one to stay out of a fight."

"She needs our help. There's a battle fleet on its way from the Lenticular and we need to do everything we can to stop it being detected."

"Fuck, what?" Rapskel said. "You didn't think to mention that earlier?"

Denev smiled. It made a refreshing change to have Rapskel off balance. "I'm mentioning it now, and she needs your help too. And mine."

Lowrans grunted. "I've already taken the liberty of ordering all monitoring of the Lenticular to come through my office. Fleet's in chaos right now. There's just too much work to do and too few resources, but even so, the Lenticular ship movements I've seen would have tripped alarm bells from Neptune to Breslaw's bedroom. I put some of my people on it. No one's noticed so far."

"I've been doing what I can at HDC too," Denev said. "We need your people to do the same, Rapskel."

"I guess I'll get right on it." Rapskel's words were heavy with irony.

"In any case," Denev said, focusing on Lowrans again, "I can't contact Rhees for a while. You'll have to tell her about Fleet's weak points."

Denev thought the expression on Lowrans's face was an amalgam of shock, fear and hope.

"I don't know if she'd want to hear from me."

"She might not want to," Denev said. "But I think she needs to."

∞

Gart was making his way back to the exit when he heard footsteps behind him.

"Wait up!" It was Denev. "I thought I'd try a way out that doesn't involve climbing a broken staircase in the dark."

"No problem. I can drop you off at your ride."

They fell into step, walking in an easy silence. Gart was still thinking about contacting Rhees. Just what was he going to say? How could he explain years of silence between them? He was the parent. It had been up to him to keep in touch.

In his peripheral vision he saw Denev looking at him, seeming about to speak.

"Something on your mind?" Gart asked.

"Not really my business," Denev said.

They walked on a few more steps then Gart stopped, feeling the pressure of the unasked question. "Come on, out with it."

Denev stopped too, looking abashed. "I was wondering how … why …"

"Why I became a traitor?"

Denev grimaced. "Not the word I'd have chosen."

"But accurate enough."

Gart considered. It really *was* none of the young man's business. But Denev had been straight with him about Rhees, and there was something about him. Gart could see in his eyes that he knew about loss. What it did to a man.

He sighed. "I guess it started round about the same time your parents died. When the ceasefire failed, the K-Chaan started in again with such fury Earthforce was overwhelmed. Suddenly they were in Sol system and our backs were against the wall. Vargas and Breslaw were giving the orders by then. Tactical genius married with complete ruthlessness. They threw the rules of war out the window and we were able to drive the K-Chaan back. But by then billions had died on the orbitals, the settlements on Ganymede, Europa, Callisto, even Mars."

Gart could still see the mass graves on Mars where his wife Catriona had died. Her body one of so many he'd never found it.

"I think we all went a little mad after that," he said. "The K-Chaan were pulling back but that wasn't enough. We chased them. We wanted to make them suffer like we were suffering. Vargas led the charge, but I was right there with him. Battle after battle. Planet after planet. We got the taste for killing and we razed their civilisation to dust."

Twenty years ago and the memories of what he'd done were still too vivid. He saw the expression on Denev's face.

"Yes, it was horrific. I told myself it was justified even as we ignored the K-Chaan's pleas for mercy. Even as we smashed planets that had lost all capacity to fight back. It was only when it was over, when I came home and tried to live with the peace we'd built from so much death, that I finally had to stop lying to myself and admit what I'd done."

Gart shook his head and started walking again, Denev in step.

"Others weren't so afflicted," he continued. "Vargas took the plaudits and, with Breslaw and the others, cemented the Central Administration in place. Their promise was that nothing like the K-Chaan would ever happen to Earth again. It was very popular but … Well, you know what the Hegemony gets up to. Under the CA, what we'd done to the K-Chaan became business as usual, along with nastier types of subversion and cruelty. I'd already lost my taste for it and one day I realised I had two choices: quit and bury myself in a hole until I died of old age; or stay and try to make things better. I can't say that's been a roaring success, but there are others in Fleet who feel like me. And over the years we've been able to find each other."

They'd reached the top of a well-lit and intact set of stairs leading down, and Gart stopped again. "So that's my whole sorry tale. But now I have a question for you."

"Anything," Denev said.

"What's my daughter *really* like?"

Denev let out a breath as they started down. "She's a great pilot, brave, handy in a fight. Headstrong and impulsive, which lands her in regular trouble."

"Telling me nothing I don't know."

Denev considered, then said, "She's a good person. I mean she *knows* what the right thing to do is. And she will do it, no matter what it costs her. I …" He sighed. "I admire her. She's strong."

Gart felt an unfamiliar pride. He placed a hand on Denev's shoulder as they came to the bottom of the stairs. "Thank you," he said. "Come on, I'll drop you off."

26

Rasa entered my office followed by her advisor, Zeluk, who looked around the room as if he'd never been indoors before. I'd met him only once and it was clear he'd suffered badly at the hands of the Hegemony. The fleshy ridge across his shoulders was ragged as if his hood had been ripped from him rather than cut. His left claws were gone, severed at the lower forearm, and one eye was blind, the iris clouded. His body plates were badly scarred and cracked as well. He was quiet – which had to be expected, given what he'd endured – but Rasa had told me he had a good mind.

"Are you ready for the meeting?" I asked.

Rasa glanced at Zeluk. "Yes," she said. "But my limited experience with aliens hasn't exactly been good so far."

I spread my feeders. "Lintal's not violent, but he can be scary in other ways." The Telsan had tried to have me arrested when I met with the Lenticular Inner Council on Telsus IV. Only Emba's quick wits had saved me.

"And how about you, Zeluk?" I asked.

The small Kresz's single functioning eye looked startled, as if he wasn't used to being spoken to. Or perhaps just not by a prime hierarch.

"I will do what I can to support Rasa," he said, looking away again to avoid further conversation.

"We can't leave immediately," I said, pressing a contact on my work table. "I have to signal the guard Isza and Gatiku are insisting we take with us."

Rasa looked amused. "We have to keep our leader safe. Which reminds me. Present from Isza."

She pulled an elongated metal disc from her travel pouch and gave it to me. It looked like the device Nok had given me to disable Kergis's empathy reflector. Two green lights blinked alternately at one end.

"Gatiku's had the Adepts place these devices in all public buildings and other sensitive areas," Rasa said. "Isza asked them to create a personal unit for you."

"Is this really necessary?"

"Isza said you'd say that. She also said you'll do what you promised your sister if you know what's good for you."

"I know better than to argue with her." I picked up my pouch from the table and dropped the device in with the few papers I needed for the meeting. "Let's go."

I'd have preferred an inconspicuous ground car, but with four bulky Defenders accompanying us we had to take an armoured wagon. Progress was slow through the narrow streets around Treaty Mount and everywhere passers-by craned to see who was in the vehicle.

I watched the people looking at the shop displays, bargaining with the owners. A group of instars walked past, all in a line with their guardians. It was all so normal. The invasion hadn't touched this street. The buildings were intact and you could almost believe Aktiuk had known only peace since the Emergence.

But then I saw what many of the passers-by refused to see. Excisees. Victims of the Hegemony, and now of our own social system, dressed in rags and sitting in laneways or standing in shuttered doorways staring into an empty sky. Lost and ignored. Free to die but not much else.

Rasa followed my gaze. "Outreach is hard," she said. "There are so many and some don't want to be helped."

I'd been like those lost excisees. I'd wandered to a Merchant street where I'd sat in the dirt waiting to die. It had seemed then that

I'd already ceased to exist for the intact and my death would mean less than nothing. But then Elrak had taken me into his shop and fed me. And ultimately he'd helped me escape. I'd looked for him after we defeated the Hegemony. Even though he'd been injured when I fled Homeworld, I'd hoped he might have survived. But his shop had been taken over by someone else and no one there had heard of him. There must be other intact who felt as he did though. Who would help a stranger who was different.

The wagon turned again and accelerated into a broad boulevard. We were clear of the older part of the city now and the streets were wider.

"What are the Telsans like?" Rasa asked.

"They look different to us and their culture differs, but for the most part they – like any other alien for that matter – are just like anyone else. Kind, arrogant, wise, stupid, greedy, benevolent. I don't really know why our ancestors barred them from Homeworld, though I suspect the same impulse for species purity that means excisees are so hated had a part to play in it. We can thank the priesthood for that. And a far more forgivable fear of the unknown for the rest. But that fear helped the Hegemony. Many in the Lenticular were unwilling to help us when we were invaded precisely because we'd refused close ties with them. Being open makes us stronger."

"It's a lesson a lot of the Council still have to learn," Rasa said.

We were skirting the spaceport's fenced perimeter now and I could see the Inland Sea ahead, its surface roughened by a stiff breeze. The road followed the shoreline, twisting and rising until finally we could see the Telsan embassy on a promontory thrust out above the water. It was a modern structure of curving steel and glass that used to belong to a senior Merchant. His wealth hadn't protected him when the Hegemony came.

A tall fence cut the grounds off from the surrounding landscape, and the gate we passed through was guarded by two Defenders. The wagon pulled up at the villa's entrance and I got out with Rasa and Zeluk. Our security detail followed, a solid wall of armour and muscle.

"Lintal is expecting you," said the small Telsan who stood in the entranceway. He was old, his fur shot through with white. His gaze drifted to our escort and he sniffed, his snout wrinkling, then he turned and – walking with a stick – led us quickly across the polished stone hall. I could see Rasa watching him curiously.

Tall doors opened as we approached onto a broad, light room furnished comfortably, with a room-length window looking out to the Inland Sea. After we'd entered, two of our guards stood in the doorway, effectively blocking it. The other two took up positions against the walls on either side of the room, trying and failing to look inconspicuous.

Lintal was standing at the window with his back to us. He must have heard us enter – the clash and rub of Defender armour plates was loud indoors – but he waited for quiet before turning.

"Welcome to the Telsan embassy," he said.

"Welcome to Homeworld," I returned.

Lintal looked at the old Telsan. "Refreshments, Shar."

Shar crossed the room and left by an internal door that was almost invisible against the wall panelling. Lintal raised a paw, indicating a group of lounges. We sat. He looked at me with his small black eyes. If Emba had been alive, he would have been the obvious choice for ambassador. But we'd have to make do.

"It's been quite some time since …" He trailed off.

"Since you told Kergis how to find me."

Lintal sniffed. "I did what was politically expedient. Which is what my job entails. Things change and here I now am, ambassador with special authority for the war effort."

It was the closest I'd get to an apology from a Telsan. And he was right. My presence on Telsus IV had made things very difficult for them. Not that I'd cared at the time. I was desperate for help.

The side door opened and another Telsan entered, younger than Shar and carrying a tray of crystal glasses and decanter. He set it beside Lintal and left.

"Arga," Lintal said, pouring the golden liquid and passing the glasses around.

Rasa took hers very delicately between her claws, no doubt worried such a fragile thing would break.

The taste of arga brought back more memories of Emba, and the night he'd introduced me to Atalna. I still felt their deaths keenly.

"Let me introduce Rasa," I said. "Leader of the House of Excisees, and her advisor, Zeluk."

"Welcome to my home," Lintal said, then to me, "I'm glad you brought others like yourself with you."

"Like me?" I was puzzled for a moment. "You mean excised?"

"Indeed." His snout crinkled. "The others," he glanced at our guards, "the empaths, always make me feel uncomfortable."

"They can't read minds," I said. "Or your emotions – that only works on other Kresz."

"I know, but I always feel at a disadvantage. As if there's another conversation going on in the room. One I can't hear."

"You don't trust them?" I asked.

"I don't understand them," Lintal said.

And yet we were fighting a war together. But that was out of necessity and a shared desire for both revenge and future safety. There were plenty of Kresz who could live quite happily without alien interaction.

"Everything is strange right now," Rasa said. "But even strangeness loses its power with the passage of time."

She was right of course. I couldn't solve everything immediately.

"Then to the future," Lintal said, raising his glass.

"To the future," Zeluk echoed, the first words he'd uttered since getting into the wagon.

Lintal drank and we joined him.

"It's the future I want to talk about," I said.

"Oh?" Lintal said.

"We want to do everything possible to encourage your embassy – and all the others – to stay on Homeworld. I think you'd agree that closer ties mean another enemy like the Hegemony would find it more difficult to attack us."

"There are those in your government who would disagree," Lintal said.

"That's true at the moment, but the lodges are more pragmatic than the houses. There's profit to be made through closer trade arrangements, and our agricultural and manufacturing processes could be made far more efficient if we had greater access to Telsan technology."

"And if you're worried about negotiating with empaths," Rasa added, "the House of Excisees would be happy to help, perhaps as intermediaries."

"Perhaps," Lintal said. "I have tried to make some initial contacts with your Cultivators Guild since I arrived. It's slow going."

I imagined it would be. Direct contact from an alien was a confronting thing for most Kresz. But Rasa was right. Her people could help, particularly those who had been members of the Cultivators Guild before the invasion. And as she'd said, not all intact shunned our kind.

"Let's look at options," I said. "If you can share details of the technology you think might help, we can work out who best to talk to about it."

Lintal drank again and I saw a flash of pointed teeth. "It could work. I'll send details to your office in the morning."

He poured himself another glass of arga and waved the decanter in our direction.

"No, thank you," I said.

He settled back in his chair. "I see another group of heavy cruisers have passed final fit-out and are already on their way to the muster point. But with the timetable, that's the extent of ships we can put in the field. Is there any way to get more allies?"

I thought about Rhees's trip to Jantri'va. "If our luck holds."

I heard a dull thud and the crystal decanter on the table rattled.

"What's that?" Lintal said.

I looked around at my guard. The two in the doorway left to investigate. One of the remaining Defenders took up a position in the doorway, while the other, Geka, crossed the room to look out the window.

"What's happening?" I asked.

"Maybe nothing," Geka said. "But —"

A crash sounded somewhere out by the front door, then a shout and the sound of blaster fire.

Geka unshouldered his weapon. "Get up," he said. "Move."

In the doorway the other Defender was crouched, firing.

Rasa, Zeluk and I followed Lintal to the side door. It opened onto a smaller room with a corridor on the other side.

Something exploded and the Defender in the other doorway was blown across the room. Geka fired into the smoke. "I don't —" he began, then the wall beside him disintegrated and a massive claw grabbed him, lifting him bodily into the air. He twisted as he crashed against the ceiling, firing down continuously. The shell of the Kresz holding him burst open in the barrage and Geka fell to the floor.

He recovered quickly, ready for another attack. But everything was unbelievably quiet after the sudden carnage.

Through the broken wall the hall was filled with smoke. A small fire was burning near the front door which was hanging open. I made to step through the opening but Geka gripped my upper arm.

"Someone's still alive. I can feel it," he said. "I'll go first." He shouldered his rifle and stepped over the remains of the dead Defender.

There was a sound from the corridor behind us and Shar and another Telsan appeared, both carrying blasters.

"You took your time," Lintal said.

"There were two groups," Shar said. "One lot tried to get in by the rear. They're all dead."

I looked at Rasa and Zeluk. What in Sakat was happening?

"We're all right," Rasa said, so I followed Geka through the shattered wall into the hallway.

The smoke was clearing and we heard someone groan. It was one of my guard. Geka kneeled and rolled the injured Defender over. His chest plate was cut in two, the edges slagged and scorched flesh beneath.

"He'll live," Geka said, and I could see from his expression that he was sharing his comrade's pain.

"Here's more," Shar called. "All dead."

There were four more bodies: my other two guards, killed protecting me, and two more attackers.

"That makes one-one all up, with the four we fought at the rear," Shar said.

"What is going on here?" Lintal demanded. "This is sovereign Telsan territory. Who did this?"

"I wish I knew," I said. Were they attacking the Telsans or me?

"I found something," Geka said. He held a dull metal four-pointed star in his subordinate claw.

"That's a Hegemony empathy reflector," Rasa said.

I still carried my travel pouch. I fumbled inside and pulled out the blocker Rasa had given me. The green lights were still alternating.

"What's the range of this thing?" I asked her.

"About a city block, Isza told me."

I looked at Geka. "You had no sense these attackers were approaching with violence in their minds?"

Geka blinked. "Nothing. Nothing when we were fighting together either." He indicated the dead Kresz lying half in the hall, half through the broken wall. "Not even when I blasted him."

There was a loud whine outside and the wind picked up through the broken doorway, clearing the last of the smoke. The small fire had died to a smoulder. A Kresz transport landed and armed Defenders jumped down to the grass.

Geka hefted his weapon. "Get behind me."

"It's all right," I said. I could see Isza and Tzek among the group.

"A little *late*," Lintal said, clearly still annoyed.

The group of Defenders entered, fanning out and checking the dead and injured, before moving further into the embassy building.

"This is *still* Telsan soil," Lintal snapped.

"It's for your own safety, Ambassador," Isza said. She stood in the doorway with Tzek, both of them surveying the damage. "Sakat, what happened here?"

"I'm still not sure, but whoever they were they wore these." I held up the Hegemony reflector Geka had given me. "And this," I held up the blocker, "was completely useless."

Isza took both devices and studied them. "This isn't a Hegemony reflector. Look, all the ones we found had the same symbol Rhees used to have on her clothes carved on one point."

I could see the metal of this one was blank. Isza passed both devices to Tzek.

"Your blocker's functioning. It was thoroughly tested before we sent it to you," Tzek said. "That suggests an alternative explanation."

"Which is what?" I asked, a little annoyed he seemed more interested in malfunctioning devices than what had happened here.

He looked at me. "That someone has upgraded the reflectors to ignore the effect of the blockers."

I was startled by a low animal growl and turned to see Lintal and Shar behind me.

"I'll ask politely one more time before my government lodges a formal complaint," Lintal said. "What is going on?"

"Ambassador, please," Tzek said, "let's find a place to sit and I'll tell you what I can."

"Very well," Lintal said, and he, Shar and Tzek went off together to the relatively intact lounge.

"Is the Hegemony doing this?" Isza asked me.

"I don't know. But the moment the Hegemony introduced this empathy reflector they damaged us more than even they could have known. This single device has negated the Emergence."

"Nowhere is safe now," Rasa said.

"If it wasn't the Hegemony," I went on, "someone else is behind this, using their tech. Improving on it. Another Kresz group?"

"An enemy we know about, or an enemy we don't?" Isza said.

"The priesthood wouldn't be behind this, no matter how much they oppose your reforms," Rasa said. "This goes against the will of Sakat. What do you think, Zeluk?"

I'd almost forgotten Rasa's advisor was with us. He thought for a moment. "Technical development of the blocker would need a skilled Adept. House Akczek has a strong relationship with the Adepts Lodge."

"Akczek is certainly vocal enough against you," Rasa said.

Would he be headstrong enough to try something like this though? "We'll need solid evidence before I accuse a hierarch," I said.

"We'll see if we can identify the bodies. In the meantime …" Isza waved one of the Defenders over. "Take the prime hierarch and his friends back to the escarpment," she ordered, then turned back to me. "It's the safest place for you."

I agreed. But as Rasa had said, was anywhere safe now?

27

Rhees realised she'd been staring at the Jantri home world for so long she'd lost track of time. There were no answers down there. Only more questions raised by the new fleet of dolphinships she'd been gifted, and she still hadn't decided where to go next. She lay back in the cockpit, the insides flowing to support her, and let her mind wander again. She might have dozed off for a few seconds, she wasn't sure, but she was suddenly wide awake when the comms interface opened up using the codestring that only Denev knew.

The face that appeared was the last person in the universe she expected to see.

"Rhees," her father said haltingly. "Hello."

"How did you get this codestring?" she said, then feared the worst. "Is Denev –"

"Denev's fine."

She was relieved, but that didn't make this conversation any easier. "What do you want, Dad?"

He looked even more uncomfortable. "I want the last dozen years never to have happened. And the same for all the mistakes I've made with you. I want you not to hate me." He stared at her. "Even though I deserve it."

Rhees's breath caught in her throat. "You abandoned me." Three simple words but she felt the pain of them as deeply as when the first realisation of it had hit her as a child. "And when I tried to make contact, you pushed me away again."

"I wanted to keep you safe. I'm a traitor to the Hegemony. I knew if they caught me they'd destroy everything I love before they finally executed me."

She felt her anger flare. "So –"

"And I'm a shit parent," he interrupted and took a long breath. "Maybe that was the real reason I pushed you away. Your mother was gone. I was too angry. Too sad. I didn't know how to be a father."

Her anger died as quickly as it had come. What would she be like if she had a child? How badly would she screw up? Fuck, she didn't have a maternal bone in her body.

"Sorry is a pathetic word to make up for the way I've hurt you," he said.

She smiled weakly. "It's a start."

She didn't know if she could really forgive him, let alone consider being a family. But she'd screwed up enough times to know everyone deserved a second chance. And Denev had given her father the codestring, which meant he'd decided to trust him.

"Maybe when this is over, we can talk," she said.

"I like your optimism."

Her smile was stronger this time and he returned it.

"How the hell did you get all the way out to the Lenticular?" he asked.

"That's a long story, and Volmar has a lot to do with it."

"That wee shite needs his neck snapped."

"No argument from me. But there's a war coming first. The Lenticular have launched a battle force. It may be suicidal, but …" She paused. "The closer they can get to Hegemony space without being detected, the better."

Gart's face split in a grin. "I'm already on it. And so is Denev." His smile faded. "What are you going to do next?"

She thought about her options, but realised she'd already decided. "I'm going to Cygnus Sector to convince the Brell, Sissilak and Totek to join the fight."

Her father's bushy red eyebrows climbed up his forehead. "I didn't see that coming."

"Hopefully neither will the Hegemony."

He nodded slowly. "It could work. There are a *lot* of ship movements right now. Things can get missed. That's what Denev wanted me to tell you. Fleet's in a bad way after the losses from the Hanloi campaign and your little action in the Lenticular. The order's gone out to pull back what ships we can to Earth as a precautionary measure, but we're vulnerable."

So Udun's battle force could have a chance, she thought. Which made it all the more important that she had some way of deflecting the killing blow if it came.

"Tell Denev where I'm going when you can," she said.

Her father pursed his lips. "I'd say take care, but that sounds kind of stupid in the circumstances. But …" He paused. "Thank you for talking to me."

"It was a good talk, Dad," she said and closed the channel.

She thought for a moment then opened a channel to Udun. He answered immediately.

"Hi from the Jantri home world," she said.

Udun leaned forward in the image. "Did you find Nok?"

"No. The planet's empty." Except for over a thousand shape-shifting dolphincraft, she thought, but she wasn't going to tell Udun that. It would make what she said next too complicated. "I'm going to be gone for a while. We need more allies, and I think I know where I can get some."

"Would you like me to send an escort to go with you?"

She smiled. "I'll be safe. But what about you? Any news on Volmar's assassin?"

"I'm not sure. Rasa and I were attacked by rogue Defenders while we were visiting the Telsan embassy."

"Fuck. Is everyone all right?"

"Yes, luckily."

"Do you know if they were working for Volmar?"

Udun blinked. "It might have been a Hegemony-backed attack, but I have plenty of homegrown enemies. They were carrying an upgraded empathy device that masked their approach. Our blocker was useless."

Rhees thought for a moment. Could the Hegemony still be delivering tech? It seemed unlikely after all that had been done to flush out HDC and Fleet ships across the Lenticular. But if there were Kresz on Homeworld who were still in comms contact with the Hegemony and had access to a manufactory … All they'd need were the fabrication details. Or maybe whoever it was had worked out an upgrade all by themselves.

"In any case, Tzek's been investigating," Udun continued. "He's on his way to see me now. And Isza wants me to climb under a rock and never come out."

"She's worried about you. So am I."

"I don't need a second sister, but thank you."

"All right," she said. At least Udun and the others were safe. "In any case, I heard from Earth. Fleet took more damage than we thought. They're weak, which gives us an advantage."

"That's good. The latest ships in our battle force launched two days ago," he said.

"I'll rendezvous with them before the fighting starts. Stay safe," she said and signed off.

Her twelve hundred dolphincraft waited in silent obedience. Time to get moving.

∞

"All the Defenders who attacked had been loyal to Dean Resgtu," Tzek said.

We were in my shielded room – what had been Czerag's shielded room – in the escarpment. Tzek looked exhausted and I doubted he'd slept since the attack.

The first night we'd returned from Lintal's, the whole house had been on high alert, expecting trouble at any moment. But none came. Aktiuk was quiet. The deans and hierarchs all sent messages or contacted me directly with some variation of relief I was alive and shock at what had happened. Akczek's sentiments seemed as genuine as the rest.

Rasa and Zeluk left the next day to return to their duties at the House of Excisees. But Gatiku increased the Defender presence there, and insisted Rasa have her own guard detail. There was an outside chance that she had been the target of the attack, though it seemed more likely it was me, or Lintal, or both of us.

"Which means they fought for Kergis," I said. "And if they fought for Kergis ..."

"They were part of the stek-la," Tzek said. "Implanted with the Hegemony empathy reflector, which had been neutralised by the blocker you carried. But this new reflector masked them all the same. After Kergis lost, these Defenders went to ground and hadn't been seen since."

I wondered how many more stek-la were still out there. "It's clear they're working for someone else now," I said. "Someone who has this new technology."

Tzek agreed. "There are a few candidates. This asset the Hegemony still has; or Akczek as your obvious opponent in Council; or someone else."

I thought about the options. It was possible the asset and Akczek were one and the same. "What houses did the attackers come from?"

"Nothing obvious there either," Tzek said. "Two from Ukat, one from Haketiug, two from Kergis and one each from Akczek and Czerag. But you know house loyalty is a poor second to lodge loyalty for Defenders."

"And the upgraded reflector – could the Hegemony be supplying them?"

"The materials appear to be of local manufacture, but it could still come from the Hegemony."

"Or one of our local Adepts," I said.

The effects of the invasion had been expressed in many different ways. There was death and suffering, but there was also exposure to new ways of doing things. New technology. The deans of the Scholars and the Adepts had both spoken of the developmental leaps possible now that we had access to the Hegemony tech and records left behind when the rebellion started.

I thought about telling Tzek how concerned Rhees had been when I told her about the attack and how she was going to find more allies for us. But I knew it would do nothing to change his opinion of her.

"So there's no definite proof. Nothing that leads us to Akczek or anywhere else," Tzek went on. "And no knowing what will happen next. It's worse than when Kergis was plotting against us. At least then we had no idea of his treachery or that such a thing as an empathy reflector existed. Now I see conspiracies everywhere and no way to prove them until our Adepts work out a counter-measure." He stood and gripped his staff. "And on that note, I have a meeting with Deans Ha'ik and Tzagse at the Academy."

I stood too. "Get some rest after that. You'll be no good to me if you collapse."

He grunted and made to leave, but turned back when I spoke again.

"You know I rely on you," I said. "I'm sorry we argued about the excisees."

"I'm sorry too. But I'm sorrier still this attack happened." The breath whistled in his spiracles. "I'd hoped we'd put all this behind us – Kresz attacking Kresz. I'll let you know what I find out."

He disappeared behind the partition wall and I heard the door open and close. Tzek might be sorry, but I could tell he still thought I was wrong about the excisees. And if his investigations found I was the target, he'd use that against me too.

I saw it differently. If this new enemy threatened my work to bring the excisees fully into Kresz society, it made that action more important still. The sooner I could normalise things, show that excisees living beside intacts didn't somehow destroy the fabric of reality, the sooner any violent opposition would be seen for what it was: terrorism attempting to advance fear and misinformation, and more of a threat to us than excisees, the Hegemony or anything else we could face.

∞

After Tzek left, I sat in my chamber lost in thoughts of traitors and excisees to no real end. I needed to get outside and see sunslight. One of the Defenders posted outside the entrance to my shielded room followed me down the short corridor to the entrance hall. It was still morning and the hall was filled with light streaming down the defile and through the open doorway. Two Defenders and a smaller Kresz stood there, silhouetted in shadow.

"I have been sent," the smaller Kresz said, "though I cannot say by whom."

"You're not House Czerag and you're not one of us," one of the Defenders said. "You're not welcome here."

I altered my path to see what the trouble was and as I crossed out of the glare of the suns, I saw the visitor was an excisee. He was old and stooped, his shell brown, and I could clearly see the scar of excision running across his shoulders. He wore a dusty travelling robe draped with a long red scarf – the colour of House Dageru.

"What's going on here?" I said.

The Defender who'd spoken turned quickly and looked instantly guilty. "He says he's been sent to see you, Prime Hierarch, but he won't say why."

"What did you mean when you said he was not one of us?"

The Defender dipped his head and wouldn't look me in the eye. We both knew he meant the visitor wasn't intact. Intolerance was everywhere, even among these Defenders who I knew would follow any order I gave them. Me – an excisee. But I was different in their eyes. An exception.

I took the old Kresz's claw in mine. "Come inside."

"We should search him, Prime Hierarch," the same Defender said. "For your security."

I looked at the old Kresz. He was clearly exhausted. "You came from Aktiuk?" I asked.

"Yes, Prime Hierarch."

"Udun, please. How did you get here?"

"I walked. I've walked and sailed from the southern reaches to see you."

"I think I'll be quite safe," I said to the Defender, and led my guest down the short passage to the vestibule of my shielded chamber.

The guard who'd remained stationed at the door knew better than to question me, and when the shielded door had closed behind us I sat the Kresz on a stone bench and asked his name.

"Isgeal," he said. The name was familiar.

"And Hierarch Dageru sent you?"

"He did. And it was my privilege to make the journey."

Something about his manner reminded me of Elrak. Tired as he was, I could see excitement and humour in his eyes.

"Things have been so hard for so long, but now … Well, you're like a miracle if you don't mind me saying so. Someone brought low like us but raised high. Though," he paused, "there's a sense of inevitability about all of this too."

I sat on the bench beside him feeling a little embarrassed. I didn't want to be worshipped, but he reminded me of my own ideas about the inevitability of social change before the Hegemony came.

"There's more than a little luck in my story," I said. "But I'd like to hear yours."

"There's some inevitability to my own story, I suppose. I was once chief advisor to Hierarch Kergis."

I drew back to look at him again. Isgeal. I'd seen him enough times, sitting beside Kergis in broadcasts from the Council chamber. But the Kresz I saw now was different. His shell was chipped, cracked and dull from his journey, and his hide hung loose on his face, drooping beneath his cheek plates and mottled with age. He seemed shrunken inward.

"Yes," he said, watching me take him in. "It's true. To my shame. Though for many cycles I felt pride whenever I thought about my role. It was my honour to support one of the great Kresz houses. And I would do anything I could to enable my hierarch to achieve his goals."

Which is exactly what Tzek would do, I thought, or any advisor to a hierarch or dean.

"Like all hierarchs, Kergis wanted power and wealth and I worked so he could get it." Isgeal placed his lower elbows on his upper thigh plates and looked at the bare stone floor. "I didn't see it at the time, but things started to go wrong when Kergis identified Hierarch Czerag as a threat. We knew he was working on some scheme but we didn't know what." He paused and his feeder claws twitched as if he were feeling the words as they forced their way out. "I implemented a program of capture, interrogation and memory suppression."

He was silent then but I didn't need details. This was how Reka had been taken in secret and questioned. He'd had his own problems, but the program had made them far worse. Ultimately it had broken his mind.

"You know I experienced that program too," I said, feeling the old anger at what had happened to me. I'd almost joined Reka in madness.

"I know. We noticed an increase of activity on Czerag lands, so we accelerated the program. You were taken because you were close to finding out about Reka. And your presence in Aktiuk made it easier." He glanced towards me but avoided my eyes. "I know it was wrong, but … I justified it to myself. I told myself it was necessary and I ignored the truth of it."

I didn't feel I could forgive him, but I suspected he didn't expect or want that. He had to live with what he'd done, and that was what he was doing.

"But I was released," I said, remembering waking in the forest and making my way back to House Czerag lands. "I never understood why."

"When the Hegemony contacted Homeworld, I encouraged Kergis to meet them. The Council rejected even the thought of close ties with new aliens. Even so, I reasoned House Kergis could benefit from trade if it was done in secret. Kergis agreed."

And wasn't that just like Kergis, I thought. Staunch defender of the old ways but ultimately driven by greed. If he'd had an inkling of what Czerag was planning, he'd have known his grip on the Merchants Lodge's monopoly was in danger. He'd needed a new revenue stream.

"Kergis insisted on going with the contact group alone," Isgeal said, "and as soon as he met with the humans everything changed. Even before he returned, closed comms meetings were held with house Defenders and then with Resgtu of the Defenders Lodge. Kergis said a war was coming and we had to be ready. I hadn't realised then which side we'd be on."

Isgeal sat up straight again and turned to me, his eyes haunted. "When Kergis returned, he brought alien devices with him. They were to be implanted in his most loyal followers here." He pulled at his chest plate, pointing at the hide beneath with one claw. "I understood that Kergis was siding with the Hegemony. I didn't know what to do. I couldn't betray my hierarch, but the more I listened to his plans the more I knew I could not follow him. He felt my reluctance of course, and finally he ordered me to implant the Hegemony device. I dissembled, and in that brief time I shut down the interrogation program and ordered you released. It was the first time I'd ever disobeyed my hierarch. I wasn't sure what you might do, but I hoped you'd be found and someone might sound the alert."

I'd tried, I thought, but Czerag had other secrets to keep.

When I focused on Isgeal again, he was staring at the wall. I'd seen that look before when talking to other excisees – when they confronted the memory of something unthinkable.

"When Kergis found out what I'd done, he took my mantle. I think I went a little mad then. But the world was mad too, so that was all right. Somehow I survived the invasion and I heard about a secret sanctuary in Dageru lands. Somewhere those like me could be safe. That's where I've been living ever since."

"Until Dageru sent you to me," I said. "Does he know who you are?"

"Yes. And much of what I've done. But not my part in your abduction, I think."

"Tell me about him."

Isgeal's feeder claws stretched wide and the look of excitement I'd first seen in his eyes returned. "He's a measured person. He always has been since first I met him in Council. Dageru acts from a place of deep contemplation. He sees the world as it is. But also as it might be."

"And you trust him?"

"I trust what I see with my eyes. There are many excisees in the sanctuary. We are well-fed and housed. Those intact Dageru Kresz who look after us are kind. I wouldn't have believed such a place existed. But its existence puts Dageru in danger from those who adhere to the old ways. By rights we should be cast out to starve in the wastes or killed. That's why it's a secret. But you –"

He reached out and took my claw in his own. By now I was used to the touch of another with no sense of what they were feeling. But I knew I believed Isgeal. He'd shared everything with me. The good and the bad.

"What does he want?" I asked.

"A way to make what he's done in Dageru lands true for all excisees. I know it's what you want to do. But how to achieve that ..."

"I know." There were ways and ways. Tzek had one view, I had another. Perhaps Dageru could see an alternative.

"Will you come and meet with him?" Isgeal asked. "Just you in secret? No one must know you're visiting. It would raise too many questions. But the other excisees – it would mean so much to them."

"Let me think about it," I said.

I stood and helped Isgeal to his hooves. We rounded the partition and I activated the shield door.

"Take him to eat and to rest," I said to the Defender waiting outside. "And make sure no one disturbs him."

"Thank you, Prime Hierarch," Isgeal said.

Back in my shielded room, I called Rasa. On the vuscreen I saw she was in her office in the House of Excisees.

"I need to take a trip to Dageru lands," I told her. "Do you feel like coming with me?"

Her feeders spread. "Just you, me and our combined guards?"

"No guards. But maybe a couple of other excisees to help. Ones who can be trusted."

She looked at me for a moment before speaking. "Does Tzek or Isza know about this trip?"

"No." This was excisee business.

"Do you think this is a good time? After the attack, I mean."

"There will always be enemies. This is too important to delay."

"All right," she said. "But how do you propose we get there *and* lose our guards on the way?"

"I have an idea. It will be an imposition, but I still feel I'm owed a favour from Lintal."

"Let me know when we're leaving," she said.

I closed the contact. There would come a time when excisees and intact lived safely side by side. I believed it.

28

"I think that went as well as we could hope," Volmar said as the car sealed and moved off from the private hypertube station.

Denev thought about the executive meeting as the dark tunnel walls of the main track blurred with speed. Lowrans had been there with Vargas. The way the two Fleet officers interacted spoke of an easy professional friendship, with no trace of the bitterness Lowrans had revealed at the dam. And Volmar and Lowrans had both been very civil to one another, despite how their meeting in Volmar's office had ended. It seemed that under Breslaw's gaze everyone at the meeting was at pains to show how much they were willing to cooperate. Bad things had happened, but the focus now was on mitigation. Volmar had won agreement for his proposal to expand HDC and Denev's risk analysis had gone down well. They had a plan to protect the Hegemony in its current weakened condition. But Denev needed to see Lowrans again in private to work out how they could access the file.

"I've been thinking about the Lenticular campaign intel leak," he said. "Rejak's clones are fully engaged reviewing HDC records, but it's possible the leak came from Fleet."

Volmar glanced up from the tablet he was reading. "Eminently possible. We need to make sure our own house is in order, especially now. But if you have some spare capacity ..."

"Thank you, Comptroller."

Volmar refocused on his tablet. In the seats behind them at the back of the carriage one of the two guards in their security detail laughed softly at a comment from the other.

"Speaking of Hel and Stin," Volmar said, still reading, "check in on them when we get back. They've found an anomaly."

The skin on Denev's scalp tightened, but he grunted agreement and looked out the window again. Asking for more detail would only make Volmar suspicious. And he wouldn't explain further anyway. He liked to keep everyone around him off balance. It was easier to control things that way.

Besides, Denev didn't have time to consider whatever it was Hel and Stin had found. Looking at the map on his own tablet, he saw they were about to pass under the Volga River.

"Nearly there," he said and adjusted the seat to hold him more securely.

Volmar stowed his tablet and did the same.

The car jumped. There was no sound of explosion in the vacuum-sealed tunnel, but the seat arms tightened to hold Denev securely as the car leaned over, tilted, then overcorrected and tilted too far the other way. The interior lights went out then shifted to emergency red, and braking engaged. The whole car jerked left, straightened, then decelerated rapidly, throwing them forward in their seats before stopping dead. The car power cut out and they were plunged into darkness again.

"Are you all –" Denev began.

The heavy thud of a shaped charge sounded. Behind them the door lifted open followed by two shots, muzzle flashes strobing against the car walls. A hum of power and the lights came on again.

Denev keyed his seat to release him and stood slowly, turning to the back of the car and lifting his hands in the air. Three men stood just inside the doorway. They wore assault gear, tac helmets with a single red eye, and held rifles levelled at Denev and Volmar. The two HDC guards were slumped dead in their seats.

"Outside," one of the men said.

Denev stepped out first, followed by Volmar. They were in an emergency siding for the hypertube. Rough, blown-concrete walls studded with safety lights and a curving platform barely longer than their single car.

The three armed men followed them out. In front of them were three more gunmen.

Someone cleared their throat and one of the gunmen stood aside, letting Ceed Felman through.

"Hypertube trouble?" Felman said. "Lucky we were nearby."

Volmar tapped his band, but Felman tutted. "No signal down here. Not since we blocked it. The hypertube sensors are fouled too."

He planted his feet and stood looking up at Volmar, a small man savouring his moment, Denev thought.

"For all anyone knows, you're still on your way to your rat's nest. You won't be missed for half an hour."

"What do you want, Felman?" Volmar spat out the name.

"I'm honoured the great Troels Volmar knows my name." Felman looked back at his men who laughed.

Denev wondered if they really shared the joke or laughed because it was expected. Felman didn't strike him as the sort of man who engendered camaraderie in subordinates. He was clearly relishing this moment. He'd made this happen and now he had Volmar completely at his mercy. Except Denev knew Felman had no intention of being merciful.

Felman turned back to Volmar, his lips twisted, any humour gone. "What I want is you brought low, cut off from your high-powered CA clique and all your dirty secrets."

Denev stared at Felman. Did he know something about the locked file? Or was he simply acknowledging what Laneaux had witnessed at the last CA meeting she'd been invited to – that Volmar was part of a club she'd never be welcome to join?

"What I want," Felman continued, "is for you to pay for what you've done. And because of your boy here," he spared a glance for Denev, "that's what you're going to do."

Denev held his breath. This was the suicidal part of bringing these two together. If Felman explained about Beloc and the hold that gave SolSec over him, Volmar would know Denev was a traitor.

Instead Volmar said, "I killed Laneaux – is that what you want to hear? She went up against me and failed."

It was typical Volmar, Denev thought. The man had ice-water for blood.

Felman's men tightened their grips on their weapons. How many seconds did they have left?

Felman took a deep breath, puffing out his chest, and raised his eyebrows in surprise. "That's very honest of you to admit it." He reached into his jacket and pulled out a small blaster. "I suppose it's true what they say: *All's fair in love and war.* Which means you can hardly complain about what comes next."

"Nor can you," Volmar said.

Felman hesitated.

The platform erupted in gunfire.

Denev grabbed Felman's blaster, twisting it from his grip, and pushed him so he lost his footing. Felman's men were dead before he hit the ground.

Surrounded now by HDC operatives, Volmar took Felman's blaster and Denev pulled the small man to his feet. Felman's eyes were wide with fear and the sudden realisation he'd been played.

"It's all very disappointing," Volmar said, "for me as much as for you. SolSec's been mismanaged for far too long but that's over now. The Security and Defence Group meeting I just attended made some important decisions. From now on, SolSec is under the direct control of HDC." Volmar placed the blaster beneath Felman's chin. "Consider this your exit interview."

There was a hiss. A bright line of laser light cut through the top of Felman's skull and he slumped to the platform.

Volmar handed Denev the blaster. "Good work, Antwer. You can go on ahead to the Datahive. There's still the anomaly Rejak's men have found. Perhaps today we'll find our leak as well as solving the SolSec problem."

"Yes, sir," Denev said. But he really hoped Volmar was wrong.

Another hypertube car was made ready for him and he rode it alone back to the Datahive. He would've preferred Volmar to be on the other end of that blaster, but in the end he'd agreed with Rapskel: better the devil you know. So he'd told Volmar that after he'd met with SolSec about the Laneaux killing, Ceed Felman had come to visit him at his apartment and laid out a simple choice. SolSec was going to bring Volmar down. Denev could go down with him or he could find himself suddenly and excessively rich. Denev was a sensible man. He chose the credits and agreed to feed Felman information on Volmar's upcoming itinerary. Then he'd reported the trap to Volmar the next morning.

Of course Denev wasn't fooled that Volmar was grateful or somehow trusted him more because he'd betrayed Felman. People were simply tools to Volmar. As long as they were useful, he kept them around. But he didn't rely on them. Denev had proved useful to Volmar's takeover of SolSec. But if he failed to find the leak, or failed the next job or the one after that, he'd be disappeared without hesitation. The fact that he *was* the leak …

The hypertube car pulled into the private station beneath the Datahive and Denev took the elevator to the basement that held the massive holo-tank. Level on level of datanooks and analysis suites rose above him in concentric rings, all the way to Volmar's empty office.

He found an unused nook on the perimeter wall and sat. The chair drew him into the unit as the neural shunt engaged. He sent a query.

The datastream twisted around him and resolved into a bright windowless room. Hel and Stin, still wearing identical grey business suits even in this virtual space, stood in the middle of a constellation of screens, readouts, maps. Scrolling realtime updates floated around them, enlarging or shrinking as the attention of the two auditors shifted among them.

One of the pair saw him and smiled brilliantly, and the data shifted to create an opening for Denev to join them.

"Specialist Antwer. Good to see you." This must be Hel, the talkative one. "I understand you've met with recent success and HDC is expanding –"

"Into the SolSec business," Stin finished.

"That's classified," Denev said, which didn't mean much given the clearance these two had, but he needed to remind them of the command hierarchy. "The comptroller said you have something."

"The anomaly," Hel said. "Very curious. An HDC operative named Elna Darrow appeared at a Fleet base on the Kresz homeworld a few weeks before everything landed in the shit." He showed his perfect teeth again. "There was some unpleasantness. A Kresz was killed and some Fleet grunts."

Rhees, Denev thought, feeling his stomach tense.

"The operative's ID was fake," Stin said.

"A very good fake," Hel agreed. "No such operative exists. But we had to dig very deep to prove it. Since that incident they've linked to the network a number of times, the most recent only a few days ago, and all from the Lenticular."

"And where is this Elna Darrow now?" Denev hadn't counted on this. It wasn't a complete disaster, but if Rhees linked to the network again …

"We don't know," Hel said.

"Your vitals are agitated, Specialist Antwer," Stin said. He waved a hand and a screen floated between them: Denev's pulse and heart rate, accessed via his datanook's monitor.

Denev swatted the screen away angrily. "Of course I'm fucking agitated," he spat. "This might be a game for you, but it's life and death for us. I want that person found."

Hel smirked at his brother and Denev wanted nothing more in that moment than to smash their perfect teeth in. He broke the contact and disengaged from the nook.

Rhees was only safe as long as she didn't contact him, and there was no way to warn her.

29

The Voss Space tunnel flashed around Rhees as she led her twelve hundred dolphincraft towards Cygnus Sector. She was making good time. The ships could travel faster in Voss Space than any Hegemony craft she knew of without causing so much as a whisper of the field-potential problems that made these passages so dangerous. So far, so simple. But what lay ahead would be far more difficult.

Cygnus Sector was Hegemony-owned and policed by the aggressive Maagba ever since Volmar had made a pact with them by sacrificing thousands of Brell, Sissilak and Totek rebels to their war machine. It was those three species she hoped to contact and recruit. But if they didn't want to listen, it could go one of three ways: they could flat-out reject her; they could report her to the Hegemony; or they could attack and try to make her ships their own.

Denev knew a lot about those species because he'd been stationed a couple of times on Herakli, the Hegemony seat of government in the sector. Rhees wished she could talk to him now, but they'd agreed not to contact one another. Still, she'd had some exposure to all three species when she worked with Denev on Herakli and he'd told her some things about them that might help.

The Brell were mammalian, looking like humanoid horses. They'd colonised much of the sector before the Hegemony turned up. Their main rivals were the Sissilak: reptiloid, covered in armoured scales and short on patience. The two species had clashed many times over planetary systems and resources. It was the Totek who prevented those squabbles from turning into outright war. Which was strange, because the Totek weren't aggressive by nature or technologically advanced enough to dominate the other two. Physically, the Totek were one of the strangest species Rhees had encountered. Short, three-legged, with no discernible face, they communicated by rapping out rhythms on an area of taut skin. Denev had told her the Sissilak deferred to the Totek in most things and the Brell listened to them too. They kept the peace. The Totek were the key.

She may not have access to the network Denev had built on Herakli, but she'd at least met one Brell before: O'Dran, the delegate who had argued with Denev for a stronger Fleet presence to keep the sector safe from the raiders, while all the time plotting with the Sissilak and Totek to build their rebel fleet. O'Dran may be dead or in prison. There was one sure way to find out.

Rhees thought about course settings and her ship obliged with a holo of the local Voss Space network. She was already headed in the general direction. Herakli was a natural hub for Voss Space channels from Earth and out to the major inhabited worlds of Cygnus Sector. It was one of the key reasons the Hegemony had chosen the world for human settlement. Rhees selected what looked like a discreet route that would limit her chances of meeting any other ships. Her fleet of dolphincraft followed.

They emerged into space just past the heliopause of the Herakli system. Here in the dark a significant concentration of cometary matter drifted: remnants of the prehistoric formation of Herakli's sun and companion planets that had avoided being broken up by tidal forces or smashing into planets. It was the perfect place to park her ships in among the dust and debris. Then she set course for Herakli, pushing her little dolphincraft as fast as it would go.

Herakli system possessed none of the gaudy beauty of Jantri space. Like Sol system it had its frozen outer worlds and moons, an extra gas giant – all of them ringed – a couple of rocky dead worlds as substitutes for Mars and the asteroid belt, and one hot, fast-orbiting planet in towards the star. Herakli was the only Earth-like world, but a little larger so gravity was five per cent above Earth normal, and the temperate zones were generally warmer.

Fleet presence had always been minimal around Herakli, but even so Rhees had expected to see more than the single Planet Class destroyer escort in orbit. As for the Maagba, their ships were nowhere to be seen. But she hadn't expected any here. Their job was to keep the non-humans in line.

Her dolphincraft had passed invisibly through enough sensors for her to know her descent wouldn't be detected as long as she avoided line of sight from the destroyer or the spaceport close to Adjubon. She set down in a semi-rural area close enough to the city, and smelled growing things in the air as soon as the dolphinship flowed open around her.

Standing on dusty ground in the shade of tall gum-like trees with papery barks, she realised she was still wearing her HDC onepiece. It wasn't exactly nondescript, even without the infinity badge on her breast.. She remembered the flowing djellaba and beautiful cottons she and Denev had worn when they were last here, just like the natives. But she had no credit. Or none she could access easily. So … what? Rip the arms off her onepiece, maybe cut the legs into shorts? Fuck, she was no seamstress and while that may make the onepiece look less like a uniform, it wouldn't make her any less noticeable. She remembered the atmosphere suit the ship had projected onto her on Jantri'va. What if …

The part of her mind that linked with the dolphincraft – or that carried a piece of the dolphincraft system inside her – reached out and the suit shimmered into place, then withdrew from her head and hands. It was like a clear film clinging to her onepiece. But as she coaxed it – without knowing *how* she coaxed it – the colour changed, first to the same rainbow fractals she'd seen on Jantri'va, then through solid colours and patterns. From her waist down the colour settled to a dark navy with the suggestion of a fine copper thread running vertically, giving the impression she was wearing pants – but close-fitting, not the baggy pantaloons that were fashionable here. The field covering the top half of her body shifted to an abstract pattern – irregular diagonal strokes of brick red, black and white. It would have to do.

The dolphincraft closed up, the hull dulling into the shadow of the trees. Rhees followed the slope of the land, emerging from the trees beside a broad roadway that curved across the contours of the countryside. The sun was shining in a clear blue sky. She could almost believe there were no enemies, no fights to be had.

She heard a low, distant whine and saw a large vehicle coming around the bend and heading towards her. As it came closer, she recognised it as one of the mass transit coaches that serviced the rural areas. Her ride to the city? Why not.

She raised an arm and the coach slowed to a halt beside her. There were only six humans inside dotted among the empty seats – two young women sitting alone, an elderly couple, and a woman with a child. Some looked at Rhees as she entered; others were more interested in the view out the window.

Rhees sat near the back and the automated system started the coach moving again. Five rows forward, a little girl with dark ringleted hair peered over the back of her seat at Rhees. Rhees smiled at her and the girl giggled, dodging down behind the seat back as her mother said something to her.

What would happen to these people in the settled worlds if the Hegemony was defeated? Would the Cygnus Sector aliens treat them kindly? Would the humans panic, fight, kill or be killed?

Every revolution had casualties, Rhees told herself. That sounded like something out of a textbook – a callous calculus for who lived and who died. People had their lives, even under Hegemony rule. The same could be said for the majority of aliens. The same could be said for slaves. What would true freedom look like? It was hard to really imagine, but it had to be better than living with a government that spied on and lied to everyone and treated aliens as if they barely had the right to exist. It had to be worth what was coming.

They were entering the city fringe now. Low-rise apartment buildings, shops and outlets, more ground traffic and foot traffic.

But even though it was more crowded, the pace of life seemed gentle. People stopped in the street to talk, while children played around their legs. No one seemed to be in a hurry.

Despite the initial friction with Denev and a couple of the other HDC operatives stationed here, Rhees had enjoyed living in the city albeit briefly. One day, when this was over, she'd like to come back. Stay for a while with nothing to do. One day. Assuming Herakli still existed after the war.

She was struck again by the enormity of what she was attempting. How everything would change. If they won the war, that would be the easy part. Building what came next would be harder.

The buildings were getting a little taller now – though nothing on Herakli was more than three storeys – and packed closer together. Rhees recognised this area, close to the diplomatic district. She stood and walked forward, waving at the little girl as she passed.

Outside, she oriented herself. In a couple of kilometres, the broad street to her left ran right past the Hegemony offices. She crossed the road, walked a hundred metres and entered a laneway to her right. This part of the city was full of branching lanes that led to small squares and more lanes. Herakli domestic architecture favoured small-windowed houses set back from paved courtyards open to the lanes and neighbours, and when the houses weren't shuttered for the storm season, much of the daily life of the inhabitants centred around these open areas. She passed knots of children standing together in courtyards, intent on whatever games were popular, while others ran across the lanes and in and out of each other's houses in a never-ending chase. As Rhees followed the twisting lanes she thought again about these children and what would happen to them.

She emerged onto another broad roadway and stopped. Yes, the Brell offices were just down to the left. She pushed through the entrance doors and crossed to the single Brell at the reception desk, struck again by how much the species resembled bipedal horses.

The Brell turned its long face to her. "Can I help you?"

"Can you tell me, is Delegate O'Dran here? I'd like to speak with her."

The Brell regarded her with dark brown eyes.

Rhees knew that O'Dran could be dead. Should be for the part she'd played in concealing ships from the Hegemony. But hers was the only name Rhees had.

The Brell leaned over and spoke softly into its desk, and someone spoke back, though Rhees couldn't hear the words.

The Brell's long ears twitched as it stood upright again. "Someone will be with you shortly."

Rhees didn't have long to wait. Another tall Brell – they were all tall – appeared and escorted her down a corridor to an open doorway at the very end. Rhees entered and the door closed behind her.

Delegate O'Dran sat behind a polished wooden table. An easy chair stood empty on Rhees's side.

"Take a seat," O'Dran said. "I remember you, of course."

"I wasn't sure if you would."

O'Dran pulled thick lips back from square teeth. "It's hard not to. What can we do for HDC?"

"I don't work for them any more."

"You'll forgive me if I don't believe you."

"You should," Rhees said. "I thought HDC would have killed you."

"Your masters believed I would still be useful. They killed my wife and my firstborn instead. My second child still lives. But it was made clear what would happen to him if I betrayed them again."

"I'm sorry," Rhees said.

O'Dran raised her left hand above the surface of the table. She was holding a blaster, pointed at Rhees. "This room is secure from your Hegemony spying devices. You could just disappear."

Rhees wondered briefly if the dolphincraft force suit would protect her. "If I was HDC, there'd still be questions. They'd know I visited your building. Have you heard about the Lenticular?"

O'Dran's ears flicked but the blaster remained steady. "Nothing on official channels. But we've heard there's been fighting. Somehow connected with the withdrawal of Fleet ships we've seen across Cygnus Sector."

There was no point holding anything back, Rhees thought.

"I was there. I fought against the Hegemony. Destroyed their ships, killed their crews. You could turn me in to them. It might keep you and your child marginally safer for a span. But we defeated the Hegemony in the Lenticular. Those planets are free. Our war fleet is headed for Earth. And we need your help."

It was impossible to read O'Dran's face, but it was clear she was thinking furiously. Slowly, she placed the blaster on the table.

"I have a thousand ships hidden past this system's heliopause," Rhees added. "I'm going to Earth. I'm offering you, the Sissilak and the Totek the chance to join us and end the Hegemony forever."

"You're either insane or you think I am."

"Maybe it's both, but I can show you my ships."

O'Dran looked into her eyes a moment longer, trying to see the lie, then she looked away. "It's not my decision."

"Then talk to whoever's it is." Rhees picked up a tablet from the table and keyed in a string of numbers. "These are the coordinates of my ships. I'll wait there two days. No longer."

O'Dran took the tablet and looked at the screen. "How do I know this isn't another trick?"

"You don't. But I swear to you, this is the only way your child will grow up free and safe."

∞

The two days were almost up when Rhees's ship called her attention to an approaching Brell Conglomerate Embassy clipper – a bird-like craft with sweeping organic-looking wings. She opened a channel and O'Dran's long, softly furred face appeared.

"You came," Rhees said.

O'Dran's ship halted, hanging just outside and below the

cometary debris cloud. "Where are you? Where are your ships?"

"Don't be alarmed," Rhees said. "I'm coming out." Slowly her ship descended out of the cloud, followed by the rest of her flight and the drones.

"Makers!" O'Dran's voice was barely a whisper. "What kind of ships are those? They don't register."

"They're part of what's going to help us defeat the Hegemony. Is your child safe?"

"Yes. Hidden where even the Hegemony can't find him. I'm to take you to meet the others. It's a short Voss Space trip."

"Will we be coming back here?" Rhees asked.

"No. If … things work out, we'll travel on elsewhere."

"Then I guess I'm bringing everything. Lead the way."

She closed the channel and fell in behind O'Dran's ship as it accelerated on an out-system course. They transited into the same chamber Rhees had arrived through, and she followed O'Dran again as the clipper chose a broad passage at the very bottom of the space.

Rhees had no expectations of what she'd face at the other end. O'Dran could have betrayed her to the Hegemony; or whoever O'Dran's "others" were may be planning to kill Rhees and take her ships. Or just maybe things would work out.

Barely an hour later they emerged close to another system with a yellow dwarf, but whiter than Sol, and O'Dran set a course for an Earth-sized world orbited by six moonlets. Approach scans showed that although the planet was in the habitable zone, the atmosphere was more like Venus with a surface scoured by extreme hurricane winds. But they were headed for the largest moonlet.

As they approached, a Sissilak Militia destroyer escort – a sleek spearhead – emerged from behind the satellite. O'Dran must have been expecting it, because she altered course straight for it and quickly docked at one of the locks dotted along the ship's side.

O'Dran's voice came over the comms. "You're welcome to dock and I'll meet you inside."

Rhees didn't believe she'd exactly be welcome, but at least they wouldn't shoot her on sight.

She halted her flight of drones, and her dolphincraft executed a curving approach to the Sissilak ship, dipping under the flanged edge of the superstructure and coming alongside a one-person lock. The skin of her ship flowed to cover the entry and make a seal. Only then did the internal wall in her cockpit pull back around the lock ring.

At the same time her force suit flowed over her – and she saw it retained the same pattern she'd chosen on Herakli, though this time her head and hands were enveloped in clear extensions. It was probably better than meeting in an HDC onepiece. She didn't need to provoke them.

When the inner lock door opened, O'Dran was waiting in the ship corridor along with a reptilian Sissilak holding a blaster pointed at Rhees. The Sissilak's scales shivered menacingly as it reared up.

Rhees held her hands up to show she was unarmed. "Easy. Just here to talk."

O'Dran led her to a meeting room. Another Sissilak was waiting there, along with holo-projected images of two Brell and a Totek.

Rhees had seen a Totek before, but not this close. It was short, only as tall as her waist. Its skin was disconcertingly fleshy pink and wrinkled except for a flat expanse that stretched across the top of its skull, assuming that was its head and contained a brain. This flat skin moved, drawing tight or relaxing into a shallow concavity. Around its rim were six evenly spaced claws oriented to bend up and over the surface. Two of them held long wooden sticks with irregular spheres on the business end. Rhees knew that was how the Totek communicated, by beating rhythms on the taut flat skin. Beneath the drumhead the body bulged out and tapered towards three legs spaced round its body like a tripod. It wore clothes, if you could call them that – a rumpled, stretchy cloth, patterned with swirls of browns and ochres, that covered most of the middle part of its body.

O'Dran made the introductions. "This is Alnat and Dalen," she said as the Brell nodded their equine heads, "and Sissilak representative Needra."

Needra hissed loudly.

Rhees remembered the Sissilak from the secret rebel meeting she and Denev had spied on. It had a temper. From what she'd seen, it was a widely inherited characteristic of the species.

"And this," O'Dran said, indicating the Totek, "is Tktkrt."

The Totek remained silent. Rhees couldn't tell if this was the one she'd seen with Needra and O'Dran before.

"O'Dran told us your story," Needra said.

"More than a story," Rhees said. "If you've had reports from the Lenticular you know the Hegemony has been pushed back there. And if you look outside, you'll see I have over a thousand ships. They may be small but they have a powerful bite."

"We know it was you that fed our ships to the Maagba," Alnat said.

Rhees had expected that, particularly as O'Dran knew her on sight. "I was with HDC, that's true. But I didn't know Volmar told the Maagba where to find your ships. And I wouldn't have agreed to it if I had."

Needra hissed again. "Words."

"No. When I argued with Volmar he gave me to the Maagba as a sacrifice. I escaped and joined the fight against the Hegemony in the Lenticular."

There were a few steps in-between, Rhees thought, but it was essentially the truth.

"It's another Hegemony trick," Dalen, the other Brell, said, showing blunt teeth.

"If it is, it's a little elaborate, don't you think?" Rhees said.

"She *was* reported killed in action," O'Dran said. "Around the time of the Maagba treaty."

So at least O'Dran was willing to believe her. What about the Totek? Its holo had remained silent.

"This is your chance to fight," Rhees said. "The way you'd been planning to before Volmar tricked you. But this time, you won't have to fight alone."

A shivering of scales made her look at Needra. The Sissilak sank down, coiling its tail on the floor. "I don't know if the fight is worth it."

Something had changed.

"From what I'd heard before, the Sissilak were spoiling for a fight," Rhees said.

Needra hissed again, rearing up angrily.

"That was before the Hegemony did what it did to Needra's world," O'Dran said.

"What it did …" Then Rhees remembered the world below them. Six moons. That was the Sissilak homeworld. But the atmosphere was all wrong.

"The Hegemony gave us two days to evacuate," Needra said. "Even with all the extra ships the Brell and Totek could spare there were still millions on the surface when the atmosphere bombs hit. The cries of those left behind didn't last long."

Rhees felt sick. This was why the Hegemony had to be stopped. The human settlers on Herakli might suffer, but she couldn't ignore what the Hegemony was for their sake.

"The Hegemony told us the same would happen to our home worlds if a rebel fleet rose again," O'Dran said.

Of course it did, Rhees thought. The Hegemony was vicious but coldly calculating. It threatened the Brell with catastrophe but sowed division between the Brell and the Sissilak, one suffering more than the other for a shared transgression. And yet here they were, still together. She wanted more than ever for these aliens to fight alongside her. They deserved it. But she needed them to listen to her.

"It would be an honour if you would join us," she said. "We are going to end the Hegemony and its cruelty will never be seen in the universe again. But we're also going to rescue humanity."

There was silence, then Needra said, "Why should we care

about Humans?"

Rhees had known – if she didn't get killed – that the conversation would eventually come to this point.

"You have no reason to, but humans like me are as much captives of the Hegemony as all of you. There are people on Earth who resist the Hegemony, who fight against it as much as they can. And who will join us when the fighting starts." She had no proof that would happen, but she knew Denev and her father would do what they could to help. "I know the Hegemony has done unforgivable things, but you've all lived among humans for a long time. You know there's good and bad in us. The good needs help now so we can defeat this evil that's overtaken Earth."

"How are we to know the difference in a fight?" O'Dran said.

Rhees had no idea, but she hoped she would when the time came. "Follow me. Do as I ask. This is the way we will defeat the Hegemony. From the outside *and* the inside."

"We have ships," Alnat said. "We kept building even after the Maagba, though we had no clear plan what to do with them."

All right, Rhees thought. She felt them hovering on the edge of decision.

The Totek shuffled on its spindly legs and one stick-wielding claw struck the middle of the now-slack skin, making a dull boom. Then the skin drew tight and two of its shorter claws struck the skin on the rim, making a double sharp rap, the second claw repeating the movement quickly to produce a sound like a snare drum.

Rhees's trink translated instantly.

"The Maagba are still here," Tktkrt said. "Even after most of the Hegemony have withdrawn. How do you plan to deal with them?"

"We'll keep out of their way. When the Hegemony is defeated, the Maagba will fall in line or we'll make them."

It wasn't a great answer, but it was the best she had right now. But Tktkrt said no more.

"We'll relay the location of our ships and rendezvous with you there," Alnat said.

And just like that, it was done. Rhees felt a burst of relief even as her chest tightened with fresh anxiety. The Sissilak, Brell and Totek hadn't exactly said they'd spare humanity. But they hadn't said they wouldn't do what she asked either. It would have to do for the moment.

There was nothing now between her and war with the Hegemony.

30

Isgeal and I left the escarpment after a quiet breakfast together. We travelled in a large half-track. Large because what I'd come to think of as "Isza's security detail" were required to accompany us.

Isza was off-planet, on what had become one of her regular patrols searching for any remaining Hegemony ships. Tzek was somewhere in the escarpment, but he'd been keeping away from me unless his duties required we meet. There was still a distance between us and it wasn't something I could fix, because I would never change my mind about the excisees.

"What do you hope for?" Isgeal asked me as we sped across the desert. "When all of this is done."

"Peace," I said.

I heard the breath hiss in his spiracles. "Yes."

Desert gave way to forest and then we were skirting Aktiuk, retracing the route to Lintal's residence. Soon we were running parallel to the shoreline of the Inland Sea. It was raining, and the wind blew stiffly from the water, gusting against the half-track. The road turned towards the headland where Lintal's house stood and came to a halt at the perimeter. The open-link fence and gate that had been here before had been replaced by a taller and far stronger wall and solid entry. Laser cannon standing on thick columns set back from the edifice swivelled to track us as we disembarked. After the attack, the Telsan government had implemented new security protocols, which suited my purpose.

Rasa stood waiting in the rain beside the gate. Zeluk stood

with her and two other Kresz I didn't know, one of them Cultivator caste, the other Scholar caste like me.

I introduced Isgeal to Rasa, Zeluk and the others. The Cultivator was named Ad'cz and the other Kresz was Rizu.

The thick security gate opened partially and Shar, the older Telsan who had greeted us at our last visit, stood in the gap, his grey-white fur slick with rain.

"Welcome," he said. "But your security detail remains here. No weapons inside the enclosure."

Geka, who was leading my security detail again, was clearly unhappy. He stepped forward. "We can leave our weapons in the vehicle."

Shar craned his neck to look up at Geka. "You're a *walking* weapon," he said and his muzzle wrinkled. "The last time you were here, one lot of you killed the other lot of you and nearly destroyed the building in the process. The prime hierarch and his party *only*. This land is owned by the Telsan government and *we* say who enters and who does not."

I turned to Geka. "Look, no one can get through that wall without coming through you first. We'll be safe. I'll call you if there's the slightest problem."

I could see him struggling with the impulse to argue further against his prime hierarch *and* the Telsan government. The moment passed. "At the slightest problem," he said.

Our small group followed Shar through the gate and along the short path to the residence. The entry and hall bore no sign of the damage the last attack had wrought, and Shar ushered us in to meet Lintal in the same wide lounge we'd met in before. Through the glass wall a flyer was visible, perched on the edge of the headland.

"I'm not going to be blamed for this, am I?" Lintal said. "Your guards out there could quite literally tear the limbs from my body."

"And cause a diplomatic incident with the Telsans?" I spread my feeder claws wide. "They won't realise we're gone for a while and they won't harm you."

"You're sure you want to do this?" Rasa asked.

I looked at Isgeal and said, "Let's go."

The glass wall parted for us and we walked onto the blustery point made windier by the downdraft from the flyer's turbines quietly spinning up. We climbed inside. Isgeal sat beside me and Rasa and Zeluk opposite, while Ad'cz and Rizu went forward to sit with the pilot. No sooner were we strapped in than the flyer lifted and immediately banked, swooping down to fly just above the white-capped waves of the Inland Sea.

"We won't be tracked," Rasa said. "Our pilot is an excisee too and he knows a few tricks." She looked more closely at Isgeal. "I know you, don't I?"

"It shames me to admit it –" Isgeal began but Rasa cut him off.

"Don't. None of that matters. You're one of us now." She reached over and laid a large claw on his shoulder plate.

I could see the effect immediately. As much as intacts reviled excisees, this was something they could learn from us. Whatever house or lodge we'd served in the past, none of it mattered. The only important fact was that we were all Kresz. All equal.

"This is the start of a new way for the Kresz," I said. "For all of us."

Tzek would have said I was being naive. But sitting here with Isgeal, Rasa and Zeluk – Kresz from different houses and very different upbringings and experiences who were united here and now – it felt more than possible. More of our kind were waiting to meet us and soon we would all be free.

The sea was still grey, reflecting the clouds above, but the far shoreline was coming closer and soon we were flying over the marshlands with the winding Resiut River to our right and beyond that the open fields of House Haketiug farmlands. The rain cleared and the day brightened as we maintained our course, still flying low and heading south to Dageru lands.

The marshes gave way to forests. As the land rose, the trees thinned until we were passing over a grassy plain crisscrossed with rivers and streams. In the distance were the foothills of the Kalead Mountains, which stretched all the way to the pole and marked the beginning of Dageru lands.

Isgeal went forward to give directions, and we banked a little and flew straight up one of a series of ravines in rough parallel with each other as if a giant had clawed the rock into deep furrows. The paths through the ravines rose and fell, zigzagging with the rock formations. Anyone on hoof could easily get lost, but Isgeal was sure of the way and he steered us across the rocky terrain until we crested a slope like any other. He pointed and the flyer slowed.

"We're here," Isgeal called back to us.

The flyer settled gently to the ground and we climbed out. It felt like we were on some desolate moon. The rocky walls of the canyon were steeply raked and the floor was strewn with flinty rocks. We stood in twilight, even though it was still a sunny afternoon above us.

"This way," Isgeal said and we followed, picking our way carefully over the uneven surface.

There was no sign of life and the canyon curved ahead so we couldn't see the end of it. For the first time since leaving Lintal's I didn't feel safe. As excisees, we could have no advance warning of a threat. Then again, there was no guarantee an intact would either, with reflectors seemingly so available.

I reminded myself of those first excisees we'd sent from the deep desert hide – they must have come this way with far less promise of a welcome at the end of their journey. And they'd come on hoof. They'd had faith. So must I.

When we reached the bend in the canyon, the position of the suns meant that half the steeply raked walls and rocky floor were bathed in light while the rest was darker than night. Even with my secondary eyelid, I couldn't penetrate the blackness. Still there was no sign of anything like a pathway leading to a hide entry. But that was to be expected. Hides were built to conceal all evidence of their existence.

And then, as we took a few more steps, the scene changed. Above us on a ledge I'd failed to see stood three Defender-caste Kresz.

Rasa pointed just past them at a rocky outcrop. "Is that it?" she asked.

"Yes," Isgeal replied. "It's a short climb."

"Let's meet Dageru here," Rasa said. I looked at her, but she didn't seem afraid, just cautious. "We've come all this way. The least Dageru could do is walk down the slope to meet the prime hierarch."

Isgeal looked uncertain.

"We'll meet here," I agreed. "Can you –"

"No need." A voice rang out from somewhere above us, and three more Defenders appeared, stepping out of the shadowy line across the canyon floor.

"If you have comms units, they're being jammed," the same voice called.

Isgeal was looking around. "Hierarch Dageru, what's –"

"Enough, Isgeal," the voice said and Dageru stepped out of the dark to stand between the Defenders. "You've done your work."

I saw all of them were armed and was sure we'd been betrayed. I'd walked Rasa, Zeluk and the others into danger.

"I don't understand," Isgeal replied.

And that was the tragedy of it. Isgeal had believed – just as I had.

"You've been fooled, Isgeal," I said, not unkindly. "We all have."

Dageru stood calm and relaxed and spread his feeders wide. "Don't feel too bad. It's easy to fool cripples like you. You take words at face value."

"But I saw them," Isgeal protested. "The other excisees. You all care for them."

I felt a dread growing inside me. "What have you done, Dageru?"

The breath hissed through Dageru's spiracles in a long sigh. "Have you any idea what it was like trying to live under Kergis's regime?" he said.

"I think we have some." Rasa's contempt was clear in her voice.

Dageru regarded her for a moment, then blinked slowly. "Yes, you suffered what the Humans did to you, but I'm talking about the slow destruction of the houses. Kergis took our children, our wealth. Soon we would have been hierarchs in name only. His Human allies made his position unassailable, but then we were visited by a wandering excisee. It seemed a rebellion – your rebellion," he looked at me, "was at least possible. Though it wasn't one I could support outright."

"In case we lost," I said. "So, what, you took in excisees secretly to prove you weren't a traitor if Kergis fell?"

"That was the beginning of it," Dageru agreed. "But after you won, it was clear you were intent on doing more damage than even Kergis would."

"You sent those Defenders against us at the Telsan's residence," I said.

"No, that was Akczek. He got the idea after that poor Cultivator attacked you in the Council chamber. We both agreed your rule should only be a temporary thing. But Akczek acted rashly and almost revealed us."

"The enhanced reflectors," I said.

"Exactly, but I shouldn't have worried. Your desire to save excisees – all excisees – was enough to bring you here despite the obvious dangers."

"What have you done to the excisees?" Rasa said.

"I've freed them."

"Freed?" Isgeal's voice was uncertain.

"I've finally given those poor half-Kresz the peace they deserve. Painless but necessary." Dageru looked at Rasa and me. "You've done so much we should be grateful for, Udun. But to think one such as you could ever rule us, or that your friends here could live among us as equals …"

"How many were there?" I asked Isgeal.

I could see the pain in his eyes as he answered. "There were two-four-four when I left."

So many. All surviving the worst the Humans could do only to die at the hands of another Kresz who called it a mercy.

"You're a monster," I said to Dageru.

"You can't understand," he said. "You lost something when they took your mantle – the knowledge of what it is to be a true Kresz. But our ancestors knew. The Way must be cleared. With you gone, Kresz loyal to my house and Akczek's will seize control of Aktiuk and soon everything will be as it was before the Hegemony came. There will be nothing to oppose it."

"Except you'll be another Kergis," I said.

Dageru lifted his arm and the Defenders beside him and on the canyon wall raised their weapons at us. "This will be quick."

Rasa grasped my claw in hers. "Udun –"

A shriek. A swift shadow passed over us and the valley was suddenly full of light. I fell to my knees, Rasa beside me.

When the glare subsided, the Defenders were gone, curls of smoke rising from the scorched ground where they'd stood. Dageru was pushing himself up off the ground. He stared at me for an instant, then turned and ran into the shadows.

I looked up. A Kresz fighter hovered above us. From around the bend in the canyon, more armed Defenders were running towards us. I saw Isza was with them.

I checked on my companions. Rasa kneeled next to me on the ground; Zeluk was on all fours in front of us, and Isgeal was beside him. Ad'cz and Rizu were unharmed too.

"No!" Zeluk shouted. He was glaring at me, his claws holding a bright flash of light.

He leaped and we tumbled together on the rocky ground. The flash arced down towards my neck, but I raised an arm. Searing pain in my claws – then Zeluk was thrown off me and I was being pulled upright.

"Udun!" It was Rasa, holding me. I looked at my arm. Two claws were gone. It could have been much worse.

"I'm all right," I said.

Isza appeared. "Sakat, brother, what do we have to do to keep you safe!"

Despite my wound I couldn't help my feeders from spreading wide. "I think Rasa's all I need."

Zeluk was being held securely by a Defender. I could still see the hatred burning in his eyes.

"What have you done?" Rasa asked him, but he seemed unable to speak.

"I think that might be the Hegemony's asset," Isza said; then to the Defender, "Take him to one of the ships, but see he's not harmed."

Ad'cz, Rizu and Isgeal had joined us now. Isgeal looked lost, as if he couldn't understand the world around him any more.

"Dageru," he said.

"He ran back to his hide," I said. "Isza, we have to find him. He's working with Akczek to overthrow the government."

"As if we haven't enough to worry about," Isza said.

"Commander!" A Defender standing half in shadow called to Isza. "We've found the entry to the hide."

"We'll go," Isza said. "You stay with –"

"No, we're all going," I said. "We have to see this."

I thought Isza would argue, but she just turned to follow the Defender and our group went after her.

Rasa fell in step beside me. "I can't understand how Zeluk would want to harm you."

It was obvious she felt guilty. Bringing Zeluk had put us all in danger, me in particular.

"He likely didn't know what he was doing," I said. "I've experienced the interrogation methods Kergis was using before the invasion. I can only imagine how much more effective those became with the help of Hegemony technology."

Once in the shadowed part of the canyon, my secondary eyelid made the way clearer. But it was only when we rounded a column-shaped boulder that the path to the hide and its entrance became visible. There was no sign of the Defenders we'd seen on the canyon wall, so three of our own Defenders entered first. Isza only allowed us to enter when they called that the way was clear.

Inside felt like the deeper parts of the escarpment. The tunnel walls showed the patterns of being cut and shaped by claw ages ago. The passage opened up into a larger entranceway with tunnels leading off in different directions. All around were signs that Kresz had been here until very recently.

More of Isza's force entered behind us and I saw Geka was with them.

"Prime Hierarch," he said. "Hierarch Rasa."

"Did you know we were going to leave you at the Telsan's house?" I asked.

He hesitated, but I could see he wasn't about to lie to me. "Isza said it was best we let you … do what you had to do."

He excused himself and left to direct the Defenders down the various tunnels. So Isza had known. Geka could have said "run off like a fool". But I appreciated his diplomacy.

"I'm sorry," Rasa said. "I was worried for you, and when I told Isza she insisted —"

"Udun!" Isza stood in the mouth of the left-most passage. "You need to see this."

A short tunnel led to a wide door that hung partly open. Inside, bodies were piled up against the walls, a tangle of broken shells, arms, legs. Yellow rusz stained the floor. The excisees that Dageru had lured here with promise of safety — they were all dead. It was a betrayal I couldn't fathom.

A gasp behind me, then a stream of whispered words I could barely understand. Isgeal had followed us into the room and now he fell to his knees, sobbing.

I felt Rasa's claw on my shoulder and I gathered her into my arms, needing something real to hold onto. We stood, breathing together. Neither of us had words for this.

Isza held a comms bar out to me. "Udun."

I left the room as I fitted the bar. I couldn't stay in there. Rasa came with me, her claws still holding mine.

"Yes?" I said into the comms bar.

"It's Tzek." Vaguely I wondered if he'd called to berate me for being so stupid. "Something's happening in Aktiuk. Armed Kresz have occupied Treaty Mount, government buildings, the Academy. They're House Akczek."

"Dageru was to give word to Akczek when I was dead," I told him. "I suppose he got tired of waiting."

Tzek grunted. "There's been no announcement yet of what they're doing."

Dageru was too busy running to do whatever it was he'd planned.

"I'm coming back to Aktiuk," I said, and turned to Isza. "I need you to fly us to Treaty Mount. Now."

"That's not wise," Tzek said.

"It's the wisest thing I'll do all day."

I had to act now before Dageru had a chance to get to safety.

31

After the meeting with the Sissilak, Brell and Totek, Rhees and O'Dran had parted ways – O'Dran returning to Herakli and her son. Now Rhees's dolphincraft were running down a long Voss Space corridor heading for the rendezvous point.

She slowed her lead ship as she approached the end of the tunnel. Voss Space opened up beyond the lip into one of the chambers that connected different routes and created stable transit points to space if the conditions were right. Line-of-sight sensors registered its vastness – it was easily capable of holding her ship group. The volume was spanned by successive columns of pure plasma, like unimaginably large energy conduits in the circuitry of the universe. No one had worked out what they were for, but Voss Space was only one extradimensional energy level among many. The columns could be the substrate of some impenetrable higher dimension. Somewhere that Nok had translated to if Udun was right.

Her ships closed up as they left the tunnel, obeying whatever sub-routine slaved them to her own vessel, and they moved together into the chamber.

A third of the way across, sensors tugged at her attention. Something was moving in the darkness above. Her vision shifted past visible wavelengths. A wide opening in the ceiling. Energy signatures, but nothing she could –

Ships streamed out of the opening, firing flights of missiles.

"Fuck."

Those horseshoe-shaped ships and the bigger craft that looked like pistol grips. It was the Maagba.

In less than a second her consciousness expanded to her attack group, giving her seventy-three different perspectives of the incoming ships. These dolphincraft oriented themselves and leaped together at the Maagba even as the rest of her drone ships scattered.

Multiple target acquisition, like pinpricks in her mind, and quicker than thought the dolphincraft unleashed a barrage of laser fire and missiles, shredding the incoming ships, driving through them and vectoring up towards the tunnel opening in the ceiling of the chamber. If she could stop the flow of incoming Maagba, set up a kill zone at the tunnel entrance, she could contain them.

She peeled off dolphinships to pursue Maagba that had evaded her first onslaught, while the bulk of her group slowed, hanging beneath the tunnel and firing, heedless of the fat dark nodes of rising field potential waxing in the space around her. The flow of ships stopped and she ceased firing as the tunnel began to distort and lost stability.

Far below, three of her craft targeted a Maagba group still flying free. Two horseshoe craft disintegrated under rapid fire, but others survived and their missiles were finding their mark. Each drone destroyed was a stab to her consciousness.

The tunnel above gave a final heave and sealed, but this wasn't over. She felt sensors register multiple movements and her ship group dropped, turning in a steep dive as more Maagba ships flooded in through the same tunnel she'd entered and other openings spaced around the chamber. Had they been tracking her?

She spread her group out and brought all weapons to bear on incoming flights, angling to protect her drones. The whole chamber lit up as Voss Space reacted to the missiles and laser strikes, forming more and more darkly twisting spheres of field-potential overload.

Still more Maagba ships streamed into the chamber. Even if Rhees had direct control of all her ships, she'd be outnumbered. The attack was playing out exactly like the one Volmar had engineered.

The Maagba had streamed down on the combined Brell, Sissilak and Totek fleet, firing indiscriminately and heedless of the dangers from Voss Space until the rebels had broken and run, transiting to space only to meet another Maagba fleet waiting to destroy them.

If she transited, the Maagba would be waiting for her. But she couldn't get all her ships safely into another Voss Space tunnel either. She kept firing, protecting her drones, feeding the field-potential nodes. She had no other choice.

Multiple nodes erupted in a blinding flash. Coruscating forks of energy lashed out at any ships caught nearby. Rhees twisted her own dolphinship away from the nearest eruption, but too late. A bolt latched onto her, licking hungrily at her hull, then sputtered and died. Others in her group had been caught in the same blast but – unlike the Maagba – they were unharmed. Something in the Jantri hull metal? She remembered Nok's station in Voss Space, sucking hungrily at multiple plasma strikes. Feeding on them.

She accelerated, spinning three of her group one-eighty, and swooped down on a group of horsehoe craft pursuing a handful of drones. A cluster of missiles took out the Maagba ships and she flew through the expanding ball of gas. The same scene played out in her segmented consciousness: evade, attack, seek new targets. Drones were still being destroyed and more Maagba ships arrived to bolster their losses. They weren't giving up, and even though Rhees's ships appeared immune to the field discharges, the whole chamber was starting to twist and distend under the onslaught. How much longer before it collapsed? And could her ships survive if it did? There was no way to escape. No way to win for either side. It was madness.

"Stop," she whispered as death bloomed around her. She spun her flight in a tight curve to avoid one of the massive energy conduits twisting towards her. A Maagba gunboat wasn't so agile and exploded in a juddering stop-frame fashion, as if reality was unsyncing from the passage of time.

"Stop," she said again, then opened a broad comms channel. "Stop!" she shouted.

She powered down all weapons, setting her attack group to evade enemy fire.

For a span of heartbeats the battle flared, then the Maagba stopped firing too. Ships hung together in a twisting space that slowly calmed, field-potential masses fading into nothing. Why had they listened to her?

She'd lost one hundred and seventy-three drones, but it could have been a lot worse. It still could.

One of the large Maagba battlecruisers approached from the far end of the now quiet chamber. The front of the ship split open and Maagba horseshoe fighters and gunboats turned away from her dolphincraft to enter its hangars. The cruiser came to a complete halt.

Rhees edged her ship forward, selecting two other dolphincraft to accompany her. They needn't know she was alone out here.

The sides of the Maagba ship slid past her and her trio penetrated its atmosphere barrier, following a light path down a broad channel and into a hangar already half-full of Maagba ships. There was a reception committee waiting for her: a group of Maagba, short, lithe-looking in oil-slick sheened onepieces, black-skinned and all with the same shaggy lion's mane of hair.

Her ship touched deck and her escort settled either side of her. The waiting group parted and at first she couldn't make sense of what she was seeing. The movement and shape looked all wrong. Then she saw a Totek standing in the middle of the group.

Only one way to find out what the fuck was going on.

The dolphincraft peeled back around her and she stepped out onto the deck, walked partway towards the Maagba, then turned to look at her ships. *Protect*, she thought. Her dolphincraft sealed up and the smooth hulls of all three were suddenly interrupted by the business end of plasma cannon pushing out from their blunt noses. Not so helpless after all.

She looked back at the Maagba.

One of them standing beside the Totek spoke. When they'd captured her before, her Hegemony trink hadn't been programmed with the Maagba language – though Volmar could speak it fluently. But the Jantri trink gave her an instantaneous translation. Had Nok known she would meet the Maagba again?

"You have surrendered," the Maagba said in a low growling voice that sounded distinctly male.

Rhees gave a short laugh. "Fuck no. We both stopped. I can take my ships back out and we can both go at it until this chamber kills us all if you prefer."

"We could," the Maagba said. "But that would solve nothing." He looked down at the Totek. "*You* deal with this, Tktkrt," he said. He looked back at Rhees, then barked a short syllable the trink didn't translate – some Maagba swearword, Rhees thought – before leading his retinue out the hangar.

Rhees didn't watch them leave. She was staring at the Totek. "What the –"

The stick-wielding claws struck the centre of the taut skin with a loud rap, followed by more sharp taps, and the trink translated. "It is necessary to do this for your own safety as well as ours."

She didn't understand, but then her band snapped open, fell to the floor and fizzed as the ceramic melted into a puddle. It was no great loss. There were any number of bands from the captured Fleet prisoners back on Homeworld she could use if she had to. But if Tktkrt was here, did that mean it had just betrayed her to the Maagba?

"You've presented the Maagba with a problem," Tktkrt said. "Follow me to somewhere we can talk." It shuffled round and started towards the hangar entrance.

The alternative was that this wasn't outright betrayal, but something else. Maybe that was what it wanted to talk about.

"I didn't expect to find a Totek on a Maagba ship," Rhees said, deciding to play along.

As it walked, the Totek rapped its short claws and longer sticks on its drumhead, which contracted and relaxed to produce different pitches of sound. It was like listening to improv jazz, Rhees thought, but it was clearly a sophisticated and efficient means of communication because the translated speech was equal to any other conversation.

"Why not?" it said. "They own us. The Hegemony gave us to them."

"But they leave you on your own. I mean, you're not locked up."

Out in the curving corridor, the Totek stopped and tilted its drumhead as if looking at her, though Rhees still couldn't discern eyes or anything similar.

"Everything has a use. We help the Maagba: the Maagba help us." It started walking again.

But what sort of help, Rhees wondered as she followed. The Totek held a position of influence with the Sissilak and Brell. Had they achieved the same thing with the Maagba? How did that work when the Maagba were doing the Hegemony's bidding?

"It just seems strange after all the Totek, Brell and Sissilak the Maagba killed," she said. "They blew up a whole system. They killed billions."

Again the Totek paused, tilting its drumhead as it considered her. A fleshy sphincter beneath the rim puckered and hissed. Then its claws got to work again. "You observe an act and determine it to be evil. You ascribe that value judgement to those who committed that act."

"Don't you?"

"It depends on whether the moral framework of the observer and the actor are aligned."

"Okay," Rhees said, feeling more confused by the second. "So you forgive them?"

"Is there anything to forgive? Did the Maagba hate us when they attacked us? Or did they simply act according to their nature? Without malice. Without evil. They had a goal: to make the Hegemony see them as equals. They achieved that. As for the deaths they caused, the Maagba are happy to die. It is not an end for them, just a change."

Rhees had a sudden thought. "So the Maagba ships that blew up the Brell sun …"

"Were fully crewed," Tktkrt said. "The Maagba don't see anything special about this instance of existence compared to any other. They treated us no differently to how they themselves would expect to be treated in the same circumstances."

"So rather than forgive them, you understand them," Rhees said.

A series of short raps. "We accept them."

Yeah, the Brell and Sissilak certainly didn't feel the same way, she thought. But maybe this perspective was what made the Totek so influential.

A door in the corridor opened and Rhees followed Tktkrt into a cabin with a broad window looking out on Voss Space.

The chamber was crowded with activity. Horseshoe fighters were scouring ship debris and floating bodies from the area. The massive plasma columns, quiet and stable now, illuminated their work. Her drones were waiting in groups, unmolested by the Maagba. Each group had a handful of her linked dolphincraft with them – she didn't know how, but she recognised them. Even though she was physically distant they occupied a non-space in her mind.

"Now we can talk," Tktkrt said.

Rhees's anger flared. "Good, because I want to know why I get attacked out of nowhere when you're the only one here who knew where I was heading."

The Totek backed away a step and she realised she was leaning over it threateningly. Claws and sticks beat a staccato rhythm. "If you defeated the Maagba, you would have proved you could help us. If they killed you, it was best it happen now before you led us into a war you couldn't win. But they stopped."

"*Why*? If you know the Maagba so well, why am I still alive?"

"I don't know," the Totek rapped. "I do know that War Leader Vatch – you saw him in the hangar – has a problem. He hasn't destroyed you. He hasn't alerted the Hegemony to your capture."

"Vatch?" That was the Maagba Volmar made the treaty with.

"He commands all," Tktkrt said simply.

Rhees knew that all right, and she'd seen what he could do.

There was a stool near the window. She sat, trying to see the connection between those statements. Was she the problem *because* they hadn't destroyed her or told the Hegemony about her? No. Because that problem was easily fixed.

"Vatch has a problem," she said slowly. "I'm still alive because I'm the solution?"

The Totek shuffled its hoofs, turning slightly. "Potential solution."

"Which is?"

The Totek folded its three legs and sat on the deck but said nothing more.

"Okay," she said. It seemed she'd have to work this out for herself.

She knew the Maagba had killed billions of Brell, Sissilak and Totek to get what they wanted: the attention of the Hegemony. When she and Denev had been captured by the Maagba, Volmar told her the Maagba had needed to fight and defeat a Hegemony force in open battle to prove they were worthy and to make a good deal. Volmar had sacrificed the Brell, Sissilak and Totek rebel ships to them instead of endangering Fleet directly. But the outcome was the same. The Maagba won. They proved themselves and Volmar made a deal with them. He gave them this sector to police for the Hegemony as partners. Again, the Maagba got what they wanted. But they still had a problem. Which meant they hadn't really got what they wanted at all. Perhaps Volmar had cheated on the deal. She could believe that.

She looked out at the field of broken ships only partially cleaned up. Maybe policing a bunch of generally peaceful – and in the case of the Totek, infinitely forgiving – aliens wasn't much of a challenge for a species like the Maagba. Volmar had said they lived only to fight.

"But they have an agreement with the Hegemony," she said.

Tktkrt rapped the centre of its now slackened drumhead with a single stick, producing a dull boom that attenuated as the skin drew tight. "Yes," the trink translated, stretching the word out so the Totek sounded like an encouraging schoolteacher.

And the Maagba had destroyed her band – a Hegemony device – for "everyone's safety".

"They can't break the agreement," she said. "It's not …" She paused, searching for the word. "Honourable," she decided finally.

Then she saw it. She stood. "Take me to Vatch."

It took a long time to get there following the shambling Totek. Rhees could have used the time to plan what she was going to do and say. But she didn't want to think about it. Because if she was wrong, she was dead.

It wasn't Volmar who had made the deal with the Maagba. Oh, he'd laid down the offer, negotiated the terms, but the deal wasn't made until the blood sacrifice – "the raktaa" Volmar had called it – was done. The blood to be spilled was meant to be Rhees's. But it hadn't played out that way. She'd killed the Maagba executioner instead. It was his blood that had stained the deck.

She remembered the other Maagba rushing in and coming to a sudden stop. They'd looked at her strangely, then their leader had pointed to the blood, said "raktaa" and they'd let her go. Volmar hadn't sealed the deal. She had. Which meant only she could offer to make a new deal. That was why the Maagba had stopped fighting when she'd broadcast in desperation. They'd recognised her. The "potential solution" as Tktkrt said.

Finally they came to another door. The Totek stepped aside as it opened. War Leader Vatch sat at the head of a long table, Voss Space shining through the window behind him. His officers sat to his left and right. They all turned to look at Rhees as she entered.

"I offer you a new agreement," she said. "Join with me in a battle to defeat the Hegemony. I will fight one of you as raktaa. If I win, you obey my orders. If I lose, you can have my ships. And I free you from your arrangement with the Hegemony."

Vatch stood and his officers turned to him. He surveyed their faces in silence, then he looked at Rhees, his lips curling back over rows of small, sharp teeth.

"Finally," he said.

32

Denev had finished his shift relatively early in the evening and was making his way to a food strip he'd heard about in the Entertainment District that served off-world cuisine. A new place had opened up with a Cygnus Sector menu and he wanted to check it out.

"Carlan! Is that you?"

Denev looked around at the shouted name and saw a figure with arm raised approaching along the laneway. Other pedestrians glanced around too, then turned back to whatever they were doing, no obvious Carlan among them.

The man was black and bald under a peak cap, dressed in a garish shirt, still waving his arm. It was Rapskel out in the open. Denev looked up at the narrow strip of sky above the laneway, scanning for drones or cameras fixed to the buildings, but there was nothing obvious.

Close now, Rapskel pulled Denev's limp hand into a shake and leaned close. "Somewhere we can talk?" He turned slightly towards a bar cryptically called The Answer, placed an arm round Denev's shoulders and walked him towards it. Denev still couldn't see any surveillance devices. A blind spot?

They pushed through retro glass doors into the bar, which was low-lit and intimate. A handful of people were slow dancing to a bass rhythm on a tiny dancefloor to the right, and an ornate glass and steel bar ran the length of the long room to the left.

"Get us a booth," Rapskel said and made for the bar.

Past the dancers was a row of privacy booths set into the wall – most of them empty and even more dimly lit. Denev sat in the last vacant booth at the rear. Had Rapskel been surveilling him? Denev wished he wouldn't. From a purely practical stand, if SolSec or HDC – which was the same thing now – noticed Denev had a tail, it would raise a lot of difficult questions.

Rapskel appeared with two glasses of what looked like whisky rocks. He sat opposite Denev and the table activated a privacy screen – a white-noise barrier to prevent eavesdropping. Useless against HDC surveillance, and Denev was sure the bar was riddled with passive sensors. He tapped his band and invoked real privacy. Nothing they said would be recorded.

"Felt we should talk," Rapskel said. "But it's too hard dragging your ass to one of our safe sites. I think you might be a little too hot for that type of trip to go unnoticed after what you did to Ceed Felman. He had a lot of friends, you know."

"So grabbing me in the middle of downtown is safer?"

"Sometimes simplest is best. Like hiding in plain sight." Rapskel raised his glass. "Congratulations on saving your boss's ass by the way."

"I took your advice," Denev said. "Now you can take some of mine."

Rapskel gave him a lopsided smile. "I thought you might feel that way. You've been getting close with your new best friend Gart Lowrans. But he's not the answer. His group is just as limited in what they can do as we are."

Denev had been careful not to push Rapskel. After all, his network had managed to evade the attention of the Central Administration for two decades. That was quite the achievement. But from what he could see, they hadn't *done* anything. The CA, SolSec, HDC were just as powerful – more powerful – than they'd ever been. As the "new boy", however, it wasn't very politic for Denev to point that out.

"I know Gart's not the answer," he said. "Neither are you. But together … there's an opportunity for us now. But we have to pool resources if we're really going to take advantage of it. Your group and Gart's can't operate at arm's-length any more."

Rapskel took another sip of whisky, watching Denev over the rim of his glass. "That separation is what's kept his people and my people safe. But go ahead. I'm listening."

Denev glanced towards the bar. This wasn't exactly the best place to have a conversation like this, but no one seemed to be watching them. "It's about the coming war."

"Of course. We're doing our piece. It's not easy tampering with sensor feeds remotely, particularly when they're registering that much ship movement."

"It's working, but when the attack fleet gets here, the CA will go on high alert. We need to keep manipulating the flow of information and blunt the CA's response. Gart in Fleet, you and me in HDC and SolSec."

Rapskel swapped his empty glass for Denev's untouched one. "I don't think you should be drinking this. You want the aliens to *win*? You know what the K-Chaan almost did to us. What's to stop these guys from blowing up the whole of Sol system?"

"Rhees," Denev said. "She can stop them."

He knew Rhees was worried she *couldn't* stop them. But somehow they had to do it.

"Okay, let's take this a step back," Rapskel said. "We *can* do what you say. The last twenty years we've been slowly putting our people in place for passive monitoring but with the capacity to act if we have to. We've been waiting for the right trigger, but this isn't it. Even if Rhees can control her big alien battle fleet, there's no guarantee they'll win if they stop short of annihilation. And the Central Administration isn't going to capitulate for anything less. They'll still be in power and all you'll achieve is a huge loss of life."

Denev sat back. "I agree. It's why we need the file."

"This again?" Rapskel's exasperation was clear in his voice.

"I believe it's exactly what we need. There's information locked away that can only be opened by the architects of the Hegemony. It *has* to be something so damaging that none of them ever want it to see the light of day. We bring this system to the brink and then we show everybody what the Central Administration doesn't want them to know. It's high risk. I know that. But I'm sure it's worth it."

Rapskel stared at Denev for long seconds, then arched his neck. Denev heard vertebrae crack. "Fuck! I have no idea if you're delusional or just plain insane. But you're right about the tactical situation. For the last twenty years we've known that even if we throw everything we've got at the Hegemony and pray to the luck gods, all we can hope for is a temporary stalemate. Now the scales have tipped a little more in our favour, but not enough. We need something more and I don't know what that is. But it's time to go all in. If your file gives us the edge, we might live to see another day. If not –" He finished the second whisky. "At least we go down fighting."

Denev let out a breath he hadn't realised he'd been holding. "All right then."

Of course he still had no idea how to open the file. But that would come later. It had to.

"You just need to live past the next twenty seconds," Rapskel said, looking over Denev's shoulder towards the front of the bar.

Denev leaned out of the booth. The street doors had been pushed open and through the crowd of bodies he saw armoured troops entering.

"SolSec tactical patrol," Rapskel said. "We've been monitoring them. Deployment is nothing special, but the thing about these guys is they're not working for new management. I told you Ceed had more than a few friends pissed at what happened to him. This is a death squad, and they're looking for you."

Denev made to stand, but Rapskel grabbed his wrist. "Relax. We were playing this game long before you decided you wanted to clear your conscience. It's handled."

The troops pushed through the dancers, long rifles tracking left and right. They wore full tac helmets which looked like metal insect heads with single red eyes. One spoke to the barman who waved vaguely towards the back of the room.

Denev wanted to run, but Rapskel held on. "Don't. Just another five seconds."

There were three of them. The other two joined the one at the bar, and they raised their rifles together, aiming at Denev's booth.

"Stop!" one shouted. They fired.

People screamed as shots hit the edge of the booth, then tracked towards the back wall, hitting and disintegrating a door.

The troops were on the move, running. As they passed the booth, one looked right at Denev – through him – and kept going. All three disappeared out the back.

Rapskel released Denev's arm and tapped the side of his head. "Augments. You know yourself any dataflow can be subverted."

"And if they hadn't been wearing helmets?"

Rapskel pushed out his bottom lip. "Then we wouldn't have been here. But this little display will have been worth it. This time, you can trust *me*."

Denev's band vibrated.

Rapskel picked up his hat and stood. "That'll be your little clone buddies. Thank me later." He left by the shattered door.

Denev dropped privacy and looked at his band. Message from Stin: *I think we've found something.*

∞

It didn't take long to get back to the Datahive by slidewalk. But despite Rapskel's assurances, Denev worried all the way. Had Rhees used the Darrow persona and given the clones a fix on her? Or had they found something more directly linked to Denev's treachery? Either way it was unlikely to be good news.

He entered reception and checked his band again. Stin had sent the location of a meeting room three levels above. Whatever it was demanded a face-to-face.

As he exited the lift, he saw the two clones through the long glass wall of the meeting room. They were standing together in the sunlight, looking out across Vigilance Plaza. Denev saw they were holding hands and wondered what sort of a relationship clones might have. Closer than brothers. He thought spending any amount of time with another iteration of himself would drive him crazy, but others might feel differently.

Then he saw the armed security guard at the meeting room door and worried again at what they'd found.

He nodded to the guard, who opened the door for him. Hel and Stin turned at his entry, separating hands and blasting him with identical blinding smiles.

"Good afternoon, Operative Antwer." Denev was pretty sure this was Hel. "We're happy to report we've found something."

"I read the message," Denev said shortly. "Has Darrow resurfaced?"

Hel's smile dimmed a fraction. "No. We've found no trace."

Which set off a whole new string of worries for Denev. Was Rhees still alive?

"We've had reports of unauthorised SolSec activity in the North-East Entertainment District," Hel continued. "Shots fired, but we're not sure why. It made us think about external system access. We'd run a full sweep before, of course, and came up empty, but," he smiled at his clone, "Stin thought it was worth another try and this time … Well, we can show you."

The exterior wall opaqued, dimming the room, and the clones sat at the long meeting table. Denev sat too as a holo formed between them. The view was from above. Buildings and shops, and in the centre of the image the utility cube where he'd accessed the Datahive and fought Beloc.

"There's a trace of an access from this building," Hel said.

Denev waited. Any moment Beloc would back around the corner and Denev would exit the cube.

Nothing happened.

"What am I looking for?" he asked.

"There's nothing to see," Hel said.

"And that's just it," Stin added. "We know physical access occurred at this building at this time stamp. But if we run the surveillance forward or back for a month, no one enters that building."

"I hope I'm not more than averagely stupid, but I still don't get it," Denev said.

The image disintegrated, turning into lines of code that disappeared as they reached the top of the holo image.

"The surveillance image has been manipulated," Hel said.

Denev knew that. SolSec had removed him and Beloc from the feed so they could blackmail him. But if Hel and Stin could uncover the real image …

"It's almost impossible to discern, but whoever tampered made a small mistake," Stin said as the scrolling code halted. "Here." He pointed at a line that obligingly turned red.

"So can you reconstruct the real image?" Denev asked.

Hel and Stin shook their heads in unison. "That's gone. But this," Hel pointed at the code, "gave us a thread to tug on."

"And it leads?"

"SolSec," Hel said, waving the image away as he and Stin both sat back. "From what Comptroller Volmar told us, SolSec have been competing against HDC for some time. This indicates their activities went much further."

Denev sat back too. "That's some impressive work."

But he wasn't complimenting the clones. He knew SolSec had tampered with the image but they wouldn't have been stupid enough to make a mistake, let alone one that led back to them. No, this was Rapskel. He'd accessed the tampered feed, taken advantage of the current situation with SolSec – shit, maybe he'd even tipped off the rogue squad so Hel and Stin would notice the disturbance – and left a clue that indicated SolSec were guilty. Thank me later, he'd said. Denev certainly would.

And Hel and Stin hadn't found Rhees — or more correctly her anomalous persona. She was still out there somewhere — either safe, facing danger, or already dead. A superposition of fates. He may never know which one turned out to be true.

33

The fighter was making best speed back to Aktiuk, far faster than our journey out. Rasa and Isza sat opposite me, and past them I could see the pilot and co-pilot in the cockpit. Both of them were intact.

"Who gave the order to kill Dageru's guards?" I said, remembering the blinding light that had filled the canyon.

"That was me," Isza said. "They were vaporised instantly. They didn't know what hit them."

Which meant no empathic backlash. Still, it was a hard thing to do. I looked at my sister, wondering how much this conflict had changed her. Rasa had admitted she'd told Isza about my plans to visit Dageru. The old Isza would have stormed into my rooms and told me I couldn't go.

"I thought you were off-planet on patrol," I said.

Isza spread her feeders wide. "That's what we wanted you to think."

"I have a feeling I've been managed. Why didn't you try to stop me?"

"You said yourself, you can't govern from inside a prison cell. We knew the Hegemony asset was out there and more assassination attempts were inevitable. They had all the advantages of secrecy. All they needed was for us to make a single mistake, and we would eventually. But if we let our guard down. Or appeared to …"

"It would draw them out," I said.

"Enough to be stopped for good. Rhees calls it 'high risk,

high reward'. But," she grew serious again, "I would never have let anyone harm you."

I believed her. She'd killed Dageru's guards for me.

The shoreline of the Inland Sea flashed by and we skirted the spaceport heading for Treaty Mount. The fighter slowed as we approached.

"Something's happening ahead," Isza said. "I can feel it."

We passed over streets and buildings in the Merchants Sector until we could see down into the market square at the bottom of the Mount. It was full of Kresz. Faces turned up towards us as they heard our engines.

Isza suddenly leaned forward and grabbed my arm. "Sakat!" she said, the air hissing loudly in her spiracles.

"Incoming comms," the pilot called and then I heard Tzek's voice. "Udun, is that you?"

"Tzek, where are you?" I asked, as Isza indicated she was all right.

"I'm below you," he said. "When you said you were coming here, I thought I'd spread the word."

"All these Kresz are here for you," Isza added. "I felt their excitement when they realised you were here."

As we descended, I saw the line of armed Defenders strung along the flattened top of Treaty Mount. Not all the Kresz here were happy to see me.

"We could vaporise them from here," Isza said.

"You've been spending far too much time with Rhees," I told her. "Besides, it wouldn't stop Akczek, and the others below would panic. Take us down."

The crowd parted to let the small fighter land. Tzek, flanked by two Defenders, stepped up onto the fighter's ramp as it opened and held his staff above his head. The crowd quietened. Then roared when I walked onto the ramp.

People of all houses and lodges were crammed into the marketplace: Adepts, Cultivators, Merchants, Defenders, young and old from the shell colours I saw, intact and excised.

Eventually they quietened and individual voices called out: "Help us, Udun!" "We are with you!" "Tell us what to do," and then, "Lead us!" accompanied by another roar from the crowd.

"It's true," Isza said, standing behind me. "They're all here for you."

I thought of all the people who had helped to bring me – us – to this moment. Emba, who'd aided me against his better judgement; Atalna, who'd lent me his strength when I had none. Rhees, the enemy who had become a friend. Nok, unknowable perhaps but dependable in the end. And Isza, who always spoke her mind. All those individuals, alien or Kresz, working together, even if we didn't trust or even wholly understand each other.

The conservative factions in the Council had argued against my reforms, saying the people had seen too much upheaval already. They claimed to know the will of the Kresz worldmind. Tzek had told me how confused the worldmind had felt since the invasion. But Isza had said it was waiting. Expectant. Change had been coming for a long time, even before the Hegemony arrived. Nok had said I was to be its instrument. I could see that now, and I felt humbled when I looked at all of those who stood before me and saw the trust and hope in their eyes. The people weren't tired of change. They were ready for it.

I looked to the Akczek Kresz visible at the top of the Mount, and everyone below turned to follow my gaze. Silence fell over the square.

I stepped down, Tzek beside me, and we walked together with Isza and Rasa and Tzek's Defenders through the crowd to the edge of the market. The Akczek Kresz looked down at us from the top of the obsidian steps, their weapons raised and trained on the crowd.

I remembered another group of Defenders at the top of these steps in a desperate last stand against the Hegemony. I remembered Isza falling to Hegemony fire on these steps as she tried to reach me. There had been so much conflict here. But cycles before, these steps had witnessed the houses joined together in peace.

"Don't be afraid," I said, and heard my words repeated through the crowd as we began to climb the steps together. The armed Kresz above were massively outnumbered, even with weapons.

"They're not wearing empathy reflectors," Tzek said. "Perhaps not enough to go round."

"Or a tactical decision," Isza said on my other side. "The Kergis traitors wore them and look what happened to them."

We were halfway to the top now, the crowd following behind in silence.

"They're worried," Isza said.

"Even without my hood, that's obvious," I said. But were they scared enough to panic and open fire?

We stopped on the top step, the line of armed Kresz in front of us. The closest stared at me above the barrel of his rifle.

"We are not your enemy," I said. "We are your brothers, your parents, your children. Would you fire on us?"

The Defender hesitated for a moment, then lowered his weapon. "Withdraw," he ordered the others and they stood back.

I took the final step and turned to face the crowd. They roared again and raised their arms to the sky.

Tzek held on to me as if to steady himself. "I wish you could feel what I feel," he said.

I looked down at the people. My people. "I feel it," I said.

I held my arm up and the crowd fell silent.

"There are other armed Kresz in Aktiuk," I said. "Go and tell them what has happened here. Tell them to go home."

"Go with them," Tzek told his two Defenders. "Tell the others and report back."

I turned and looked at the doors to the Council chamber building. The scene etched into them showed the moment when the Kresz houses laid down their weapons as the empathic bond of the Emergence blossomed and took hold. The moment war was banished from Homeworld.

All societies could seem unchanging for generations and then change in an instant. The hierarchs hadn't understood then, and they didn't understand now. But the people did. Even if Akczek's Defender had killed me at the top of the steps, it would no longer have made a difference. The old ways were dead.

34

Datahive, Cape York Conurb, Earth / Sol Sector / Hegemony

Denev sat in nook immersion listening to the deep space and Voss Space sensors. So far so normal. Traffic moved in and through Voss Space, transponders checked out, and pre-filed flight plans matched realtime coordinates. But it was a lie. Beneath the calm surface was a deeply buried data substrate that told a different story: one of lethal-looking vessels moving purposefully to converge near Sol system. The truth was wrapped in an elegant algorithm that compressed the data into a blind spot, like the space where the optic nerve passed through the back of the eye. According to the nook, Denev was working on a completely different area of the datafeeds.

Denev prided himself on his technical expertise. He'd soaked up the HDC's system infiltration training like it was mother's milk, aced whatever tests they'd thrown at him and successfully deployed his skills in the field against all kinds of alien code. But the approach Rapskel's group used was like nothing Denev had learned in class. Whoever had come up with it was a genius. It was as if there was a glass ceiling above him and standing on that level was another Denev, interacting with the system and working on whatever analysis HDC required of him. As he worked, he cast a shadow down through the transparent floor and it was in that shadow that the real Denev worked unseen, changing orders, diverting craft and clearing a path for the Lenticular group. In this null space he sensed other operators – Rapskel's people exploiting the same weaknesses. It was how they had been able to avoid detection for two decades.

Slowly Denev withdrew, and the synapse shunt closed down

and returned him to the real. While Hel and Stin pursued their leaker in SolSec, he was pursuing another line of enquiry – that the leak came from Fleet. To that end, he had an appointment with Admiral Gart Lowrans.

Denev took a public hypertube out to the eastern coastal beaches. Coming up out of the station, he followed a group in Fleet fatigues onto a base ground bus. They glanced at his uniform but kept their opinions to themselves and their voices low in case he was spying on them.

At the base perimeter checkpoint Denev's band buzzed briefly and the bus barely slowed. Gart's office had arranged his clearances.

Finding the ship was a little harder, but one of the ground crew eventually pointed it out to him. It was a squat cargo lugger – big engines with a bulbous hold slung between them, topped by a small cockpit like a pimple on a hill. The bay doors were wide open but the interior was almost bulkhead to bulkhead with cargo crates, leaving only a narrow corridor leading to a ladder to the cockpit. Ninety-nine-point-nine per cent of the cargo headed for space used the commercial or government-owned space elevators, but there was still some cargo classed as too dangerous to transport that way. This route was more direct for Denev and avoided a lot of eyes in the elevators, but he hoped whatever they were hauling was well stowed.

A comm buzzed at the bay door. "Who's that?" A woman's voice.

"Operative Denev Antwer. Permission to come aboard?"

"My extra cargo. Come on up, cargo. You can ride with me."

By the time he got to the top of the ladder, his thigh muscles were beginning to feel the climb. He poked his head through the open hatch. The pilot was already strapped into her crash-seat, angled so her back lay along the floor Denev was climbing through. The instrument panels and cockpit window curved close above his head.

"No frills here," she said. "I'm Golder. Strap in."

Denev lay in the second chair, swung his legs over his head and slid his feet under boot grips. He busied himself tightening his seat harness.

"Won't be long," Golder said. "Just on final checks."

She concentrated on her boards and traded words with the control tower. She was maybe in her sixties or seventies, tan skin and white blonde hair cut short and swept back. Her sleeves were rolled up and as she opened and closed contacts above her head he could see the muscles of her thin arms rippling.

"Hold tight," she said, finally satisfied with whatever the tower was telling her.

Beneath them the engines exploded and then got louder. Denev felt the push in his back as the ship lifted, slowly at first but picking up speed fast. He could see nothing but blue sky through the window.

Beside him, Golder kept up a steady interchange with flight control. It all seemed very old-fashioned. Surely whatever information they were exchanging could have been shared by automated systems. But it was an old ship. And she was an old-school pilot. Maybe she just preferred it this way.

The ship tilted and the acceleration eased a little.

Golder looked over at him and took a deep breath. "You're HDC," she said.

It didn't sound like a question so he didn't reply.

"Tell me, what the fuck is going on with you guys and SolSec? You both run out of people to spy on so you turn on each other?" The smile that accompanied her words was far from friendly.

"I hear Fleet got its ass kicked out in deep space," Denev said.

Her smile soured into something worse. She flipped a contact and a giant sat on his chest as the ship accelerated again. Her obvious lack of interest in making further conversation suited Denev fine. Let her complain to her friends about the arsehole HDC operative she had to ferry up from Earth. Everyone took comfort in perpetuating stereotypes, and didn't question or look too closely as a result.

The old animosity between Fleet and HDC, HDC and SolSec, and any arm of CA you'd care to mention against any other, was built in part on a feeling of moral superiority. Fleet prided itself on fighting the Hegemony's enemies out in the open, not stabbing them in the back like HDC. HDC saw their work as surgical – achieving outcomes with the minimum of damage. A scalpel to Fleet's club and so – again – ethically better in the long run. But they – *we* – are all just killers, he thought.

The sky blue thinned and faded to space and the thrust cut out completely. They were chasing a star, but very quickly it became more than that. Fleet central control. Panops it was called. Some said the name derived from "panopticon"; a tall, windowed building from where prison guards could watch everything their prisoners did. Certainly Panops' location in low Earth orbit meant it could see everything on the spinning planet below and in all of space above. Others said more prosaically that it was a shorter version of "pan-operations". Whatever the derivation, Panops was the biggest object in LEO, casting an artificial dusk on the land it passed over when the conditions were right.

The structure was complex and composed of three elements. A large saucer section, curved like a shield but topped with an eight-pointed star whose points protruded past the rim and formed vast entry ports for hangars and cargo bays. Four long arms angled down from the underside of the shield, then bent at elbows to thrust outward, forming long gantries that supported larger ship-repair facilities. A Hurricane Class corvette and a Planet Class destroyer escort were currently docked there. And thrusting down from the centre of the disc, a long thin column ending in a bulbous pommel like the hilt of an ancient two-handed sword.

Golder trimmed their approach efficiently, heading for one of the star points on the saucer. Denev's body pushed against the harness as the ship turned, the cockpit facing up towards empty space again, and drifted sideways towards the cargo bay. The leading edge of the star point came into view and then they were in the brightly lit hold, slowing and descending as the artificial gravity took hold.

The ship came to a halt. Denev unharnessed and glanced at Golder. She was staring studiously at her instruments and flicking contacts.

"See ya, cargo," she said, without looking at him.

Out on the deck, a smartly uniformed woman with collar-length black hair waited for him. "Welcome to Panops," she said and sounded like she meant it. "I'll take you to meet Admiral Lowrans."

He followed her out of the dock and into a waiting lift in the corridor. The car moved smoothly sideways and then down a long way. Denev suspected he was in the sword hilt section.

Exiting the elevator, the officer pressed a contact on a nearby door. It opened onto a large office. Denev's attention was drawn instantly to the window. Earth curved away to a far horizon along the bottom half, and closer in at the top left the corvette was visible clinging to one of the giant gantries.

Gart Lowrans was seated behind an expanse of desk cluttered with flimsies.

Denev's escort stood at parade rest and he followed suit. "HDC operative Denev Antwer to see you, sir," she said redundantly.

Gart nodded his large head. "Thank you, Sasha. You can leave us."

She glanced at Denev.

"It's all right," Gart said, rising. "The big bad HDC man isn't going to eat me."

She smiled, said, "No, sir," and left.

As the door closed, Gart came round the desk and gripped Denev's hand and elbow in a firm handshake. "Thank you," he said.

Denev could see an intensity of feeling in the older man's eyes. "You spoke to Rhees," he said, feeling his own relief as Gart's face split in a broad smile.

"I did. She's good. We're … I can't say we're good, but we're better than we were." He took a deep breath and sighed. "I can't tell you how relieved I am, after thinking she was dead for so long."

"I think I have an idea," Denev said.

Gart finally released his hand and gestured to a couple of easy chairs by the broad window. "It's safe to talk here."

"Where is she?" Denev asked.

"Last we spoke, on the way to Cygnus Sector."

"Cygnus?" Rhees could always surprise him.

"She was hoping to enlist help from the Brell and Sissilak. I read the reports. You two had a bit to do with them."

"We helped Volmar stop a revolt, and killed a lot of aliens as a result. But if they still have ships …"

"And Fleet's pretty much withdrawn from the sector. We're relying on the Maagba to keep the peace."

Denev remembered the fierce Maagba attacks they'd witnessed. It wouldn't be easy allying with the Sissilak and Brell with the Maagba around. But Rhees must have felt it was important.

"She's worried about the Lenticular forces," he said. "After what the Hegemony did to them, they're likely to wipe humanity out if they can. Rhees has been looking for a way to stop that happening. If she has a second force under her command …"

Gart nodded. "Aye, I can see that. It's risky but."

"Try suicidal," Denev agreed, but he'd told Rapskel she could do it.

"In any case, if she's moving a second attack force from Cygnus Sector she'll need the same kind of cover we've been giving the Lenticular group," Gart said.

"That complicates things, but … I guess it's doable."

"It'll have to be. I've already alerted my people. We've worked a long time to get into the right positions. A fleet runs on accurate and timely information. How many ships you have is secondary to that." He sat forward. "But when the attacking force gets here, that's a bit harder. We need to be in control by then. That's where your secret file comes in."

"You still agree it's the key?"

"It fucking better be. But yes, like I said, something happened back then that no one talks about. I've seen the looks pass between them over too many years."

"The file can only be accessed by Volmar, Breslaw, Vargas and Rejak," Denev said. "And they need to open it together."

"But they don't need to *be* together when it's opened."

Denev thought about that. "Not physically, no. They need to be connected to immersion so the system can verify brain scans."

"Still, it makes it a bit easier. Especially since your pal Volmar is now head of SolSec as well. It gives him certain duties if Earth is under attack."

"And that's good because …?"

Gart grinned. "Let me explain a couple of things about disaster planning."

35

Rhees was about to try to kill a Maagba in single combat so she could make a deal with them. A deal that meant attacking Earth and more death and destruction. What series of fucked-up decisions had led her here? How far back would she have to go? Someone like Nok could piece it all together maybe. After all, he'd known Rhees well enough to include Maagba in her trink.

Had she become as evil as Volmar? Or was it like the Totek said: did it depend on the moral framework you used to judge the action? It seemed to Rhees that she had no choice but to do what she was doing. What did that say about Volmar?

The Totek had returned Rhees to the room they'd spoken in, and one of the Maagba had left her a weapons belt that held two of their black batons, both with a single contact stud. The executioner on the first Maagba ship had carried one of these and she'd used it to kill him and free herself.

When she activated the batons, the air around the business ends vibrated in a coherent, faintly glowing energy column. One column, from the larger of the two batons, was about eighty centimetres long; the other was about thirty centimetres. It was basically a sword/dagger combination.

She'd done *some* sword training at the Academy, both rapier and katana, but it was sheer luck she'd been able to kill a Maagba with one of these the last time. She switched off the sword baton and moved the knife across the back of a chair. It sliced through the material like it wasn't there.

The door opened to reveal two Maagba waiting outside. Rhees strapped on the weapons belt, took a last look at Voss Space outside and stepped between her Maagba guards.

They led her to what must be a cargo bay, but it was empty of any cargo. Another Maagba waited at the far end, wearing a weapons belt like her own. At least they weren't tying her to a pole this time like a sacrificial goat. Still, the outcome would be the same. One death. She felt more nervous than ever before. *Don't*, she thought, taking a deep breath. She'd gotten this far. All she had to do was keep going.

The guard left and the door closed. Now it was just Rhees and her opponent.

Had the Maagba volunteered for this or been ordered? What were its wants and needs? Did it have a family?

No. She couldn't think like that. She *had* to win. She'd chosen this fight. The Maagba at the other end of the hold wasn't an enemy, just an obstacle between her and her objective.

She walked forward, removing the batons from her belt and activating both blades, arms out so the tips pointed towards the deck.

Her opponent hadn't moved yet. Hadn't drawn its batons. She had no idea how skilful it was. How skilful Vatch needed it to be.

The last time, Vatch had simply needed blood to be spilled. But there was a choice this time. If Rhees won, the Maagba would follow her into war. If she lost, they were free. But free to do what? Vatch wasn't above setting up the parameters of the contest to favour a desired result.

Rhees stopped in the centre of the hold and brought her right baton to shoulder height, the longer energy blade angled across her body. Her left arm was lower, holding the knife close to her hip, ready to thrust.

"Are you going to join me?" she asked.

The Maagba took a step, then hesitated.

War Leader Vatch's voice echoed across the hold. "Begin."

The Maagba drew both batons and, with a roar, ran at Rhees. It ignited the blades, holding both out to its left as it closed, still yelling, then swept the blades towards her. Columns of energy screamed as she met blade with blade.

The Maagba was strong and she pushed back, then stepped left so the blades skittered along each other. Momentum carried it past her and she turned to follow, holding her batons in defensive position.

The Maagba mirrored her and they both stood beyond the sweep of each other's sword tip. Rhees had the height advantage, but the Maagba was stronger and the joints in its limbs were made differently, bending and pushing in unexpected ways.

She lunged forward, swinging her sword down in an arc towards its head. It blocked her blade and she had to jump back as its knife swept towards her at stomach level.

The Maagba roared again and ran at her, blades swinging in wild arcs across its body. Rhees stepped back and back, parrying with sword and knife. The attack was wild and aggressive but lacked any accuracy, and when the Maagba stopped its advance it was panting noisily.

They began to sidestep round the space between them. Rhees had no doubt that if this guy was an expert with energy swords she'd be dead by now. But they seemed evenly matched. Part of Vatch's design?

The batons were light but her arms were already starting to tire. She had to get in close, past the arc of the blades. Go hand to hand.

The Maagba lunged forward with another sweeping sword cut and she jumped back quickly. She'd nearly been sliced in two. *Concentrate for fuck's sake.*

She threw her knife baton at the Maagba's head and stepped in as it flinched. Its sword swung back in surprise, then swept forward towards her shoulder. She blocked it with her own sword, pushing hard, and with her free hand grabbed the Maagba's knife arm that was already thrusting towards her. She kicked down hard on its leg while pulling its arm past her left hip and they overbalanced, falling together. She landed hard on it with her left shoulder, still holding its knife hand, then rolled off to a stand and stamped down on its sword arm. Slowly she pointed her own vibrating sword tip at its neck.

She was panting for breath. Wasn't this enough? She'd bested their champion. But it was like some gladiator contest in ancient Rome. Nero wanted blood. The Maagba wanted raktaa. She had to kill her opponent so she and War Leader Vatch could get what each of them wanted.

Rhees made it quick. The Maagba died, and she threw her baton aside and walked towards the opening door. Maybe a Totek could justify it, but she knew she was no better than any of them. She was a killer like Volmar. Like all humans.

Tktkrt stood in the entrance. "The Maagba you killed was happy to die," it rapped.

Presumably it was trying to make her feel better. It didn't work.

∞

As we made our way through the empty auditorium, Isza told Tzek what had happened in Dageru lands and about Zeluk's attack on me.

"Even if he is the Hegemony's asset, there may be others," Tzek said as we entered my room beneath the Council chamber.

"Perhaps," I said. "It doesn't matter much now. You saw the people out there. They're united – all houses, all lodges, intact and excised alike. The old systems that kept us apart no longer hold meaning for them. The change is complete. I'm not needed any more."

"We'll need your leadership for cycles to come," Tzek said.

"Perhaps." I sat on the nearest bench. I felt tired, but I also felt at peace for the first time in a long time. "We need to call a full meeting of the Council."

"I can arrange the sitting, but we need to deal with Akczek, and Dageru when we find him," Tzek said.

"Akczek's fate depends on how his people behave. If they withdraw like they did on Treaty Mount, then what is he guilty of?"

"A failed coup. An assassination attempt on you from what Isza said."

"So, two failures. And how much of what he did was because of Dageru's influence?"

"But why not prosecute him?" Isza said.

"Sometimes it's not good to push things too hard." I looked towards Tzek. "My advisor told me that once."

Tzek seated himself beside me and his feeders spread wide. "As you say. We'll see how his people behave."

The comms at the far end of the table announced an incoming transmission. The screen showed random lines, then flashed twice and Rhees appeared. I was glad to see her, but she looked different. Human expressions were still hard for me to interpret but I'd spent a lot of time with Rhees. She looked drained.

I tried to lighten her mood. "I'm glad to see you're still alive." But there was no sign of anything I'd come to associate with a smile.

"I shouldn't be," she said. "I called to let you know I've found allies. A lot of them."

A tension I hadn't realised I'd been holding inside eased. If Rhees had succeeded …

"They'll fight for us?" Tzek asked.

"They'll fight for me. Which amounts to the same thing," Rhees replied. "But if the Hegemony surrenders and the Lenticular forces decide to finish the job and destroy Earth, I'll stop you."

Tzek grasped his staff tightly and struck the floor with its end. "How dare you threaten us after what your people did to the Kresz."

"Tzek," I said and he quietened.

"We agreed not to use each other," Rhees said.

I remembered what we'd spoken of on the way to Homeworld to find Tzek and all the other Kresz in hiding. We'd agreed to make each other's goal our own. Rhees had done so much for me. For all Kresz. But I also understood Tzek's anger.

"What if the Hegemony refuse to surrender?" Tzek said. "We're not going to stand down just because you say so."

Rhees looked at me for a long moment and drops of water ran from the corner of each eye down her cheeks. "I know," she said.

"Rhees, what is wrong?" I'd never seen her like this.

She sat back and wiped the trails of water from her face. "I'm tired. I want to go home, but going home means death. And I've lived with this fear for so long, hoping I could find some way to stop the Hegemony that doesn't mean killing millions. But that's what humans do."

I thought about what Dageru had done to the excisees. And about all the Kresz who had died on the Plain of Ak'ra fighting Kergis. Humans weren't the only species to kill their own. I'd had enough of death too.

"I remember our agreement," I said. "If you believe humanity is worth saving, I'll do everything I can to help you."

"Udun. How can you even think that?" Tzek said.

"Because things have to change. Here and everywhere." I looked back at Rhees. "But you have to convince the other Lenticular battle leaders."

Finally her mouth turned into a smile. "I know. Nok told me the same thing what feels like a lifetime ago. And it's not going to be easy. Thanks, Udun. We'll talk again at the muster."

The comm ended.

"I'm not questioning your judgement," Tzek said. "But what happens if she can't convince the Telsans or the Svestans to trust her as you do?"

"We must make sure that doesn't happen," I said. "Lintal has been helpful so far. Let's start with him."

Air hissed slowly through Tzek's spiracles. "Then it shall be as you say." He pushed against his staff to stand before me. "Udun, I lost your trust when I forgot how to be a good advisor to you. I want you to know I'm sorry."

This time I felt he was truly on my side and I could forgive him. "Thank you, Tzek."

"Come on," Isza said to Rasa. "I see my breach brother is safe enough for now. Let's leave them to their plotting."

But Rasa hesitated in the doorway, then turned back to me. "I know Dageru said when you lost your mantle you lost the knowledge of what it is to be Kresz," she said. "But I can see you gained much more than you lost. And all of us have a great deal still to learn from you."

Even for a Kresz without a mantle, the emotions in the room were too much for me. Feeling awkward, I walked round my table to sit on the other side, ready to face the hierarchs, the Hegemony and whatever came after that.

36

Rhees was smiling as she broke the contact, surprised she could still feel hope after everything she'd done, and with everything she still had to face. At least Udun would back her. One step at a time.

Her dolphincraft split open and folded down around her, and she stepped out into the Maagba battleship hangar. All of her dolphincraft were here, settled in long rows that filled the entire bay. She walked quickly down the corridor to the room where Tktkrt waited, perched on a stool in front of a comms array. The window beyond was crowded with ships. The entire Maagba fleet was hers to command because of the life she'd chosen to take.

"I've been in contact with the Brell and Sissilak," Tktkrt rapped out on its drumhead. "What ships they have will join us."

"Least you could do after selling me out to the Maagba," Rhees said. She still didn't know how to take the Totek. "I need to speak to Hegemony Fleet Command."

"We have the comms protocols," Tktkrt said, claws tapping at the console.

Of course they did. The Maagba had been authorised to do Fleet's work out here.

A comms window opened in front of her showing the Fleet insignia. "Thanks," she said and Tktkrt hopped nimbly off the stool.

Now they were linked to the Fleet channel, it was easy to enter a particular ident codestring and request full privacy.

The image flashed and her father appeared. He looked at his screen, then quickly up. "You can go, Duncan," he said. "I'll take this alone."

When he peered into the screen again, his voice was urgent. "Are you all right?"

"I'm okay."

"You look terrible. I mean …"

Fuck, she must look bad if her father was worried. "I'm fine. The last few days have been rough."

Yeah, she'd raided a dead planet, found a fleet of magic spaceships and got into a Voss Space battle that ended in single combat to the death.

"I'm in charge of a Maagba space armada and we're headed for Earth."

She expected Gart to pepper her with questions, but he just nodded. "Things didn't go exactly to plan then."

"A little wrinkle. The Totek, Brell and Sissilak are joining in too."

"You'll be rendezvousing with the Lenticular force?"

"Yes. How's Denev?"

"He's fine. Together we're clearing the way for you. But when you get here …"

"I know." She felt the tension take hold in her chest again. "A lot of people are going to die. I'll do what I can to stop it, and some in the Lenticular force are on board with that. But if we get the upper hand and the Hegemony refuses to surrender …"

"It'll be bad," her father finished. "Where bad is shorthand for outright fucking disastrous. Look, Denev and I have a couple of things on the go here. At worst we can blunt the Hegemony war machine. But at best, we might be able to bring it to a grinding halt."

Rhees sat back. "That would be a miracle."

"Aye. No promises, but we'll give it our best shot."

She broke the contact, took a deep breath and let it out slowly. Tempting as it was, she couldn't rely on Denev and Gart. The Lenticular force needed the strongest battle plan possible.

She turned to Tktkrt. "There's something else you can help me with. Last time I was here, we followed Delegate O'Dran to a secret meeting with other Brell, Totek and Sissilak. And to get to the meeting place, we passed through a weird unmapped Voss Space tunnel."

She remembered how O'Dran's ship had seemingly vanished from the tunnel they'd been following her down with no transit signature. They'd almost lost her until they saw the sphincter-like portal in the tunnel roof. It had turned out to be a short cut to the meeting place.

Tktkrt stood still, one clawed toe tapping on the deck.

"Come on," Rhees said. "You still owe me for the Maagba. A fleet of ships isn't enough."

Finally Tktkrt's sticks rapped on its drumhead. "We can create stable bridges between Voss Space tunnels."

"How big and how long?"

"We haven't found a limit yet. There are certain conditions that must be met. A minimum space-time curvature to make it possible."

She sat back. "Okay, explain the whole thing to me."

∞

Gart stared out his Panops office window for long minutes, but he didn't see the maintenance gantries, the Fleet ships docked there, or the vacuum-suited figures and drones drifting around them. His mind was with Rhees somewhere out in Cygnus Sector, but on the way here. It was the calm before the storm and he wondered about the changes that were coming. How would it all play out? Who would win and who would lose?

His door chimed and he looked over to it, disoriented for a moment.

"Come in," he said, and was surprised to see Sasha enter with Colonel Anyo. "Brok," he said, standing, "what brings you all the way from Jupiter?"

Anyo shook Gart's hand. His smile looked pasted on. "Took the opportunity to hop on the milk run and surprise Devra. It's our anniversary tomorrow."

"And you're wasting time visiting *me*?" Gart smiled to show he was joking, but all Anyo could manage was a grimace.

Anyo glanced at Sasha and said, "Can we talk in private?"

Yes, Gart thought, definitely something off kilter here. "There's nothing you can't say in front of Sasha. But," he closed a contact on his desk before taking his seat again, "we won't be overheard if that's what worries you."

Anyo sat opposite and Sasha remained standing at parade rest.

"It's the monitors," Anyo said.

"Of course it is. What about them?"

"We're masking the data, but – Gart, have you seen how many ships are coming?"

"Oh, I've seen them."

"A lot of people are going to die."

Gart sat back and sighed. "Do you remember when you came to see me after Cracis IV? What you said?"

"I said I was disgusted. I was ashamed to be part of what was done on that planet."

"Yes. But I suppose memory fades. In some of us at least."

"No," Anyo said. "It doesn't. I can still smell the bodies, but …"

"But it's our people who'll be dying now? What do you think revolution means?"

"I know what it means," Anyo snapped back. "But this … If we let these alien ships in, they'll destroy everything. Us included."

Gart considered Anyo. They couldn't afford a weak link. Too many men and women in the network would be exposed.

Behind Anyo, Sasha's right hand dropped to her flechette pistol. Gart shook his head just a fraction. Killing Anyo would be impossible to cover up here. Besides, that wasn't who they were.

Anyo had served under Gart as his exec for five years, through some of the worst action he'd experienced. He knew Anyo had doubts sometimes, but was sure he wouldn't break. And to be honest, the worries he expressed were worries Gart shared. Everything turned on Denev and Rhees now.

"Do you trust me, Brok?"

Anyo took a deep breath, sat straighter. Mentally pulling himself together, Gart thought. *We all have our dark days.*

"I do, sir," Anyo said. "Can we pull it off?"

Gart had no idea. But he had faith in his daughter. If she failed, it wouldn't be for want of trying.

"I need you to hold the line," he said. "And be ready to act when I give the order."

37

The ground car deposited Tzek, me and our obligatory guard at the edge of the market so we could climb the steps to the top of Treaty Mount. Three days had passed since Dageru had fled and he was still missing. In the meantime, Akczek and his advisor, Czel, had been at pains to distance themselves from him. The appearance of armed Akczek Kresz that day had been a reaction by Hierarch Akczek to "reports he'd received" that I had gone missing. His only aim had been to preserve order until I could be located. Tzek could find no evidence to the contrary, and there was nothing that definitively linked Akczek to the attack at Lintal's residence either. No doubt Czel had worked hard – even while plotting with Dageru – to protect his hierarch if things should go wrong. He'd done his job well.

Halfway to the top of the mount I paused and looked back. The market was full: a sea of coloured fabric shading the stalls, and between them a press of Kresz from all houses and lodges, browsing, sampling, haggling. I remembered a very different marketplace shortly after occupation. The few traders that remained had been fearful of the Hegemony soldiers – the cruel new owners of Homeworld. And earlier still, the sudden appearance of excised Kresz in the square below during our last stand on Treaty Mount against the invaders. We hadn't understood at that moment what the Hegemony had done to us.

We continued our climb, the breath hissing loudly in Tzek's spiracles. When we reached the top, Isza and Rasa were waiting for us.

"Udun," Isza said and embraced me, holding me tight against her shell.

She let me go and moved on to Tzek, and Rasa embraced me too. She held me just as tightly as Isza had and I felt she could keep holding me for as long as she liked. Rasa must have felt the same because it was only when Isza said, "Shall we?" that we broke apart. I saw Isza was smiling at me.

"I feel I should say something profound before we all go inside," I told them.

"Save it," Isza said. "You'll need all your good words for the Council."

We passed the extra guards in the entry hall and entered the sunken auditorium of the Council chamber. Isza left us to sit in the gallery, and Tzek, Rasa and I descended the steps together to the central podium.

Rasa left us to take her bench alone. The other lodge deans and house hierarchs were already there, sitting on their assigned benches or clustered in whispered discussion.

Ha'ik of the Adepts and Hebv, dean of the Merchants Lodge, were standing with Hierarch Akczek and Czel, who turned to watch our descent then turned back to his conversation.

"He's layer upon layer of schemes, that one," Tzek said. "Worse than Dageru if you ask me."

"He's not the only one," I said. "Even if things go our way today, there are many who will need close watching."

Tzek's feeder claws spread wide. "I'll be happy to oblige."

I left him and climbed the two steps up to my bench. Tzek struck the stone floor with his staff and the remaining Council members took their seats. All conversation stilled. But as soon as all was quiet, Akczek stood again to address us.

"Prime Hierarch," he began, then paused, looking round the chamber to make sure he commanded everyone's attention. "I speak for all in this assembly when I say how relieved and grateful we are to see you safe and well. And I personally am glad that the actions House Akczek took to safeguard the institutions of your government were ultimately unnecessary."

And keen to make sure the Akczek version of events makes it into the Council records as quickly as possible, I thought.

"It pains me to see that recent events have left you further diminished," he continued.

I took it he meant the loss of two of my claws. Clearly Akczek had an agenda.

"I, like many here, was shocked at the reports of what occurred. That you had been tricked by a notorious excisee and former advisor to the war criminal Kergis. And that the advisor to the hierarch of the House of Excisees should injure –"

"I'll stop you there," I said, standing.

"But Hierarch," Akczek insisted, still on his hoofs.

"*Prime* Hierarch," I said. "Be seated."

Akczek sat and Czel leaned over and whispered to him.

"I just need to know one thing, Akczek. And they'll know if you are lying." I swept my arm round to indicate the hierarchs and deans. "Did you know Dageru was planning to kill the excisees he'd hidden in his lands?"

Akczek looked at Czel but saw no help there. "No," he said.

"And what about you, Czel?"

Czel sat upright but didn't speak, though the answer was clear to every intact in the room. I looked at Tzek who blinked slowly in the negative.

"Then you may keep your positions," I said, and turned away from Akczek as if he no longer existed.

"I can understand Hierarch Akczek's desire to portray recent events as somehow being caused by excisees," I said to the rest of the hierarchs and deans. "No doubt he would have gone on to explain how my own nature as an excisee made me blind to what was going on around me. I can understand it, even though it sickens me. Some here cautioned me to slow my reforms, saying the Kresz were not ready for another change. What Dageru did – the two-four-four Kresz he slaughtered like feed animals – was an act of evil that belongs in a past that must never be repeated. Change is here. This is a moment of history; like the moment of Emergence when battle suddenly ceased on the Plain of Ak'ra."

"You think you're history?" Czel shouted.

I turned to him. "I am an instrument of history. The people showed they were ready for this change three days ago when they joined me in the market below this place. They are sick of the in-fighting between houses. They are sick of intacts being told to hate excisees. They want peace. The houses and lodges must change too. You've resisted it for too long. Never again will one Kresz harm another just because they are different. The lodges will be open to Kresz of all houses equally. Excisees will be free to rejoin their house or remain under the care of Hierarch Rasa. And any who oppose this will find themselves on the wrong side of history. Like Kergis. Like Dageru."

I sat, and Tzek stood as we'd arranged.

"The reform package debated at our previous session is tabled unchanged," he said. "The vote is called."

"As temporary hierarch of House Czerag," I said, "I support the reforms."

Loyal Tzulak, now Hierarch Haketiug, stood. "Support," he said.

"Ukat supports."

"The House of Excisees supports," Rasa said and she looked at me, feeders stretched wide, as she sat.

The Kergis hierarch stood. "Our house has no vote here, as it should be. But if we did, I would vote to support. To heal the damage House Kergis did to our way of life, for all Kresz but in particular to the excised. The innocents whose forgiveness we do not deserve."

House Dageru had no vote until the hierarch could be found.

That left Akczek for the houses. He got to his hoofs like a Kresz who had run out of choices. "Akczek supports."

The lodges were next.

"The Defenders Lodge supports," Gatiku said.

Ha'ik and Hebv were both keen to put the close ties they'd had with Dageru behind them and each voted to support the reforms.

Djudsu for the Cultivators stood, his long-legged body towering above us all. "Labour is labour," he said. "We support."

"The Scholars support," Tzagze said, which left only Gulatesi, the high priest of Sakat.

He stood and looked round the room. I expected him to rebuke me, all of us, for losing our way. Instead he said, "Perhaps this too is the will of Sakat. Support."

I looked at Tzek. We both knew this was only the beginning. But it *was* a beginning.

I stood again. "I thank the houses and lodges for their support. Now, we have a war to win."

∞

The tactical briefing of the battle fleet was held in a virtual space. There was no way the leaders of the Lenticular species that formed the fleet could meet in person; their ships had approached the Hegemony through many different Voss Space ways and channels.

Hooked into her dolphincraft, Rhees could "see" the network, the disposition of the ships, how the tunnels linked and branched and where they led. She was lurking on the edge of the meeting space while the other leaders phased in. It felt like immersion but also like she had another body in another place, a place that was ill-defined beyond this circle of grey floor illuminated by directionless light.

Adke'ul, the Defender-caste commander of the Kresz flagship, *Will of Sakat*, greeted the commanders of the Telsan, Aphsan, Dray and P-vvarni forces as they arrived. The Kresz contingent of ships was small – they'd been hit hardest during the occupation – but the Lenticular governments had agreed that Adke'ul would command the combined battle group.

The goal was clear: make sure the Hegemony never came back to the Lenticular. The simplest way to achieve that was to wipe out humanity. It was certainly how Earth had dealt with the K-Chaan. Every conflict came down to brute strength: who had the biggest guns and wanted to win the most. The firepower the Lenticular had mustered was impressive, frightening even. But going on the latest intel from Gart, it wouldn't be enough. The addition of Rhees's dolphincraft and the Cygnus group with the Maagba, Sissilak, Brell and Totek ships doubled their strength and made it an even fight with the Hegemony. Problem was, Rhees didn't want species genocide.

"We're just waiting for Tol Imnan," Adke'ul said, then, as Udun stepped into the light, "Prime Hierarch!"

Adke'ul sounded surprised. Rhees was too, but she was happy to see Udun. As Udun said, "I hope you and the other commanders don't object to my joining the meeting," she committed fully, appearing opposite him in the rough ring of commanders that had formed.

Udun didn't miss a beat. "And you all know Rhees."

Tol Imnan of Svesta appeared. "What is *she* doing here?"

Rhees wouldn't be surprised if he'd been lurking like her, waiting for the right moment. "I didn't realise Svestans had such a short memory," she said to him. "You do remember we fought together before?"

"I remember you stopped us killing Humans," Tol Imnan said. "That's not going to work here."

"I asked Rhees to attend the meeting," Udun said.

It was a small lie but Rhees appreciated the backup. It silenced the Svestan for the moment. And since she had everyone's attention

. . .

"It's always been my intention to be with you at the end of this fight," she said. "I fought alongside Udun and the Kresz to help retake Homeworld, and I've fought across the Lenticular against the remains of the Hegemony forces after their defeat. What you don't know is that I'm not the only human that is trying to help you."

Tol Imnan grunted with what to Rhees's ears sounded like derision. But, for the moment, the others were silent.

"That's why you've been able to travel so far without challenge," she continued. "Humans, working inside the Hegemony, have altered the sensor alerts and diverted patrols to give you safe passage. Humans who – like me – don't support the Hegemony's philosophy that aliens are somehow beneath them, to be used or killed without remorse."

"Maybe it's as you say, or maybe the Hegemony fears to attack us," Tol Imnan said.

Rhees dipped into her dolphincraft systems and threw up a tactical view of Sol system above the heads of the commanders. "We hurt them in the Lenticular, but they're still strong, especially here. They've drawn every ship they can back from Hegemony space to protect Earth in case of an attack."

"They *do* fear us then," Tol Imnan said.

"We've got them worried, but that's not going to help. I don't know if you hunt on your world, Tol Imnan, but a beast is at its most dangerous when it's cornered. I know you've deployed ready to transit outside Sol system, move in together and slug it out with the Fleet. But they'll see us coming from light minutes away."

She looked up at the planetary system above them. At this point in their orbits, all the planets were on the same side of the sun.

"The biggest contingent of Hegemony ships is between Earth and Mars," she said, and a pulsing circle appeared where Gart had told her Fleet had deployed. "But there are three other battle groups in-system. One out near Jupiter; one trailing the orbit of Venus; and one on the other side of the sun completely." Three more pulsing circles appeared. "They're ready to deploy to wherever they're needed. A conventional approach will give them time to engage us in the outer system and keep us well away from Earth. That's the planet they have to protect at all costs. But if we can get close enough to Earth quickly enough, they won't be ready for us. That's why I want to use transit points."

"That's madness." This was the Aphsan commander, a mound-shaped being that Rhees found even more alien-looking than Tktkrt. "Any transit points in Hegemony space are controlled by the Hegemony. If we use them, they'll destroy them."

"Yes, and leave whatever ships make it through stranded without an escape route or any chance of backup," Rhees said. "But there are other humans helping us. We start the attack with a conventional incursion out past the edge of the system. There are two Hegemony-controlled transit points in the outer system — one in Jupiter orbit near the Fleet group there, and one below the ecliptic trailing Neptune's orbit." As she spoke, the points appeared above her. "There should be enough time to get small groups through both those points before the Hegemony shuts them down. With three incursions in that volume of space, the Fleet groups at Jupiter and Venus will move out to intercept. Some of the main force near Mars will move out as well to provide support. There's another military transit point above the ecliptic between Mars and the asteroid belt. That's where our main force will come through."

"There won't be time before the Hegemony destroys that point too," the Aphsan said.

"They could if they still control it. But they won't. The humans like me will." As long as Gart could deliver. Otherwise the fight would be over before it had properly started.

"They'll keep the point open," Rhees continued. "My ship group will go through first and we'll create a defensive sphere for the rest of our ships to transit. The group in the outer system will tie up the Fleet forces out there, which leaves us to deal with the Fleet between Earth and Mars."

And at some point, Denev and Gart will do what they're doing, she thought. *If* they can do it. If not ...

"If we can get enough ships through the Fleet and within striking distance of Earth, I'm sure we can force a surrender," she finished.

The Telsan commander spoke up, the feed naming him as

Enklo. "It could work. But we're not deployed to use those transit points. And it will take days to backtrack through Voss Space even if we can find the way through the network."

"You're right," Rhees said. "But I have the Totek from Cygnus Sector with me. And they have a way of creating Voss Space bridges from wherever you are now to where you need to be."

Silence. It looked like she had them thinking about it at least. A surprise attack was always better than a slow, visible advance.

She glanced at Udun. He at least knew what she was going to say next. "But when we do force the Hegemony to surrender, I need you to agree that we won't destroy Earth."

"You don't tell us what to do," Tol Imnan said.

And that was the crux. She could win the war, but how could she stop the killing that came after?

"With all respect to Adke'ul," Udun said, "Rhees is your new battle commander. I've already spoken to your governments and they've agreed."

Tol Imnan rumbled. "The Svestan Concordance w–"

"Have also agreed," Udun interrupted. "We are *not* the Hegemony and we will not kill innocents, or other Humans like Rhees who are trying to help us. If the Hegemony Fleet does not surrender, I am confident Rhees will do everything she can to defeat them. But after that, it will be time to make peace. To break the cycle of revenge."

Rhees was as stunned as everyone else. She knew Udun hadn't done this just for her, but … it was more than she could have hoped for.

"We can't simply forget what the Hegemony have done. To any of us," Enklo said.

"Agreed," Rhees said. "The Hegemony has to be held to account. That includes the leaders, the command structure, everyone who has willingly supported them and helped them achieve so much evil in the galaxy. But that's not all of humanity. It's not even all of the Hegemony Fleet."

"If you fail us," Tol Imnan said, "I will personally kill you."

Reasonable, Rhees thought, but unnecessary. "If I fail, it'll be because I'm dead."

"Does anyone have a better plan?" Udun asked.

When no one spoke, he turned to Rhees. "I'll leave you to finalise details with your commanders." And then he was gone.

Rhees looked at the other aliens. They were all waiting expectantly, even Tol Imnan. She linked to Tktkrt and the Totek appeared beside her.

"Okay, Tktkrt will explain how this is going to work."

38

Denev hadn't seen Hel or Stin for days. They were still off somewhere chasing down their SolSec conspiracy lead. Volmar had likewise been sequestered away, establishing his authority through the SolSec network. So Denev had been left to his own devices – linking to his nook, masking his true activity and watching the approach of the still undetected Lenticular fleet and, coming on a different vector, Rhees's combined Maagba, Brell, Sissilak and Totek group. Denev had no idea how she'd managed it, but if they all survived the next few days he'd demand she tell him every detail.

When it happened, the whole thing was beautifully coordinated: mass ships transiting together at multiple nodes at Jupiter, Neptune and past the heliopause. Even on their own, the ships from the Cygnus group that appeared inside the orbit of Jupiter were formidable. Eight Maagba battleships, two giant Totek transports and six Sissilak battlecruisers, supported by Sissilak and Brell destroyer escorts and gunships and countless singleships: Sissilak Talon fighters, the distinctive Maagba horseshoe ships, and something else, moving like quicksilver, that he'd never seen before.

Now it was time to drop the curtain. He felt rather than saw the signals from Rapskel's group and withdrew, his awareness flicking to become that other Denev in whose shadow he'd been working. Less than two seconds later, the alarms started.

Denev disengaged from the nook and stood on stiff legs to head for the lifts. This level and the levels below were suddenly active: analysts and operatives streaming into the galleries towards opening nooks. He stood aside as one of the elevators opened to disgorge more of his colleagues, who moved quickly to take up their stations. Then he entered Volmar's private elevator car and rode it to the top level.

Volmar was talking to someone on his tablet as Denev arrived. "Just fix it now. Work out the 'how' later."

He pierced Denev with his icy gaze. "Somehow a fleet has just transited at the edge of Sol system, and we've had incursions through the transit points at Jupiter and below Neptune orbit."

"Fuck," Denev said, hoping the word carried the right blend of shock and incredulity. "How?"

"The how doesn't matter for now. We've closed those points down but we have a fight on our hands. I'm going to Panops with Breslaw. That'll be the command centre."

It was vital Volmar didn't take Denev with him. He had other places he needed to be.

"We're leaving now?" he asked.

Volmar looked at him, eyes narrowed and calculating. Finally he looked down and slipped some flimsies into a clear valise. "No. You stay here. There's enough to do on tactical evaluation."

"Of course," Denev said.

Volmar collected his things, strode past Denev and was gone. Denev let out a long sigh, then headed for the basement hypertube.

The station was busy. He waited for the car to empty of HDC personnel called in off-shift for the emergency, then boarded with a smaller group of operatives heading for other destinations. The car sealed and sped into the vacuum tunnel. Far above in a very different vacuum, Rhees and her allies would be starting their attack run. They may even have engaged the Hegemony ships by now.

Denev stood as the hypertube slowed for the first stop. He was the only one disembarking here. Coming out of the station, he saw it was already dawn. He heard a whistle and saw a figure with arm raised standing beside a ground truck in the gloom.

Rapskel greeted him as he approached. "Beautiful morning for a coup."

They climbed in through the truck's side door as the engine hummed to life. Rapskel indicated a bench.

Denev sat opposite a thickset red-haired man with a square jaw and freckles across his broad nose.

"This is Banq. Pol's up front driving," Rapskel said.

Banq nodded but kept quiet.

The truck slowed and stopped. "Checkpoint," Rapskel said. The truck started again. "The shit's hit the fan, and everyone's too freaked out to notice what's going on on the ground."

"And the ship?" Denev asked.

"Requisition went through on the system. Flagged covert. No flight plan required. I imagine there's a lot of that going on right now. Fat cats making for their twenty-year-old K-Chaan bunkers, thanking god they kept them well-stocked and maintained."

"And you checked Rejak's at home?" Denev felt his stomach tighten. There was too much at stake here.

Rapskel cocked his head. "Relax, Operative Antwer. Rejak's at home. Safest place for him since he lives on top of an ancient bunker dug into a fucking limestone mountain."

The truck swerved to a halt and the side door slid open.

"Looks like our ride's fuelled and ready," Rapskel said as he and Banq jumped down to the ground. Banq hefted a heavy kitbag onto each shoulder.

The ship was the same kind Denev had used to escape the Laneaux assassination: a tapered arrowhead, hypersonic and stealth-active.

"You requisitioned *this*?" he said, climbing out of the truck. On the other side of the main hangar, a low rumble announced lift-off for a suborbital.

"*You* requisitioned it according to the records," Rapskel said, a lazy grin spreading over his face. "I figured after today your cover's burned, so …" He shrugged.

Rapskel was right. Ever since Denev had decided to find out

how his parents had really died and what Volmar's involvement was, there'd been no going back.

They were joined by Pol, a short woman with close-cropped brunette hair and a nose that had been broken more than once. The way she stood told Denev she knew how to handle herself in a fight.

Together the group climbed the ramp at the rear of the ship and it closed behind them. The craft could be remote-piloted – which was how Denev had ridden it before – but it also had a pilot's chair at the tapered end. Pol sat in it and fired up the engines. Within seconds they were airborne and accelerating.

Rapskel hunkered over one of the kitbags Banq had dropped on the deck between them. He pulled out two Fleet-issue assault rifles and two tightly compressed shimmer suits, and passed one to Banq. Unlike the suit Denev had used before, these had hard flight shells fused to the spine.

Banq opened the other kitbag and slid out a long, heavy-looking spearhead missile. It was matte black with a flared faring at the back, the smooth casing pierced on either side where turbines sat in the housing.

Denev reached into the bag and pulled out the one piece of equipment he'd requested: a portable nook. Really just an immersion helmet with a hinged visor, but as soon as he sat back on the bulkhead webbing and closed it over his head the synaptic shunt engaged and he was logged into the HDC tactical feed.

Out near Jupiter, fighting had already begun and other ship groups were moving to intercept. But he could see there was conflicting data on enemy ship disposition and movement – Rapskel's people were still doing their thing. Line-of-sight observation trumped everything though, and as both forces engaged and those two datapoints failed to agree, some bright spark would work out what was happening and they'd lose that advantage. Then it was down to Denev, Rapskel and Gart to give Rhees the edge she needed.

He linked with ship sensors briefly. They were flying over the

Arabian Sea, the nearby coastline ablaze with light. Then he keyed the codestring for Gart.

The admiral appeared and it felt like they were in the room together.

"Good to hear from you," Gart said. "We're ready for the party up here. I'm just about to welcome our guests."

"I'll call you when we're there," Denev said. He broke the contact and pushed back the visor. "All set," he said to Rapskel.

Rapskel showed his teeth in a predatory grin. "I'd say a prayer if I believed in god."

∞

The transport landed feather-soft on the Panops hangar deck. Breslaw, Vargas and Volmar – three of the most powerful men in the Hegemony – stepped out and walked quickly towards Gart and Sasha. Another two men emerged from the ship behind. They wore high-end tailored business suits and transparent wraparound visors and looked like senior government functionaries, but Gart knew they were Breslaw's personal bodyguard, no doubt armed and definitely dangerous.

"Gart," Breslaw said. The use of his first name sounded friendly enough but Breslaw's expression was stern and cold, like a cobra considering its next meal. "Everything ready for us?"

"Yes, sir." Gart nodded a greeting to Vargas and Volmar as he led the party into the corridor.

"What's the current situation?" Vargas asked.

"Three incursions," Gart said. "One out-system and two smaller ones through the Jupiter and Neptune transit points."

"What the hell was Anyo doing?" Vargas asked.

Gart knew exactly what Anyo was doing – altering the incursion data – and he had to keep on doing it for as long as possible.

"The ships came out of nowhere," he said. "There and through before anyone could react."

"Sloppy," Volmar said.

"It seems your Maagba allies have turned on us as well," Gart said with no small amount of satisfaction. "And they've brought half of Cygnus Sector with them."

Volmar had no smart response to that.

Gart led them past guards stationed at the open doorway and into tac control – a circular room dominated by a long holo table. Officers sat at immersion stations around the wall. Gart gestured for the others to sit and activated the display. Breslaw's bodyguard took position either side of the door and Sasha stood with them.

The holo spun up a view of Sol system and zoomed in to the space between Jupiter and Neptune orbits.

"Fleet units round Jupiter are engaging, and some of our ships closer in are using the Mars point to hop out as backup," Gart said. "The Venus group's on a hard burn to intercept."

"Not ideal," Vargas said, studying the display. "But containable. It's just a matter of time."

Time. That was in short supply for all of them, Gart thought.

39

"Going subsonic," Pol said.

Rapskel and Banq stood to check the flight shells on each other's suit.

Denev turned off the internal lights and the vessel's floor became transparent. They were flying over a long thin body of water that reflected the moonlight. But then it was lost beneath a bank of clouds that seemed to roll on forever, pierced only by snow-capped ridges and peaks ahead.

"One minute," Rapskel said, strapping an assault rifle across his chest and pulling his flight hood down.

Banq passed Denev and Pol earpieces. As Denev pushed his in place he heard Rapskel say, "Comms check," and gave him a thumbs-up.

Ahead, a long ridge climbed above the cloud with an illuminated roadway. The rear ramp of the craft opened and wind tore at Denev. He grasped the hull webbing.

Rapskel and Banq ran out the opening and were gone. The turbines on the spearhead missile fired up and it shot out into the night after them. The ramp sealed over.

Denev pulled on his immersion hood and linked with Rapskel's heads-up. The sky was a perfect bowl of darkness, the full moon shining like a searchlight and obscuring all but the brightest stars. Rapskel angled his body down and Denev saw a soft blanket of cloud covering everything below fifteen hundred metres. The illuminated road came into view, leading up to a promontory thrusting out above the cloud and the house that stood there. Then the flight shell deployed and Rapskel's descent jerked and slowed.

Denev pulled off the hood. "They're almost down," he said to Pol.

"So are we," she said.

The craft turned gracefully as it descended to a pad at the terminus of the mountain roadway. They landed and the rear ramp opened again. There was snow on the ground.

Denev stood and brushed self-consciously at his HDC uniform.

"Good luck," Pol said.

He nodded to her and stepped onto the snow. There was no doubt their landing had been observed, but he hoped Rejak was distracted by whatever was going on in space.

A path lined by pine trees led to the house, which sat on the rocky promontory over a bright sea of cloud. Denev hurried down it. The house was illuminated, lights showing in the small windows on the back wall. He ran up a short flight of steps to the left and along a stone-arched gallery to the door. It stood open.

He stepped inside the hallway. "Secretary?" he called, but there was no answer.

A quick sweep of the bottom floor confirmed it was empty. There was a half-drunk glass of wine in the sitting room. A fire still burned in the hearth.

He backtracked to the gallery.

"Rejak?" Rapskel's voice in his comm.

"Not here. Probably already gone to the bunker," Denev said.

"We'll be in position."

Denev followed a path down the side of the house; the land fell away steeply to his right. The path opened onto a courtyard at the front of the house. Above him, large picture windows took in the view. Beneath and cut into the rock was a broad tunnel. The arch at the front was dressed in the same stone as the house so it looked old, but the short run of tunnel to the thick alloy door that closed off the entry showed the perfect smoothness of being shaped by modern excavating lasers.

A callscreen was set into the wall. Denev closed the contact and waited. And waited.

Finally the screen cleared. Rejak's face peered out through his antique glasses frames.

"Secretary Rejak," Denev said.

The eyes narrowed. "I know you. You're Volmar's man."

"Yes, sir, Operative Antwer. The comptroller sent me to get you to safety."

"Safety?" Rejak echoed.

The best way to lie is to use a truth. Denev tried to put as much sincerity into his words as possible. "There's a rogue SolSec squad on its way here to kill you. It's blowback for Laneaux's assassination. They've already tried to kill me. If you can let me in, I have a stealth flyer waiting."

The door remained solidly closed.

"I really feel safe enough in here," Rejak said.

"Steady," Rapskel said in Denev's comm.

Denev froze and instantly a hail of fire hit the rock beside him, sweeping down and left. "They're here!" he shouted. "Let me in, Secretary! There's still time."

Rejak looked scared, but still the door didn't open.

More fire peppered the wall.

"I'm sorry, Antwer," Rejak said. "It's not safe out there." The screen went dead.

"Slimy fucker," Rapskel said.

Denev turned to see Rapskel and Banq standing in the courtyard, their hoods pulled back, their shimmer suits deactivated.

"Just as well we brought Plan C," Rapskel said. "Come on."

He and Banq ran back to the side of the house and Denev followed them. He could hear the rising tone of the spearhead missile's turbine. Both men were hunkered down on the path, pressing their backs to the bare rock. Denev joined them. The turbine got louder.

"This isn't going to kill Rejak, is it?"

"I hope not," Rapskel said. "But we've got to get through that door. And it's a tough one. We were limited in the ordnance we could misappropriate and bring to site. Here it comes."

The spearhead missile shrieked and the mountain jumped beneath Denev's feet, night turning into day with a deafening roar. Then silence.

When Denev opened his eyes again, Pol was with them.

"From all the noise you're making, I figured you need these," she said. She handed him a rifle and his immersion hood, which he hung over his shoulder by the strap.

Back in the courtyard, they could see the spearhead had done its work. Beyond the fire-blackened arch of rock, the door had shattered. Tangled metal lay on the corridor inside, and the wood panelling in the entryway was on fire.

"Impressive," Rapskel said. "He should have listened to you."

Pol took point and they jogged past the ruined door and along a tunnel. Beyond the fire the wood panelling was hung with old paintings of men in uniforms that Denev didn't recognise. Ancient history.

Up ahead and to the left a door swung open, spilling light into the passage. Someone fired and Pol returned short bursts. There was a shout. A stocky bald man fell to the floor and the door started to close over.

Denev ran full pelt, Rapskel and the others behind him, and smashed into it, throwing whoever was behind it flying.

More guards inside, bringing weapons to bear, then Rapskel and Banq were firing. The sound was deafening and then it was over.

Rejak stood in the middle of the room, a look of horror on his face. Six guards lay dead around him.

"Sweep for others," Denev said, and Rapskel and Banq moved past him, ignoring Rejak who seemed frozen to the spot.

Pol took the secretary's arm and pushed the business end of

her rifle into his side.

Rejak came out of his daze. "Killing me won't get you anything," he said.

Rapskel and Banq re-entered. "All clear," Banq said.

Denev levelled his rifle at Rejak. "We have something else in mind for you, Secretary."

Rejak's show of defiance slipped into fear again. Let him sweat, Denev thought.

40

Getting here had been hard enough, although Tktkrt's bridge technology had worked beautifully. Getting through and out would be harder. And what lay beyond that …

Thinking was not helping right now. Rhees gave the signal and her flight of dolphincraft moved towards the edge of the Voss Space chamber. She didn't hesitate at the edge. It was either going to work or it wasn't. Her flight streamed into the chamber.

Sitting at the centre like a misshapen metallic spider was the transit station: a heavily weaponed Fleet facility controlling access to Sol system beyond.

Dolphincraft sensors tugged at her consciousness as they registered point cannons on the superstructure gimballing to track her advance. More ships streamed into the space behind her. If the station was going to open fire …

A second passed and nothing. Her father had been true to his word. The door was open.

Rhees flew straight at it, activating her command channel. "Transit. Transit. Transit."

Voss Space shifted around her and then she was in realspace. Mars far below and off to one side, and – coming up to meet her – a wall of Fleet ships.

More of her battle group transited behind her and spread out, forming a defensive shield as she punched for maximum acceleration, her dolphinships leaping at the oncoming enemy.

Fleet weapons fire cut loose as soon as she was in range

and then the rest of her battle group engaged, moving quickly to close-quarter fighting. It was a shitstorm. Rhees's dolphincraft looped wildly, throwing off a pursuing ramcraft in a sky too full of ships. Laser blasts, missile trails and superheated railgun charges crisscrossed in a constantly changing tapestry of light around the blossoming flowers of explosions.

If she'd been limited to conventional feeds and situated on the bridge of a flagship, Rhees would be hard-pressed to understand the shape of the battle from minute to minute, but Nok's gift to her kept giving in surprising ways. She'd allocated a handful of Maagba-piloted dolphincraft drones with each of the attack groups. Somehow she felt a whisper of the contact she had with her own flight of dolphincraft. It was enough.

Adke'ul commanded the battle group that had transited out past the edge of the system; it was engaging with the Fleet hard-burning from Jupiter orbit, which had now split, some turning back to face the smaller Lenticular group that had used the Jupiter transit point before it blew.

The Fleet group trailing Venus had moved off to engage the third transit group below Neptune. Rhees had put Tol Imnan in charge of that. He'd been happy enough and she knew it would keep the Svestans away from the main action, where they could do the least damage. Those Fleet ships couldn't backtrack to help the force near Mars without being harried all the way by Tol Imnan's ships.

It wasn't going well for Rhees's group. Surprise had helped them all safely transit, but the heat of battle was too frantic to allow any cohesive action after that. Individual ships and small groups engaged with whatever enemy was closest. They desperately needed to push through to threaten Earth. But Fleet wasn't giving an inch.

Three elegantly knife-shaped Sissilak battlecruisers linked somehow, and coruscating bands of plasma formed a triangle of energy between their tips that shot out, raking an incoming Fleet light destroyer and shearing off the port weapons stack.

Rhees lost sight of them as she expanded into her dolphincraft flight – or they filled her with multiple viewpoints. Some of her craft swooped in to pace a Totek militia gunship, providing covering fire as it accelerated towards and through a pack of Storm Class gunboats amid a swarm of Typhoon ramcraft. Then her flight took multiple vectors, climbing, dropping and dodging inertialessly as their nose cannons fired, sending ramcraft in all directions. The Totek ship erupted in a brief fireball and she broke off. There was nothing she could do and others needed her help.

"Incoming three-twenty-eight, dec four," she said on the general band.

Three Sector Class battlecruisers were moving in to join the Fleet force. Massive hammerheads built for the sole purpose of carrying as much firepower as possible. The other Fleet ships deployed to make room for the newcomers.

All three battlecruisers carried insanely powerful railguns and these fired in tandem, catching a Telsan Congress gunboat as it turned side-on, shredding its tiered superstructure like tissue before it erupted in flame.

The battle seemed to pause for an in-breath. Then the sky burned bright with weapons as opposing ships re-engaged with increased frenzy.

The battleships used their heavy armaments to blast at whatever Lenticular ships strayed too close, but their firing patterns were dictated by the host of other Fleet ships in the way. Rhees relayed that intel to her group and the close-quarters fighting gained an added level of complexity, with captains keeping one eye on the relative position of the battlecruisers. But just one slip and singleships, corvettes or even destroyers were vapourised by the concentrated firepower of those behemoths. She had to stop them.

She signalled the Maagba-piloted dolphincraft to continue defensive cover of the Lenticular group – the ships dodged so fast that even the battleships' weapons couldn't follow them – and collected her flight. They accelerated up and out of the mayhem of battle, arced briefly above in a deceptively quiet part of space, then dropped and burned hard down on top of the battleships. She couldn't hope to destroy their heavily armoured engines – that would be like hitting an armoured ground car with a hammer – but she could target sensors and weapons, especially the massive railgun tracks.

She split her flight into four. Three groups took runs at the exposed rails of each ship where they emerged from the heavy shielding, while the fourth kept watch for whatever support came. It didn't take long for four Storm Class gunboats – basically big fucking cannons with wings – to emerge from the main melee, burning hard towards the battleships.

Rhees kept up the runs on the battleships, and peeled off her fourth group to engage the gunboats, corkscrewing towards them in a manoeuvre that would have torn apart a ramcraft. Nose cannon fired as clouds of pinhead missiles deployed, homing in on the gunboats and targeting engines. There was a flare from each gunboat's drive and they started to drift. At the same moment she slagged the last railgun track.

The battlecruisers were down to lasers and missiles – still a lot of firepower. Then more ramcraft vectored in and she had to break off.

Each dolphincraft turned and turned at maximum acceleration in a way the ramcraft couldn't hope to follow, then targeted the small ships' engines, leaving them dead in space, just like Rhees had done around Homeworld and countless sorties after that.

But other ships and pilots were dying – on both sides. It was too much killing. She had to stop it. But she couldn't. No power on Earth could. She needed a miracle.

41

They may have been inside a mountain, but Rejak's sitting room was comfortably furnished with everything a senior government official could need during an enforced isolation. Only the dead guards on the thick carpet spoiled the ambience.

Denev took Rejak by the upper arm and led him through an archway into a much larger room with one long wall dedicated to a full comms bank with terrestrial and Voss Space transmission capacity. In one corner stood an immersion chair, but without the full faring that enclosed the user in the Datahive models. That was good. It saved Denev the bother of removing it.

He pushed Rejak forward. "Take a seat, Secretary. Make yourself comfortable."

Rejak half-turned, his eyes full of fear. "Whatever you're doing it won't work. You'll all be arrested and killed."

"No one's coming to save you, Rejak," Rapskel said, placing his rifle against Rejak's head. The older man flinched at the touch of cold metal. "We jammed your alarms, and your friends are a little busy fighting a fucking alien invasion. You're going to help us or I kill you right here."

Denev knew Rapskel wouldn't. He couldn't. But his words had the desired effect. Rejak sat in the immersion chair.

Denev kneeled beside him and activated the chair. Then he unslung the immersion helmet from his shoulder and placed it over his head.

"Wish me luck," he said to Rapskel.

"Luck."

Denev pulled the visor down and slaved Rejak's chair to his control, entering the codestring Gart had given him as the synaptic shunt engaged. He could feel Rejak in the dataspace beside him, riding along like a silent co-pilot.

The codestring was accepted, which meant Gart would receive the signal that Denev was online.

There was the flash of connections and handshakes, then he was looking down at the main tactical control for Panops. Fleet officers sat immersed at stations around the curved bulkhead, linked to comms and sensor feeds, and at the tactical table in the centre sat Gart Lowrans, Antonus Breslaw, Ten Vargas and Troels Volmar. They were staring intently at a holo display of Sol system with battle lines and floating coloured points scattered across it.

∞

"The Mars transit point is *still* open," Volmar said. "If we can't blow it remotely, can't one of the cruisers be tasked to take it down?"

"Impossible to get within firing distance," Vargas snapped, so consumed by the holo battle that he didn't spare Volmar a glance.

"Then why didn't your Fleet detect them sooner?" Volmar bit back.

"Gentlemen," Breslaw said calmly, "there will be a full accounting at the proper time. But right now …"

Gart's band buzzed once. Denev was ready.

He tapped his band. In his peripheral vision, Sasha pulled her flechette pistol, pressed it against the neck of the closest bodyguard and fired. The man went down.

His colleague pulled a small blaster and swung it up in an arc towards Sasha, before his arms flung wide. On the other side of the room, one of the officers stood beside his immersion station, a newly fired strafer in his grip.

Vargas twisted in his seat as the second guard fell lifeless to the deck. He glared at Gart then saw the stinger in his hand. "What in hell, Gart!"

The Fleet guards outside the room entered and sealed the doors behind them. They levelled their strafers at the holo table.

"Everybody remain seated, please," Gart said, pointing his pistol at Vargas, Breslaw and Volmar in turn. "No sudden moves."

Sasha took up position behind Volmar, pistol in hand. Two more officers disengaged from their immersion stations and hurried to stand behind Breslaw and Vargas.

Vargas half-stood and the officer behind him drew back ready to fire, but halted as Breslaw raised a hand.

"Sit down, Ten," Breslaw said.

Gart could see the permanent head of the Central Administration was neither shocked nor afraid. He looked like a man who knew he could control any situation.

"Check, I think," Breslaw said, turning in his chair to face Gart. "We're in the middle of a war. Are you leveraging that fact for a promotion, Gart?" He turned back to Vargas. "Ten, would you step aside for Gart as chair of the joint chiefs?"

"I would have in time," Vargas said. "Not now."

"Come, Ten, we can't begrudge him his ambition," Breslaw said. "You could go much further in civilian life, Gart. But your advantage is transitory at best. It's check, but it's not checkmate. Harm us and you won't leave this station alive."

Gart pursed his lips in disgust. "It's always the same with your kind. Everything has a price. But I'm not playing fucking games."

He activated a table control and the holoprojectors wiped the image of Sol system, instead projecting an image of Denev seated between himself and Vargas.

"Antwer," Volmar said. For once he looked shocked. "What in hell are you doing?"

"Finding out the truth," Denev said. "Something happened on my father's last mission. A ceasefire had been brokered with the K-Chaan and he travelled to Talos III to open negotiations. But the truce broke down almost immediately."

"What are you talking about?" Volmar sounded exasperated.

"You were there."

"I –"

"You were listed on the manifest of the Earthforce Heavy Carrier *Lincoln*."

"Antwer, stop this nonsense," Volmar said.

"And there's a record of what happened on the planet."

Volmar was suddenly silent and Gart saw a look pass between him and Breslaw.

"Don't insult me by denying it," Denev said.

When Volmar spoke again there was a coldness in his tone. "That file can't be opened."

"Not unless I know the exact file name and location, and you, Breslaw, Vargas and Secretary Rejak are linked into the system together," Denev said.

No one spoke.

The transmission widened to show Rejak beside Denev in immersion. "I'm with Rejak now."

Volmar twisted in his seat, grabbed at Sasha's arm and pointed her gun at Vargas. She punched Volmar in the face with her other fist, but the pistol fired, flechettes raking across Vargas's shoulder. Volmar fell to the floor and Sasha grabbed him by his uniform and hauled him to his feet again.

Vargas clutched his shoulder, his face twisted in pain. Blood was soaking through his jacket, but Gart could see the wound wasn't life-threatening. But if Volmar had been able to kill him, Denev's file would remain locked.

"We're going to link you all into the system and see what that file tells us," Denev said. Then he looked directly at the comptroller. "Rhees Lowrans says hello."

Volmar's eyes widened and he glanced at Gart.

"Aye," Gart said. "She's out there now. And she's the reason you're all fucked."

There was a sudden banging at the control room door.

"I think we'd better get a move on." Gart nodded to his officers and they dragged Volmar, Breslaw and a stooped Vargas to the waiting immersion stations.

"Initiating the key sequence now," Denev said.

Gart focused on Denev's image. "This better be what you think it is."

The contact broke and Gart sat at the table again and activated the tactical feed. Fleet was still fully engaged in the battle with Rhees's aliens.

"Sasha, see that my ship's ready for immediate launch," he said. Whatever happened in the next few minutes, he was going out to find his daughter.

Check, but not checkmate Breslaw had said. He'd read the situation wrong. This was the endgame.

42

Rhees could see the rhythm of the battle was changing. Ships attacked each other viciously, heedless of the broken hulls and other debris spinning between them. A Sissilak battlecruiser listed dangerously, atmosphere and flame streaming from a long tear in its side as its support Talon fighters raked the attacking Hurricane Class corvette with laser fire. Below her a flight of Maagba dolphincraft brought nose cannon to bear on a Planet Class destroyer, strafing the bridge section at the rear and heedless of the retaliatory missiles that destroyed half their number. She could feel the dolphin drones dying. More than three hundred now.

She'd briefed the Maagba and the other Cygnus Sector ships under her direct command to target weapons and drives and leave crews alive – just like she'd done countless times in the Lenticular – but the fighting was so fierce now, all pretence at minimising casualties was gone. She couldn't blame them. They were fighting for their lives and she'd killed … she didn't know how many since the battle began. It wasn't her fault. She knew that. But it was senseless, brutal – death and destruction for its own sake. Much longer and everyone would be caught in some fucked-up blood lust that wouldn't be satisfied until the last ship was blown apart.

The dolphincraft prodded at her mind. She brushed the intrusion away and leaped her flight forward through an expanding ball of plasma that had been a corvette, and vectored down to take on a group of ramcraft harrying a Totek gunship. But her dolphincraft kept at her – a distracting pull in her consciousness.

She pulled her flight up, snarling, "What!"

The comms window opened and she saw a face, struggled for a moment to recognise it, to remember something other than flying and killing. Denev!

"It's time," he said. "Gart's going to pull back Fleet. Or try to anyway. You have to break off. Incoming broadband transmission. I've flashviewed it. It should help."

Rhees's heart leaped as she opened her command channel to the battle group. "All ships break off! Repeat, break off now! Withdraw!"

Ships still fired indiscriminately at each other as if her transmission had failed. But then she saw it – a lessening as attackers veered away, trying to find some navigation solution that would take them safely through the field of dead ships. Rhees felt dazed at the sudden change. Was sure others must too.

And then the Fleet broadcast was incoming and her father was speaking. He looked dishevelled, and there was a spatter of blood on his face.

"To all Fleet ships. This is Admiral Gart Lowrans. Admiral Vargas has been stood down on my orders. The permanent head of the Central Administration and his conspirators have been arrested for their part in a traitorous act that killed countless Fleet personnel and civilians in a needless war. The evidence is before you now."

The scene changed to a video image with the ident of the Earthforce Heavy Carrier *Lincoln* and timestamped … It was twenty years old, Rhees realised. Location read *Talos III*.

The feed showed the inside of a pavilion of some sort; a red-soiled barren plateau was visible between the structure's supporting columns. The image was frozen, but she could see people. Three humans. A man, a woman and … Volmar. Much younger, but easily recognisable. And at the other side of the pavilion, the unmistakable shapes of three K-Chaan.

Words scanned over the bottom of the image: *Ceasefire Negotiations – Earth K-Chaan War*. Rhees was looking at history.

The K-Chaan had called a ceasefire at Talos III, then attacked the Earthforce ships there when their defences were down. It was the most infamous event in a war full of infamous events.

The image leaped into motion. Volmar looked at the other man, then pulled something from his jacket. Something metal that flowed and morphed into the unmistakable shape of a weapon. He fired at one of the K-Chaan. The alien fell dead and all hell broke loose. The two remaining K-Chaan fired and the other man – Denev's father, Rhees realised – disintegrated, what was left of his body crashing into Volmar so both fell to the ground.

Volmar rolled free of the corpse, looked once at Denev's mother cowering now beneath the table, and ran.

We could have had peace, Rhees thought. How many tens of thousands died when the truce was broken? And in the battles since then?

Volmar had forced the resumption of a war that Earth had almost lost, then formed a replacement government with Vargas and Breslaw that turned the tide but led to the complete annihilation of the K-Chaan, and all the death and suffering that flowed from that. Those three men were the heroes of what had become the Hegemony. And it was founded on a lie.

Her father was speaking again. "All Fleet ships are to disengage and stand down. I'm declaring martial law. Any ship that does not comply with the stand-down order will be fired upon."

Seconds ticked by and no ship fired. Whether because of the broadcast or simple exhaustion, it seemed Fleet no longer wanted to fight. That was fine by Rhees.

"Stand down," she said over the comms to her battle group. "It's over."

We've won, she thought. We've all won.

Spacetime shuddered. The dolphincraft's sensors blanked out and she felt a jolt as the inertial dampers were almost overwhelmed.

Visual sensors cleared and she tried to make sense of what she saw.

Her craft had been thrown back on the periphery of the intrusion. Other ships were tumbling away on all sides, and the three Fleet battlecruisers were gone, vapourised instantly along with whatever else had been there when their atoms were displaced by the arrival.

Calling it a ship conveyed nothing. It was bigger than any craft Rhees had ever seen. Kilometres long, ridged, organic-looking with ripples passing along its length. It glistened wetly. Like a sea cucumber maybe, if the tumbling ships and debris around it were no bigger than microbes.

Comms came back online, garbled, searching for signal. A Fleet band, filled with static, words drifting in and out, then steadying for a moment. One word clear: "Hanloi".

The Hanloi were here. The Hegemony had attacked them out past Lenticular space. And now they were returning the favour.

∞

Denev pulled off his immersion helmet, shocked at the sudden arrival of the Hanloi. He'd seen what one of those ships could do out near galactic centre.

"What's happening?" Rapskel asked.

Denev shook his head, trying to reintegrate into his physical reality. "It was working but ..."

"But?" Rapskel's voice was loud, insistent.

"New player on the field," Denev said. "Nothing we can do from here. It's down to Gart and Rhees to handle it."

Christ, he hoped they could. They'd been so close to ending this, he'd started to think they'd all come out of it alive.

Rapskel sighed. "What do we do about this motherfucker?"

Rejak was still seated in the nook, looking up at them like a cornered rat.

"Bundle him up, fly him back with us," Denev said. "Assuming we're not all obliterated in the next ten minutes, there'll be war crime trials. Justice seen to be done and all that."

"Assuming we survive," Rapskel echoed.

"Wait," Rejak said, "I can testify. There's things I know about Breslaw. All of them." His eyes darted between Denev and Rejak, pleading.

"Nah," Rapskel said. He shouldered his rifle and fired a short burst.

∞

"Fuck!" Gart stared at the new arrival in the holo display. It was massive.

The sudden appearance had scattered ships and changed the topography of the battlefield. Alert flags blossomed against Fleet ships. Three battlecruisers were just gone. Rhees's attack group had been hit badly too. He had no way of knowing if she was still alive.

Instinct took over. "Open a channel to all remaining Fleet ships," he ordered.

"Open," Sasha said. Her eyes were wide, frightened.

"This is Admiral Lowrans. Target the Hanloi ship. Hit it with everything you've got."

43

Rhees's sensor feed dimmed automatically as coruscating beams of energy lanced out from the rippling body of the Hanloi behemoth, carving through Fleet ships, Lenticular ships and debris alike. On the periphery of the displacement, those craft that were still functional turned, forgetting they lay alongside enemy vehicles they'd been frantically battling only a few minutes before, and accelerated towards the Hanloi.

A Totek Militia gunship flew alongside two Fleet Hurricane Class corvettes – one with a mangled stump where its port weapons nacelle should have hung – and opened fire on the Hanloi ship. It ignored them, carrying on the work of blasting everything nearby to fine powder, impervious to the mass laser and missile fire its attackers brought to bear. Then it seemed to register the approach and a single one of its beams licked out and the three ships were gone.

The dolphincraft fed Rhees tactical data. A lot of her battle force were so badly damaged by the fight or the sudden transit blast they were no use. The Fleet ships were in a similar state, and anything that could still move and fire couldn't hope to stand against the Hanloi's energy blast. But her dolphincraft had avoided the worst damage from the shockwave. She was down to twenty-eight in her own flight, and the Maagba-piloted drones … she still had contact with six hundred and thirty-two scattered across local space, not counting the few with the other two battle groups. Fighting out by Jupiter and closer in had stopped, but both forces were too far away to help.

Sensors showed Vatch's heavy cruiser somewhere on the other side of the Hanloi ship. Could she do this? Pile death on death? But if they couldn't stop the Hanloi here, their next target would be Earth.

She opened a channel and the Maagba war leader appeared in the window.

"Vatch," Rhees said, "you want the biggest fight of your life? This is it. If we destroy the Hanloi ship –"

"You have a plan, battle leader?" Vatch interrupted, leaning closer and baring his teeth.

She had to give it to the Maagba – they were true to their word. Bloodthirsty and borderline insane, but that's what she needed.

"Order all your pilots in the dolphincraft to burn hard for the Hanloi ship. Collision course."

Vatch didn't even hesitate. "It will be their honour."

Suicide mission isn't a problem when death is meaningless, Rhees thought.

"The order is given," Vatch said, and the window closed.

All across the battlefield Rhees saw dolphin drones moving – tiny and insubstantial among the debris, and certainly against the massive length of the Hanloi invader.

She sent the rest of her own flight with them. The sleek craft surged forward like captured lightning. Six hundred and fifty-nine ships dancing through the debris, dodging energy lances. Six hundred and fifty-nine ships firing at the Hanloi behemoth as they screamed towards it: nose cannon, missiles, energy beams like neon fans. Closing. Closing.

She felt small deaths as individual drones or craft in her own flight dodged too slow, vapourised in the furnace of energy being thrown out by the Hanloi.

Close now. Now.

She gave the order: *Self-destruct.*

For the second time, sensors were overwhelmed. Visual feeds

blanked out. Her ship was caught in the blast, spinning wildly, the inertial dampers overwhelmed.

Rhees felt her consciousness bleed away.

∞

Somehow she was still aware. Was this what death felt like?

… alive …

Everything hurt. Rhees didn't even want to open her eyes. But she heard the voice again. And this time it spoke her name.

… hear me … Rhees …

She was still in her dolphincraft, but lying on her side in darkness. Her eyes couldn't focus. The interface was down and she felt the barest of touches on her consciousness from her ship. Then it was gone. Pinpricks of light punctured the darkness, growing and joining as her craft disintegrated. Returned to its original form.

She was lying in a drift of diamond pebbles. But there was a larger room around her. A hangar? She could feel the vibration of engines through the floor.

Strong arms picked her up. The tiny rocks fell from her as she was held close and carried. She could barely make out shapes but she smelled a scent that carried a long ago memory.

"Dad?"

"I've got you," Gart Lowrans said.

A door hissed and then she was lowered to a chair, lying back as the form arranged to support her. She blinked again and detail jumped into focus. Gart was kneeling beside her, still holding her hand.

"I didn't think we were going to find you in time," he said.

"The Hanloi —"

"Gone. Your other ships destroyed it."

All the Maagba pilots, so willing to die. Vatch would be proud.

"The Hanloi are gone, the fighting's stopped, and," Gart flashed a quick smile, "you're looking at the new commander of the Combined Hegemony Defence Force. Self-appointed and temporary of course, until we get a provisional government sorted."

Rhees felt like she was in a dream. That none of this had happened – Petar dying, Volmar and Denev, the fight with the Maagba. Or maybe it *had* all happened and she was still in her crippled dolphincraft, waiting for life support to run down.

Gart squeezed her hand. That felt real, at least. It felt good.

"Hey," he said, and she could see the concern in his eyes.

"We did it," she said. It felt like a question.

"*You* did it," Gart said. "Come on. Let's get you home."

44

The formal garden spread out in concentric circles dotted with private memorials to the dead. Far off and over the top of the surrounding fir forest, the gently sloping Cairngorm range sat beneath a blue sky. This was the crash site of the only K-Chaan warship to breach orbital defences during the Battle for Earth. The deep scar it had ploughed into the soil was long covered over, but the ship's hull was still here. It had been refashioned into a tall obelisk-like structure that towered above the manicured lawns. Two words were etched into the metal: *Never forget.*

Denev had visited here only once before. He'd been five or six, and Petar was still a baby. The war was over and their parents' bodies had been reclaimed from Talos III and interred in a place of honour close to the memorial. His five-year-old self couldn't understand the connection between the parents he remembered holding him close who were now gone and the gleaming black headstone.

He hunkered down to read the inscription.

Here lie Varic Antwer and Ellan Summers.

Heroes of Earth.

Never forget.

Beside the stone, a holo scrolled their story. Sent to Talos III to parlay a ceasefire. Betrayed and murdered by the K-Chaan.

It was a lie. All of it. All of this. Even the K-Chaan had been victims of the Hegemony, of a handful of men who wanted nothing but power.

Knowing the truth should help, shouldn't it?

His band vibrated and he stood. A rising wind pushed against him, bringing a chill of snow off the mountains.

Rhees would be landing soon. Another survivor like him. He knew she felt guilty about the things she'd done, and about Petar's death. He felt guilty too. But they'd both been given a second chance.

Denev was determined not to waste it.

Epilogue

"Don't stare at the aliens," I told Isza.

"I'm not staring, I'm observing," she said. "I've never seen so many species in the one place."

I hadn't either, though the alien enclave on Mars came close. I wondered briefly if Ephes Dreh, the alien who had betrayed Atalna and me, was still there.

The pale sun of this world shone in a clear and empty sky. But I knew countless ships occupied the space above us: the remains of the Hegemony Fleet and the Lenticular and Cygnus forces, and more that had come after the battle – from every system in what had once been the Hegemony, and from those Lenticular worlds that had not been directly involved in the war. Their representatives filled the broad plaza before us. As Isza said: lots of aliens.

Beside us at the podium stood Rhees's father, Gart Lowrans, who I had only just met. He was speaking of the war crimes tribunals and reparations commissions that had brought us all to Earth. There would be more significant meetings and assemblies in days to come, but on this first day it was important to speak the simple truth of the destruction and anguish the Hegemony had caused and how things must be different from here onward.

There were others I knew sitting in the crowd. The Telsan Lintal, the Kresz battle leader Adke'ul, even the Svestan Tol Imnan, his spine-covered body ensuring those seated around him kept their distance. And near the front was Rhees, sitting beside her friend Denev and holding his hand in her lap. We owed both of them so much.

Gart Lowrans finished his speech to polite cheers, and I grasped Isza's claws and pulled her with me off the dais. We pushed our way through the suddenly milling crowd until we were within reach of Rhees.

Isza bent forward and gathered her up in her arms.

"Easy," Rhees said, grunting a little as Isza lowered her to the ground again.

I thrust out my claws in a human gesture to Denev and we "shook". I wasn't sure what to say to them. There was no easy way to acknowledge what we had done together. That we were all alive seemed like a miracle.

It was Rhees who broke the silence. "Who's looking after Homeworld with the two of you here?"

"Rasa," I said. "With Tzek's help."

"House of Excised in charge," Rhees said. "Things have changed for the better."

"Here too, it seems," I said.

"Early days," Denev said.

"Hey, Volmar's stuck in a cell not far from here. We could go visit. You could rough him up a little if you like," Rhees said, her teeth bared in a human smile.

"I'd enjoy that," Isza said.

"Beyond the trial he'll face for his crimes, I'd rather not waste any more time on him," I said. "There's more important work to do."

"And there's still the Hanloi out there," Rhees said.

"Yes. I've been thinking about them," I said. "Don't you think they appeared at a very convenient time?"

"Pretty *in*convenient," Rhees said. "We'd only just stopped fighting."

"And then our attack force and the Hegemony Fleet had to immediately band together to fight a new threat. It demonstrated how effective we could be as allies."

"You think the Hanloi *meant* to do that?"

"Perhaps someone did. Someone who could influence the actions of an ancient civilisation at the centre of the galaxy."

Rhees folded her arms, considering. "Nok?"

"I have no proof either way, but it's a comforting possibility. That he's still out there somewhere, in some form. That a part of what he is now still cares about what happens."

"Another test then," Rhees said. "Do we really need another threat to keep our new coalition together?"

It was a good question. Rhees and I had been chosen by Nok because we were different. We'd both rebelled against what was considered normal. For personal reasons, we'd been agents of change in our respective societies. But we'd gone beyond that role when we agreed to make each other's cause our own. That was what had finally brought us all together. That was what had made today possible.

"We can fight the Hanloi," I said, "or we can choose a new path. There are so many species in this new coalition, so many perspectives and ways of thinking, there must be at least one who can suggest a different approach. One that might work to open a dialogue with the Hanloi."

Rhees laid a hand on my lower elbow. "We're stronger together."

"The Hegemony is finished," I said. "What do we call this new thing we have created?"

Rhees looked at Denev and Isza, then back at me. "I don't know. Maybe something like … Alliance of Worlds?"

"That sounds good," I agreed.

We turned and regarded the crowd together. All different species, joined here in a desire for peace. The Alliance of Worlds.

I wasn't naive enough to believe there wouldn't be difficulties between us – or between the houses and lodges at home. But if we could truly find a common understanding, surely there was no limit to the wonders we could accomplish together.

Glossary

Adjubon	Capital city of the main landmass on the planet **Herakli**.
ah'lok	Kresz small, feathered reptilian flying creature.
Ah'lokna (season)	Kresz season when the ah'lok swarm and mate in the desert reaches. Weather is dry and hot.
Aktiuk	Chief city of the Kresz Homeworld. The Treaty City where the houses made peace after the **Emergence**.
Aphsan	Lenticular sentient species, resembling cone shape mounds with a thick brow ridge of sensory tissue. Close trade partners of the Telsans.
ataz	Largest of the Kresz Homeworld's three suns; golden yellow in colour.
at'heka rod	Kresz ceremonial stick adorned with long braids and bleached and dyed ah'lok feathers, used to initiate peaceful parlay between rival houses pre-Emergence.
auto	Hegemony term for automobile or small, personal ground vehicle.
Battle for Earth	A pivotal moment in the Earth–K-Chaan war, when the enemy penetrated the Solar System and almost invaded Earth before being driven back.
Betlaan	A peaceful planet and home to **Atalna**. Due to political infiltration by the Hegemony, the rightful government was overthrown and replaced with a puppet government controlled by HDC.

Brell	Cygnus Sector alien species from the Brell Conglomerate. Bipedal but horse-like. Tall, covered in fine brown hair, long-necked and long-headed with long ears. Their home planet is **Brell Prime**.
Central Administration (CA)	The executive governmental body of the Hegemony.
communion	A full empathic sharing between Kresz.
compensator	Hegemony ship device that assesses the stability of a Voss Space chamber in three-dimensional space and selects an exit point out of Voss Space.
Cygnus Sector	A region of space that was annexed and settled by the Hegemony shortly after the defeat of the K-Chaan. Home to the **Brell**, **Sissilak** and **Totek**.
czidak	Kresz curse word, literally 'withered limb'.
czid-ga	Kresz traditional weapon: tapered lance with hooked end to pull at enemy, and sharp outer edge to slash between armour plates.
Cz'kras Park	An area of Aktiuk set aside for Kresz house funeral ceremonies.
Datahive	HDC headquarters and main surveillance and analysis facility, situated on Earth in Cape York Conurb.
datanook/nook	Immersive data conduit for HDC operatives. It connects directly with the operative's mind, establishing a **synapse link** that enables them to interface directly with the data architecture in cyberspace. The nook imposes a **neural brake** on the user during interface with the datastream to still any involuntary muscle movement while connected.
dean	Title for the head of a Kresz lodge.
Defence Force	The combined Kresz defence fleet, comprising all ships owned by Kresz houses and lodges and controlled by the Defenders Lodge when required.
djel	Second in size of the Kresz Homeworld's three suns; red in colour.
Dray	Lenticular sentient species.
Elysem	A domed city on **Telsus IV**.
Emergence	The moment in history when the empathic link manifested between all Kresz.

endar	A type of tree on the Kresz Homeworld with blue foliage.
Endikar	A **Brell** colony in Cygnus Sector.
Fvel	Lenticular sentient species.
gaszti	Kresz traditional weapon – a long knife, carried in a sheath.
ha'ga	Kresz traditional weapon: long club with heavy weights at end, used for smashing through shell.
Hanloi	An alien species that inhabits galactic centre. A Hegemony mission to Hanloi space was lost, presumed destroyed.
Herakli	Hegemony-settled planet in Cygnus Sector.
Hierarch	Title for the head of a Kresz house.
House Akczek (Kresz)	House colour: white; house lands: the northern reaches of the planet. The Akczek hierarch controls lands with an abundance of gem stones and precious metals; consequently they have much to do with the Merchants Lodge and strong ties with the military.
House Czerag (Kresz)	House colour: brown; house lands: the escarpment and the deep desert. The Czerag are traditionally nomadic, producing much of what they need in hidden areas of the desert. Their main trade item is tekla, an ore which they mine and refine. It has good properties for spaceship hulls particularly for Voss Space craft.
House Dageru (Kresz)	House colour: red; house lands: the southern reaches. The Dageru lands occupy the southern pole and extend around a major proportion of the far southern landmass. Dageru lands produce textiles and electronics.
House Haketiug (Kresz)	House colour: yellow; house lands: plainlands to the east of the Inland Sea. The Haketiug are traditionally agriculturists.
House Kergis (Kresz)	House colour: green; house lands: the equatorial belt of tropical rainforests. The Kergis hierarch holds the title of Protector and commands the combined Kresz armies and fleets in war.

House Ukat (Kresz)	House colour: blue; house lands: the Inland Sea and the southern shores. The Ukat hierarch oversees cultivation and harvest of the Inland Sea.
Jantri-va	Lenticular sentient species. From a highly radioactive planet. Always wear radiation armour when interacting with other species.
Kalead Mountains	A range of mountains in the southern hemisphere of the Kresz Homeworld that mark the beginning of **House Dageru** lands.
Kareee (season)	Kresz season of rains. The drought breaks and, particularly over the Inland Sea coastal regions, there is heavy rainfall. Temperatures begin to fall. Planting begins for the growing season.
Kedisz Ocean	Kresz Homeworld's southern ocean.
K-Chaan Empire	Aggressive alien species in the Earth–K-Chaan war.
Kresz caste: Adept	Professional disciplines such as scientists, lawyers, technicians, pilots etc.
Kresz caste: Cultivator	Agents of agriculture and fishing. Cultivators have elongated limbs and are taller than most Kresz, except for female Defenders.
Kresz caste: Defender	Defenders are the tallest of males, despite lacking a second knee joint and mid-calf. Their armour plating is thicker and they have an oversized arm – usually the left – which ends in a massive pincer. Prior to the **Emergence**, Defenders were a warrior caste who fought for their house hierarch.
Kresz caste: Merchant	Agents of manufacturing and commerce.
Kresz caste: Priest	The priests are devoted to maintaining the teachings of the Kresz god, **Sakat**.
Kresz caste: Scholar	Academics, researchers and scientists, Their claws are thin and delicate and their feeder claws are similarly longer, used for manipulating delicate instruments as much as for eating.
luk'ah	Kresz fish and a valuable food source. Also the name of a Kresz-style singleship similar to a ramcraft.

Luk'ah (season)	Named after the indigenous luk'ah fish which is the primary food source from the Inland Sea. Luk'ah is the period when these fish are harvested. The cooler weather is coming to an end. Temperatures are rising as the rain ceases to fall.
luk'ri	Larval stage of the luk'ah fish.
Luk'ri (season)	Named for the larval stage of the luk'ah fish which develops along the shores of the Inland Sea at this time. The weather is hot but changeable and thunderstorms predominate.
Mentari	Lenticular sentient species.
neural brake	See **Datanook**.
Oclath	Lenticular sentient species.
Ophids	Lenticular sentient species whose technology is far behind most others.
Plain of Ak'ra	Occupying territory between the Inland Sea and **House Czerag** lands, the Plain was the site of the last great House War.
podule	A standard-sized cargo unit used across the Lenticular.
processor	Kresz computer.
Prox Base	HDC intelligence gathering post, second only to the **Datahive** in importance.
raktaa	Maagba term for agreement by blood sacrifice.
realspace	Kresz term for space, as opposed to **tenspace**.
Resiut River	Kresz river running from southern shore of Inland Sea, between the marshlands and House Haketiug arable lands to the west.
rikla	An edible Kresz fern, the heart is considered a delicacy.
Rikla (season)	The season of drought. Harvest occurs during the first few weeks before the heat and lack of rain take their toll. The season is named for the rikla fern which withers at this time.
rusz	Kresz blood analogue. Thick and yellow.
Sakat	The Kresz 'god of death'. Also the name of the season at the end of the Kresz year associated with rebirth.
Sakat (season)	The season of rebirth. Crops benefit from cool days and mild nights and regular rainfall.

setzla	Kresz animal. A predator, the size of a large dog. Known for its cunning.
shield metal	A dense bluish metal that blocks Kresz empathic signals when of sufficient thickness. It is used to line the offices of house hierarchs and lodge deans and other sensitive facilities.
Sissilak	Cygnus Sector alien species. A reptilian analogue, resembling human-size snakes but with four arms. The scales that cover their bodies are thick like an armadillo's plate armour.
skystalk	A space tether and orbital elevator between the Kresz Homeworld city of **Aktiuk** and the **Hub**.
SolSec	Sol System Security: an arm of the Hegemony's Central Administration.
stek-la	A pre-Emergence Kresz dialect word meaning 'a person or group that is close to the middle'.
stinger	Fleet standard-issue flechette pistol.
stonewood	A type of tree on the Kresz Homeworld known for its strength.
sura	Third and smallest of the Kresz Homeworld's three suns; blue in colour.
Svestans	Lenticular sentient species. Methane-breathers, large, covered in thick bony skin bristling with spines. Aggressive.
Talos III	Barren world in neutral territory used as a ceasefire meeting place in the Earth–K-Chaan war.
tekla	An ore mined only on the Kresz Homeworld. It has unique insulating properties over a wide range of temperatures and is favoured in ship-hull construction and mining and other heavy industrial applications.
Telsans	Lenticular sentient species. Small, furry and sharp-toothed. Generally brusque in nature.
Telsus IV	A molten world in the Telsan system. The Telsans scoop the abundant minerals from its surface in floating manufactories. They have also constructed cities such as **Elysem** and other habitable areas on suitable floating plates of the rocky crust, covered with crystal atmosphere domes to keep out the deadly air.
tenspace	Lenticular word for **Voss Space**.

Totek	Cygnus Sector alien species. Look like walking kettle drums; communicate by rapping a beat on tightly drawn skin across the top of their body.
trink	Hegemony tech. A translator link, worn in the ear, that provides instant translation of programmed alien languages. See also **voder**.
voder	Ubiquitous Lenticular tech. A voice decoder that enables instant translation of Lenticular languages for the wearer. See also **trink**.
Voss Space	Also known as **tenspace** by the species in the Lenticular. A space that exists above/below/between space – dimensions other than the four dimensions of spacetime. Access to Voss Space enables ships to travel to other parts of space more quickly than by conventional means.
vuscreen	Kresz term for visual display.
yoq	Kresz animal. A beast of burden similar to a buffalo.

Acknowledgements

And so Udun's story is complete. Or this part of it at least. I began writing about Udun and the Lenticular over two decades ago – although a lot of living got in the way between then and now. I'm a relatively slow writer, but not *that* slow. But one thing kept me coming back to the Lenticular. My promise to Udun that – after all the hardship I'd thrown at him – I'd see the story through and give him a happy ending. I'm glad I've been able to keep my promise.

But I couldn't have done it on my own. First I have to thank my editor, Nicola O'Shea. Her input on successive drafts has been invaluable in helping me pull Udun's and Rhees's stories together over the three books. She's also my fantastic partner.

My friends in the Serapeum writers' group also provided early, honest – and sometimes brutal – feedback on what became *Traitor's Run*. I wasn't always completely grateful for the feedback I received at the time, but it all went into the mix and ultimately made the story stronger. So my deepest thanks go to Andrew Macrae, Adam Browne, Brendan Duffy, Rjurik Davidson, Peter Hickman, Matthew Chrulew, Jason Nahrung and the wonderful Paul Haines, who we all still miss very much.

If you've enjoyed The Lenticular, please leave a review on Goodreads, Amazon or your website of choice. Thanks for reading!

About the Author

Keith Stevenson is the author of the science fiction thriller *Horizon* and The Lenticular Series. His short fiction has appeared in *Andromeda Spaceways Inflight Magazine*, *Aurealis Magazine*, *Oceans of the Mind* and the Agog! Press anthology *Agog! Fantastic Fiction*. He's a past editor of *Aurealis – Australian Science Fiction and Fantasy Magazine*, hosted the Terra Incognita Speculative Fiction Podcast, and edited and published *Dimension6*, the free Australian speculative fiction electronic magazine.

WWW.KEITHSTEVENSON.COM

Also by Keith Stevenson

H O R I Z O N

Thirty-four light years from Earth, the explorer ship *Magellan* is nearing its objective – the Iota Persei system. But when ship commander Cait Dyson wakes from deepsleep, she finds her co-pilot dead and the ship's AI unresponsive. Cait works with the rest of her crew to regain control of the ship, until they learn that Earth is facing total environmental collapse and their mission must change if humanity is to survive.

As tensions rise and personal and political agendas play out in the ship's cramped confines, the crew finally reach the planet Horizon, where everything they know will be challenged.

"Refreshingly plausible, politically savvy, and full of surprises, *Horizon* takes you on a harrowing thrill-ride through the depths of space and the darkness of the human heart." – **Sean Williams**, New York Times bestselling author of the Astropolis and Twinmaker series

"Crackling science fiction with gorgeous trans-human and cybernetic trimmings. Keith Stevenson's debut novel soars." – **Marianne De Pierres**, award-winning author of the Parrish Plessis, Sentients of Orion and Peacemaker series

Available as a print book and ebook

www.ingramcontent.com/pod-product-compliance
Lightning Source LLC
Chambersburg PA
CBHW020328120726

47904CB00002B/320